CARLENE THOMPSON

If She
Should Die

HODDER

First published in Great Britain in 2013 by Hodder & Stoughton
An Hachette UK company

1

Copyright © Carlene Thompson 2004

A CIP catalogue record for this title is available from the British Library.

Book ISBN 978 1 444 77877 9
eBook ISBN 978 1 444 77878 6

Typeset by Hewer Text UK Ltd, Edinburgh
Printed and bound by Clays Ltd, St Ives plc

Hodder & Stoughton policy is to use papers that are natural, renewable
and recyclable products and made from wood grown in sustainable
forests. The logging and manufacturing processes are expected to
conform to the environmental regulations of the country of origin.

Praise for Carlene Thompson

"Mary Higgins Clark fans take note: loaded with more
mystery and suspense than the real thing."
Kirkus Reviews

"Thompson pulls no punches showcasing her high caliber
writing gymnastics and leaves her imprint for those iconic
writers in the suspense/thriller genre."
Examiner.com

"Thompson creates smart, interesting characters the reader
cares about within a gripping suspense story."
Judith Kelman, author of *After the Fall*

"Sure to please readers who pride themselves on sniffing
out clues. Definitely . . . for fans of Mary Higgins Clark."
Library Journal

HAVE YOU READ . . .?

SHARE NO SECRETS

After her husband's death four years ago, Adrienne Reynolds and her teenage daughter Skye moved to the quiet town of Point Pleasant, West Virginia. But their newfound sense of safety is brutally shattered when Adrienne discovers the body of her best friend Julianna in an abandoned hotel.

SINCE YOU'VE BEEN GONE

Clairvoyant Rebecca Ryan became famous a decade ago when, still a teenager, she helped the police solve a number of high-profile cases. But when her younger brother was kidnapped she was mysteriously unable to provide any information. Rebecca made a new life for herself in New Orleans, but when she experiences dark and disturbing visions again, she knows she must return to her hometown even if that means putting herself in danger.

Also by Carlene Thompson

All Fall Down
Black for Remembrance
Don't Close Your Eyes
If You Ever Tell
In the Event of My Death
Last Seen Alive
Last Whisper
Nowhere to Hide
Share No Secrets
Since You've Been Gone
The Way You Look Tonight
To the Grave
Tonight You're Mine
You Can Run . . .

To Pamela Gray Ahearn

For years of guidance and encouragement

Thanks to Russell Crump, Kelsey Thaler Brown, Jennifer Weis, and Keith Biggs.

And thanks to Rhiannon, who sat on the back of my chair as I wrote every word.

,

PROLOGUE

Her name was Dara. Her mother, Eve, had claimed when she looked into the baby's eyes two minutes after birth, she'd known this child was *daring*. The baby's father had wanted to name her Angelina, but Eve knew the girl was no angel and Eve's will had prevailed.

Now Dara Prince sat on the rail of the rotting wooden bridge crossing Crescent Creek and looked up at the Black Moon. In one of her rare spells of patience she'd tried to explain to her "inherited" brother, Jeremy, that according to the teachings of Wicca, any time new moons occur during a single month, the second new moon is referred to as the Black Moon and is considered the strongest.

In spite of his nodding and smiling, though, she didn't think Jeremy had really understood. At seventeen, he had an IQ of around 70. People told her he had the emotional and intellectual development of a child of eleven or twelve, although the age assignment was arbitrary. In many ways, he was not like a regular kid of that age. Dara didn't fully understand his disability and she had little interest in it beyond the fact that he wasn't normal.

She sat on the old dirty bridge rail, sipping vodka from a small flask she'd brought along and desperately wishing her father had not become the legal guardian of Jeremy and his older sister, Christine, when their parents died in a small plane crash four years ago. Jeremy deeply embarrassed Dara. She always feared people would think he was her natural brother. At least he didn't have Down's Syndrome. Those people often had strange-shaped heads and mouths that hung open. He did possess the saving grace of extraordinary good looks, sort of like Brad Pitt, only taller and more muscular. Dara often thought of what a joke God must have had making Jeremy tall, handsome, nice, strong, and dumb. God could be such a jerk sometimes, she mused. A real funny guy. Only the jokes were all on humans.

Jeremy's older sister, Christine, wasn't such a joke, though. She was twenty-one and although certainly not prettier than Dara, she was smarter, at least when it came to intellectual matters. People also admired her mature air, poise, and sense of responsibility. Teachers loved her. Dara thought with disgust that Christine had probably never made anything except an A+ in her entire school career.

"Of course I never gave a *damn* about grades!" a slightly drunk Dara announced with aplomb to her small black cat, Rhiannon, who sat on her lap. "You get some teacher who likes you, they put down an 'A' instead of a 'D' on your grade sheet, and everybody loses their minds with joy. Hell, you could have copied someone's paper and gotten the A."

She took another sip of vodka and leaned her head back and stared at the moon. While she loved studying her mirrored image in sunlight, night was her favorite time. Night was soft, caressing, beguiling, and magical. Tonight she'd enjoyed the quiet for a while, staring at the stars and the Black Moon and listening to the spring peepers. Rhiannon leaned against her, and she ran her hand over the black cat, feeling her back arch in response. Then Dara stood and retrieved her boom box. After all, the bridge over Crescent Creek was far enough from any houses that she could play loud music without disturbing anyone. Not that she cared about disturbing people. She just didn't want to get caught in her secret place at 11:00 P.M. when she was supposed to be studying for an English lit course she was about to flunk.

Dara put in a compact disc and the song "Rhiannon," by Stevie Nicks of Fleetwood Mac, cut through the warm, quiet night. She'd chosen the newer version with the lilting piano introduction. It was Dara's favorite song, with its haunting melody and lyrics, and she played it endlessly.

The darkness and the warmth of vodka temporarily soothed her. She stood and swayed seductively beneath the moon, her hair flowing, her hips rotating, her eyes closed in pleasure. Unsupervised, Rhiannon ran up a tree, perched on a branch, covered her front paws with her tail, and watched the scene with huge golden eyes.

Dara danced on in complete abandonment, running her hands through the silk of her hair and lifting her face to the moon. Nowhere else did she have such freedom. That's why she loved this place. She believed the area was mystical, because it was once the home of ancient Indians. A peninsula of land lay on the other side of Crescent Creek. For over a century, parts of the land had been used for farming. Equipment was brought across the bridge until several years earlier, when both the land and the bridge had been abandoned after the land had become fallow and the bridge was deemed a danger not worth fixing. After this desertion, an archaeologist had managed to get a grant and with his team excavate a promising piece of the peninsula.

She hated every history course she'd ever endured, but for some reason she'd never fathomed, Dara had become fascinated when the archaeologists discovered and excavated an ancient village built by the Indians known as the Mound Builders. She vividly remembered creeping over to the site every morning. No one had sent her home. Most of the workers were amused by the beautiful twelve-year-old girl enchanted by the dirty artifacts, always careful never to touch anything or walk where she shouldn't, ever willing to fetch cups of water for sweating diggers, often offering misshapen chocolate chip or peanut butter cookies she'd baked.

And then had come the most spectacular time of her life—the week they'd entered a burial mound and found eight skeletons, six adults and two children, all lying on their left sides facing west in accordance with their burial rituals. Dara had stayed at the site until after sundown, too mesmerized to care about her worried and work-obsessed father, who had no idea where she'd been spending her days.

Afterward, when he'd discovered what she'd been up to, he'd banned her trips to the creek and the peninsula. The old bridge wasn't safe, he said. Vagrants wandered the area. Copperhead snakes lived in the weeds. Groups of skunks carrying rabies roamed around. Dara had burst into uncontrollable giggles at the last objection, claiming she'd never heard of a gang skunk attack, and to her surprise, her usually doting father had almost slapped her.

At the time, Dara was stunned that her father couldn't take a joke like her mother. Later Dara thought he'd been unnerved by the discovery of the skeletons and frustrated that he couldn't keep her away from the place that secretly frightened him. But even now nothing frightened Dara except the thought of getting old and losing her looks, and that was not an immediate concern. She was only nineteen. Middle age seemed a century away.

The song "Rhiannon" ended and on her way back to the CD player to replay it, Dara heard a noise. She stiffened. Several times Jeremy had followed her out here at night. She never spoke sharply to him. She hated to admit it, but one look at his defense-less face and adoring eyes and she couldn't force herself to be mean. She had told him of snakes and witches and other horrors she'd hoped would scare him off, though. They hadn't. He always wanted her to show him where the ancient Indians had lived. He was almost as fascinated by the place as she. Worst of all, she couldn't complain about him trailing along without giving away her own trips to the creek after she'd convinced her father she'd abandoned them. Miraculously, Jeremy had kept the secret about her continued visits.

She looked up at Rhiannon. The cat's golden eyes moved toward the creek and Dara heard another sound. Water splashed as a small animal—a muskrat or a mink—jumped into the water. She was disturbing the woodland life, she thought. Didn't the creatures realize she was one of them—wild, native, full of animal energy trapped in human form? She smiled. She was getting downright poetic like her "almost" sister, Christine. But Christine was not moved by this place. She didn't like it. Christine was an outsider who didn't belong here like *she* did.

Except for tonight. Dara knew she'd only heard an animal. Still, she felt uneasy. Her breath quickened. Every sense seemed to snap to life, quivering with primal instincts of danger and the need for preservation. She shut off the CD player and moved away from the bridge, heading for the tree where Rhiannon sat tensed on a branch.

Dara stooped and from a flat, dry rock picked up a heavy glass sphere tucked in a burgundy velvet bag. It had belonged to her mother, Eve, when she'd dabbled in witchcraft "just for fun," she'd told Dara. When she was young, Dara had been half-afraid of the witchcraft, but when her mother died, she'd insisted on having the sphere, an actual crystal ball the size of a small cantaloupe. Dara loved to hold it up to the sun and the moon to see watercolor-tinted light flash through the facets. Sometimes Dara kept the sphere near just for luck, or to remind her of her mother. Right now, though, she was thinking of it more as a weapon than an object of divination. But there was nothing to fear. Or was there?

Apprehension cold as a dead finger touched Dara's neck. She'd felt so anxious lately. An intense fear had overtaken her, a fear she'd never felt before in her life. And she'd brought it on herself, she thought. She'd been playing a risky game, a game that had gotten dangerously out of hand. She'd pushed things too far. She deeply regretted it, but she didn't know how to fix her situation.

Unless she left this town, she thought. After all, since last week nothing held her to the place anymore except her father, whom she'd never forgiven for remarrying a much younger woman so soon after his first wife's death. Or for taking in Christine and Jeremy. But strong as Dara's attachment to him was, she couldn't turn to him now. He would be infuriated. He would be disappointed in her. Humiliated. He would never understand.

He would probably hate her, and that she couldn't bear.

Yes, she should leave, she told herself firmly. She'd made tentative plans the last few days, thinking of where she might go, withdrawing $10,000 from her bank account full of money she'd accumulated from generous lifelong Christmas and birthday gifts. Still, she'd hesitated. Leaving the place she'd always known was a big step. Considering the bad vibes she'd been getting lately, though, she felt like leaving tonight. She felt like she *needed* to leave tonight.

But she was frightened. Frightened to stay, frightened to leave. God, what a quandary. She sat down on the flat rock and let hot pent-up tears slide down her cheeks.

The breeze picked up, heavy with rain. Late March always brought rain. Every few years so much rain came that Crescent Creek flooded and rushed, as if exultant with its temporary strength, into the swollen Ohio River. This felt like one of those years. A flood would bring excitement to this calm West Virginia town, Dara thought, but the last thing she craved was more excitement.

From her perch on the tree branch, Rhiannon growled low in her throat. Dara looked up in surprise. Rhiannon was an amazingly quiet feline, meowing softly only two or three times a week, seldom purring, even more rarely growling or hissing.

Dara glanced around. Someone stood on the narrow, sloping path leading down to the bridge, someone whose stiff form was only nebulously limned by star- and moonlight.

"Jeremy?" Dara called shrilly, abruptly rigid with unreasoning panic. God, she was really spooked tonight, she thought, in spite of the usually calming vodka. But aside from Jeremy, her only visitor in this place was Streak Archer, an eccentric friend of her father who jogged at night and always called out to her before approaching.

"Streak?" she asked anyway. Streak did not answer.

"Christine?" Dara tried again, her voice cracking. Christine didn't come here, but maybe Jeremy had told the secret and Christine was playing watchdog tonight because Dara's father and stepmother were out for the evening. The figure was tall, and at five-ten, Christine seemed like an Amazon to petite Dara. Yes, it must be Christine, who'd tracked her down and come to drag her home.

The figure stood perfectly still, its face lost in shadows. Then a voice rang out: "Dara, I couldn't see you hiding under that tree!"

Dara didn't know whether to be frightened by the person's presence or relieved by the congenial tone of voice. She decided to act nonchalant. "I wasn't hiding. I was just sitting here enjoying the night. But a storm's coming. Feel that wind!"

No answer. Dara's eyes narrowed. The visitor's body bore an odd tension. The voice wasn't normal, either. Too cheery. Strained. Dara grew wary. Something was wrong. "It's time for me to go home, though. I'll walk back with you!" she called casually, her perspiring hands picking up the crystal sphere. Once more to Dara it had become not a memento but a weapon and somehow an object of spiritual protection because it had belonged to her mother. Dara stood and took a few steps forward, wind whipping her hair across her face, her fingers trembling, wondering if she was really in danger or just crazy from the influence of the second new moon of the month.

Rhiannon's golden eyes remained fixed on the visitor. Slowly the cat stood up on the branch. Her eyes turned to slits, her back arched, her tail bushed, her ears flattened. She hissed again and again.

Twenty minutes later, just as raindrops were beginning to splash into the already swollen waters of Crescent Creek, Rhiannon daintily walked along the railing of the bridge. Her ears remained flattened. The shining black hair along her backbone stood up. And she left a path of bloody paw prints behind her as the boom box played loudly, sending the haunting sounds of "Rhiannon" into the empty darkness and up to the Black Moon.

I

Three Years Later

Christine Ireland struggled to clasp the silver-and-garnet line bracelet around the customer's plump wrist extended to her. She was successful, and blood vessels in the woman's hand immediately distended. "Wilma, this bracelet is lovely, but it's only seven inches long. I believe you might need an eight."

Wilma Archer burst into jolly laughter. "Oh, Christine, didn't I say this is for my granddaughter's high school graduation in two months? Good heavens, if I wore this for a day I'd be a candidate for amputation."

Christine breathed easier and smiled. So many women who came into Prince Jewelry tried to force wrists and fingers into jewelry that was far too small for them, then became insulted when a clerk suggested a larger size. Christine had known Wilma Archer for years, though. The woman didn't have a vain bone in her body.

"Are you sure you wouldn't prefer the bracelet in gold?" Christine asked as she gently unfastened the tourniquet-like bracelet.

"Of course I'd like it in gold with a few diamonds for accent, but that would triple the cost and my granddaughter will be keeping the bracelet in the dormitory. It could be lost or stolen."

"She's living in a dorm?" Christine asked as she placed the bracelet on cotton in a long navy blue box bearing a small gold crown logo. "Isn't she going to college here in town?"

"She had aspirations for Princeton because Brooke Shields went there, but her grades kept her here at Winston University. Not that Winston isn't a good school."

"It's my alma mater," Christine said.

"And you graduated summa cum laude, which I'm sure my granddaughter won't manage. You were also sensible enough to live at home." Wilma scowled. "Her parents will be paying a fortune to let her stay on campus in some cramped little dorm room when her home is fifteen minutes away from the school." Wilma sighed. "Oh well, I doubt she'll last more than a year, but if she miraculously graduates, I'll buy her a bracelet, a ring, and earrings in gold, garnet, *and* diamonds!"

"That should be incentive enough for her to get a degree," Christine laughed.

"I hope so, but I'm not holding my breath." Wilma glanced casually around the showroom. "My husband bought my engagement ring here when old Mr. Prince managed the store." She raised her eyes to the ceiling. "Listen to me—*old* Mr. Prince. He was younger than I am now, but he seemed old as the hills to me back then. And very grave. He made every purchase seem as if it were the most important thing that had happened to him all week. You would have thought that ring with its little chip of a diamond was one of the crown jewels," she said wistfully. "It's such a shame Ames didn't go into the business. I know Mr. Prince wanted the store to pass from generation to generation. But at least Ames didn't sell the place."

"His heart is in the law, Wilma, and he's generated quite a practice in a city of only thirty-five thousand," Christine said. "He *must* be good."

Wilma grinned. "Is he as good a guardian as he is an attorney?"

"You know he is, and I'm grateful to him every day for taking in Jeremy and me."

Christine remembered being seventeen and feeling like she was plunging down into a dark, cold pit when a doctor entered the hospital waiting room where she and Jeremy had been sitting for five hours. With a grave face and gentle voice he'd told them both their parents were dead from the crash of her father's small plane. Jeremy had begun to cry in a low, monotonous whine.

Christine had pulled his head to her shoulder, her grief and horror mixed with the weight of knowing that above all she must take care of her mentally disabled brother and not let him be swept into a system that would let him wither for lack of attention and love.

"I don't know what we would have done without Ames," Christine told Wilma. "I hate to sound self-pitying, but the few elderly relatives we had didn't want us." The relatives didn't want Jeremy, she meant, in spite of their sizable trust fund.

"Shameful!" Wilma burst out. "Family is the most important thing in life, I say." She tapped her pudgy fingers on the glass showcase for emphasis. "The *most* important. I complain about mine sometimes, but I cherish them."

"Even if they throw around their money?"

"In *spite* of all their flaws!" Wilma declared, grinning.

Christine giggled and Wilma said, "It's so good to hear you laugh, honey. You don't do it often enough, a beautiful young lady like you. Actually, you're more like Ames Prince than his own daughter was. Responsible and sensible."

Wonderful, Christine thought. Dara Prince was a laugh a minute. I'm responsible and sensible. Dara was a sexy red spike-heeled pump. I'm a sturdy brown oxford.

Wilma laughed good-naturedly and patted Christine's hand. "Oh, sweetie, if you could see your face! You think I wish you were more like Dara, don't you?"

Christine felt her cheeks warm. "I know how much fun she could be."

"Sometimes Dara was fun. But there's a time for levity and a time to be serious . . ." Wilma trailed off as sadness flashed in her usually merry eyes. "If she'd been around longer, she would have learned that not all of life is fun and games."

"It seems her mother's death would have taught her that," Christine said softly.

Wilma nodded. "I know. But Eve's death had the opposite effect. Afterward, Dara seemed almost reckless. Maybe Ames indulged her too much." Wilma shook her head as if clearing it. "Enough sad talk."

"I agree. Do you want this bracelet gift-wrapped?"

"No, dear. I don't like that garish wrapping paper Ames makes you use for all occasions. I don't know why he insists on it."

"Because Eve picked it as Prince Jewelry's trademark paper. Frankly, I don't like it, either. Over half the customers decline it, but I can't budge Ames on the matter."

"You are the manager of the store, for heaven's sake!" Wilma huffed. "He should listen to you. But I know how stubborn he can be. *I'll* speak to him about it. Sometimes I have great influence on him."

"Most of the time, you mean."

Wilma couldn't hide a slightly self-satisfied smile. "Where's young Jeremy?"

"In the back working on some pieces."

"Who would have guessed that boy had such a talent for jewelry design?"

"Not me," Christine said. "Artistic talent doesn't run in the family."

Both women looked up when the front door opened and a tall man strode in wearing a tan raincoat and carrying a black umbrella. Christine cringed as he shook the umbrella vigorously, dousing the pale gray carpet and a nearby chair covered in hyacinth blue silk. He had started to tramp across the showroom when Wilma Archer said commandingly, "Ames Prince, maybe you own this store, but you should treat its furnishings with a little respect. Wipe your shoes on the mat, put the umbrella in the stand, and hang up that dripping coat."

Christine tried to stifle a smile as Ames glanced at Wilma with surprise etched on every line of his aristocratic hawklike face, then did exactly as the woman ordered. When he'd finished, he looked at Wilma without animosity and said, "Is that better?"

"Much. I'm sure Christine appreciates it. She went to a great deal of trouble redecorating this place last year, and it looks beautiful. I won't have you spoiling it with your carelessness."

"Yes, ma'am," Ames said meekly, his thin lips twisting with a rare burst of amusement. Few people could have gotten away with speaking to the dignified Ames Prince that way. But when Ames was an only child with a quiet, aloof father and a mother slowly dying of multiple sclerosis it was Wilma Archer who had welcomed him into her warm home and treated him like one of her own boisterous brood of four. He'd spent more time with the Archers than with his own father even after the death of his mother when he was ten. "What are you doing out on an awful day like this?" Ames asked her.

"This is the fourth dark, rainy day in a row. I felt if I didn't get out of the house, I'd scream. Besides, I don't think it will be safe to come into town after today."

"You're right," Ames said. "The river is three feet below flood level. I think they'll be putting up the sandbags soon." He looked at Christine. "Jeremy doesn't want to help with the sandbag operation, does he?"

"Yes, he does," she said, regretting that Ames always acted as if Jeremy were physically twelve years old, not just mentally.

"It's too dangerous for him out there. He could fall in the river and drown," Ames pronounced.

"He's an excellent swimmer," Christine offered.

"Not when the current is so swift. And he panics."

Wilma rolled her eyes at Christine. Ames had become overprotective of Jeremy, especially after the disappearance of his daughter Dara three years ago. Foul play had never been proved. For all anyone knew, she'd simply run away. After all, she'd threatened it often enough and many of her clothes and belongings were missing. But Christine knew the specter of his daughter's possible death constantly lingered over Ames.

Rain had blown under his umbrella and dampened his hair. Seeing his hair wet made Christine realize how thin the silver-laced brown strands had become in the last couple of years. Moisture glistened on all the new lines etched around his cool gray eyes and bracketing his thin lips. His cheekbones jutted starkly beneath unhealthily pale skin. Dara's disappearance had taken a noticeable physical toll on Ames. His feelings he kept to himself.

"Business slow today?" he asked Christine.

"It's four o'clock and Wilma is my fifth customer."

Ames frowned. "Hardly worth opening the store for."

"Well, I like that!" Wilma declared with mock outrage. "I'm not worth opening the store for?"

Ames smiled. "Please pardon my discourtesy, madam. I would keep the store open all day for you alone. But I think we should go home early today. And tomorrow we'll open at ten instead of nine."

"Good," Christine said. "I'll have time to go to the gym before work. I haven't been there for over a week."

"As if you young, skinny things need to work out," Wilma said. "I think you could stand to put on ten pounds, Christine. And you could do with twenty, Ames. You are entirely too thin—"

"Wilma, I'm afraid you're going to have an unpleasant trip home. It's pouring and there are flash flood warnings," Ames said abruptly to stem one of Wilma's tirades about everyone's weight.

"I'm a fine driver and I've been maneuvering these roads since before you were born," Wilma returned tartly.

"You're going to drive home all alone in this downpour?" asked Ginger Tate, the twenty-year-old red-haired sprite Christine had hired as a clerk two months ago. For the past hour she'd been polishing an ornate silver tea service on this slow afternoon. "I don't think driving by yourself is a good idea, Mrs. Archer. What if you have a flat tire?"

"I know how to fix a flat tire, young lady."

"When you're being pelted with rain?" Ginger shook her head and grimaced. "It'll blur your vision and you can't see. It'll mess up other drivers' vision, too. Gee, someone might run right over you. *Splat!* Then how would you feel?"

"Probably not too well," Wilma answered solemnly.

"Right. And aside from you getting hurt, the other driver would feel crummy for running down an elderly lady," Ginger added, polishing diligently. She went at every task enthusiastically. "They'd feel guilty for the rest of their lives."

Ginger was too busy polishing to notice that Christine and Ames were now on the verge of laughter along with Wilma.

Wilma's tone was grave: "I guess I'm being appallingly selfish. I hadn't given any of those possibilities a thought. You're a very astute young lady, Ginger."

"Yeah, well, my dad says I analyze everything too much, but I can't help it. It's just my nature."

"It's often a fine trait," Wilma said. "All right, Ames, Ginger has convinced me I'm taking unnecessary risks. But before I go home, I have some things to drop off at the church for families who've already been flooded out of their homes. Blankets, canned foods, some clothes. You can follow me home from there and make sure I don't cause any disasters."

"It would be my pleasure," Ames said, "but we should get going. Driving is more difficult in this rain when it gets dark, and at the most we only have about a couple of hours of daylight left."

Christine handed Wilma the box containing the bracelet and Ames was shrugging back into his damp raincoat when the front door opened. A tall, lean man entered the store and looked quickly around. He carried no umbrella and rain glistened on his short, thick brown hair. He wore a yellow rain slicker and water-spattered uniform trousers with the distinctive black stripes down the sides.

"Be sure to wipe your feet," Wilma instructed.

The man looked down at his shining black shoes. "I've had on rubber boots until two minutes ago," he said. "I left them outside the door."

Wilma squinted at the broad-brimmed hat he carried. "I was introduced to you last year at the Sternwheel Regatta. You're Deputy Sheriff Michael Winter, aren't you?"

"Yes, ma'am."

"I'm Wilma Archer. This is Ames Prince and Christine Ireland."

He shot Christine one quick, keen glance after which she was certain he could describe in detail her short blond hair, light aqua eyes, straight nose bearing a smattering of freckles, above average height, and white silk knit sweater.

He turned his gaze back to Wilma. "We did meet at the regatta, ma'am," he said in a deep, smooth voice as he held out his hand to the older woman. "The weather sure was nicer then."

"Oh, it was beautiful! And what a fine turnout we had. I do love all those pretty boats!" Wilma sounded young and slightly flustered. Christine recalled her going on a few months ago about meeting the new deputy in town, clearly with matchmaking on her mind since she'd added excitedly that he was young, divorced, and handsome and had moved to Winston from Los Angeles, where he'd been a detective. Please don't let her announce that I'm single, Christine thought, not without provocation. Wilma's determination to find her a husband had embarrassed her in front of several single men. But when the deputy sheriff began to talk in a businesslike tone, her fear of humiliation vanished. He wasn't going to give Wilma a chance for any small talk.

"I need to speak to you, Mr. Prince," Winter said almost grimly as he looked at Ames. "I was told at your office you might be here."

"And so I am," Ames said casually. He seemed calm, but Christine felt a small clutch of fear caused by the discomfort in Winter's eyes, the formality of his tone. "How may I help you, Deputy?"

"I wonder if we might speak alone."

"I'm not under arrest for some heinous crime, am I?" Ames's voice was strained. "You're not trying to spare me the humiliation of arresting me in front of a crowd?"

"No, sir, certainly not. But I have some news I thought might best be delivered to you in private."

This was something about Dara, Christine thought with a dark, certain dread as she saw color seep from Ames's face. He sensed it concerned Dara, too, and he was afraid to hear the news alone, although he would never admit it.

"I have no secrets from Miss Ireland and Mrs. Archer," Ames said stiffly. He completely ignored Ginger, who'd stopped polishing and watched with huge eyes. "Please don't drag this out any longer."

Michael Winter's slender face tightened. His dark eyes gazed unflinchingly into Ames's for a moment and Christine saw his right hand curl into a fist, then relax. He swallowed and said gently, "Mr. Prince, about an hour ago an object washed up on the riverbank about half a mile south of town. It was tightly wrapped in plastic." He paused and Wilma's breath drew in sharply. "Unfortunately, I wasn't present when it was retrieved and therefore couldn't stop some of the local men from unwrapping it—"

"Probably a cow or a dog or a goat or a ..." Wilma interrupted before her voice trailed off and she looked apprehensively at Ames, who seemed frozen, not even blinking.

"It's not an animal, ma'am," Deputy Winter said gently. "It appears to be an adult female."

"Oh!" Wilma exclaimed. Michael Winter did not look at her. His gaze remained fixed on Ames, who swayed almost imperceptibly.

"The body has been in the water for a while," Michael Winter went on softly. "Maybe years. There's a lot of decomposition in spite of the heavy plastic wrapping. However, Mr. Prince, I regret to say we believe it might be the remains of your daughter, Dara."

2

1

Nearly ten seconds ticked by while Wilma Archer went rigid and Ginger gasped. Christine felt an odd plunging sensation, as if all her blood were draining to her feet, but Ames Prince merely stared at the deputy with a small detached smile. "I'm sorry I snapped at you earlier, Deputy Winter. I appreciate your coming to tell me this personally, but that unfortunate person can't be my daughter. I just got a letter from her last week. She's in Arizona. Phoenix, to be exact."

The letters, Christine thought in despair. They'd been coming three or four times a year since a month after Dara's disappearance. They were always posted from a different part of the country, and they were typewritten. Ames had placed all his faith in them. Christine could not believe they were really from Dara.

Deputy Winter gazed unwaveringly at Ames although his voice was still gentle. "Sir, I've heard there's some doubt about those letters actually being sent by your daughter."

"That's ridiculous," Ames said loudly. "Who else would send them? Who's been saying they aren't from my daughter?"

"I don't suppose you've had them checked for fingerprints—"

"No!" Ames was almost shouting. "I know my daughter's writing style, her signature. Having them checked would be a waste of time! Besides, she left a good-bye note in her room before she left."

The deputy took a deep breath. "Well, I don't know much about the letters or the note, sir. All I know at this point is that we've retrieved the remains of what appears to be a female around five feet, four inches tall, which I know from her file is your daughter's height, with long black hair like your daughter's."

"Black hair," Wilma whispered.

"Dozens of women have black hair," Ames said in a dry, metallic voice. "Hundreds of women. And who can tell what color the hair actually is after a long time in the water? It might be brown hair that's just dirty."

Christine flinched inside, knowing how genuinely alarmed Ames must be to come up with such a weak excuse for the corpse having black hair. "Was she wearing any jewelry?" Christine ventured. "Dara always wore a ring. A heart-shaped ruby surrounded by diamonds."

Deputy Winter turned depthless brown eyes on her. "I really can't describe effects recovered. Mr. Prince will have to identify any items found with the body as well as the body itself."

"Oh, dear lord," Wilma moaned. "We have to go down to the riverbank and look at this *thing*?"

"No, ma'am," Winter said gently. "It's procedure for bodies to be sent directly to the state medical lab in Charleston. Mr. Prince will have to go there to look at the body."

"To Charleston?" Wilma demanded in a rising voice. "Why not a local funeral home? Why all the way to Charleston?"

"It's procedure, ma'am—"

"Wilma, it's quite all right," Ames said calmly. "I'll drive to Charleston tonight, look at this body, and confirm that it isn't Dara, and everything will be fine. It only takes an hour to get to Charleston. I'll be there and back by nine o'clock. It isn't the end of the world."

But it *was* the end of his world, Christine thought in misery. She knew in her soul Dara had been found at last, and tonight, when Ames looked at the remains of her body, he would be forced to face a horrible truth he'd desperately outrun for three years.

"Sir, I hate to ask you this," Winter went on, obvious dismay in his voice. "But I mentioned the extreme decomposition.

There's a chance you might not be able to identify the body even if it is your daughter. We'll probably have to do DNA testing, so we'll need a hair or tissue sample from Dara. Would you happen to have anything—"

"Excellent idea!" Ames boomed. "Her bedroom has been shut off since the night she disappeared. She took many things with her when she ran away. Clothes, personal items. All missing since that night. But her brush is still on her dresser. A lovely silver-backed thing my father gave her. There's still hair in it—" He broke off. "We'll stop at my house before going to Charleston, you can get hair samples, and I'll take them with me to Charleston—"

"Sir, that's not procedure. I can collect them and send them tomorrow—"

"To hell with procedure!" Ames suddenly seemed almost giddy. "There's no need to wait until tomorrow. The sooner the better, because DNA testing will show absolutely that this corpse is not my daughter. That will settle things. How soon will we get back the test results?"

"West Virginia doesn't do DNA testing, sir," Winter said cautiously, as if not knowing what reaction to expect next. "We send most of our samples to a lab in Pittsburgh. We won't have an answer for four to six weeks at best."

"That's a damned long time. No sense in our not being able to do our own testing." A new idea seemed to pop into Ames's mind. "How about dental records? That would be much faster."

"The corpse's teeth are missing, sir."

"Missing?" Ames seemed to draw back for a moment before he grasped at another straw. "Then maybe it's the body of an old person whose teeth have been extracted."

"No, sir. They look as if they were smashed out, probably to prevent identification. The fingertips were cut off, too."

Christine flinched. Teeth bashed out? Fingertips cut off? Dear God, please let the person have been dead when those atrocities were committed, she thought.

"Look here," Ames began again. "You said the body's badly decomposed. Then you tell me it's the body of a female. Now how do you know it's a female?"

Winter took a deep breath. "The length of the hair. The height. The shape of the pelvis—"

"Some boys these days have long hair," Ames announced. "And you're not a doctor. What do you know about the shape of a pelvis?"

"Not much, sir. That's why we need an autopsy." Ames glared at the deputy as if the situation were entirely his fault. "Mr. Prince, I really don't think we're accomplishing much here except alarming everyone," Winter said evenly. "If you would just agree to go to the medical examiner's in Charleston—"

"All right, all *right*!" Ames stormed. Then he closed his eyes and breathed deeply, as if he were counting to ten. Finally he touched Wilma's shoulder. "Dear, I'm afraid I won't be able to follow you home."

"I can get home by myself," Wilma said shakily. "But I don't want you driving all the way to Charleston in this rain and as upset as you are."

"I'll be fine, just fine. I'm not upset. This is all just a terrible mix-up that I will have straightened out in a few hours."

"I can go with you, Ames," Christine volunteered, although she dreaded an acceptance.

"No. You have Jeremy to look after," Ames said. "And I don't need a nursemaid. Wilma here seems in much worse shape than I am."

"I'll take you home, Mrs. Archer," Ginger said unexpectedly.

Wilma looked surprised. "Oh, honey, that's not necessary."

"I'll just drive behind you to make sure you get home safe and sound. You won't have to actually sit in a car with me listening to me prattle, because I know that's what you're really afraid of. My dad says I could talk the ear off an elephant, and that's a mighty big ear."

She ended with a wink and Wilma actually managed a weak smile. Christine could have kissed Ginger, who wasn't always so sensitive to other people's needs. Thank heavens she'd come through this evening, Christine thought as Ginger herded a shaking, watery-eyed Wilma out the door. Ames followed briskly, saying in an abnormally hearty voice, "Wilma, don't go to pieces. This person *isn't* Dara. It just isn't. I'd know if my daughter were dead, wouldn't I? It *isn't* Dara."

2

After they left, Christine stood rooted behind the counter. Deputy Winter had made no move to leave the store. She looked at him, tried to smile, failed, and pushed her short hair behind her ears for the third time, a nervous gesture. She seemed cold to the bone in spite of the store's comfortable temperature and her warm sweater. Her fingers felt sharp and icy.

At last, Deputy Winter asked, "Do you know anything about these letters from his daughter Mr. Prince has been receiving?"

"I know everything about them," Christine said. Winter looked at her in mild surprise and she realized she had not explained her relationship to Ames. "I'm Christine Ireland. Mr. Prince was a good friend of my parents and took in my younger brother and me when they were killed seven years ago. Ames became our legal guardian."

"But he didn't adopt you."

"No. But my brother, Jeremy, is now twenty and still lives with Mr. Prince and his wife, Patricia."

"Patricia Prince," Winter said thoughtfully. "I believe I've met her. She's not Dara's mother, is she?"

"Oh no. Patricia is far too young. She's Ames's second wife. Dara's mother, Eve, died of cancer when Dara was twelve. Eve insisted on spending her last weeks at home, and Patricia was her nurse. She and Mr. Prince were married less than a year after Eve's death."

"Did Patricia and Dara get along?"

"They tolerated each other," Christine said carefully, seeing a flash in the deputy sheriff's eyes that meant he knew she was evading the complete truth. In reality, Dara and Patricia couldn't stand each other and argued constantly.

"You don't still live with Mr. Prince, Miss Ireland?" Winter asked.

"No. I have a house on Cardinal Way."

"Nice area. New. Not many houses." Deputy Winter shifted from one foot to the other. Christine didn't know whether to ask him to sit or to offer tea or coffee in this situation. It was hardly a social call. But he seemed weary.

"I've just made a fresh pot of coffee," she said. "You look cold. Would you like a cup?"

He hesitated, then said with a grateful smile, "I'd love a cup if it wouldn't be too much trouble. I take it black."

Christine went into the small closet they called a kitchen with its sink, microwave oven, coffeemaker, and miniature refrigerator. In a moment she returned and motioned for him to sit at the table where Ginger had been polishing silver. "Sorry I don't have any pastry to offer. We always get a fresh selection from the bakery in the morning, but we've been so bored today, we've eaten it all. It's a good thing every day isn't like this or we'd be the pudgiest staff in town."

Winter rewarded her with his first genuine smile that even reached his eyes. He took a sip of coffee, muttered, "Good," then asked, "Will you tell me more about these letters Mr. Prince has been receiving, supposedly from Dara?"

"Well, the letters are brief and noncommittal, written on a small piece of stationery, usually something with flowers or cupids or bows. That *is* the kind of paper Dara would choose. But they're typewritten except for an ornate *D* at the end, always done in ink."

"Was it Dara's habit to type her letters?"

"No. She hated to type. And she loved the name Dara. Ames says her mother chose it because when she first saw her daughter, she said the baby would grow up to be a *daring* young lady. Anyway, I've never known of Dara to sign anything with just a *D*."

"Mr. Prince said the last letter came from Phoenix, Arizona."

"They're always from a different place, some large city where it would be hard to find her."

"What do they say?"

Christine closed her eyes, trying to recall the letters. Ames hadn't shown her one for over a year. "They're vague. 'Having a great time.' 'Doing well, so don't worry.' Terse, really nothing more than notes, although Dara was a chatterbox. Of course, the way people speak and the way they write aren't always the same."

"What about requests for money?"

"None that I know of."

"Reference to a job or a boyfriend?"

"No," Christine said. "And no explanation about where she's living—apartments, houses, hotels."

"Did she have credit cards?"

"No. She was only nineteen. But she had a sizable bank account accrued from bonds and cash gifts from friends and relatives. She'd withdrawn ten thousand dollars from it two days before she disappeared. She left a couple of hundred in the account, to keep it open, I guess."

Winter raised his eyebrows. "I can't imagine having ten thousand dollars of my own at nineteen."

"Neither can I." Christine's parents had left eight hundred thousand in trust for her and Jeremy and a hundred thousand in life insurance. The terms of her father's will did not give her possession of the money until she was twenty-two, though, and Ames had always kept her on a tight leash where money was concerned. Technically she'd been financially well off at nineteen, but actually she was like a child with a small allowance. This hadn't been the case with Dara, though, and Ames had grasped at the large bank withdrawal as another sign that Dara had run away and needed the money to finance her "escape."

"Ten thousand would have lasted awhile," Winter was saying.

"Yes, but not three years."

"You don't think Dara could have gotten a good job, one that paid so well she didn't have to ask her father for money?"

"If so, why does each letter come from a different part of the country?" Christine asked. "Besides, she really had no skills to get a high-paying job. And if she'd married a man who was well off, I believe she'd boast about him."

"A lover?"

"You mean a rich sugar daddy? No, she'd boast about him, too, only she'd say they were engaged so she wouldn't enrage her father." Christine shook her head. "Nothing about those letters makes sense to me."

"You clearly don't think she's sending the letters. Does Mr. Prince believe they're from his daughter?"

Michael Winter looked at Christine intently. His voice was deep yet with an intimate, sincere quality that made her feel as if she could tell him anything. Christine had nothing to hide, but she reminded herself that she did not know this man, either. Just how truly his voice and gaze revealed his personality was yet to be seen. Until then, she felt she must watch her step for the family's sake.

"Ames certainly wants to believe they're from Dara."

"But he doesn't really?"

"I can't read his mind, Deputy."

"But you've known him for years. Certainly you can make a guess about whether he believes they're from his daughter."

Christine sighed. Ames Prince was a hard man to know, and in spite of her years in his house she felt he held her and Jeremy at a distance. He was fond of them. He'd taken his responsibility as their guardian seriously. He'd always maintained an interest in their activities. He'd been unfailingly patient and kind to Jeremy, whom he liked to have around, especially after Dara disappeared. But he had never in any way been like a father or, at least, like their warm, demonstrative father had been. She knew Ames didn't love them, maybe because Dara had so jealously hoarded his parental affections. Christine wasn't sure she

and Jeremy felt anything for Ames beyond friendship and gratitude. But she couldn't say all of this to a man she'd only met
twenty minutes ago.

"Ames desperately wants to believe the letters are from Dara.
I think he's almost convinced they are."

"But not quite."

She shook her head. "He's too smart not to realize something
is wrong about them."

"That's why he won't allow them to be tested for fingerprints,
isn't it? He's afraid Dara's won't be on the letters."

"Yes, I think so."

"What about this farewell note she left the night she
disappeared?"

"That night, Ames only glanced in her room and saw she
wasn't there. None of us actually went in, so we didn't find the
note until the next day. It was on her dresser and said: 'Time for
this bird to fly. Don't worry.'"

"Signature?"

"Just *D*."

"So you don't believe she wrote the note?"

Christine frowned. "The handwriting looked like hers if she
was really nervous or in a hurry. But once again, the terseness
bothered me. I think if Dara were really running away, she'd say
something a lot more melodramatic than 'Time for this bird to
fly.'"

"Did you ever consider kidnapping?"

"Ames and the police did for a while, but if she was, no one
ever asked for a ransom. There were no signs of a struggle in her
room or anywhere in the house."

"But you don't believe she just ran away."

"I think her taking off voluntarily is really unlikely. She'd
threatened it, but she always said dramatic things to get her way.
Like a child. But actually running away would mean being out
in the world on her own with only ten thousand dollars. That
might sound like a lot to us, but it wouldn't to her. She spent
money like water." Christine shook her head. "I'm rambling.

This news about the body has thrown me. Maybe I can talk more clearly when I've had time to calm down. But—" Michael Winter raised his eyebrows. "But I wouldn't want Ames to know I've been discussing the letters and the farewell note. He considers it all family business. He'd be furious."

"He won't hear it from me." Michael Winter smiled at her again. His dark eyes went from hard and inquisitive to understanding, and the chiseled planes of his face softened. His teeth were even and white, and shallow lines framed either side of his mouth. Christine noticed he had a mole beneath his left eye that looked almost like a tiny dark tear. She found herself wanting to trust him in this awful situation. She found herself afraid of taking the chance.

"Would you like more coffee?" she asked abruptly.

"I really should get going, although I've been out in this mess since early this morning."

Christine looked out the front windows at the rain falling against a dull gray sky. The few trees lining Main Street bore young, droopily wet leaves, and signs hanging in front of buildings flapped in the cold, brisk wind. Cars splashed dirty water onto the sidewalks. Suddenly an image of Dara, beautiful and laughing, flashed through Christine's mind. Her stomach did a small flip at the thought of what lying in dirty river water for three years would have done to Dara's lovely body. The picture was gruesome.

"What's wrong?" Winter asked. "Your face went completely white."

"I was thinking of Dara in the river." She folded her arms across her chest almost protectively. "If this body found today *is* Dara's, how could she have remained in the water so long? Surely she would have surfaced before now."

"The plastic wrapping could have gotten caught on something. Maybe trapped in tree roots sticking out under the water. This is the first flood for three years. The rush of water could have dislodged the body. And there's a tear in the outer layer of plastic. It's possible the body was weighted down with a concrete block or something else heavy. The bundle, for lack of a better word, could have come in contact with something sharp that ripped the plastic and the weight fell out, allowing the body to finally surface."

Christine swallowed hard at the idea. She and Dara had certainly never been friends, but the thought of her beautiful body slowly decomposing as it lay trapped in plastic and filthy water made Christine sick. But maybe it wasn't Dara after all. Maybe Ames, with all his seemingly irrational optimism, was right about Dara being alive.

"What's going on? I thought I heard you talking about Dara."

They looked up to see Jeremy Ireland standing in the doorway leading to the showroom from the back rooms of Prince Jewelry. He was even taller than Deputy Winter, with blond hair a few shades darker than Christine's but the same aqua eyes. Jeremy's handsome square-jawed face was now pale, the mouth slightly open in surprise and dismay.

"Deputy Winter, this is my brother, Jeremy," Christine said quickly, going to her brother and placing her hand on his arm. "Jeremy, the flood washed up a body. It could be Dara, but the police aren't sure it's her. No one is sure."

"But it could be!" Jeremy's voice rose. "Dara could be dead!"

Christine stroked his arm. "We don't know that, so you calm down and think good thoughts, because it's probably not Dara." She glanced at Winter, who studied Jeremy with a faint frown. Obviously, he noticed the slightly childish tone of Jeremy's speech, which did not belong to a man of twenty. She wondered if anyone had told the deputy sheriff that Jeremy Ireland was mentally disabled, that he had the intelligence of a twelve-year-old, although that age assignment was arbitrary. In many ways, he was not like a regular kid of twelve.

"I wanna know about the body," Jeremy demanded.

"Let's not talk about it now." Christine tried to smile at him. "Let's talk about it later when we're home and comfortable."

"I'm not a little boy," Jeremy said solemnly. "I want to know what's happening *now*."

Christine sighed. No, at his level of intellectual development Jeremy wasn't exactly a little boy. But he wasn't an adult, either.

Winter came forward, hand extended. "I'm Deputy Sheriff Michael Winter. Glad to meet you, Jeremy."

"Glad to meet you, too," Jeremy said, shaking Winter's hand. "Dara was sort of like my sister, but not really. Her father is our guardian."

"Your sister told me."

"So what's goin' on?" Jeremy asked edgily.

"Well, Jeremy, I'm afraid the flood has washed up something unpleasant," Winter went on without a hint of condescension. "The body of a female wrapped in plastic. It's been in the water a long time. We can't tell a lot about it except that it's the right height to be Dara and it has black hair. But it might not be Dara."

"Why can't you just look at the body and see if it's Dara?"

"Because the body has been in the water a long time. There's been decomposition . . ." Winter looked at Jeremy's frown. "The body has been damaged, Jeremy. In spite of the plastic wrapping, the water caused the skin on the body to—"

"Rot," Jeremy supplied bluntly. "She's all rotted down to bones."

"Well, not completely—"

Tears welled in Jeremy's eyes. "Christy, I feel sick."

"Go to the bathroom and splash some cold water on your face."

"Cold water won't help if Dara's all rotted—"

"The body hasn't been identified," Winter interrupted. "Jeremy, I want you to keep in mind that it may *not* be Dara."

"But you said there was black hair."

"Lots of people have black hair. It's not proof that the body is Dara's. Now do what your sister said. Go splash water on your face and think positive thoughts."

"Positive thoughts?"

"Don't think about it being Dara's body until we know for sure. Stay strong. I'm sure everyone in your family is depending on you to be strong."

Christine looked at Winter sharply. Was he making fun of Jeremy by telling him the family was counting on him? Was Winter patronizing him? But the deputy's expression was open and guileless. Either he was a good actor or he was genuinely trying to give Jeremy strength and encouragement.

Jeremy nodded. "I'll be strong; I promise."

He turned and walked briskly toward the back of the store. When Jeremy closed the door behind him, Winter looked at Christine. "Miss Ireland, I'm sorry to have delivered this news. I'll be in touch with your family as soon as I know anything. In the meantime, I'm trying to keep this as quiet as I can to spare Mr. Prince more grief, although it's hard to keep a lid on news like this."

"I know. So does Ames. But we appreciate your efforts, Deputy Winter."

The deputy rose from the table, grabbed his poncho and hat, and strode out the front door, head bent against the cold, pouring rain. Christine stood staring after him as if his exit couldn't possibly be the end of the scene.

"What's wrong?" Reynaldo Cimino asked, making Christine jump. She hadn't heard him enter the showroom. With his black hair, high cheekbones, and perfect smile, he looked more like a movie star than a gem artisan who created beautiful pieces for Prince Jewelry. He'd spent the first thirteen years of his life in Florence, Italy. At age twenty-eight he still had not completely lost the accent that so intrigued many of Winston's female inhabitants. "Christine, Jeremy's in the bathroom throwing water all over his head and saying he has to be strong, and you're white as a ghost. What's wrong?" Rey asked again.

Christine floundered for a gentle explanation to give the man who'd been in love with Dara three years ago when she vanished. He'd been frantic for weeks, then retreated into near-silence for several months. It was over half a year before he began seeing Tess Brown, whom he then abruptly married. Most people thought he'd wed without love and on the rebound. Everyone was certain he'd never recovered from losing Dara.

Christine finally found her voice. "Rey, a body wrapped in plastic washed ashore. A deputy was here. He believes it might be Dara."

So much for gentleness, Christine thought. The blunt words had simply spilled unchecked in a taut, crisp voice that didn't sound like her own. Rey stared at her, his olive skin paling, his body going completely still as if he'd turned to stone. Finally he drew a deep breath and murmured, "He said the body was Dara's?"

"He said it *could* be Dara's. No official identification has been made yet. The body has been taken to the medical examiner's in Charleston. Ames is on his way there to view the . . . remains."

"Remains?" Reynaldo repeated roughly. "What identifiable remains would be left after three years in the water?"

"I don't know. There was the plastic wrapping—did I mention the body was wrapped tightly in plastic? It's horrible . . ."

Christine trailed off as Jeremy re-entered the showroom. His face was ruddy from the sting of cold water, and his shirt collar and the front of his hair were wet.

Rey didn't seem to see him. "She was wrapped in plastic?" Christine nodded. Rey made the sign of the cross. "Mother of God."

Jeremy went to him, touching his shoulder. "Maybe it's not Dara. Don't cry."

"I wasn't going to cry," Rey nearly snarled.

"You looked like you were," Jeremy said innocently. "Or maybe you just looked scared."

"What would I be scared about?" Reynaldo demanded, suddenly hostile.

"Scared that it's Dara. What else?" Jeremy asked.

Rey was pale as death, and a tiny muscle in his right eyelid twitched. "I'm going back to work," he announced between clenched teeth.

"Never mind," Christine said. "It's four-thirty and pouring rain. We won't have any more customers today. We're closing early."

"Thank goodness." Rey stood motionless, but his hands had begun to tremble.

"Yes, I think that's best," Christine said inanely. "None of us could concentrate anyway."

"You never liked her," Reynaldo burst out. "What do you care?"

Christine's eyes widened in surprise. "What?"

"You never liked Dara. You don't really care that she's dead."

"Rey, that was a mean thing to say," Jeremy chastised fervently. "Why do you want to hurt Christy's feelings? She didn't do anything."

"Rey, Dara and I didn't get along very well, but you can't possibly think I wanted her *dead*." Rey didn't look at Christine. "Well, do you?"

Rey continued to look at the floor. "No. I'm sorry. I'm just . . . Hell, I don't know how I feel."

Christine tried to regain some of her composure and said evenly, "You're shocked, like all of us."

"Yeah, that's it. Shocked."

She wanted desperately to say something comforting, but she couldn't think of anything appropriate. Rey had loved Dara. But he was married to Christine's best friend. The subject was too sensitive. Instead she said woodenly, "Why don't you go next door and make Tess close early?" Rey's wife owned the adjoining bookstore, whimsically named Calliope for the antique musical instrument on display in her showroom. "Take her out for dinner at the Tudor Rose."

"I went there for my birthday," Jeremy offered. "Me and Christine and Ames and Patricia. They had really good food, and after I finished my meal waiters and waitresses brought me a cake and sang happy birthday to me. It was great."

Rey looked at them angrily. "I can't believe you two!"

"What?" Jeremy quavered. "What did we do?"

"Dara's body is found and you want me to take my wife out to dinner and eat, drink, and be merry?"

"Rey, we didn't mean to offend you," Christine said. "It was just a thought, something to take your mind off things until we know something for sure. After all, we don't *know* that the body is Dara's. I thought you understood that."

"I do. But still . . . if nothing else, out of respect . . ." Rey ran a hand over his forehead, then stalked to the coat tree and whipped free his raincoat. "I'm outta here."

"Don't let Tess see how upset you are," Christine said.

"In here I take orders from you, Miss Ireland. Once I'm out that door, I'm my own man," Rey snapped.

She and Jeremy watched Rey slam out the front door. Jeremy frowned. "He must be really mad to call you Miss Ireland."

"No kidding."

"Today's been a real bummer, hasn't it?" Jeremy asked.

"It sure has, and I can't wait to get out of this store."

"I don't feel like working anymore, either. Hey, Christy, I don't think Rey loves Tess as much as he loved Dara."

"Unfortunately, I don't think Dara loved him," Christine said as she put on her silver-gray raincoat and drew the belt tight. "But she was very young."

"Yeah," Jeremy said. "But even if she didn't love Reynaldo, she wouldn't have loved me instead. Sometimes that used to make me mad."

"It did?" Christine asked casually, although a finger of alarm touched her neck. "How mad?"

"Oh, pretty mad sometimes. Then she'd be real nice to me and I wouldn't feel so mad anymore that a girl like her wouldn't ever want me for a boyfriend. I guess it was okay just to be her friend."

"Yes, sometimes it's better just to be someone's friend," Christine said, hearing the false brightness in her voice. "Like Sloane and me. We were engaged and I wasn't very happy. Then I broke the engagement, we didn't get married, and now we're good friends and I'm happy. Happier than I was when I was his girlfriend."

Jeremy shook his head. "Sometimes I don't get all this love stuff. Love like men and women have, not the way I love you and Rhiannon."

"Me *and* Rhiannon?" Christine asked with a smile as she handed him his tan raincoat. "Who do you love more? Me or the cat?"

"I love you both the same," Jeremy said with great kindness. Then his face grew troubled. "Do you think my dreams will stop now?"

"Your dreams?"

Jeremy slipped into his tan raincoat. He was as tall as their father, Edward, had been and just as handsome, but he and Christine had their mother Liv's Scandinavian coloring. "I said something to you about my dreams a long time ago. You said not to worry, but now I wonder about them."

"Tell me about the dreams again, Jeremy. I don't remember all the details."

"You weren't paying close attention like you expect me to do all the time," he said with reproach.

"I'm sorry. You're right. So tell me once more as we lock up, and I'll pay very close attention."

"Okay." Jeremy paused, gathering his thoughts. "Ever since Dara went away, I've been dreaming about water," he said in a slightly anxious voice. "Dark, cold water that won't let me see or breathe. And something that won't let me move, something wrapped all tight around me. But in the dream, I'm alive. I know I'm gonna die and I'm awful scared, but I'm still alive." A haunted look clouded his clear blue eyes. "I always thought I was dreaming about me, but now I think I was dreaming about Dara. But how could I have known she was in the water all wrapped up in plastic, Christy? How did I know?"

3

1

Christine stiffened. "Jeremy, don't tell anyone else about those dreams."

Jeremy looked puzzled. "How come?"

How could Christine tactfully explain the conclusion some people might draw? Many thought the mentally challenged were capable of anything. Christine had been protecting Jeremy from that ignorant type for as long as she could remember. Now he was talking about dreams that might lead people to believe he'd killed Dara and thrown her body in the river, then didn't have enough sense not to talk about it.

"People can misunderstand things," Christine said casually. "They might not realize you were talking about *dreams*. They might—"

"Think I hurt Dara," Jeremy interrupted sagely. "Some people are really mean."

"Yes. And some just aren't too smart."

"Like me."

"No, not like you. You're smart in all the ways that count. A lot of other people aren't." They walked through the showroom to the storeroom and the rear entrance. "They get things all turned around in their minds, or they think they know a lot about subjects when they really don't have a clue."

"Is Deputy Winter like that?"

"I don't know. I just met him."

"He seemed nice."

"Yes. But as I said, we don't know him. So I especially don't want you mentioning the dreams to him."

"Because he's the police?"

"Because we don't know him," Christine ended lamely. Of course because he was the police. Three years ago, Sheriff Buck Teague had been convinced Jeremy had done something to Dara. He was probably still convinced. God only knew what Deputy Winter thought. She could tell he was sharper than Teague. And he'd been a detective in Los Angeles before he came to Winston. *Why* he had come to Winston was a mystery. So was he. A mystery that could pose a threat to Jeremy if the body turned out to be Dara's and Winter held the same opinion of the mentally challenged as Sheriff Teague.

"You look worried," Jeremy said as they stepped out the back door onto the small parking lot. "Are you worried about my dreams?"

Christine raised her umbrella, then locked the back door of the store. "It's been a bad day. The rain, the flooding, the body. I'm just a little depressed."

"I don't feel too happy, either." They hurried to her small car in the rear parking lot. Jeremy tucked his rangy body into the bucket seat. She opened her side, shut the umbrella, tossed it onto the backseat, then climbed in to meet Jeremy's look of childish appeal. "I really wish you'd get a car like Reynaldo's."

"That's a vintage 1957 Thunderbird he spent about three years restoring. I'm not up to the job. It's also expensive, and I just bought us a fairly big house."

"And wouldn't that T-Bird look cool sitting in the driveway?" Jeremy persisted winningly. "It's even red, my favorite color."

"I agree that it's a great car," Christine said, thinking of how much Dara had loved riding around in it when she'd dated Reynaldo. "Unfortunately, my *uncool* little blue car will have to do for now."

"Well, maybe someday we can have one like Rey's," Jeremy said wistfully. "Christy, I feel real bad for thinking about food when Dara might be dead, but I can't help it. I'm really hungry and nobody's home."

"Nobody? How do you know Patricia isn't home?"

"This morning when she brought me to work she told me to fix a sandwich for dinner. She said she had to go out."

"Out where? To dinner?"

Jeremy shrugged. "I don't know. She doesn't tell me things and I haven't heard Ames asking her about being gone so much."

"She's gone a lot?"

"Yeah. Lately lots more than usual. Anyway, I'm *starving*."

"Me, too," Christine lied. She certainly didn't want to drop Jeremy off at the empty Prince home to scrounge dinner for himself and think about Dara. "How about going to Gus's Grill?"

"Good. I'll have a cheeseburger and a banana split."

Half an hour later they sat in a dark green booth in the intimate Gus's Grill, whose decoration scheme could only be described as eclectic, a mixture of the Mexican, Chinese, and French restaurants it had been in past lives over the last fifteen years. Christine was particularly fond of the renovated mural along one wall showing a woman in a kimono serving spaghetti and meatballs. They ordered loudly above the theme song from *Exodus* Gus had blaring over the speakers.

"I'll tell him to turn the music down," the waitress said to Christine after she'd repeated her drink order for the third time.

"Don't hurt his feelings," Christine said. "I know it's his favorite song."

The waitress rolled her eyes. "Gus's feelings are made of steel. Couldn't hurt 'em if you tried. And if *I* have to listen to that song one more time today, I'm going to hit him on the head with a frying pan."

Jeremy laughed uproariously and the waitress smiled at Christine. She always tried to get a laugh out of Jeremy when they ate at Gus's.

A few minutes later, when the waitress delivered their drinks and the music had been lowered a fraction, Christine asked Jeremy where he thought Patricia went so much of the time.

"Don't know." Jeremy noisily sucked Cherry Coke through a straw. "Nobody tells me anything. I get pretty bored and lonely at home, Christy. I only stay because Ames likes me around. Well, sometimes. Other times he acts like I'm invisible."

Which wasn't good for Jeremy, Christine thought. She knew her brother needed constant stimulation and a sense of purpose. She particularly disliked his being lonely. Ever since she'd bought a house late last summer, she'd planned to have him permanently move in with her. The basement was large and with an abundance of windows, giving it an unusual amount of daylight for a basement, and offered both inside and outside entrances. She'd decorated the whole area to look like a big loft apartment to give Jeremy a feeling of maturity and privacy while still living with her.

Before the holidays she'd told Ames she wanted Jeremy to move in, but Ames had begged her to let Jeremy stay until after Easter. "I'd miss him too much on long, dark winter evenings," Ames had said. But today had changed a lot of things. Even if this body did not turn out to be Dara's, the fear that it had been was likely to throw Ames into a depression Jeremy didn't need to be around. And it sounded as if Patricia wasn't home much, although she rarely went out of her way to entertain Jeremy. While Christine forced down half a cheeseburger she didn't want, she decided the time had come for Jeremy to move in with her.

"You're hardly eating," Jeremy commented. "You usually eat as much as me, maybe more."

"That is not true!" Christine retorted heatedly, then noticed Jeremy's twitching lips. He was trying to get her to smile. She obliged. "I happen to be watching my weight, smarty. I haven't been going to the gym as much as I need to."

"But you're not fat. Just tall."

At five feet, ten inches, Christine had always felt like an Amazon beside petite Dara, in spite of her vigilant maintenance of her weight. Danny Torrance, the gym manager, told her she was perfectly proportioned although she needed to be more diligent about her workouts to build strength. But then, Danny had been a family friend for years and could be counted on for a compliment.

As soon as he'd finished the very last drop of his ice cream, noisily scraping the sides of his glass dish, Jeremy looked at her and frowned. "I don't really want to sleep at Ames's house tonight. I'd rather come to your house. Is that okay?"

"Sure," Christine said promptly. "And it's *our* house." Jeremy beamed. "I'd be glad for the company, and I know Rhiannon will be happy to see you."

Months after Dara had disappeared, when Christine graduated from college and moved out of the house, she had taken Dara's black cat, Rhiannon, because Patricia detested her. So did Patricia's obnoxious little dog, Pom-Pom, who never gave Rhiannon a moment's peace.

"I can't wait to see Rhiannon," Jeremy said enthusiastically. "And can I watch *Buffy the Vampire Slayer*?"

"Certainly. I like it, too. But you have to call home first to let them know you're with me. If no one is there—"

"I know. Leave a message on the machine." Jeremy sounded like a beleaguered teenager. "I don't have to be told stuff a million times, Christy."

"Sorry. I didn't know you were so sensitive."

"It just wears me out when you say things over and over." Jeremy sounded slightly cranky, something Christine didn't want to deal with tonight.

"I won't keep repeating myself. I promise."

"Good." Jeremy wiped his mouth and scooted out of the booth. "Now I'll make my call."

"Where are you going?"

"To the payphone."

"Where's your cell phone?"

Jeremy's face reddened. "I left it at the store."

"Jeremy, it's very important for you to keep the cell phone with you." She stopped. She was about to deliver a lecture he'd heard a hundred times. "Sometimes I forget mine, too. Do you have—"

"Money for the pay phone? Yeah," Jeremy said over his shoulder as he headed toward the front of the restaurant and the pay telephone. "For Pete's sake, Christy!"

Christine smiled to herself. When others treated Jeremy like a child, she got annoyed, but she did it herself. Constantly. It irritated him with good reason. He was twenty now. It was time for her to stop hovering over him.

"It looks like this is the place to be tonight."

Christine looked up to see Sloane Caldwell standing beside her booth. Sloane was an associate in Ames's law firm, and a few years ago they'd been engaged. She'd broken off the engagement only weeks before the wedding, but they'd remained friendly, if not close. "The place does seem to be doing a booming business tonight," she said. "I think it's so gloomy, people hate to go home. Have a seat. Jeremy's gone to use the phone."

"Forgot his cell phone again?"

"Yes," Christine said without defensiveness. Sloane had always been kind to Jeremy, and during their engagement he'd seemed happy at the prospect of having Jeremy live with him and Christine. Not many men would have been so accepting of a woman's mentally challenged younger brother. "He's decided to spend the night at my house and wants to let Ames know."

Sloane sat down. He was a big, rugged-looking man with broad shoulders and a deep, booming voice that served him well in court. He had thick, curly brick-colored hair, an open smile, and a dozen lines shooting from the corners of his dark hazel eyes as if he'd been looking into the sun too long. His nose bore a bump from a long-ago break and a thin scar traversed his chin, both imperfections the result of his playing high school football. In spite of the designer suits he favored and his flawless manners, Christine had always thought Sloane looked like he should be spending his days hunting in the mountains instead of sitting behind a desk in a law office. He'd never married after their broken engagement.

"You look beautiful, as always, Chris, but I can tell when you're troubled," he said kindly. "Want to tell me what's wrong?"

"You'll hear soon enough, if you haven't already. A body wrapped in plastic washed ashore today. They think it might be Dara."

Sloane's lips parted and he stared at her for a moment, his eyes seeming to go flat with shock. "Good God! One of the secretaries told me a deputy came to the office looking for Ames. I guess that's what he wanted to tell him."

Christine nodded. "He tracked Ames down at the store. Ames demanded to be told right in front of everyone, then he insisted the body couldn't be Dara's. He was badly shaken, though. I was glad Wilma Archer was there. She's like a mother to him, you know."

"Yes, she is," Sloane said distractedly. "Did this deputy tell Ames the body was definitely Dara's?"

"It was Michael Winter, that new guy from Los Angeles, and he didn't say the body was Dara's. He said it was the right height and had long black hair, but there was a lot of decomposition in spite of all the plastic wrapping. After all, if it *is* Dara, she would have been in the water three years."

"If she was wrapped in plastic, she didn't drown accidentally. She was murdered," Sloane said. "But she could have been murdered later—weeks or months after she disappeared."

"I hadn't even thought of that possibility. If she did run away and came back a while later, though, no one saw her."

"At least no one who came forward."

"That's true. You're always so good at seeing all the angles."

"It's part of my job," Sloane answered. "Sometimes it's necessary in a client's defense."

"Yes, I guess it is." Christine ran a hand over her forehead. "Anyway, the body was sent directly to the medical examiner's in Charleston. Ames is there now to see if he can identify her. I think it's cruel to make him look at the body if there's been massive decomposition."

"There's no point in blaming the police, Chris. It's procedure."

"It may be procedure, but that doesn't make it less awful," Christine said dully, feeling like a cold wind was blowing over her.

Sloane shook his head. "Someone should have gone to Charleston with Ames."

"Me. I should have gone. But there was Jeremy to deal with—"

"I didn't mean you, Chris. I'm the one Ames should have called."

Yes, Christine thought, Sloane was incredibly strong. It was so easy to lean on him. But leaning on Sloane became a double-edged sword. It made him think he was in charge of every situation, a trait Christine had learned she couldn't live with and that was partially responsible for making her decide she couldn't marry him three years ago.

"I'm sure he'll be all right if there's no way he can be sure the body is Dara's," Christine said with more hope than certainty. "And he won't be alone when he comes home. He has Patricia."

Sloane pulled a face. "Yes, the devoted and sensitive Patricia, who couldn't stand Dara. She'd probably be a great comfort."

"Jeremy says she's gone all the time anyway."

"Is she getting bored with the good life already?"

"Maybe. She's a lot younger than Ames, and he hasn't exactly been a barrel of laughs since Dara disappeared."

"Chris, I doubt if Ames was ever a barrel of laughs."

"No, that's not his style. Still, he's gone from serious to gloomy. God knows how he'll be if this body turns out to be Dara's."

Jeremy appeared at the table. "Hi, Sloane."

"Hi yourself. Haven't seen you for a while."

"I'm really busy at the store. You heard about my job, didn't you? I'm not just a stock boy. I get to design jewelry."

"Of course I heard about it. Ames is really proud of you."

"Did Christy tell you about Dara?"

"She said a body was found, but no one's sure it's Dara. Don't think the worst, Jeremy." Sloane stood up quickly and Christine was glad he wasn't going to linger on the subject. "I've got a ton of work to do tonight, so I'd better get going. It was good to see the two of you. Drive carefully tonight. Those roads are treacherous."

"Christy drives *real* slow," Jeremy complained. "It takes us forever to get anywhere."

"Well, it's better than going too fast, having a wreck, and not getting there at all. Goodnight, folks."

Jeremy scooted into the booth after Sloane left. "Nobody was home, so I left my message."

Christine knew Ames was in Charleston, but where was Patricia? She should have been with Ames, of course, to help him through this horrible experience. Instead, no one seemed to know where she was. She might not have even heard about the body.

"You look sad," Jeremy said.

"Too much rain and too many gray skies."

"And too much bad news. About the body in the water. It's creepy." He looked away for a moment, then said with one of his abrupt changes of subject, "I want to go home and see Rhiannon."

"Me, too. But don't tell her you had a banana split or she'll pout all evening."

Jeremy's deep laugh boomed and his whole face seemed to light up. He looked like a male version of their beautiful mother, and Christine often felt bad when girls approached him based on his striking adult male looks only to find they were talking to an adolescent. But Jeremy rarely seemed to mind, thank goodness. He was remarkably adept at accepting his life.

Christine paid the bill and they set out for home. The rain had tapered off to a drizzle, but she still drove slowly while Jeremy listened to the radio, bobbing his head and singing along with even more gusto than usual to "Fly Away" by Lenny Kravitz, which happened to be his favorite song. Jeremy loved rock music and his voice was fairly good. Unfortunately, music annoyed Ames. Jeremy had to content himself with a boom box and a karaoke machine she'd bought him for Christmas, and even those things Ames had banished into a dingy back room of his basement.

When they entered Christine's large modern stone and sand-colored wood house the cat shot from behind a chair and flung herself at Jeremy's feet, rolling upside down and stretching her legs into the air.

Jeremy dropped to the floor and picked her up. "Rhiannon, I missed you!" The cat rubbed her mouth along his jaw to leave her scent. "Everybody thinks Dara just named you for that song she liked so much, but I know Rhiannon was really a witch."

Christine was surprised Jeremy recalled Dara telling him about the witch of Celtic legend, but then, what he remembered often surprised her. "Rhiannon is happy to see you," she said as the cat lolled happily in Jeremy's arms.

"I miss her all the time. I sure wish she could stay with me at Ames's house, but Patricia won't let her. She only likes Pom-Pom."

Christine, who loved almost every dog she saw, definitely found Pom-Pom an exception. The dog was eight pounds of sharp teeth, ear-shattering yips, knotted grayish-white hair, bad breath, and bad temper. Christine had no idea what misbegotten canine mix had created the ankle-biting monstrosity Patricia inexplicably adored and no one else could bear.

"You got any clean clothes for me to wear tomorrow?" Jeremy asked.

"I have some older things, but I just bought two new pairs of slacks and two shirts at the Gap three days ago."

Jeremy brightened. "You did? Are they downstairs in my room?"

"Yes. And I've just about finished decorating it. Run down and see what you think."

With the cat still in his arms, Jeremy immediately dashed to the kitchen and the upstairs entrance to his basement "apartment." Christine hoped that within a month he would be living here full-time.

Christine walked into her kitchen and felt a rush of pleasure at the sight of gleaming chrome appliances and the walls painted in cheerful shades of pistachio green and lemon yellow. Ames, with his inflexible traditional taste, didn't like the modern lines of her home, but he had almost quailed at the sight of this shining, vibrant room. Christine remembered having trouble hiding her amusement at his efforts not to express his overwhelming dismay that she'd spent so much money on a house he considered a frightful concoction of strange angles and loud colors.

While she poured water into a huge fern hanging at a window, Christine gazed beyond the deck and into the backyard, which she hoped would be a riot of colorful flowers come summer. On this dismal evening, though, that scene was hard to imagine. The wall of evergreens bordering the back of the lawn raised dripping limbs against a gunmetal sky. A forlorn sparrow sat on the edge of the bird feeder, and rain had beaten down the heads of six daffodils that had bloomed too soon, tricked by a few early warm days. Water stood in all the cracks between the flagstones of the walk leading down the slope to the patio outside Jeremy's basement entrance, a patio she hoped would accommodate some summer barbecues.

Christine filled the coffeemaker, and in a few minutes the smell of Jeremy's favorite raspberry-chocolate blend coffee filled the kitchen. She took his favorite thermal mug out of the cabinet and her own sturdy earthenware cup she favored over china.

"The place looks so cool!" Jeremy exclaimed as he bounded up the basement stairs and into the kitchen. "You didn't tell me you got me a ping pong table!"

"Early birthday gift," Christine managed as Jeremy gave her a bear hug. "You can have your friends over to play."

"Like Danny. Since he doesn't live beside Ames anymore, I hardly ever get to see him. And I've got my own door to the outside, too. People don't have to go through *your* place to get to *my* place!"

"I'm glad you like it."

"It's super. Hey, will that coffee keep me awake? 'Cause I have to go into the store early tomorrow."

"We're not opening until ten."

"I have to go earlier."

"Why?"

"It's a secret. Let's go watch TV."

Christine pretended to concentrate on shows that seemed to enthrall Jeremy, but she really wasn't paying the slightest attention. All she could think about was Ames in Charleston viewing a ravaged body that might be his daughter's. At ten o'clock she felt ready to scream with tension when the phone rang. She leaped from her chair and grabbed up the receiver. "Hello?"

A ragged voice emitted a couple of agonized sounds before Ames said, "H-her."

"Ames? I can barely hear you."

"The body. It's . . . it's Dara."

She'd been sure ever since Deputy Winter told them about the body being washed ashore that it was Dara's. Now her mind did not want to accept it. "You can't be sure," she said quickly, wrenched by the sound of his tormented voice. "Not until they've run tests. They have to do DNA testing—"

"The ring."

"What about the ring?"

"In the plastic wrapping they found her ring. The ruby-and-diamond ring I gave her for her high school graduation." He sounded like he was choking before he ground out, "It had her initials engraved inside. *DMP*. Dara Marie Prince. And the graduation date . . . Oh God, Christine—"

"Ames, are you on the road?"

"No. Home."

"Is Patricia there?"

"What? I don't know."

"If she isn't, I'm coming right over." Jeremy stood by her side now, his expression frightened. "You shouldn't be alone."

"Don't come over."

"Yes, I insist—"

"Don't come, Christine." Patricia's voice, crisp and cold, had replaced Ames's. "I'm here. I'll take care of my husband. You look after Jeremy. We don't need him here on top of everything else."

The phone clicked in Christine's ear.

And so the hope Ames had held on to so fiercely for three long years had been crushed on a cold, rainy March day when the Ohio River washed up the forlorn remains of his once-beautiful daughter and left them on a soggy bank like a grotesque offering.

A desolation that surprised her washed over Christine. She turned her face into Jeremy's chest and cried.

2

An hour later they'd trudged off to their respective bedrooms. Christine had finally controlled her weeping, and Jeremy had retreated into silence. He took Rhiannon downstairs with him, though. Christine knew he would find comfort in Dara's little black cat, who always curled beside him to sleep.

As she changed into a nightgown and washed her face, Christine was certain the sleep she wanted so badly wouldn't come for hours. She was too disturbed and shaken. But after she forced herself to read a few pages of a less than gripping murder mystery, the book toppled from her hand and she slid sideways against her stacked pillows.

She was dreaming of arguing with Dara over Sloane Caldwell. The dream was a playback of the last contretemps she'd ever had with Dara, when the girl had openly flirted with Sloane and even sat down on his lap during a party, stroking his face, rubbing her breasts against him, and licking his ear. Christine had been furious at the display, letting her temper get the best of her as she called Dara a tramp. Dara had laughed at her. "It's not my fault you can't hold on to Sloane," she'd jeered. "He'd rather have me and you know it!" Sloane had looked acutely embarrassed but said nothing.

Christine had slammed out of the party, refusing Sloane's attempts to take her home, asking a friend to drive her instead. The next day she'd broken off her engagement to Sloane. Less than a week later Dara had disappeared.

The phone rang and Christine awakened abruptly, Dara's sneering face dancing vividly in front of her own. She jerked up in bed and grabbed the phone on her bedside table. "Yes? What is it?"

"Did I wake you?"

"No." Christine always said no whether or not she'd been asleep, as if she felt guilty for not being alert at all times. "Who is this?"

"You *were* asleep or you'd know my voice. It's Streak." Streak Archer? Wilma's son? And what time was it? Christine peered at the bedside clock. Twelve forty-five. "Chris, I'm with Jeremy," he said urgently.

"Jeremy is downstairs in his room."

"No, he isn't. Now wake up and pay attention. He's down at the bridge at Crescent Creek with the cat. I found him when I was jogging."

"At the creek? What's he doing?"

"Don't ask questions. Just come. Your brother is more upset than I've ever seen him. He needs you *now*."

4

1

Christine bolted from bed, pulled on jeans, a sweatshirt, and a jacket, and rushed to her car. The constant rain of the last four days had stopped, but she didn't notice. The streets were nearly deserted, mist creating halos around streetlights. The Prince home was only a half-mile from her own. She passed its large brick facade and saw two lights burning, one in Ames's study and another in Patricia's bedroom. Patricia had probably retreated to her room to let Ames suffer alone. Or maybe he'd sent her away. Ames couldn't bear for people to see him as anything but strong and controlled.

Christine turned down Crescent Creek Road, a narrow asphalt lane that ran beside Ames's property. Only three small homes sat along the lane before the asphalt stopped and the gravel began. Her car, a light blue Dodge Neon, bounced over the road damaged by the heavy rain of the last week and a hard winter. Some trees appeared on either side of the road, mostly small locusts. She rounded the final curve leading down to the creek. Here the trees and undergrowth were denser, everything gleaming moistly in her headlights. She stopped the car, put on her emergency brake, and stepped out onto a slick patch of mud and gravel. Immediately she spotted, leaning against a tree, the ten-speed bike Jeremy kept at her house.

"Christine." She looked up to see Streak Archer in a running suit. At fifty-three he looked at least ten years older, with thick, silver hair and deep lines running across his forehead and down his cheeks. A scar bisected his right eyebrow. His real name was

Robert, but people had called him Streak since he'd been the fastest thing anyone had ever seen on the Winston High School track team.

"Where's Jeremy?" she asked anxiously. "Is he all right?"

Streak came to her and put his hands on her shoulders, gazing at her with his sad, hooded eyes. "He's not hurt and he's calming down some. I'm just glad I had my cell phone with me. I hate the damned thing, but Mom made me promise I'd carry it when I ran in case I ever got hurt in some desolate spot." He smiled wryly. "Guess she knew best. It came in handy."

Streak was the son of Wilma Archer, who had been in the store earlier that day. Streak and Ames Prince had been friends since childhood, when a young, lonely Ames had found comfort in the Archers' warm, noisy, openly loving home so unlike his own with his austere father and invalid mother. Wilma was like a mother to him and Streak like a brother.

"Jeremy is upset about Dara, isn't he?" Christine asked tensely.

"Yes. Mom called and told me about their finding the body, then about Ames identifying it as Dara's."

"Jeremy got very upset in the store when he found out about the body, but later this evening at my house he calmed down. Then Ames called. Jeremy seemed unnerved but under control. Maybe he was too calm when he went to bed. I should have known that was a bad sign."

"When I found him he was sobbing, throwing petals from silk flowers in the creek, saying he was sorry and talking about a dream with dark water and not being able to see or breathe."

Dread washed over Christine. "Apparently that's a recurring nightmare. He's mentioned the dream a couple of times since Dara disappeared, but he didn't seem too distressed by it, and frankly, I didn't pay much attention. Today he went into more detail about it. It's awful." She sighed. "Streak, sometimes it's hard to know what's bothering him. He'll get upset over something trivial but not say a word about something that deeply troubles him like this dream. He must have had it again tonight and it set him off."

"I think you're right."

"I need to see him."

"Sure you do." Streak put his arm around her. "Watch your step. This gravel in the mud is treacherous."

"I'm surprised you're out jogging tonight."

"I jog every night unless there's pelting rain or a snowstorm. Helps keep my own nightmares away."

Nightmares of Vietnam, Christine knew. Streak had been only nineteen when news came from an exotic place called Qui Nhon that he'd been shot in the head and the bullet had lodged in his brain. He was sent from the field hospital to Saigon, and although he was alive, doctors warned there was next to no hope. Ames told Christine that a deeply religious Wilma had spent all her time in church and Streak's father had put in compulsive eighteen-hour days working the farm while they waited for the inevitable news that their son had died. But Streak had hung on, although doctors again warned that if he survived, he would be brain-damaged, maybe little more than a living corpse.

Streak was eventually sent to Hawaii, where he continued to astonish everyone by gradually recovering, struggling through an agonizing rehabilitation where he relearned to walk, to feed himself, and to talk. Fourteen months later he returned to Winston with the only visible signs of his experience being a couple of scars on his forehead and a mane of silver hair that had been black two years earlier. But he had changed in a way that was not immediately noticeable. He suffered memory lapses and was plagued by insomnia. He endured shattering migraines. Most shocking was that the once-gregarious Streak was now taciturn, growing distraught and suffering panic attacks in the crowds he'd once loved. During one boisterous surprise welcome home party thrown by some rowdy old friends, Streak had started to sweat and shake and ended the evening curled in a corner, whimpering. So people said he'd gotten strange and a little scary, and they left him alone.

That had been a long time ago, but he'd never lost his new love of solitude. Now he was close only to his family and to Ames, along with some contact with Jeremy and Christine. Streak spent his days at home designing brilliant computer programs, providing himself with a very healthy income, and a good part of his nights he filled with jogging to keep at bay nightmares of his horrifying injury and the hell of his recovery.

Christine and Streak started down the slope to the bridge. They'd only gone a few feet when Jeremy ran toward Christine with an odd lumbering gait she'd only seen him use a few times when he was distraught. "Christy!" he cried, enfolding her in his strong arms. "Dara is dead."

"I know, honey." She patted his back. "But Dara has been gone a long time. We knew it was possible she was dead."

"But Ames got those letters, so I thought *maybe* she didn't die. If she didn't send those letters, who did?"

"I'm sure everyone would like to know that," Christine answered.

"She used to be real nice to me sometimes. She'd tell me about magic. And she sang with me on my machine."

"Your karaoke machine?" Christine asked. He nodded. "I didn't know that."

"She sang really pretty. But she'd get the giggles."

His eyes filled with tears again and Christine took his hand. "Jeremy, why did you bring Rhiannon and come here in the middle of the night?"

Jeremy drew back and gave her a long intense look, his eyes troubled. "Because this is the last place where Dara was. She brought her boom box. Then she was gone."

2

Christine's heart gave an uncomfortable thud. Streak's brown gaze met hers over Jeremy's shoulder. "Jeremy, you don't know that Dara disappeared from this spot. No one knows where Dara was before she . . . disappeared."

"*I* know."

"*How* do you know?"

Jeremy frowned. " 'Cause Dara was upset. She'd been upset a couple of days. And the evening she went away, she was *real* upset."

Christine searched his face. "Jeremy, I don't remember Dara being upset."

"You prob'ly didn't even see her. But I saw her leaving the house with Rhiannon and her boom box. She always took her boom box to the creek."

Christine's anxiety grew. "You told everyone you didn't see her that night."

"I said I didn't *talk* to her, and I didn't. But I knew where she was going because of the boom box and it being Black Moon night and everything." Jeremy hung his head. "I did say Dara *might* be at the creek. Remember? We went and looked and she wasn't there." His expression grew even more troubled. "Later, when she didn't show up at all, I knew I should've told about her being upset, but it seemed too late then. People would have thought I was making it up. But I came back here and looked a hundred times."

"Jeremy, just because Dara came to the creek that evening doesn't mean she disappeared from here," Christine said, trying to sound calm.

"But it *is* the place where she left."

"What makes you so sure?"

Jeremy looked miserable. "I don't know, Christy. It's a feeling, that's all. At least, I think that's all. I can't really explain what it is."

Oh, dear God, Christine thought in despair as her hands grew cold. Was Jeremy merely experiencing a vague feeling of guilt because he hadn't been completely honest at the time of Dara's disappearance? Or was he dredging up a dark memory of what had happened to her the last night she'd been seen alive?

3

"Jeremy, you don't *know* that Dara *disappeared* from this spot," Christine repeated slowly and emphatically, emphasizing the word *disappeared* so as not to upset him even more with the word *murdered*. "I don't want you to tell *anyone* that you know she definitely was here."

"Why not?"

"Because it could be misleading," she said quickly, feeling Streak's gaze on her.

Jeremy's forehead wrinkled. "I don't understand."

"Look, Jeremy, maybe she did come down here with her boom box before you went next door to play ping pong at the Torrance house with Danny."

Jeremy nodded. "Yeah. That's when she left."

"Okay, let me finish. Let's say she came down here, but it started to rain and before you came home from Danny's, she went back to the house. Maybe she was really upset about something and she'd decided to leave home. You know she was always threatening to run away." Like a nine-year-old, not a nineteen-year-old, Christine thought. "She came back and no one was home, so she packed up some of her clothes. You know things were missing from her room—things she would take if she were leaving. And she wrote the good-bye note. You saw it. Then she had someone pick her up in a car. They picked her up at the house, Jeremy, not here."

"Nobody ever said they picked her up."

"She could have sworn them to secrecy, made a secret pact. Remember when we used to make secret pacts?"

"Yeah." Jeremy was not to be placated so easily, though. "But we were kids. Grown-ups don't make pacts so much, and everybody knew how scared Ames was that she might be dead, so they wouldn't have told him they took Dara away from the house." Jeremy shook his head vehemently. "Nobody helped Dara run away, and *I* know this is the last place she was."

Christine stared at her brother, panic racing through her.

Three years ago when Dara disappeared, Sheriff Buck Teague and some other Winston citizens were suspicious of Jeremy. Many people knew he'd had a crush on Dara. And Jeremy was big. And retarded, they said. Who knew what a big retarded guy might do if he was rejected, angered, hurt? Ames had quieted a lot of the speculation by letting it be known Dara constantly talked of leaving Winston and that many of her clothes and possessions were missing. He'd also told everyone of his acquaintance about the first letter he'd received supposedly from Dara, postmarked Miami, Florida. Wilma Archer had also spread the word to her many friends, but Christine knew not everyone was convinced Jeremy Ireland had not harmed Dara. Now he was insisting he knew where Dara had been on her last night in Winston, which would certainly stir up old suspicions. Dangerous suspicions.

Fear for her brother struck so deep that suddenly Christine couldn't speak. She stood staring at him while he looked back with an injured expression growing in his blue eyes. Christine could have kissed Streak when he said easily, "Jeremy, why don't we just hang around the creek for a while and talk? It's quit raining and the stars are out. And you've got Rhiannon with you. Let's make this a fun midnight adventure."

Jeremy hung his head. "I don't feel like having fun."

"Oh, come on, I know you like adventures." Streak took Jeremy's arm and began walking toward the creek with him. "I think looking at a flooded creek at night in the moonlight is really cool. Don't you?"

"I guess," Jeremy said listlessly, as if all the emotion had abruptly drained out of him.

"Don't you think it's cool, Christine?" Streak prodded.

"Oh yes," she said tonelessly, following them to the creek bank. "Sort of spooky cool. Jeremy loves spooky cool things."

"Like on TV," Jeremy said with a tad more enthusiasm.

"Yeah, like on TV. I love having exciting experiences like the ones on TV," Streak went on, knowing that cajoling Jeremy out of a mood took patience and verbal repetition.

"Don't you feel sad that Dara might be dead?" Jeremy asked Streak.

"Right now I'm not thinking of Dara. I'm having fun."

"I've heard people say you're weird and you don't like to have fun."

Jeremy with his complete honesty and lack of tact, Christine thought, hoping Streak wouldn't take offense.

But he laughed. "Jeremy, some people say lots of things that aren't true. The people who say I don't like to have fun have probably never even met me."

"People say things about me, too. They say I'm stupid."

"Those are the people we ignore. What they say can't hurt us." Streak pointed at the creek. "Look how high it is."

"And still," Christine said. "You expect rushing water in a flood."

"The water from creeks does rush into the river until the river gets so full, it backs up the creeks like a big plug. The more the Ohio River rises, the more water will be forced back into Crescent Creek."

Which meant Dara could have been killed in this very spot, thrown in the creek, and remained trapped there until the rushing water of this flood carried her into the river. And once the river had made its awful delivery, it was coming back into the creek, Christine thought fearfully. Jeremy could be right. This could have been the site where Dara had died. Or rather, been murdered.

Christine shuddered and forced thoughts of the possible logistics of Dara's murder from her mind. Moonlight shimmered on the dark water that was higher than Christine had ever seen it. Not that she'd seen it often. She'd always avoided this place. Something about it made her edgy, as if she were intruding on sacred ground. The feeling probably came from the stories Dara had told her and Jeremy about the Mound Builders who had lived on the other side of the creek.

Christine had crossed the bridge on foot only twice with Dara to look at the mounds built by the Indians hundreds of years ago, and each time she'd been unnerved, although she tried to hide her apprehension from Dara. Dara would have laughed at her—with good reason. No ghosts of ancient Mound Builders lurked around protecting their burial grounds. Still, Christine hated the creek and the peninsula on the other side. Unfortunately, Jeremy had always seemed as drawn to it as Dara had been. And now he was vehemently declaring he knew this quiet, gloomy spot was the last place Dara had been. Christine shivered.

"What's wrong?" Jeremy asked.

"I'm a little chilly," Christine said.

Jeremy frowned. "But you're wearing a sweatshirt and jacket. I don't think it's cold. Do you, Streak?"

"I'm not freezing or anything, Jeremy," Christine lied, knowing it wasn't the temperature but her conscience that turned her hands and neck icy. For years Christine had not let herself think about the time immediately before Dara's disappearance when she had allowed her long resentment of the selfish, spoiled girl to boil over at the party where Dara had flirted with and fondled Christine's fiancé and he had not resisted. Afterward, she'd treated Dara with cold and self-righteous disdain, publicly blaming Dara for having to break her engagement. She'd hated herself for the lie; she'd known for some time that she didn't love Sloane. She'd been looking for an acceptable excuse to break off with that generous and intelligent man who would have given her a steady, comfortable life, but whose dominating personality would have suffocated her.

When Dara caused the scene and Sloane allowed it to happen and said nothing, Christine had jumped at the convenient justification for canceling the upcoming wedding. Ironically, Dara had done her a favor, but everyone except Jeremy had been mad at Dara. Christine had been ashamed by her manipulation of the circumstances, in spite of years of Dara's hauteur and slights, but she'd played the hand and was still playing it when Dara vanished only days later. Now Christine's guilt over the incident came flooding back like the dark, dirty water of the creek. She knew she'd wronged Dara. She knew she'd never find peace within her own mind until she'd tried in some way to make amends. But how did you do that when the one you'd wronged was dead?

"Do you want to come, too?"

Christine realized Jeremy was talking to her. "What?"

"I knew you weren't listening!" Jeremy said fretfully. "I hate it when you don't listen."

Christine mentally shook herself. She had come here to help her troubled brother, not indulge her own guilt. "This place just seems kind of strange to me and I got distracted," she said. "I'm sorry."

Jeremy appeared to think this over before finally muttering, "Okay."

"Thank you. You asked if I wanted to go. Do I want to go where?"

"This summer when everything dries up, Streak said we could go over and look at the mounds."

"Jeremy, I know you'd enjoy that, but I don't feel comfortable about your going to the peninsula at night."

"It doesn't have to be night," Streak said.

"You mean you'd go out in the *day*?" Christine asked in surprise.

"I'm not a vampire, Chris," Streak said in mock reproach. "I won't burst into flames if a sunbeam hits me." Jeremy, whose favorite show was about vampires, laughed out loud, and Christine felt relief. Laughter was a good sign that Jeremy was getting his anxiety in check. "I can go out in the day," Streak continued. "I just usually choose not to. But I'd go over to the mounds with Jeremy and you."

"I haven't been over there for a few years," Christine said. "I guess I could tag along with you guys. In the *day*. No power on this earth could get me over there at night."

" 'Fraidy cat," Jeremy teased. "But we can go in the day if you want. Maybe we could even have a picnic." Christine couldn't think of a place she'd less like to have a picnic, but she would do it to please her brother. "And we'll look for more Indian graves."

"I draw the line there," Christine said. "Absolutely no grave-hunting."

"We wouldn't move the bones or anything," Jeremy assured her. "Even though they're not scary. Dara said the ones she saw a long time ago weren't scary."

"Maybe they weren't scary to her, but they would be to me," Christine said faintly, unable not to link the idea of Dara with skeletons. The body washed up from the river had been badly decomposed . . .

A few minutes earlier a mist had risen and now it curled through the undergrowth, giving the surroundings a hazy, dreamlike quality. Something about the atmosphere felt ominous to Christine, almost as if the mist were trying to grab hold and drag her down into the dark earth that smelled of rotting leaves and stagnant water. A cold tingle quivered through her. She felt as if malevolent eyes crawled up and down her body. She glanced nervously around, sensing some kind of presence. A *presence*? In spite of her dislike of this place, she was really letting her imagination run wild, she thought in annoyance. The only presences around were those of animals. Squirrels. Opossums. Perhaps even a fox. But a fox wouldn't attack a human unless it was rabid, in which case it wouldn't have stayed quiet and watchful for so long. She was being ridiculous. Still, the feeling of being watched persisted. The hairs on her neck tickled.

"Jeremy, your sister looks tired." Streak's interruption sounded entirely normal, although Christine guessed she looked worse than tired. She felt jumpy and deeply apprehensive, and Streak didn't miss much.

"I really would like to leave now," she said. "I'm sleepy." Another lie. "Are you ready to go, Jeremy?"

"Yeah, I guess," he said reluctantly. "But I thought we were gonna have an adventure. Standing on the creek bank isn't much of an adventure."

"We'll save the adventure for our picnic." Christine smiled. "I might even get up my nerve and help look for graves. How about that?"

Jeremy smiled. "That sounds like lots more fun!"

"Grave-hunting. My idea of a good time," Christine muttered, then looked around and asked Jeremy, "Where's Rhiannon?"

"Prob'ly hiding. I'll go find her."

Streak stared as Jeremy walked away through the brush, his gait easy and coordinated again. "Dara always brought that cat down here to the bridge at night. I used to take a break from my run to talk to her."

Christine was surprised. "I didn't know you two were friends."

"Chats at the creek were about the only socializing Dara and I did," Streak said quickly. "I don't know if you'd call us real friends."

"Did you ever tell Ames about your visits with Dara?"

"No. He'd forbidden her to come down here. I didn't want to start a fight between them by ratting her out. But I understood his concern. This isn't a good place for a girl to be hanging around by herself at night. So I always ran by, although I don't think she ever guessed I was watching out for her. I always tried to make it seem casual, like I was just hanging around and shooting the breeze while I took a breather." He looked slightly melancholy. "We had a few good talks."

"About what?"

"Oh . . . nothing really. What I'd thought of her mother when I met her. What her father had been like when he was young."

"And about Jeremy and me. Don't try to tell me she didn't have quite a few complaints about us."

Streak grinned. "Your name might have come up once or twice. She pretended not to like you, but I think deep down she admired your maturity and intelligence."

"You could have fooled me. What about the night she disappeared? Did you see her then?"

"I didn't run that night. I was working on a difficult piece of software—something to do with fuzzy logic—and decided to skip my run so I could get it done. You don't know how much I've regretted that burst of diligence."

"You sound like Jeremy, as if you're certain she disappeared from the creek area."

"No, but if I'd met her here, I would have gotten a chance to talk to her, seen what kind of mood she was in—rebellious, ready to leave home, or frightened. And if something *did* happen to her here at the creek, maybe I could have prevented it."

"I see what you mean," Christine said slowly. "But don't you think you should have told the police you saw her out here regularly?"

"I did tell the police. I just didn't tell Ames. He would have been furious with me for not telling him she came here all the time, although telling him wouldn't have accomplished anything except to cause more trouble between him and Dara. Things were pretty tense back then, if you remember."

"Oh, I remember," Christine said dryly. "I never understood why she didn't just move out into a small apartment."

"A small apartment where she'd have to do her own cooking and cleaning?"

"I'd rather cook and clean than fight with people all the time."

"But you're not Dara," Streak said. "She had a little bit of the princess syndrome."

"More than a little, and it bothered everyone except Ames and Jeremy." She frowned. "I hope Jeremy doesn't tell everyone he *knows* Dara disappeared from down here. Sheriff Teague has always been convinced Jeremy did something to her, even though he had the whole Torrance family and several other teenagers to confirm that he was at a party at their house, playing ping pong, until after Ames and Patricia got home and Dara was gone. But Teague kept saying that with all the commotion, Jeremy could have slipped out of the party and no one would have noticed."

"I remember the grilling Teague put Jeremy through. It would have been worse if Jeremy hadn't had Ames there to protect him."

"And now there's this new guy, Winter, who seems pretty interested in the case."

"Winter?"

"Michael Winter. He's the deputy who came to the store and told Ames about the body. He came to Winston from LA. I'm sure there's a story behind that move. He seems nice enough but tenacious. I just have a bad feeling . . ."

"Chris, you don't think Jeremy hurt Dara, do you?"

"No! Of course not!"

"Well, if anyone else asks you that question, try to act like you're not protesting too much." Christine looked down and took a deep breath, wondering just how large was that ugly tendril of doubt about her own brother's innocence. "But I understand why you're upset. And I agree that Jeremy has to stop talking so much about Dara. You've got to keep him busy at the store. And let him stay at your house a lot. He can also spend some time with me. He likes computers."

Christine looked at Streak gratefully. She knew how much he valued his routines and his privacy.

"He'll love getting to visit you." Christine plunged her hands in her pockets. "And I'll love getting away from here tonight. This mist is giving me the creeps."

"I thought you women loved mists like on the moors in *Wuthering Heights*."

"You can have your mists and your moors, Streak. I prefer hot, sunny days."

They both turned to look at Jeremy tramping back through the undergrowth. "Rhiannon's hiding really good tonight," he said. "I couldn't find her."

"How did you get her here with you in the first place?" Christine asked.

"Easy. I put her in the basket on my bike. I wrapped her up in that little wool blanket you have in her bed and left her head out. She loves to ride that way."

"She also loves to climb," Streak said, gazing beyond Christine. "She's running up that old wild-cherry tree after a squirrel."

"Oh, wonderful," Christine moaned. "We'll never get her."

"I can," Jeremy assured her. "I'm great at climbing trees."

"Not that one," Christine warned. "It's old and fragile and covered with damp honeysuckle vines."

"The vines aren't blooming," Jeremy argued, standing beside the tree.

"They're still slippery."

"It'll be okay."

"No, it won't. Jeremy! Streak, stop him!"

Streak ran to the tree, but Jeremy was already four feet off the ground. Short of grabbing his ankles and yanking him loose, Streak couldn't get Jeremy down. "If that tree starts creaking under your weight, drop immediately," Streak ordered. "I'll catch you."

"I'm too heavy! I'd mash you flat, Streak Archer!" Jeremy laughed. "Don't worry. I know what I'm doing."

Christine closed her eyes, envisioning the tree along with Jeremy crashing into the flooded creek below. Jeremy was an excellent swimmer, but if the tree fell on top of him . . .

"The squirrel went in a hole and Rhi's trying to go after it!" Jeremy called. "C'mere, you little witch cat. You're not going in that hole!" Christine heard an enraged *meow* before Jeremy yelled, "Got her! Oh! Here's something else!"

"Leave the something else and come down right now," Streak said. "It could be a snake."

"It's not a snake or an animal." *Meow* and *hiss* from Rhiannon. *Creak* and *groan* from the tree. Christine held her breath. "It's something in plastic!" Jeremy called.

Plastic? Christine's thoughts immediately jumped to the plastic shroud on the corpse in the river. "Jeremy, come down this instant!" she ordered. "Leave the cat and the plastic thing."

"You always think I'm gonna get hurt." Jeremy began his descent. "I'm *fine*. I know how to climb a tree." As he neared the bottom, Rhiannon leaped from Jeremy's arms, throwing an obligatory enraged hiss at Christine and Streak before she ran to the side of the road and began vigorously grooming. While his feet were still three feet above ground, Jeremy let go of the tree and thudded into the weeds, dragging a handful of honeysuckle vines with him.

Christine's patience finally snapped into shrill carping: "Well, I hope that was worth it, Jeremy! You're a *mess*! Do you know how dangerous that was? You could have fallen in the creek! You've probably sprained your ankle—"

"Gosh, Christy, will you chill out?" Jeremy stood up and scraped off the damp, clinging vines. "Let's look at this thing in plastic."

"I don't want to look at it," Christine continued stridently. "It's dirty. Put it down."

"It looks like a book," Jeremy said.

"A book?" Christine drew closer, curious in spite of herself.

"It's in one of those plastic bags you put in the freezer." Jeremy wiped off the bag with his hand. "Got your flashlight, so we can see it better, Christy?"

"I don't want to see it better," Christine snapped, nevertheless pulling a penlight from the pocket of her jacket. "I just want to go home and make sure you're all right. And sleep might be nice. It's nearly dawn and I am *so* tired—"

"It isn't nearly dawn," Jeremy said testily, taking the penlight from her. "You sound like Patricia. Gripe, gripe, gripe." He flipped on the instrument and shone a thin stream of light on a navy blue book cover bearing golden print. He read in a halting, hushed voice:

"*Diary of Dara Marie Prince.*"

5

"What?" Streak sounded shocked. "Dara's diary? You've found Dara's diary?"

"I remember this," Christine said slowly. "Patricia gave it to Dara that last Christmas. I never saw the diary after Dara disappeared. I thought if she did leave Winston voluntarily, she must have taken it with her."

Streak frowned. "I used to see her writing in it when I'd stop by on a run. She was always quick to close the cover."

"I remember it, too," Jeremy said, holding the plastic bag almost reverently. "She said I must never look in it, and I never did."

"Has this been here for three years?" Christine asked no one in particular. "Why wasn't it found?"

"The police searched this area after Dara went missing, but their search wasn't too enthusiastic," Streak said. "High water, lots of mud. It was a mess here. Besides, who would look in a vine-covered hole in an old tree?" Streak drew closer, peering down at the book. "She must have kept it here all the time, wrapped in this bag. No doubt she suspected that Patricia did regular searches of her room."

Christine quirked an eyebrow. "You mean she gave Dara a diary to encourage her to bare her soul so Patricia could read it?" Streak nodded. "I remember thinking when Dara opened the gift that a diary seemed like something for a young girl, not a nineteen-year-old. I thought Dara would sneer about it to me when Patricia wasn't around, but Patricia must have known

Dara better than I thought. Dara started writing in it immediately."

"Patricia didn't know her very well if she thought Dara would leave it around for her to read," Streak said.

As Christine gazed at the dirty bag in Jeremy's hands, she felt dread descend. "We have to take this to Ames. If he's asleep, though, I don't want to wake him."

Streak said thoughtfully, "Maybe it should just be left alone, like Dara wanted."

"You mean put it back in the tree? Streak, that's absurd. Do you know what this would mean to Ames?"

"Of course we won't put it back in the tree. But I could take it and give it to Ames someday when the pain of all this is past. It seems almost cruel to give it to him now."

Christine hesitated. The diary was meant to be private. Privacy should be respected. Then she thought of Sheriff Teague's conviction that Jeremy had done something to Dara. His conviction would only grow stronger if the body was identified as Dara's, because she'd obviously been murdered. Add to the mix the things Jeremy was saying about knowing from where she vanished and her being in the water—things he would keep saying although she'd told him to stop—and the situation could prove disastrous for her brother.

But the diary could contain information they'd never known, never guessed at—things going on in Dara's life that could have led to her murder. And if they could discover who killed Dara, the dangerous suspicions about Jeremy would be lifted. His freedom, his life, could depend on it.

"You know, Streak, there could be significant clues in this diary," she said urgently.

"Clues about what?"

"Who Dara was seeing. What she was into back in those days." She paused. "Maybe who could have had a motive to murder her."

Streak seemed to recoil at the word *murder*. "Chris, that's a real stretch."

"No, it isn't. It's a real possibility."

"You think that if Dara believed someone was going to murder her she would have written it in her diary but not told anyone? That's crazy."

"I didn't mean she'd say anything so direct. But maybe reading about what she did, who her friends were . . . I don't know. *Anything* might give us an idea of someone who was dangerous to her, even if she didn't realize it."

Streak looked troubled for a moment. Finally he said, "Okay, let's say it is. What do we do with the thing?"

"Give it to the police."

"The police!" Streak's raised voice cut through the night. "But it's so personal. You can't have the police reading Dara's most private thoughts!"

"You *can't* read that diary," Jeremy said stridently. "Dara said not to. She made me promise. She wouldn't like it. If you read it, she might even come back from the dead and . . . and do something bad to you!"

"Jeremy, why don't you round up the cat so we can leave?" Christine said gently.

"You're just trying to get rid of me!"

"No, I'm tired and I want to go home and we can't go without Rhiannon. You don't want her to spend the whole night out here in the dark and the wind and the rain and the cold, do you?"

Christine had added every persuasive objection she could think of to drive home Rhiannon's pitiful state if left at the creek. "I guess she *would* be scared. We could just wait on her," Jeremy said.

"I can't wait. I'm too tired. I'm going, even if Rhiannon doesn't."

"I think you're being mean," Jeremy announced hotly.

"Maybe. I'm tired."

"*Okay,*" Jeremy huffed. "I'll go *look* for her."

"Thank you." She extended her hand. "I'll hold the diary."

"Don't you dare open it," Jeremy warned. "Don't forget what I said about Dara coming back. This is a ghost hangout, you know. She'd be back here lickety-split if you read her diary."

"All right. I believe you. Now don't let Rhiannon get away again. I'm not staying out here half the night."

"You really are crabby tonight," Jeremy muttered as he tromped off after the cat.

Streak looked at Christine. "There could be things in here that would be excruciatingly embarrassing to Ames, things that can't hurt Dara because she isn't here. Ames still is and he's been through enough."

"Which doesn't change the fact that Dara was murdered. Information in this diary could lead to her killer." Christine felt growing confidence in her belief. "That's why it has to go to the police."

"I see your point if there really is something important in here. But the diary might be full of nothing but a teenage girl's silliness. Not that at nineteen Dara should have been all that silly, but in some ways she seemed much younger than her age."

"In some ways she seemed like she didn't have a brain," Christine couldn't help snapping. "But in others she was very sophisticated. She wasn't a bad person, Streak, but she was self-absorbed and she never thought about the consequences of her actions. She was also extremely impulsive."

"You really did hate her," Streak said softly.

"I did not!" Christine's anger rose. "I am so tired of being accused of hating Dara. I tried to be friends with her when we first came here, and she let me know in a hurry she wanted nothing to do with me. And she kept letting me know it. She made fun of me. She shunned me. She rubbed my face in the fact that she was beautiful and popular and had a doting father. She hurt my feelings. She made me jealous. She made me mad. So no, I didn't *like* her. But I didn't *hate* her."

Streak held up his hand as if to stem the tirade. "I shouldn't have said that. I saw her goad you over the years. You had every right to dislike her. But I was out of line to say you hated her. I'm sorry."

"All right. Apology accepted. But my prejudices against her aside, Streak, you know she got a thrill out of taking risks, and I'd bet my life she was up to some things she shouldn't have been."

"Things that could have gotten her killed?"

"Maybe."

"So you're planning on running to Sheriff Teague with this diary?"

"Absolutely not. Buck Teague is an idiot. Besides, the diary could be full of things that have absolutely no bearing on Dara's murder."

"Then what's your solution?"

Christine said firmly, "We should read the diary first. We don't want the whole police department reading about family squabbles that have nothing to do with Dara's death. If that's the only kind of thing she wrote about, we don't need to give this to the police."

"But if there's something suspicious—"

"Then we have no choice, even if the family does suffer some embarrassment."

Streak's face turned grim. "I don't like it, Chris. It's sneaky. It could cause Ames untold humiliation."

"What does some humiliation matter if it leads to finding who killed Dara, wrapped her in plastic, and threw her in the river?"

The force of Christine's brutal words seemed to freeze Streak's objections. Of course Ames loved his daughter and wouldn't want her reputation besmirched in any way, even by something trivial. But even more than protecting her reputation, he would want her killer found and punished.

Christine could see the conflict going on behind Streak's hooded eyes. "Streak, I want *us* to read it first," she tried again. "I want you to come home with Jeremy and me. You and I will read the diary and then *we* will decide what to do."

Christine knew how intrusive Streak must find such a request. After all, he really didn't know her well. Also, he was comfortable only two places—in his home and on his lonely runs. His visits were limited to his mother's house and Ames's, and they were always short.

Streak looked extremely reluctant and Christine almost withdrew the request, then forced herself to take a stand. She needed help with this matter. "Please, Streak. I know you don't want to do this, but I don't feel right about deciding all on my own whether to take the diary to the police. You're more like family to Ames than I am. There's no one else I'd really trust to help me with this decision."

Finally, Streak said with a slight smile, "Going to push the responsibility off on me, are you?"

"If it goes to the police and Ames has a fit—"

"He definitely will, Chris."

"I know. Anyway, in that event, I'll take full responsibility for the decision. He won't even know you were involved. I promise."

"I was teasing, Chris. I don't like displeasing Ames, but he doesn't scare me. And I'm more of a man than to push the responsibility off on you. If we decide to give the police the diary, I'll own up to my part in the decision."

"Okay. But I have one condition. If it goes to the police, I want to give it to Deputy Winter, not Sheriff Teague."

"Winter? I thought you didn't trust him."

"All I said is that he struck me as being tenacious. But as for trust, after one brief meeting with him I trust him more than I do Teague. Our sheriff has it in for my brother."

"Yes, he certainly does. All right. If the diary goes, it goes to Winter. But are you sure you want to start reading tonight?"

"I can't possibly sleep after all this. I also don't think we should hang on to the diary for long if there's something in it that could tell us what happened to Dara."

Streak nodded, then turned. Jeremy was tramping toward them with Rhiannon in his arms, her golden eyes looking huge in the moonlight. "Your sister has asked me to come home with you two. I'll ride your bike back. You and Rhi go in the car."

"How come you're going to our house? You've never been there before," Jeremy asked suspiciously.

"It's part of our adventure."

"Oh." Jeremy's suspicion faded and he looked pleased. "Maybe you don't know which house is Christy's. You can ride in the car with her and I'll take my bike."

"I know which house is yours and I *really* want to ride your bike. It's a beauty." Christine knew Streak had no great desire to ride Jeremy's bicycle. Just an hour earlier Jeremy had been an emotional wreck, and now Streak wanted to make sure he returned home safely. "Riding the bike is part of the adventure for me," Streak said enthusiastically.

"Oh, sure, I get it," Jeremy said approvingly. "Do you know how to ride my bike?"

"This ten-speed is a lot fancier than anything I ever had, but I think the old-timer can make it. See you at the house in a few minutes."

As soon as they left the creek area, the vitality seemed to drain from Jeremy. Christine imagined the adrenaline that had pushed him into overdrive earlier had abruptly dissipated, leaving him exhausted. He was yawning hugely when they got home. He and the cat nearly tumbled from the car, and as soon as they got inside, he said, "I'm sorry to mess up Streak's adventure, but I'm too sleepy to stay up and visit. Do you think he'd be mad if I just go to bed?"

"Of course he won't be mad. There's plenty of time for other adventures." Christine had expected an argument with him about their reading the diary. With relief, she realized that if Jeremy went to bed, a spat could be avoided. "Make sure the basement doors to the outside are locked," she called as Jeremy headed downstairs with Rhiannon.

Christine put on another pot of coffee and waited for Streak. "Thank goodness the rain has stopped," he said after putting Jeremy's bike in the garage and sitting down at the kitchen table. "That could have been a nasty ride home."

"No rain means no more flooding."

"Not necessarily. The rain has just moved north. The river will still rise. The trouble isn't over yet." She set a mug of coffee in front of him and he immediately took a sip. "Unfortunately, we don't have a flood wall like that town down the river. I think the Army Corps of Engineers will order sandbagging to start tomorrow."

"And Jeremy will want to be in the midst of the activity."

"Don't sound so worried. He's strong and capable. You can't hover over him forever, Chris." Streak grinned. "Even the notorious recluse Streak Archer will turn out to help."

"That should cause talk."

"Hopefully enough to drown out talk about the body."

"I don't think anything could do that." Christine sighed as she sat down with her own mug of coffee. "Can you imagine what Ames must be feeling tonight?"

"No, but then, Ames has always been good at closing his eyes to what he doesn't want to see. He didn't even cry when his mother died, although I know he adored her."

"What about when Eve died?"

"Pretty much the same. He said he couldn't cave in to his grief because he had to be strong for Dara, but I think giving in to emotion to him was the same as admitting Eve was gone. And he couldn't let go of her, so he turned to her nurse. Patricia was just a link to his first wife."

"A young and pretty link."

"Yes. And one that Dara liked until Ames married her."

"Do you think Patricia loves Ames?"

Streak shook his head. "She came from a dirt-poor background, detested nursing although she was good at it, and saw a comfortable landing place with an older, financially successful man."

"Not so comfortable a place with Dara around. They rarely got through a day without some kind of blowup. I remember how anxious it made me when Jeremy and I came to live with Ames. I thought Ames might decide Jeremy and I were responsible for all the trouble and get rid of us. Everything had been so peaceful and loving in our home. The Prince house was fairly crackling with tension."

"Tension Dara probably wrote about in the diary." Streak picked up the plastic bag and carefully slid out the book. "Think we should get started?" Christine nodded and he pushed the diary toward her as he leaned back in his chair. "You begin. Then I'll take over."

Christine opened the cover. The first page was covered with Dara's familiar large, loopy handwriting done in red ink. Christine read aloud: "'I received this diary on December twenty-fifth, another merry, scary Christmas in the Prince home. Here we are, all acting like we're a loving family when most of us hate each other. But that's nothing new. What's new is how I feel.'"

Christine's gaze darted ahead and then she paled. Streak leaned forward. "What does it say?"

She drew a deep breath and read, "'I feel like someone wants me dead.'"

2

Michael Winter lay staring at the ceiling. He'd been going since five in the morning, it was now after midnight, and he still couldn't sleep. His eyes felt gravelly, his legs ached from all the walking he'd done, and he was more tired than he had been for a year. But his thoughts churned and he couldn't sleep.

"Well, hell," he muttered, flinging back his sheet and blanket. He walked barefoot into the kitchen, got a beer out of the refrigerator, popped open the can, and drank deeply. Its cold bite felt remarkably satisfying. Michael rarely drank, but he realized he'd been craving a beer since he came home three hours earlier.

He wandered into the living room, picked up the television remote, and faced the twenty-five-inch screen. Immediately he saw a woman with bared breasts the size and shape of grapefruits wearing a nurse's cap as she climbed into a delighted elderly patient's hospital bed. "I can make you feel lots better then those old doctors can," she cooed.

Michael tapped buttons on the remote. Suddenly a hot police pursuit was in progress, the cop's car spinning wildly around corners, the cop looking iron-jawed and deadly. On another channel, well-dressed teens screamed their way down an alley, fleeing from some kind of roaring creature with tentacles. "One more try," Michael muttered. A young woman burst into view, frolicking through a meadow and tossing her long auburn hair. Apparently, her fabric softener had thrown her into a fit of ecstasy. Michael's mouth opened slightly as she turned, flashed a brilliant smile, and batted her lashes over heart-stopping large green eyes. "Good God, it's Lisa," he said as his ex-wife beamed to all the world.

He and Lisa had been divorced for almost two years, yet seeing her smiling at him in the night still shook him, still made him feel empty. She'd written to him about getting the commercial, but he'd forgotten. Or rather, he'd purposely blocked the idea that he might see her on television. She looked so young. Too young to have been the mother of a two-year-old girl who'd drowned. The woman on television looked like she'd never known a moment of unhappiness, much less the shattering trauma that had torn them apart.

The commercial had vanished to be replaced with a doctor yelling to people only inches away, "Three hundred joules! Clear! *Clear!*" Michael didn't see him. He still saw Lisa skipping through the meadow and remembered how she'd looked when they met five years ago in Los Angeles. She'd rear-ended him at a stoplight. He'd thrown his car into park and flung out of it, ready to blast the ignorant jackass who shouldn't even have a license to drive. And there she'd stood with her long hair and big eyes, looking contrite, afraid, and absolutely beautiful. He'd smiled and said, "Looks like we've had a little accident," then thought about how foolish he sounded. But she'd smiled tremulously and his heart had melted. Three months later they were married. A year after that they were parents of a perfect baby girl they'd named Stacy.

The ache of loss washed over Michael as if Stacy had died two days ago instead of two years. Well-meaning people had told him that time heals all wounds. They'd been wrong, he thought as he drained the can of beer and went back to the refrigerator for another.

"Two is the limit, Winter," he said aloud as he walked back into the living room with his fresh beer. It had been a long, hard day and he had another one starting again in a few hours. He needed to be sharp.

He turned off the television, although Lisa's image was long gone. He didn't want to chance seeing the commercial again. He needed to focus on something immediate, not replay that torturous tape of the past. And what was most immediate? The finding of the body in the river.

Michael had seen his share of dead bodies when he was a detective in Los Angeles. He'd gazed at the remains of people who had been shot, strangled, and stabbed. He'd looked with cool professionalism at the dreadful wounds one human being had inflicted on another. He'd sat in on autopsies where pathologists had plunged hands into corpses to withdraw organs, each measured and weighed. But nothing had ever sickened him as much as the putrid atrocity he'd seen lying in a shroud of filthy plastic this afternoon. Of course, it shouldn't have been unwrapped, but eager volunteers did not know police procedures and had loosened the smothering cover only to jump back in horror and revulsion. By the time Michael got there only minutes later, two of the men had already thrown up and a third barely stood—shaking, sweating, and white-faced.

Now came the job of finding out who had sent this hideous offering into the Ohio River.

In spite of the gorge that had risen in his throat when he first saw the body, part of Michael had been able to stand off and observe. That part had judged the body to measure between sixty and sixty-five inches long. The tangled mess at one end was the remains of longish black hair. As he'd watched, flesh had begun falling away from the bones. One of the men who still hung near the site had said hoarsely, "I'll bet that's Ames Prince's girl, sure as I'm living. I knew she hadn't never run away."

Before he left police headquarters that day, Michael had retrieved the file of Dara Prince. He now picked it up from an end table, took another sip of beer, then sat down in a chair and opened the file.

The first thing he saw was her picture. Her head was slightly tilted, her lips shiny with gloss, her incredible violet eyes seeming to gaze challengingly into his. She looked insouciant, defiant, and just a bit vulnerable around the mouth. She had been a sophomore at Winston University, where she made average to low grades. According to her father, life at the Prince home was one of sweetness and harmony with Dara enjoying a lovely relationship with all members of the family. The comments of outsiders gave a different picture. People said Dara hated her stepmother, Patricia, and resented Christine and Jeremy Ireland, her father's wards. Dara had few girlfriends and was, according to some, "a shameless flirt." Michael smiled faintly. That prissy assessment certainly hadn't come from anyone under sixty.

Dara had dated jewelry designer and employee of Prince Jewelry Reynaldo Cimino for a year. According to several sources, although Cimino was clearly serious about her, she didn't seem quite so devoted to him. Most people couldn't point to one particular man, though, who'd captured her attention, with the exception of Sloane Caldwell, who was engaged to Christine Ireland. Michael took another sip of beer. Now that was an interesting, although scanty, piece of information. Exactly what kind of attention had Dara given the man?

Michael read on. Dara had been nineteen years old when she disappeared on a stormy March night. Her father and stepmother had gone to a movie. Jeremy Ireland was next door with the neighbors. Christine Ireland had been in the university library.

In the early hours of the morning, Ames Prince had reported

his daughter missing. A search of her bedroom revealed missing clothing, a missing suitcase, missing cosmetics. There had also been a brief farewell note. Her stepmother said Dara often talked of leaving Winston. However, Christine Ireland, twenty-one years old at the time, insisted things remained in the bedroom and bathroom that Dara would have taken with her if she'd run away.

At this point Michael would have liked to see some details about what "things" of Dara's remained, but nothing had been noted. He took another sip of beer, thinking. Christine Ireland no doubt remembered exactly what remained that Dara wouldn't have left behind if she'd run away. He remembered Christine's clear, open look in the store. She'd appeared shaken to hear of the body but also well in control of herself. She seemed sensible and smart.

She was also the sister of Jeremy Ireland, who Michael knew from a brief talk with Buck Teague this afternoon the sheriff believed had killed Dara Prince. "You know how those retards are!" he'd boomed at Michael, his big face even redder than usual. "Hot-headed. Out of control. He probably tried to kiss her or rape her and she screamed and he lost what little mind he had. You mark my words, Winter. If that body turns out to be Dara Prince's, our killer's been right in Ames Prince's own house for years and that sister of his has known what he did all along."

Michael decided to talk to Christine again within the next twelve hours. Teague's scenario didn't make sense to him. If Christine knew her brother had murdered Dara, but there was no body, she'd be relieved so many people assumed Dara had run off. She'd encourage that line of thinking, not insist possessions of Dara's remained that she would have taken with her if she'd run away.

He'd already received word that at the medical examiner's, Ames Prince had identified the body as Dara's. Of course, this identification was not considered official because it was based on the presence of a ring like one Dara Prince owned, not on identifying features of the body itself, like a pin in a once-broken bone. Or dental records, Michael thought, since the killer had knocked out the teeth. Still, Michael felt in his gut that Dara had finally been found, and he wanted to know who had brutally killed and tossed in the river the beautiful girl with the challenging eyes and the vulnerable mouth.

6

1

"What?" Streak blurted out.

Christine's heart pounded, but her voice was calm as she read again, "'I feel like someone wants me dead.'" She looked at Streak. "That's the end of the entry."

"Who's she talking about?"

"Streak, lower your voice or you'll wake Jeremy. I have no idea who she meant, but isn't this the kind of thing we were looking for?"

"Yes," Streak said slowly, "but it came as a shock to hear it right off the bat. Damn. She was afraid for her life and she said nothing? I don't believe it. She must have been exaggerating."

"People usually exaggerate to impress another person. Dara didn't expect anyone else to read this diary."

"Maybe she just felt that someone disliked her so much they wouldn't care if she died. Patricia, for instance. Or you."

"I didn't—" Christine broke off. She'd already stated her feelings about Dara to Streak. She wasn't going over it again. But she couldn't help saying, "Dara had to know I didn't wish her dead."

"Read some more," Streak said without expression.

Christine turned her attention to the diary, skipping to New Year's Eve, when Dara had attended a party with Reynaldo Cimino: "'He's so possessive. We went through the whole song and dance about him thinking I'm seeing someone else. I got him quieted down because he wants to believe everything I say. I get tired of him, but he's such an Adonis. That's what I call him. He loves it. Oh well, what the hell. He's a big boy. He can take care of himself. And I can take care of myself.'"

Christine looked up at Streak. "She doesn't sound afraid of Rey. She doesn't sound afraid of anything now."

"Seems like bravado to me," Streak said, getting up to pour more coffee for both of them.

"When she sounded afraid, you thought she might be exaggerating. When she doesn't sound afraid, you think it's bravado."

"All right, at this point I don't know what to think." Streak set down the coffee mugs. "Do you?"

"No. Dara was moody. I'd almost forgotten that about her, but I think her entries reflect her mood swings."

The next four entries were petulant rants about Patricia, whom Dara called Wicked Stepmother or most often W.S. Dara complained that W.S. was a gold digger. She was running through "Daddy's" money, spending it on clothes and jewelry and a suspicious number of trips to see her mother in Florida. Dara said she'd thought about hiring a private investigator to have Patricia followed, "but that would be *so* expensive!"

Christine frowned. "Patricia did go to see her mother a lot before Dara disappeared. She said her mother wasn't well. Something about her heart. But Patricia rarely leaves home now, although her mother is still alive."

"So you think something was going on back then? Patricia wasn't really going to Florida?"

Christine shook her head. "I don't believe she would have risked telling Ames she was going to visit her mother if she wasn't. He called her in Florida sometimes. I just wonder why she stays so close to home now and not then." Christine flipped a page in the diary and read: "'Things getting sticky with the Brain. I wonder if this affair was a good idea, although the sex is great.'"

Streak looked taken aback. "Who's the Brain?"

"I have no idea. She called Reynaldo Adonis. I don't know why he'd suddenly become the Brain." She glanced at Streak, who stared out the sliding glass doors at the misty darkness beyond. "Didn't she ever mention any guy she was interested in when you had those talks at the creek?" Christine asked.

"No. What makes you think she'd talk to me about her love life?"

Streak's voice was sharp. Christine wondered if he thought she was accusing him of withholding secrets. "Dara didn't talk to me about guys, either," she added casually. "And although I lived in the same house with her, I didn't pay much attention to her comings and goings. I was a senior in college when she was writing in this diary. I was going for a four-point average and pretty consumed with studying and planning my wedding that never happened."

"You were too young," Streak said. "I was glad you didn't go through with it."

"Yes, I think things worked out for the best." Christine was deliberately vague, not wanting to think again tonight about the ending of her engagement to Sloane and how she'd blamed Dara. She flipped through pages of the diary. "The next few passages look fairly benign. She hates school. She hates Patricia. Can't stand the Amazon. The Amazon would be me."

"Reading that would make you think she was a real sourpuss."

"She was no day at the beach, Streak," Christine said dryly.

"At least she wasn't one of those bleak kids who feel nothing. She had passion."

"Maybe too much. Listen to the entry for February fifth: 'Dangerous, heavenly day with S.C. Am I crazy? Crazy in love!!!'"

"Sex is good with the Brain, but she's in love with S.C.," Streak muttered almost angrily. "Who the hell is S.C.?"

Christine sat unblinking. Finally she said softly, "Sloane Caldwell."

"Surely not Caldwell. He was engaged to you."

"Can you think of any other people with the initials *S.C.* in her world?"

"I didn't know her world, Chris. I don't think you really did, either."

Christine's mind spun back to those winter days three years ago. She was twenty-one and felt as if she'd been walking on eggshells ever since she and Jeremy moved into the Prince home. She'd barely known Ames Prince, in fact had seen him only a few times before her parents' funeral. In the space of one week she and Jeremy had been orphaned, then lifted from their cozy, peaceful home in North Carolina and dropped into the turbulent Prince home, where neither Patricia nor Dara wanted them. Christine had tried to see to Jeremy's every need so he wouldn't get on anyone's nerves while she also strove to prove her worth by distinguishing herself at school, even deciding to go for a master's degree.

Still, she'd been afraid that Ames would ask her to leave and take Jeremy, thereby relieving some of the tension in the house. Her father had left plenty of money in trust for her and Jeremy, but he'd set the arbitrary age of twenty-two, when he was certain she'd be married and have a "sensible" man to look after her. She'd loved him, but he was maddening when it came to the subject of women's independence. The result was that she hadn't known how she could both get her master's and manage Jeremy's needs along with his special schooling. There would be no time to handle it all, which any social worker would see, and she'd worried that Jeremy might be taken away from her. Those who did not know how Jeremy had backslid after his parents' deaths might not understand what another disruption like a separation from his beloved sister might now do to all the mental strides he'd made in recent years.

And in the midst of Christine's turmoil had come Sloane with his patience, kindness, stability, and complete acceptance of Jeremy, and she'd seen a healthy and happy way out for her and her brother. Christine told herself that Sloane was exactly the kind of man her father would have wanted for her and for Jeremy. She'd told herself that affection was a good enough basis for marriage, that in the years to come she would learn to love him deeply, and she'd accepted his proposal in September.

By February she was almost certain she couldn't go through

with the wedding. She didn't love Sloane. She'd also realized that although her delicate mother had always told her a woman needed a strong man to lean on, she could not pledge herself for life to someone she didn't love. She had to believe she was strong and capable enough to look after herself and Jeremy without anyone's help. Still, she couldn't see a painless way out of the spring wedding. Sloane seemed to want her so much, and he'd been so wonderful to her and Jeremy. For Christine, every day had been an agony of conflict, frantic need to break free warring with her equally strong desire not to hurt Sloane. No, she had not been thinking too much about Dara back then. She'd been consumed with her own problems.

"Chris, are you still with me?"

She closed her eyes for a moment, then looked at Streak. "Yes. I was just trying to remember as much as I could of that time. You're right—I didn't know most of Dara's friends. But the initials *S.C.* coupled with the way she acted around Sloane make me wonder."

"I think Dara probably came on to all men."

He'd made a statement sound like a question. Christine realized he was curious about Dara's behavior around men. "She was forward, but how she acted with Sloane was different. She seemed even more blatant. And Sloane never discouraged her."

"Did he *encourage* her?"

"No," Christine said slowly. "But Sloane isn't a passive man. It's not his style to let something he doesn't like slide past him. And he didn't seem heartbroken when I ended our engagement."

"I've only been around him a couple of times, but he seemed to be a proud guy. I don't think he'd beg no matter how much he wanted to marry you. And he's never married anyone else."

"I hope someday he finds the woman who's right for him," Christine said. She didn't want to think about Sloane anymore. "Back to the diary."

"I'll take over." Streak reached for the diary. He skimmed a couple of pages, then said, "Here's something interesting for February fourteenth: 'Ladies and Gentlemen, presenting Dara

Prince, Juggler Extraordinaire! How does she do it? How does one small, beautiful girl handle three lovers on Valentine's Day? Very carefully! And I'm pretty sure I pulled it off. I'd better have pulled it off.'"

"*Three* lovers?" Christine echoed. "Rey was one. I guess the other two were the Brain and S.C."

Streak looked shocked. "Ames would have had a stroke if he'd known what his little girl was doing."

"I get the feeling each lover would have had a stroke if he'd known there was someone else. She said she had to juggle them. But she also sounds worried that she didn't do a good job of it."

Streak shook his head. "You know, I feel like a fool. I used to think I knew Dara. But she was too clever for that. She was pacifying me and I never caught on."

"Pacifying you? Why would she have had to pacify you about having three boyfriends?"

"I guess I said that wrong. I mean she never told me anything she thought I'd feel compelled to tell Ames." He quickly looked back at the diary and read: "'Hell of a nightmare last night. In it someone was following me, watching me, hating me more and more each day. I knew I should get help and I'd try to run, but I couldn't find anywhere bright and safe. The person was always in the shadows. And he or she wanted to kill me and I knew it and I couldn't do anything about it. I woke up in a sweat and couldn't get back to sleep. All day I've had the creeps and been looking over my shoulder. Am I crazy? Or psychic? I'd rather be crazy, because then I'd know I was just imagining it all, not foreseeing the future.'"

"So Dara was having anxiety dreams," Christine said. "She must have been really worried, and she wasn't the type to worry over nothing. Just the opposite. She usually didn't take things seriously enough."

"I'd say she was more than worried. She was scared."

The next few pages were filled with innocuous passages until the March 5 entry:

I was in the library today and someone followed me into the

stacks. There I was up on the sixth floor with all those musty bound periodicals and no one in sight and I felt eyes on me. I could feel *hatred* in the look. I was so creeped out I headed for the elevator. I heard rustling behind me and someone drawing a deep breath and sort of mumbling a lot of gibberish. I looked around and caught a flash of blue. Like a periwinkle blue. I thought I would faint. That awful mumbling came closer. I almost fell into the elevator. Back on the main floor I ran into a friend who wouldn't stop talking. Then I saw Christine get off an elevator and head for the front doors. She had on a *periwinkle* blue sweater!!

Christine gaped at Streak. "Dara thought I was stalking her?"

"Sounds like she did on this day. Do you remember being in the library wearing a blue sweater?"

"Blue is my favorite color. One Christmas when I was in college I got three blue sweaters as presents. And I went to the library a lot. I could concentrate better there than at home."

"Did you go to the sixth floor?"

"At least a dozen times." Christine felt herself bristling. "Streak, you're interrogating me!"

"I didn't mean to. I was trying to figure out if Dara could have seen you and put a false spin on the situation, or if she was just imagining things."

"If she did see me on the sixth floor, I certainly wasn't lurking behind her mumbling gibberish. That's absurd."

"So you think she made up the whole incident?"

Christine paused, thinking. "No. Not completely. Her fear sounds too real. Maybe someone *was* following her in the library. Or more likely, she'd just gotten herself so spooked by this time that she thought someone was after her."

"Mumbling gibberish."

"Like a lunatic. Now that *does* sound like imagination."

"Well, we can't know exactly what really happened and how much is exaggeration." Streak glanced through a couple more pages. "March tenth is the date on this entry: 'I feel like things are getting out of control. Maybe I bit off more then I can chew. Maybe I've pushed everybody too hard. I'm having a really hard time sleeping.'"

"I do remember her looking tired and being jumpy around that time," Christine said. "Patricia called attention to it at dinner one night. Dara got mad. But then, they were always sniping at each other. I mentioned Dara's condition to Ames after she disappeared, but he said he hadn't noticed anything wrong."

"And if he had, he would have ignored it." Streak sounded impatient. "He's a master at hiding his head in the sand. Listen to this: 'Today Rey proposed. I couldn't believe it and I burst out laughing. The look he gave me! I don't know how to describe it except it scared the daylights out of me. I told him I was too young. That we should wait. He knew I was just putting him off. I've felt weird about him all day.'"

Streak said, "In this March eighth entry even her handwriting looks shaky: 'I think I'm losing it. I keep getting the feeling someone's watching me. I smuggled some vodka up to my room. After a couple of shots, I don't feel so frightened.'"

"Dara wouldn't keep up an exaggerated scenario for days," Christine said. "I don't think she was being melodramatic. I think she really believed someone was watching her."

"I do, too. But who? One of the lovers?"

"That's my guess. Except she seemed to think I was tracking her in the library." Christine rubbed her eyes, which were stinging from lack of sleep. "Anything important in the next entry?"

"Something about shopping for a dress for a party."

"That would have been Tess's birthday party."

"Tess?"

"Reynaldo's wife. She was in love with him back then, but he belonged strictly to Dara."

"Too bad Dara didn't belong strictly to him. Maybe she'd be here today if she hadn't been so greedy."

Christine smiled. "Dara was greedy about everything,

especially people's emotions. I'm not sure she was capable of real love, but she certainly couldn't get enough of it to fill herself up. I've always thought that's why she was so tolerant of Jeremy. He adored her, and she reveled in it."

"I'll never know what made her so insecure." Streak lit another cigarette. "Eve and Ames loved her beyond reason."

"But Ames is so undemonstrative. Was Eve?"

"No. You always knew exactly how Eve felt. But before she got sick, she was a real overachiever. She belonged to a dozen clubs. She was always working on some project, always learning something—gardening, dance classes, art classes, music lessons, toward the end, witchcraft. Whatever she tried, she went at with a vengeance. I think she might not have paid enough attention to Dara during those times." His gaze went back to the diary and he read the next entry: "'God, what a close call this evening! I was making love with S.C. when the Brain came to the door! Knocking and knocking! I thought my heart would stop. S.C. not too upset, but I had to get out of there as soon as I could. I have a feeling the Brain *knows*. That would be a disaster.'"

"No wonder she was getting jittery," Christine said dryly. "I wonder where she was making love with S.C. when the Brain came to the door. S.C.'s house?" She pictured Sloane's house on the other side of town. Had Dara spent evenings there while Christine was at the library? Could that explain her flagrant flirting with Sloane and his lack of rejection? Christine pulled herself back to the present as Streak began to read again: "'I know I went too far this time. Tess's party. I drank before I went, because I was so nervous; then I drank too much there. Tess was drooling over Rey. Christine was like a giant Goody Two-shoes with her fiancé. I made a real spectacle of myself. I danced all by myself; I sang raunchy songs; I sat on Sloane's lap and kissed and fondled him. Amazon and Rey went ballistic. Amazon broke her engagement. Tess told everyone about the party. I think the whole town knows. Rey is furious. S.C. is furious. The Brain is furious, which is worse. And I'm scared.'"

"Oh, that party," Christine groaned. "It was awful."

Streak tapped ashes off his cigarette. "Was she really so bad?"

"She was horrible. And she didn't appear drunk. Just ... manic. I hadn't thought of that until this minute, but her behavior wasn't just outrageous. It had a frantic quality. Maybe Sloane realized something was wrong and that's why he didn't get rude with her."

"He never explained himself?"

"Oh, he offered a couple of excuses, but I was too angry to listen." I was too desperate to grab onto any excuse to get out of marrying him, Christine thought again with a prickle of shame. "But Dara says S.C. was furious. If Sloane was furious with her, he sure didn't act it. And she sounds more worried about the reaction of the Brain." She sighed. "I'm getting a headache."

"No wonder. We've only got one more entry. Let's get it over with. It's dated March twenty-fourth."

"The night *before* she disappeared," Christine breathed with a rush of foreboding.

"'I am *so* tired. Nightmares about whoever is following me, what they want to do to me. Or maybe I'm so strung out from not sleeping that I'm hallucinating. The looks Amazon gives me! They'd be funny if I wasn't so spooked. I can't stand everybody being so mad at me, even Daddy. He said something about me being like Mama after all. What did that mean? Then, to top it all off, I find out *this!* How could I let this happen? I didn't take the pills right, I guess. Too buzzed on vodka to keep track. I told him. Don't know what I expected. But there are no proud fathers in this family. He said I have to get rid of it, but I'm afraid I'll die. And I don't know how to arrange things like that. Practical things. Messy things life makes you do to keep going. But he's so mad. And if anyone else finds out—

"'I wish my mother were here because without her, I'm lost. It's all gone wrong and I just know now that no matter what I do, I won't be around this time next year.'"

Streak slowly closed the diary, his dark eyes sad. "And she wasn't around at that time the next year. Or even the next week," he said with a gravelly edge to his voice. "Damned exasperating high-spirited girl."

Christine swallowed hard, her own pity rising. Dara was not only frightened by the idea that someone was following her and wanted her dead; she'd also found out she was pregnant. The pills she hadn't taken properly were birth control pills. She'd told the father, who clearly had been less than thrilled. And when she'd written that passage, she'd been reduced to a frightened little girl who thought only her mother could protect her.

Dara had been selfish, greedy, and appallingly careless with her life and the other lives she touched. Christine had seen for herself, though, that Dara had been reared to believe she could have whatever she wanted. Her father rarely said no to her. Probably her mother hadn't, either. She'd been beautiful, adored, and indulged to the point where her personality never matured beyond that of a spoiled child. She didn't seem to understand the concept of accountability. Still, no matter what her human failings or how she'd come by them, the state she'd reached when she wrote her last diary entry was tragic. The hot tears Christine now felt blurring her vision, though, were caused only partly by pity. She also felt at fault, as if she'd been indirectly involved in what happened to Dara, although she couldn't figure out quite how.

"I never guessed she was pregnant," Christine finally said. "And obviously afraid to have an abortion." Streak stared off, his cigarette smoke circling in front of his eyes. "Did you know she was pregnant?"

Streak seemed to snap back to the moment. "Pregnant? How would I have known that?"

"I thought maybe she said something down at the creek that made you wonder."

Streak's voice was harsh. "She didn't. I told you she didn't talk about her love life."

"Okay," Christine said mildly. "What do you think Ames meant about her being like Eve?"

"Like Eve? Well, Eve was an extrovert. I was shocked half to death when Ames brought her home to marry. He was so staid—good, kind, trustworthy, but staid. Eve was just the opposite. After a few years, their personality differences began to take a toll on the marriage. Eve went from being an extrovert to being flamboyant, flashy, and . . . well, sort of familiar with men."

"Familiar?"

"Flirtatious. She just seemed to come alive around them and she had this way of acting like she knew you intimately. Even Ames couldn't ignore her behavior, although there were never any public scenes that I heard of. I know he didn't approve of the way she acted, but I never doubted he loved her. I'm not sure Eve loved him after the first few years. I think she got bored with him. Then she got cancer. For almost two years she went downhill, until there was very little of the old Eve left."

"Do you think before she got sick she had affairs?"

"No." Streak's voice was clipped. "But then, I don't seem to know much about women."

He sounded faintly bitter, as if he'd been hurt. Most women did not want to get involved with such a reclusive man. Also, he hardly went anywhere to meet women. But what about Eve? She would have been in his immediate circle. He was a handsome man. A brilliant man. The romantic wounded war hero. Could Eve have turned to him when she got frustrated with her aloof husband?

"Something wrong?" Streak asked sharply.

"No. It's just hard to take all of this in."

"Yes, it is. But we wanted to know what was in the diary. Now I almost wish we didn't."

"So do I, but we know it's important that the diary go directly to the police, not to Ames," Christine said. "With the information about Dara having *three* lovers, I don't think he'd let it into the hands of the police."

"He definitely wouldn't."

"We can't even let him know about it now, much less trust him to turn it in himself. I'll take it to Deputy Winter tomorrow.

The sooner I get this thing out of my possession, the better I'll feel. At least I think I will."

"I hope so." Streak stood up from the table and stretched. "It's two-thirty and you look tired enough to fall on the floor, Chris. Time for me to go home."

"I'll drive you."

"It's only a mile. And I didn't get my run out tonight."

"Streak, taking this diary to the police is the right thing to do, isn't it?"

His forehead furrowed. "You having doubts all of a sudden?"

"Yes. Ames will see it as the act of a traitor."

"I'm afraid he will." He paused. "But the police should see it. We both know that."

Christine nodded. "Okay. It's settled. Sure you're not too tired to walk home?"

"Not too tired to *run* home. The old guy's got some life in him yet. Goodnight, Chris. Try to get some sleep."

Christine closed the front door after Streak. She could hear him padding rhythmically down her front walk, not a hint of fatigue betrayed by his steps. When she could no longer hear him, she went back to the kitchen and picked up their coffee mugs. She hadn't drawn the vertical blinds against the sliding glass doors leading out to a wooden deck, and she noticed that the mist had grown even heavier, frothing under the dusk-to-dawn light.

Something glinted sharply through the mist, and she stopped, her eyes narrowing as she peered into the night. Perhaps it was someone with a flashlight looking for their pet, she thought. The people who lived two houses down had a cocker spaniel who occasionally wandered into Christine's backyard. She walked slowly to the glass doors and slid one back, listening. No one called for a dog. She called, "Buddy!" a couple of times, but the ancient cocker spaniel didn't come to her as he always did if he'd gotten lost.

Christine stood at the open door, casually looking for what had caused the glint of light. She heard nothing. Of course, if someone was walking in the patch of woods behind her house, he would be stepping on a carpet of wet ground covered with rotting pine needles and soaking dead grass. She couldn't expect to hear anything. It had probably been nothing—

With an abruptness that startled her, Christine felt naked, totally exposed to a spying, unfriendly world. Her neck tingled as if someone touched it lightly, teasingly. The same frightening sensation of being watched she'd had in the creeping mists around the creek rushed over her.

Rhiannon let out a loud hiss behind her, and she choked down a scream. She jerked around to look at the cat, who sat on the table, her golden eyes fixed on the mist beyond the door, her tail bushed out in alarm.

Christine grabbed the handle of the sliding glass door, slammed it shut, flipped the lock, and slid in the safety bolt at the top. The cat now let out a low growl followed by an eerie yowling sound that triggered a primitive, unreasoning fear deep within Christine. Danger. The cat sensed it. Christine sensed it. Rhiannon hissed again. Her sharp white teeth showed and the gleaming black hair along her spine stood up. Then she leaped off the table and ran from the room.

Christine reached for the cord and yanked, sending the heavy vertical blinds swinging into place. Glass and plastic and cloth, she thought. Fragile shields against the night and what lurked beyond the glow of the dusk-to-dawn light, a light she'd always found too bright and that now seemed maddeningly feeble. Still, whatever was out there didn't want to come into its glow. *Whatever?* Christine folded her arms across her chest and backed away from the doors, telling herself she was being ridiculous. *Whatever* was probably only a squirrel.

Only it wasn't. Rhiannon wouldn't have reacted so violently to a squirrel, a mouse, or even an opossum. The presence out there was human. And still watching with malevolent eyes.

My God, Christine thought, chilled to the bone. This is how Dara must have felt during the last weeks of her life.

2

A tap at the car window awakened Reynaldo with a jerk. He blinked, rubbed his eyes, and looked out to see a crinkled elderly face peering in at him with a mixture of annoyance and concern. Rey rolled down the window. "Yes?"

"Locked outta your room?"

Rey frowned. Then the weathered board siding of the Riverside Inn came into focus. "No."

"Then what're you doin' here?" The old man peered closer. "Hey, I know you. Used to come here all the time."

"Yes."

"Recognized the car. It's a beauty. Thunderbird. Nineteen fifty-six?"

"Nineteen fifty-seven."

"Yeah, that's what I thought. Sure would give an arm and a leg to have her. So, what you doin' back after so long? Used to see you here ever couple a weeks. Never stayed the night, though. Only a couple a hours." He tapped his temple. "See? Memory ain't goin' yet."

"It sure isn't."

"Your name's Orman, ain't it? I remember that."

"Yes," Rey said to the false name he'd always given.

"And I remember one time you speakin' to that pretty girl you used to bring. You called her Farrah. Like Farrah Fawcett on *Charlie's Angels*. I sure did love that show, but the wife never let me watch it."

Rey remembered the time Dara had trailed into the office while he was registering. In his surprise, he'd slipped and said her name. "Yeah, that was it," he told the old man. "Farrah."

"So why ain't I seen you around for a while? Get married?"

"No. Not to . . . Farrah."

"Oh." The old man gave his version of a leer. "*I* sure wouldn't a let that little honey get away. Maybe you didn't have no choice, though. That's the way it goes. When I was young, I had me a real looker. But she took off with a no-account that had a lot more money than me. Years later he dumped her when her looks failed her. Guess I shouldn't a felt bad for her, but I did. Never told the missus. She woulda been jealous."

"I'm sorry. About the looker, I mean."

"That's life." The old man frowned. "Look, I hate to be an old crab, but the missus doesn't like you just sittin' out here. Gives me hell when I don't do what she tells me. I gotta ask you to move on if you ain't gonna take a room, even though it's not like we're full-up or anything. And I figure you're just reminiscin'. Ain't no harm in that. But she don't wanna hear it."

"I *was* reminiscing."

"Yeah. Had that look on your face. And I'm real sorry about makin' you move on. But the missus, you know. She can make things awful uncomfortable if I don't toe the line. You know how they are. Or maybe you don't."

"Unfortunately, I do."

The old man cackled. "No wonder you're thinkin' back to better times. So do I, only even at her best my gal wasn't quite as good-lookin' as Farrah. 'Course, I wasn't no movie idol like you, neither, even if you're lookin' awful pale this morning. You didn't get no bad news, did you?"

"Real bad," Rey said, turning the key. The Thunderbird started with a satisfying purr. "I got some real bad news from the past."

The old man shook his head. "That's the trouble with the past, son," he said dolefully. "Just when you think the worst of it's long gone, it jumps up and slaps you right in the face. Yes sir, right in the face."

Tess Cimino's eyelids snapped open. Immediately she reached over to touch her husband, Rey. He was gone. Then she realized a clatter in the kitchen had pulled her from sleep. She glanced at the digital clock by the bed. Five thirty-five.

Tess climbed from bed, threw on an old blue flannel robe, and went into the kitchen. It was dark and she flipped on the overhead light.

"God, turn that thing off!" Rey snapped, shielding his eyes. "It's blinding."

"It's no brighter than usual and there's no other light in here." Rey squinted at her. His ebony eyes were bloodshot and circled by mauve hollows. He hadn't shaved since yesterday, and his skin looked pasty beneath dark stubble. "You've been drinking."

"A little."

"More than that."

"I'm not drunk."

"I didn't say you were drunk. You were drunk about three hours ago. Now you're sobering up and obviously feeling like the devil. I'll make some coffee."

"Whatever."

Tess began dumping grounds into the coffeemaker basket. "Where have you been?"

"I told you. Having a drink."

"Since ten last night? The bars closed hours ago."

"I got it to go."

"And drank it while you were driving around?" Tess flipped on the coffeemaker. "You could have been arrested."

"I went somewhere private."

"Where?"

"I have places. If I told you where, they wouldn't be private anymore."

"Well, aren't you the mysterious one?" Rey shrugged. "What you mean is, if you told me where they are, I'd be able to track you down."

"Sometimes a man needs to be alone, Tess. You always come looking for me."

"You make me sound like a bloodhound." He shrugged again. "You took the Thunderbird. You drive that car about four times a year."

"I want to keep it looking new. Is that coffee about ready?"

"Two minutes. Then you need a shower. And a change of clothes. The bottoms of your pants are damp."

"Thank you, dear, for telling me when to shower and change clothes."

Tess looked at him as she poured milk in his coffee cup. Even in his current state, he was still the handsomest man she'd ever seen. She'd fallen in love with him the first time she met him. He looked like he'd stepped from the pages of a fashion magazine. With young and beautiful Dara on his arm.

"Rey, don't you think this excessive mourning over Dara is just a tad inconsiderate of you?"

"Inconsiderate?"

"Inconsiderate of my feelings. *I'm* your wife, now. And you're going off the deep end over another woman."

Rey's dark eyes flared. "A woman who was *murdered*."

"Three years ago. And don't say the idea never occurred to you. That she was dead, at least. But I don't see anyone else going on alcoholic benders because of it."

"And just how many people have you seen since we got the news?"

"None." She poured the coffee and set it in front of him. "You rushed us right home after you heard about the body, jittered around here until ten, then took off without a word. I was *so* worried, but I'll bet you never gave me a thought. I knew you'd go off and drink."

"Why would you know that? I hardly ever drink."

"You had that *look*."

"Oh," Rey said sarcastically. "That *look*."

"I considered calling the police to look for you, but I didn't want to embarrass you."

"At least one of us is considerate."

Tess sat down at the table and put her face close to his. "Rey, I love you, but I can't put up with behavior like last night's. You were acting like a crazy person."

Rey glared at her and raised a trembling hand. "Don't ever say that about me."

"Why? Because your father wasn't the picture of mental stability?"

"You shut up about him."

"Rey, I wasn't comparing you to him. Mental illness is not inherited."

"I don't want to talk about my father!" Rey stood up, his whole body quivering. "Jesus, Tess, do you have to bring him up *now*? After all of *this*?"

"After they've found the body, you mean. For God's sake, Rey, you don't even know if it's Dara."

"It is. I know it is."

"Dara," Tess said coldly. "Dara. Always Dara. I am sick to *death* of Dara Prince."

"Why? I don't talk about her."

"No, but you're always thinking about her. I can tell. She's always here, always with us, even in bed. I feel like you're making love to her, not to me." Tess took a deep breath. "Dara was a tramp, Rey. A selfish, spoiled, immoral, unprincipled tramp who never did anything but play you for a fool—"

The sting of Rey's hand on her face knocked her back two steps, not from force but from shock. Her hand flew to her reddening cheek, and tears flooded her eyes. Rey glared at her, his eyes burning in his pale, taut face.

"You've . . . you've never touched me in anger before," Tess managed shakily. "*Never*. You're not that kind of man, Rey. You're not violent. You're not cruel. You . . . are . . . not . . . your . . . father."

"Oh yeah? Well, maybe I am," Rey ground out before stalking from the kitchen. "Maybe I am and you really don't know a damned thing about your own husband."

7

1

Christine dozed fitfully until dawn. As the birds began to chirp, she sank into a deep sleep. An hour later Jeremy stood at her bedside. "Christy," he said, touching her shoulder. "Christy, it's time to get up."

"No, it isn't," she mumbled. "My alarm hasn't gone off. What's wrong?"

"Nothing. I want to go to the store."

"We don't open till ten today."

"Please, Christy? I gotta get my cell phone."

"You can do that later."

"And there's something I want to work on. I should have finished it yesterday. I want to surprise Rey and have it done when he comes in."

Christine groaned and put the pillow over her head. "Do you have to be so conscientious?"

"I couldn't understand a word you said under that pillow."

"I said—"

"I want to go to the store."

"In a couple of hours."

"You don't have to take me. I can ride my bike. It's not raining."

Christine knew argument was useless. When Jeremy decided he must do something, he became maddeningly tenacious. She took the pillow off her head. "You can't ride your bike. It's too far."

"But I *have* to go, Christy. I have—"

"Something important to do." She looked closely at his expression for some sign of the disturbance last night to account for his burning desire to get to the store, but he appeared placid. And determined. She said in resignation, "Okay, but I need some coffee before we go and you need some breakfast."

"I can fix it. You want an omelet?"

"Jeremy, your talent does not extend to the kitchen. You are a terrible cook." He grinned. "You open a can of food for Rhiannon. I'll be down in five minutes."

"I'll go ahead and make the coffee," Jeremy said.

"No, Jeremy, wait—" He was gone. In ten minutes she would be drinking coffee strong enough to remove varnish from wood. "Oh, crap," she muttered. "What a wonderful beginning for the day."

She started to get up, then fell back onto the bed as the events of the night before seemed to rush at her and hit her with the force of a blow. Dara had been found.

And her father had seen her after she'd lain in the river for three years.

"Oh, Ames," Christine moaned, knowing the hell he must have endured last night. She wondered if he'd even want the store opened today. It was certainly too early to call. Perhaps she should drop by the house around nine to see how he was getting along.

Immediately she knew that would be the wrong thing to do. If he'd only fallen asleep near morning, as she had, she didn't want to disturb him. And she didn't want to deal with Patricia right now.

And she really didn't want to see Ames before she turned over Dara's diary to the police. Being with him might weaken her resolve to do something she knew was necessary, although hurtful to Ames. No, she would take Jeremy to the store, go in at ten when Ginger and Rey would be there, and then give Ames a call. She would not see him until later in the day, after she'd done what she felt was her duty with the diary.

She got up, walked stiffly into the bathroom, and gazed gloomily into the bathroom mirror. She looked awful. She'd clearly slept on her abdomen and face, and the pillowcase had left creases on her cheek. Her eyes were slightly bloodshot and wreathed by dark circles, her skin was pasty, and even her lips seemed to have lost color.

She glanced at the shower, then decided to put off bathing until she'd had a long-overdue bout at the gym. She might be able to get her mind off Dara and the diary for a while, and she certainly looked as if she could use a workout.

Christine washed her face, brushed her teeth, applied some pink gloss to her pale lips, ran a wet comb through her hair, trying to make her bangs lie down, and slipped into a sweatsuit. After her workout, she would come home and prepare for the day.

When she got downstairs, she saw that Jeremy had opened the vertical blinds across the sliding glass doors. She gazed out almost fearfully, only to see her familiar backyard. It looked cheerless and messy, but not at all menacing. She was a bit ashamed of the terror she'd felt only a few hours ago when she thought someone lingered in the mist.

When she *knew* someone lingered in the mist.

"What are you saying?" Jeremy asked.

She realized she must have spoken her thought aloud. "I said I didn't get much sleep last night."

"That's *not* what you said. You said something about mist—"

"I'm going to the gym after I drop you off at the store," Christine interrupted. She wasn't going to say a word that could frighten or upset her brother. "Gee, I've always loved black toast, Jeremy."

"The toaster doesn't work right." He looked at his own toast with distaste. "I think we need a new one."

"I think we need to push the adjustment back from dark to light. Here, let me make some more."

"No, I want to make the toast. Put the knob in the right place. And I couldn't find any of Aunt Wilma's jam."

"So she's gotten you to call her Aunt Wilma. She's been working on me, too, but I can't get used to it."

"She's like an aunt. Like Mom's Great-aunt Peony."

"The one who said children were evil and she'd rather take in two wolves than us after Mom and Dad died? The one who wore that bag of stinky herbs around her neck to keep germs away? The one who took a bath once a month because she was afraid she'd catch a cold and die? *That* Aunt Peony?"

"Well, I guess not," Jeremy said slowly as he brought the old harridan forward in his mind. "Anyway, there's no jam."

"We ate it all. We'll have to wait for summer when Wilma makes some more. Right now it's Welch's grape jelly or nothing, sir."

Five minutes later, Christine told him he had jelly on his chin. He dutifully wiped his face as she fished in her purse for the store keys and handed them to him. "Now, Jeremy, I want you to be very careful with these. If you lose them—"

"Somebody could rob the store." Jeremy growled low in his throat. "You only tell me that every time I *look* at a set of keys."

Christine sighed. "You see what comes from getting up too early? We're cranky." He gave her a half-smile. "You do your important work at the store and I'll exercise at the gym, and in a couple of hours we'll feel great."

As they walked outside to the car, Christine noticed that the rain had not resumed. Nevertheless, the cool air still felt weighted with moisture. An ashen sky hung low and bleak. Atop a telephone pole a lone black crow cawed with loud harshness into the dreary morning.

"A lookout crow," Jeremy commented. "I wonder where his friends are."

"Back in the trees planning a day of meritorious duty," Christine said. The crow cocked his head, looked at her with beady eyes, and cawed sharply. "I don't like you, either," she called to him, and Jeremy laughed. How she loved that sound, especially after his misery of the night before. He hadn't mentioned Dara this morning, and Christine wanted to keep the subject at bay. "I'll be glad when it's summer."

"It seems like it's been winter for about a year," Jeremy commented as he tucked his large frame into the small car and fastened his seat belt. "I don't think it'll ever be hot again."

"You won't be saying that in August when it's in the nineties every day." A sharp gust of wind blew wet leaves across the hood of the car. Christine pulled her jacket tighter and tossed her gym bag into the backseat. "And to top it all off, we have a flood. Bad for the town, not to mention our business."

"I thought you said we did a landfill business at Christmas."

"A *landslide* business, thanks to that lingering slick snow that kept people from going to the mall in Charleston. At least this year's accounting books won't reflect the slump we're in. I want to prove to Ames I'm doing a good job as manager."

"He knows you are, Christy." Jeremy smiled encouragingly. "I heard him tell Patricia so the other evening."

"Really?" Christine backed out of the driveway onto their deserted street, Cardinal Way. "And what did Patricia say?"

"I don't remember." Which meant she'd said something nasty that Jeremy didn't want to repeat. Oh well, Patricia's opinion didn't matter anyway.

At six-fifteen the downtown area was deserted. Christine pulled into the alley that ran behind one block of Third Avenue's stores and stopped at the back door of Prince Jewelry. She handed Jeremy her gold-plated key holder. "Now be sure—"

"Not to lose them," Jeremy said, beating her to the punch. "I will guard them with my life. Maybe I'll even swallow them after I get the door open."

"I don't think such drastic measures will be necessary," Christine said wryly. "Don't work too hard."

"I'm not kissing you good-bye here in front of everybody," Jeremy announced.

Christine looked around. "No one is here, Jeremy, but I understand that you have an image to maintain. See you later."

She pulled out of the alley and headed north. The gym, more properly known as the Winston Fitness Center, sported only two cars in the parking lot near a row of winter-ravaged shrubbery. The vehicles no doubt belonged to Danny Torrance, the manager and onetime neighbor of the Princes, and Marti, the fitness trainer. Christine had a suspicion they were lovers and spent nights in the small apartment at the back of the sprawling building that had been erected only five years ago. The owner didn't mind. Their constant presence discouraged prowlers and writers of graffiti that might deface the structure's cream stucco facade.

Christine parked her car at the side of the building to avoid the vehicle being covered with soggy leaves the sharp breeze brought down. When she entered the fitness center Danny stood behind the half-moon counter. "Hey, Christine, kind of early for you, isn't it?" he asked with a smile displaying perfect teeth.

"Ames is opening the store late, so I have some extra time," Christine answered, wondering how he could look so unbearably alert and cheerful at this time of morning.

He turned serious: "I heard about the body that was washed ashore yesterday. It isn't Dara, is it?"

Christine looked at him. To most people she would have given a vague answer that shut off further questions. But Danny had grown up beside the Princes. He'd known Dara all of his life.

"Ames went to Charleston last night. He says the body is Dara's."

Danny closed his eyes and shook his head. "Damn. I can't believe it. I mean, I can. It never made sense that she'd just run off and not come home for three years. But I hoped . . ."

"We all did."

"She was murdered, wasn't she? I mean, if it was an accidental drowning, she wouldn't have been wrapped in plastic."

"No, she wouldn't have been. But I don't know how she was murdered. Stabbed or shot or . . ." Christine drew a deep breath, feeling queasy.

"Enough talk about Dara," Danny said briskly. "Go do your workout. You need to get some color in those cheeks."

"I need more than color in the cheeks. Today I feel like I need a whole makeover." She signed in, noting that hers was the only name on the register. "Looks like I'll have the equipment to myself."

"Business has been off the last few days, but I can understand it. People are thinking of more important things than working out. They're trying to ward off the flood. If the Corps of Engineers orders us to start putting sandbags in place, I'll have to turn the place over to Marti and go do my civic duty," he informed her, referring to the attractive trainer. "I hope it doesn't come to that, though."

"You want to miss out on all that exercise?" Christine said lightly. "It would be good for you to be out in the trenches instead of working out here in the lap of luxury."

"You're a sadist, Christine," Danny laughed.

"I try. But honestly, if we need to sandbag, Jeremy will be right in the middle of the action. He's strong and eager and he could be a big help. I won't try to stop him. But I'd appreciate your keeping an eye on him."

"He could probably handle twice as many sandbags as I could and think it was fun. You'd better ask him to look out for me." Danny grinned at her. "But sure. I'll work by his side, even if I can't keep up with him and he'll make me look bad."

"You're a fine and gallant man, Danny Torrance." Christine laid down the pen and picked up her gym bag, forcing a smile. "Off to the wars."

"Are you going to do your usual routine, or do you want help with something new?"

"Nothing new today. I don't have the physical or mental enthusiasm."

"Okay. Enjoy yourself. Marti and I were just sharing some juice and bran muffins in the back. If you need anything, give us a shout."

As Danny disappeared again, Christine walked through the empty exercise room and back to the dressing rooms, where she placed her gym bag. No need to secure everything in a locker, she thought. There weren't many chances of theft on such a slow morning. She put an elastic band on her right wrist, which she'd broken when she was nine and fell out of a tree house. To her frustration, she'd never regained full strength in that wrist.

Next she climbed on the scale. At five-ten, she'd felt like a clumsy giant next to the diminutive, sylphlike Dara with her delicate bone structure, but the scale topped at 135. According to the fitness experts, she was maintaining a good weight. Still, she'd never shaken her teenage wish that she were shorter and thinner.

She remembered being astonished when the devastatingly cute Sam Parks with his sleek body and wavy dark hair had asked her to the freshman prom. At fifteen, she'd already reached her full height, while Sam remained a stolid five-foot-six. Her mother had bought her a new dress, an exquisite aqua creation that exactly matched her eyes, and she'd felt like a princess walking into the dance. Then she'd heard a cluster of guys snickering to Sam, "So what are you doing here with *her*?" And blushing, Sam had replied, "Our mothers are friends. My mom told me if I didn't bring the Incredible Hulk, I'd be grounded for a month." Christine had never told anyone what she'd overheard. For the next few weeks, though, hurt feelings and humiliation had sent her into silent tears after she went to bed.

Oh well, the indignity was long past, Christine thought. Besides, she'd had the satisfaction of running into Sam when he was twenty-two and still five-foot-six with an extra thirty pounds packed around his waist and his wavy hair already thinning. "There really is justice in the world," she murmured to herself before padding back into the exercise room in heavy-soled aerobic shoes.

She caught a glimpse of herself in a mirror and cringed. Some women came to the gym looking like they were ready to tape an aerobics video, with perfect hair, careful makeup jobs, and colorful scanty Lycra outfits. Christine always opted for gray sweatpants and shirt. She was here to work out, not look glamorous, and the loose clothes allowed for more comfortable movement. Still, on a day when she already looked tired and colorless, the drab outfit did nothing to help. She hoped she could finish before anyone else came in.

Danny, a firm believer that everyone exercised better to music, preferably songs of the eighties, had turned on the sound system. Wang Chung's "Everybody Have Fun Tonight" boomed through the large exercise room. As Christine did her warm-up yoga, she found herself bouncing along to the music in spite of her best efforts to hold her stances without motion. Dispensing with the yoga, she moved on to livelier activity.

She mounted one of the stationary bikes, pedaling rapidly to Robert Palmer's "Addicted to Love." The bikes faced the large front windows. She looked out at the nearly empty parking lot where a few dead leaves, an orange Frisbee, and a yellow-and-red disposable cup blew wildly in the rising wind. Across the street a small deserted park lay dotted with puddles. A rusty swing set sported swings whipping violently back and forth as if possessed by riotous ghostly children. Among the play equipment, trees lifted skeletal limbs to the darkening sky. Another storm was coming.

When she'd broken a sweat on the bike, Christine turned to the treadmill. As she walked briskly on the rotating rubber, thoughts of her certainty of being watched last night crowded into her mind.

The question was whether she'd been the victim of a random Peeping Tom, or if the watcher had a specific purpose in observing her. True, citizens had been complaining for a couple of months about a group of teens who'd been spying into people's houses as well as creating "malicious mischief." Christine could have been the victim of these vexatious young people who could find nothing better to do with their time than cause trouble.

But what if the person had been outside for some time watching her and Streak pore over Dara's diary? Watching two people read couldn't hold an audience for long, she thought. Not unless what they were reading had some significance for the watcher. If that was true, it probably meant that she, Streak, and Jeremy had been under scrutiny not only at home, but also at Crescent Creek when she'd had the uneasy feeling of being watched. Or had the watcher been around even before Streak and Christine arrived? Had someone watched as Jeremy cried and threw his pitiful silk flowers into the swollen waters, babbling about the creek being the place where Dara had vanished? The thought set Christine's hands trembling and her heart racing.

Christine quickly abandoned the treadmill, sat down to draw a few calming breaths, then headed toward the weights as "Relax" by Frankie Goes to Hollywood began echoing loudly through the room. She placed twenty-pound weights on either side of the rod, lay down, and lifted. Lowered. Lifted. She worked out regularly and felt little strain in her upper arms. This won't do at all, she thought, remembering her Great-aunt Helga, whose flesh had dangled at least three inches below the triceps muscles on her arms. Such a fate would not await Christine, she vowed. She stood up and added another weight to each end of the rod, then lay down again, this time pressing a total of sixty pounds.

Danny would have a fit if he saw her, she thought. Bench-pressing was definitely not a good idea without someone to spot her. There was always the chance she would drop the rod and the entire sixty pounds would come crashing down on her chest. But no one was around and she didn't want to disturb Danny or Marti. Actually, she didn't want to make conversation. Besides, she wouldn't be at this particular exercise for long.

Christine had raised the bar for the fourth time when a slight chill rushed over her. She was not alone in the room. She drew a deep breath and told herself to calm down. This was a public exercise room. Someone else had finally arrived.

Five lifts, six lifts. Suddenly her heart seemed to jump in her chest. Someone was near. Too near. She heard the intake of breath, felt the tingle of a gaze traveling up and down her body. Panic racing through her, she started to reach back in order to place the rod on the rests when something heavy and wet dropped over her nose and eyes.

"What—" she got out before terry cloth was jammed into her mouth, nearly choking her. She tried to scream around the material, but nothing emerged except a few faint garbled squeals. Blind and mute, she knew she was too disoriented to replace the bar in the holds. She slanted her arms to the right, trying to drop the rod so that it missed her head, but strong hands grasped her elbows, forcing them into extension directly above her chest. She was trying to rise at the waist when someone sat down heavily on her thighs directly below her pelvis. She squirmed beneath the hot body, barely able to move. Her attacker had firmly pinned her lower body against the vinyl-covered bench, while forcing her to hold the sixty pounds of weights directly above her chest.

Saliva poured into Christine's mouth only to be absorbed by the cloth. She jerked her head to the side. The heavy, wet mass of material over the top of her face shifted slightly but not enough to give her a view of her attacker. Music pulsed through the room. The throbbing bass seemed to shake the floor. "Relax, don't do it," the singer commanded to the beat. "Relax . . . relax . . ."

Christine knew everyone's weakness with the weights came during the time of lifting and lowering. Once the lifter had gotten the rod aloft, she'd achieved a position of strength. Under normal circumstances, Christine had the capacity to hold the bar directly above her chest for at least ten minutes. Probably more. But now her hands perspired treacherously. If they slipped . . .

The music pounded on, then stopped while the sound of spewing water thundered through the room. Then the singer let out a shout before the beat began again. Oh God, where is everyone? Christine's mind screamed.

Her attacker blew a stream of cool breath over her sweaty arms. Up to the hot skin of her throat it crept, tickling, teasing, almost caressing. Revulsion filled Christine and her arms had begun to tremble under the heavy weight she'd so foolishly added to the rod. Whenever she tried to kick, the bulk of a body ground painfully against her thighs, twisting and pinching the delicate skin.

"Please stop. Please," she tried to say around her gag, but nothing emerged except meaningless gibberish. Above her someone sighed with sickening satisfaction.

If I drop these weights, they'll break my ribs, Christine thought frantically. The ribs could puncture my lungs. Dear God, where is Danny?

The weight, but mostly the fear, suddenly sent violent tremors through her arms. She gagged. She felt as if she were going to throw up. If she did, the vomit could roll back down her throat, choking her. And she was probably about to be raped. Hot tears gathered in her closed eyes. She had never been so terrified in her life.

Then the seemingly unbelievable happened. Her attacker lifted the rod bearing the weights and placed it back on its rests. With one weakened, shaking hand Christine made a futile swipe for the heavy, sopping material covering her face. With the other arm she struck outward, connecting only briefly with flesh before a shattering blow to the temple sent her into darkness.

2

"My God, Christine!" The words floated to her from far away. Daddy, she thought. Daddy's come to save me. "Marti, call the paramedics! Christine, babe, wake up! It's Danny!"

A mouth covered hers and she panicked, bucking with tremendous force and cracking her forehead against the one above hers. "Ouch! Damn it, Chris!"

Slowly Danny's pained young face came into focus. Christine drew a deep breath and collapsed backward. "Sorry," she gasped. "I thought it was him."

Danny rubbed the reddening spot on his unlined forehead. "I was trying to give you mouth-to-mouth. I didn't mean to scare you. What happened?"

"Someone made me hold the weights." Her mind felt fuzzy, her thoughts a tangle of disconnected images. "Sat on me. Hit me."

"Who?"

"Don't know." She tried to raise her head, but Danny gently pushed it down. "Threw something over my face . . ."

"A wet terrycloth robe."

"Stuffed something in my mouth."

"A washcloth. Didn't you see *anything*? Not even a body part?"

"Nothing. It all happened so fast." Her thoughts began to coalesce into a meaningful pattern and she touched her temple. "Danny, I have one hell of a headache."

"No wonder. There's a bloody weight lying beside you."

"He hit me. There's blood?"

"All over the place. Scalp wounds bleed profusely. It may not be as bad as it looks, although you're a mess."

"You're such a comfort."

Danny didn't smile, but his perpetually tanned fine-boned face lost some of its anxiety. "At least you're being as sarcastic as usual."

"I try. Danny, I need a couple of aspirins."

"Not until you get to the hospital."

"I may be dead by then."

"No way. You're tough as nails."

"Again with the silver tongue." Christine kept talking because she was afraid if she didn't, she would lose consciousness. "I'm going to look fabulous tomorrow."

Marti rushed in and threw a white blanket over Christine. "Paramedics will be here any minute." Her cute pixie features had turned so pale her freckles looked the color of chocolate. "Chris, I'm so sorry we let this happen to you, but I don't know *how* it happened. A buzzer goes off in the refreshment room where we were when the front door opens. We didn't hear a buzzer. And both back doors are locked."

"Locked?" Danny echoed. "They can't be."

"Well, they are."

"Are you sure?"

"Of course I'm sure," Marti returned, hotly defensive. "I guess I can tell if a door is locked or not."

"Maybe a window's unlocked, but I'm sure I checked them." Danny stood up. "I have to look for him. He might still be hiding in here."

"You will do no such thing!" Marti shrilled. "He could kill you, or worse." Christine wondered what was worse. "I called the police. They'll be here in a few minutes. Let *them* look for him!"

Christine was vaguely aware of someone coming into the exercise room and, after a moment, crying, "What on earth's happened?"

Tess Cimino, Reynaldo's wife. Christine would have recognized her loud, husky voice anywhere. "It's just me, Tess!" she called. "I've had a slight mishap."

Tess rushed to her side and looked down at her with frightened blue eyes. "Chris, you're bleeding!"

"So I'm told."

"Did something fall on you?"

"Yes. A great big man I think wanted to rape me."

"*What?*" Tess blared.

"Mrs. Cimino, please," Danny said in a quietly pained voice. "We're not exactly sure what happened, but Christine seems to be holding her own. The paramedics are on their way and the less excitement we have, the better it will be for Chris."

"I'm not doing anything to hurt her!" Tess blasted.

"Actually, you are," Christine replied with what she hoped was a sweet smile. "Could you lower your voice? My head is killing me."

"Oh, I'm sorry," Tess abruptly whispered. She reached forward and brushed Christine's hair back from her forehead. Her fingers were long and cool. "Do you want a glass of water?"

"Yes."

"No," Danny said firmly. "Nothing until the doctors say it's all right."

"I want to stand up." Christine rose slightly. "I feel stupid lying here with everyone gathered around me."

Danny gently pushed her back. "No. Not yet."

"You're a tyrant," Christine muttered. Actually, just lifting herself a few inches off the board had brought on a wave of dizziness, although she wouldn't admit it. "Is my sense of time skewed, or is it taking the EMS van a hell of a long time to get here?"

"They're pulling into the parking lot now!" Marti called from where she stood near a front window.

"It'll be all right soon," Tess said, still whispering. She'd pulled her brown hair back in a ponytail, and like Christine, she wore sweatpants. Without makeup she looked washed out, and even in her groggy state Christine noticed the new fine lines and shadows around Tess's eyes, the slight puffiness of her face. At thirty-five, she was seven years older than her handsome husband, Reynaldo, and worried obsessively about the age difference, always certain he was admiring younger, beautiful women.

"He's not, you know," Christine said as fog seemed to close in.

"Who's not what?" Danny asked.

"Rey loves you."

Danny's eyebrows raised. "I'm thrilled. Chris, I think you're passing out again."

And she did.

8

Christine didn't remember the ride to the hospital. Awareness returned only as she was wheeled down a hall with what seemed like a hundred faces peering down at her. She shut her eyes. She hadn't been in a hospital since her parents died, but she wasn't worried about herself now. She only feared someone would tell Jeremy what had happened and bring him here. This was not a scene for him.

"My brother," she murmured. "Can't tell my brother."

"We'll let your brother know as soon as possible," a sweet-faced nurse told her. "Just give us his name."

"*No*. I don't want him here. Where's Tess? Did Tess come?"

"I'm here!" Tess called. "They're trying to make me to sit in the waiting room, but I won't leave you!"

The sweet-faced nurse looked annoyed. "You *must* wait in the other room, miss."

"It's *Mrs*. Cimino and I'll do nothing of the sort. The patient is Christine Ireland. I have her purse with her identification and insurance information—"

"Then take it to the front desk and be good enough to call her brother."

"Don't give me orders!" Tess glared at the young nurse, then looked at Christine. "Don't worry, Chris; I'll take care of everything. Do you want me to call Ames?"

"No. Don't bother him. Call Reynaldo. Tell him to go to the store. Jeremy went in early. He can give Jeremy an excuse about why I'm not coming. And . . ."

She felt herself sliding again, cool oblivion replacing the noise and confusion of the hospital emergency room. It seemed only seconds later when she awakened to face an older man with a red, shiny face and hard little eyes. "You have a concussion," he said sternly, as if it were her fault.

"I thought so."

"You're lucky it wasn't worse."

"Will I have any lasting effects?"

"The radiologist didn't appreciate any signs of brain damage in your CAT scan. Never really know about these things, though. I guess time will tell."

"That's comforting. What about my brother?"

"I don't know anything about your brother. Was he hurt, too?"

"No. I'm just concerned—"

"I don't know anything about him if he wasn't hurt. I didn't treat him. Your family can tell you something."

"When can I see them?"

"Later. You will, of course, have to spend the night in the hospital." He looked pointedly at her naked left ring finger. "Unless you live with someone."

"I could stay with my guardian—"

"Your guardian?"

"Ames Prince. But no, now isn't the time to be piling in on him."

"Ames Prince is your guardian?" the doctor repeated, his expression softening. "Ah, Mr. Prince. I caught a glimpse of him in the waiting room. A fine man, Mr. Prince. I didn't guess that he'd come here about you."

"I didn't seem worthy of the fine man's time?" Christine asked sourly. Her head hurt badly. The doctor gave her the kind of forbearing look one saves for a badly behaved five-year-old. "May I see Mr. Prince now, Doctor?"

"Briefly. Then the police want to talk to you, Miss . . ."

"Ireland. It's on my chart."

The doctor gave her a hard look. "Five minutes with Mr. Prince," he said curtly. "Then the police."

Ames entered the room slowly. His face was lined and

haggard, and a strange haunted look filled his gray eyes. "Christine, are you all right?"

"I'm holding my own."

"Thank God."

"No, thanks to my attacker's lack of knowledge about my anatomy. He went for the hardest part of my body—my head." Ames managed a slight smile. "I'm so sorry you had to be dragged out to the hospital today."

"I'm not an invalid, dear, and I had to see you, to make sure you're all right. I don't know what I'd do if something happened to you, too."

Christine reached out and took his hand. The skin felt paper-thin and cold. "I'm fine, Ames. Don't worry one more second about me. I'll be here tonight with doctors and nurses just minutes away if I need anything. And by the way, my doctor seems quite impressed with you."

"Ah, Dr. Holt." Ames cast a glance at the empty doorway, then lowered his voice. "I handled a case involving his son. I can't discuss the details, but I got the boy off with just proba-tion, which I'm not so sure was in the best interests of society."

"Since the doctor is so grateful, maybe you could talk him into letting me have something delicious for dessert instead of Jell-O."

"I don't think my influence goes that far, dear. Besides, isn't Jell-O good for you?"

"Jell-O is gelatin. Gelatin is made from ground-up horses' hooves."

"Good God!" Ames made a face. "I didn't know that!"

"It's a deep, dark secret, but true."

"Well, aren't you a treasure trove of knowledge? Although I think I'd rather not have known about gelatin. I'll never eat the wretched stuff again," he said with a grin and a wink.

Christine felt suddenly self-conscious when Michael Winter entered her room. She hadn't looked in a mirror, but she knew her face was bruised, her hair matted and discolored with blood.

But Winter wasn't here to admire her appearance, she reminded herself sternly. She was being vain and foolish.

"Hello, Mr. Prince," he said.

Ames nodded. "Deputy."

Winter looked at Christine. "I'm sorry about what happened to you," he said simply. She was struck by the lean, handsome lines of his face, his square-cut jaw, and the almost ebony eyes. Although he didn't look as worn as he had yesterday at the store, he still appeared tired. "Your doctor told me you're going to be fine."

"Right now my head doesn't feel like it'll ever be fine again, but I hope he's correct."

"Hi! Mind if I come in?" Tess was in the room and standing by Christine's bed before anyone had time to say a word. Winter looked slightly annoyed. Christine knew he was waiting to question her about the incident. Tess frowned ferociously. "Oh, Chris, you look *awful*!"

Christine laughed. "Tess Cimino, the soul of tact."

"Hello, Mr. Prince," Tess said. Christine could see doubt in Tess's face. She didn't know whether to mention Dara, but Ames saved her from her quandary.

"Thank you for coming to the hospital with Christine and for calling me immediately," he said in his somewhat formal tones.

Christine's mind suddenly flew to her brother. "Ames, Jeremy went into the store early. He'll wonder why I don't show up and I don't want him to know I'm hurt."

"Don't worry about him," Ames said. "Tess told me he was at the store. I'm closing it for the day and I've sent Patricia to pick up Jeremy. She's to tell him I sent you to Charleston on some important errand for me."

"I hope Patricia doesn't slip and say something she shouldn't to Jeremy about what's happened to me."

"Patricia is quite good at keeping secrets when she wants to," Ames said with a trace of acerbity. A mixture of curiosity and alarm nibbled at Christine's mind. Was the marriage in trouble? Jeremy said Patricia was gone a lot.

"Rey could have taken Jeremy home," Tess said. "He was already at the store."

Ames shook his head. "I'm afraid not. Just before you phoned me from the hospital, I got a call from him saying that he couldn't reach Christine and he wanted her to know he wasn't well and wouldn't be in to work today."

"Rey left the house at the same time I did," Tess protested sharply. "He should have been at the store by seven-thirty."

Ames gave her a placating smile. "He thought we weren't opening until ten o'clock. Perhaps he ran an errand and found that he didn't feel well enough to work today."

"What errand could he run at seven-thirty?" Tess demanded. "Nothing's open."

"Convenience stores are," Christine offered.

"What would he go to a convenience store for?" Tess continued. "He doesn't buy anything at convenience stores."

"Gasoline. He probably filled up the car, then went back home."

"He's not home," Tess insisted. "When I couldn't reach him at the store, I called home twenty minutes ago to tell him what happened to you. Where could he have been?"

Ames looked slightly baffled by the barrage of anxious commentary and questions. Christine was accustomed to Tess jealously keeping tabs on Rey's whereabouts. She knew Tess was envisioning Rey involved in some early-morning tryst. However, she was also slightly alarmed by the alert look that had sprung into Deputy Winter's eyes. She guessed he might be speculating about where Rey Cimino was during the attack on her at the gym.

"Tess, I'm sure there's a good explanation for why Rey wasn't home when you called," she said. "Rey probably went to the drugstore for Pepto-Bismol or Alka-Seltzer or cough syrup if he wasn't feeling well."

"We have all that stuff at home," Tess snapped.

Christine felt abrupt deep frustration with Tess for making a scene. Deputy Winter was staring hard at the unduly agitated woman. Ames shuffled, cleared his throat, then said hastily, "Christine, Deputy Winter is waiting to talk to you and you're looking tired. We should all clear out so he can question you and then you can get some rest." He turned to Tess and gently but firmly took her arm. "May I walk you out, Mrs. Cimino? It seems like *such* a long time since I've seen you. I don't get to your bookstore nearly often enough. Tell me, have you gotten in that new biography of Churchill by Renson? I plan to give it to Patricia for her birthday."

Oh, she'll do cartwheels over that gift, Christine thought dryly. Still, Ames had deftly removed an increasingly annoying Tess from the room. Christine's headache could not have withstood much more of her loud insecurity.

"Is she always like that?" Winter asked after Ames had closed the door.

"Yes. She's madly in love with her husband and jealous beyond belief."

"Does she have reason to be jealous?"

"Not at all," Christine said adamantly. Too adamantly, she realized when Winter's gaze flickered again, but she couldn't think of anything to mitigate the false-sounding intensity of her denial.

"I don't suppose you've caught the guy who did this to me," she said quickly, hoping to divert his attention.

"I'm afraid not. Unfortunately, it's a bad morning. Another storm was blowing up and there weren't any pedestrians in the area. Drivers were concentrating on the road. You were the only guest at the gym."

"Just my luck." She paused. "But I guess I *was* lucky. That blow to the head could have killed me."

"Yes. We're all very glad it didn't." He gave her a slightly weary smile, then flipped open a notebook and poised a pen above a page. "I know you're in pain and this is the last thing you want to do, but please tell me everything about the attack you can remember."

Christine recounted the experience slowly, trying not to leave out any details, even the embarrassing ones about the assailant grinding his hips painfully and suggestively against her thighs. "He didn't say a word," she added. "He didn't even grunt or mutter under his breath. I can't tell you anything about his voice."

"Most people don't think about voices," Michael Winter said approvingly. "Voices can often tell us a lot, if you'll forgive the pun. It's a shame this particular jerk didn't make a sound." His eyebrows drew together, causing two creases above his nose. Worry lines, her mother used to call them. "What about smell?"

Christine knew smell was the strongest of the five senses, the one most likely to evoke memories, but she hadn't thought about her attacker's smell. Until now. She closed her eyes, forcing her mind back to the scene, the feel of the person grinding into her thighs, the smell of . . . "Dirt," she said. "Musty dirt. And . . . yeast."

She opened her eyes. Winter had leaned slightly closer to the bed and she realized she'd spoken softly as she tried to conjure the memory. "What do you mean by *musty* dirt?"

"Dirt that hasn't been in the sun. Sort of the way the dirt smells in the stand of evergreen trees behind my house. Dirt with moss mixed in. And a slight pine scent."

Winter nodded. "Great. How about the yeast?"

"Well, it wasn't a fresh yeast scent like you'd get if someone was baking. It was stale." She paused. "Maybe like . . . beer. Yes, like he'd had beer, but not immediately before. It was more like the beer was partially digested and being sweated out of the pores."

"You're very good at this."

"Maybe if Ames ever decides to close the jewelry store I can get a job as a police dog."

Winter actually grinned as he wrote quickly in his notebook.

A thought struck Christine. "Marti at the gym said the buzzer didn't go off the way it does when someone comes in the front door, and the back doors were locked. Have you figured out how he got in?"

"A back window had been cut open, then unlocked."

"Cut open?"

"A sharp instrument is used to slice a circular hole in the window and a suction cup is attached to pull out the glass. That way there's no sound of glass crashing. The person reaches through the hole and unlocks the window."

"But doesn't the gym have an alarm system?"

"Mr. Torrance said he turned it off at six A.M. when the gym opened."

"Oh, of course he'd turn off the alarm during the day."

Michael Winter looked at her intently. "Can you think of anyone who would want to hurt you?"

"No, not really."

"Not really?"

She hesitated, then guiltily gave him a highly altered version of the finding of Dara's diary. She told him that she and Jeremy had gone to the creek just to look at the high water and had run into Robert "Streak" Archer, who often jogged that way at night. She went on about the cat running up the tree, Jeremy pursuing, and then finding Dara's diary in the hollow of the tree.

"That was quite a coincidence. All three of you being out there at night, that is," Winter said expressionlessly.

"I didn't know it, but Streak runs by there almost every night," Christine said, hoping she didn't appear guilty, careful to look directly into Winter's eyes. But didn't too steady a stare always betray that one was lying? She was overthinking and tried to smile guilelessly. "It turned into a bizarre little group, especially with Rhiannon the cat along."

"And her running up the tree. And Jeremy finding the diary."

Skepticism was written all over his face, and Christine decided hedging wasn't wise with this man. He saw, or sensed, too much.

"Yes. The diary. I first considered taking it to Ames, but then I thought there might be something in it the police should see. I suggested to Streak that we read it."

"Why did you want Streak to read it?"

"Because he's known Ames most of his life. They're like brothers. And I didn't want the entire responsibility of deciding whether the diary should go to the police."

"Because there might be things in it that would be embarrassing to the family?"

"Yes. Embarrassing but not important to the murder investigation. In that case, I wouldn't have given it to the police. But if there was possibly crucial information in the diary, I would never have withheld it. Still, I wanted Streak's opinion on the contents. I know a lot of people in town think he's odd, but he's really a very levelheaded person. I trust his judgment."

"Okay, so you found the diary and then what?"

"We went back to my house and read it. There are things in it that . . ." She hesitated. "Well, we thought the police should see it. But not Ames. He would want to protect Dara's reputation, and the diary wouldn't do much for that cause. He'd never turn it over to the authorities. So, we decided I'd bring the diary to you today. Streak left. And then . . ."

Michael Winter lifted an eyebrow and Christine felt her face getting warm. She didn't want to sound foolish to this man. "After Streak left, I had the sensation that someone was watching me through the sliding glass doors facing the dining room table where we'd been sitting. I hadn't closed the blinds, you see. Anyway, it was an eerie feeling, but I put it down to exhaustion and imagination. Then the cat came in, jumped up on the table, looked out, and started hissing. She only hisses when she senses danger. Or when Pom-Pom chases her. Pom-Pom is Patricia Prince's dog. He and Rhiannon hate each other." She was rambling and stopped herself. "Anyway, I'm sure someone was out there watching. They probably saw Streak and me reading the diary."

For the first time, Winter's face lost its impassive expression. "Miss Ireland, you said you thought the diary should be given to the police. Is that because you felt it pointed to someone who might have murdered Dara?"

She drew a deep breath, gathering the courage to dismiss Ames from her mind and take what she knew was the wisest course of action. "Yes. There were definitely damning passages about more than one person. Dara was involved with at least three men, none of whom knew about the others. She seemed to think it was fun at first. Then she got scared. She thought she was being followed. She said she'd gotten in over her head." Christine paused. "Her Christmas entry says she felt like she'd be dead in a year."

Winter's dark eyes flickered. "Do you think she could have been exaggerating?"

"Well, yes. Dara could be melodramatic. But in light of what happened . . ."

A quick glint in his gaze told Christine he accepted the importance of Dara's declaration. "Who were the three men with whom she was involved?"

"I don't know. Dara was really into using nicknames and initials. She was openly dating Reynaldo Cimino. He's a jewelry designer at Prince's. Very talented. Very handsome. She called him Adonis. I'd heard her use that nickname. He was crazy about her and devastated when she disappeared. Now he's married to Tess Brown, who owns Calliope, the bookstore next to Prince's. The woman who was in here earlier."

"How soon after Dara's disappearance did he marry Miss Brown?"

"About six or seven months. People said he was on the rebound. I hate to think that was true. She's one of my closest friends."

"All right," Winter said slowly. "Who were the other lovers?"

"As I said, she didn't name them. She called one the Brain and the other she always referred to by the initials *S.C.*"

Winter looked up from his notebook. "Any idea who the Brain is?"

"None. I never heard her use that nickname."

"Know anyone with the initials *S.C.*?"

"Well, I'm sure a lot of people have those initials. They aren't uncommon. You know, like *Z* or *U* or *Q* or—"

"Miss Ireland, you might as well tell me who you have in mind."

So much for dodging the truth with this man, she thought. "Sloane Caldwell."

"The attorney."

"You know him?"

"I've met him."

"Oh. Well, he used to be engaged to me." Michael Winter merely stared at her, clearly waiting for her to continue, and she couldn't have stopped herself if she'd tried. "I was twenty-one. He was twenty-six. We were engaged for seven months. I broke off the engagement. I broke it off a week before Dara disappeared."

She could have bitten her tongue for that last revelation. Her guilty conscience about the drama she'd created over Dara and Sloane at the party had nagged her into a confession that hadn't been lost on Winter.

"Did your ending the engagement have anything to do with Dara?"

"Not directly. I'd decided I was too young and making a mistake. And Dara was flinging herself at Sloane." *Flinging?* She decided she must really be flustered. She sounded like a character in a Victorian novel. She plowed on self-consciously. "Sloane never rebuffed her and to some people it could have seemed as if we broke up over her." Winter again raised an eyebrow in question. "Okay, as a matter of fact, we had our final blow-up about her."

And now he's going to ask about the details of our final argument, Christine thought with dread, but he surprised her. "Has Mr. Caldwell been seriously involved with a woman since Dara's disappearance?"

"Seriously? Not that I know of. But he's dated other women. Quite a few, actually."

"So you've kept track of his romantic life."

Christine's face flamed. "Certainly not!" she said hotly. "But we've remained friends and it's a small town, where you hear gossip, not to mention that he works in my former guardian's law firm."

"Ames Prince never struck me as a gossip."

"He's not!" Christine's voice was rising while Winter remained totally offhand. "But I know one of the legal secretaries. And another lawyer in the firm. They mention things sometimes. Not because I'm quizzing them, mind you. Just casually. I do not pry into Sloane Caldwell's life. I have no interest in it except that he be well and happy—"

"You don't need to get so wound up, Miss Ireland," Winter said easily as his lips curled in a maddening, barely perceptible smile.

"I'm not wound up! You just made it sound like I'm a lot more interested in Sloane Caldwell than I am. That's all."

"All right. I didn't mean to offend you." He looked calmly back at his notebook as Christine glared at him. He'd managed to fluster her with a few innocuous words. And piercing looks, she fumed. The man seemed like he could look right through you. She hated it.

"You're asking me a dozen questions about old issues," she snapped, deciding to go on the offensive. "How about what happened to me this morning? Aren't you interested?"

"I'm very interested," Winter returned evenly. "That's why I was asking so many questions about the diary. Did you have it with you at the gym?"

"No. It's at home. Why?"

"Because your gym bag had been torn apart as if someone was looking for something. I didn't know what. Now I think it could have been the diary. There's also your car."

"What about my car?"

"I suppose you locked it, because someone used the same razor and suction cup method to cut a hole in the driver's side window to get in. The contents of your glove compartment are scattered everywhere and some of the carpet has been torn loose. The trunk lid has been popped open and some of the carpet is torn loose there, too."

"Oh no," Christine groaned. "That means I have to contact the insurance company and then get a rental for a week while mine's being repaired."

"I think Mr. Prince has already notified your insurance company and had the car towed in with a promise that you'll have it back in a couple of days."

She smiled. "Thank heavens for Ames. He's always so capable in an emergency. Except for yesterday."

"You'd have to be superhuman to keep your head in a situation like yesterday's," Winter said kindly. "Now, back to the diary. Where is it?"

"At my home."

"You say you'd decided to give it to the police. Since your doctor tells me you won't be released until tomorrow, may I have permission to enter your house and get it?"

"Certainly."

"May I borrow a key?"

"Sure. They put my purse in the bottom drawer of that little chest beside the bed." Michael Winter withdrew the purse and handed it to her. She found her key ring and removed the house key, handing it over to the deputy.

"I'll bring it back to you this afternoon."

"That's not necessary. Just leave it on the kitchen counter. My friend Tess will probably be picking me up in the morning, and she has a key."

She smiled and refastened her purse, feeling she was being not only virtuous in turning over important information to the police but also highly professional about the whole matter.

Deputy Winter looked at her expectantly. She smiled back. Finally he asked, "Where *is* the diary, Miss Ireland?"

Her image of professionalism shattered. "Oh. Well, it might be hard to find." Winter looked at her questioningly. "When I got the feeling I was being watched last night, I hid the diary. There are no windows in my laundry room. There *is* a big box of powdered laundry detergent. The diary is buried about two inches under the powder."

Now she felt like a complete fool. Hiding the diary in a box of laundry detergent sounded ridiculous. Paranoid. Adolescent.

Winter looked at her steadily. "You should have been a spy, Miss Ireland."

"I guess I watch too much TV," she said sheepishly. "I just thought if someone wanted the diary and broke into the house, they'd never look for it in a box of laundry detergent."

"That was pretty smart. If you'd taken it with you to the gym, it would be gone. If the perp entered your house, which we haven't verified yet, he would have looked for it in a drawer or some obvious place and found it immediately." He paused again. "Are you fairly certain someone was looking into your house when you and Mr. Archer were reading the diary?"

"Yes, but only because when we found it at the creek I had the same sensation of being watched. It could have been a coincidence that someone saw us find the diary. We weren't keeping our voices down when we talked about it. Then he could have seen us leave with it. If he had an interest in Dara's murder, it makes sense that he would have followed us."

Winter nodded and made more notes. Then Christine asked, "When will Dara's body be released?"

"No time soon, I'm afraid."

"Why? Ames identified her."

Winter looked at her. "He identified her on the basis of a ring found wrapped in the plastic with the body, not on the basis of any identifying marks about the body itself. It could be Dara's ring that somehow ended up with another body. Therefore, Mr. Prince's identification isn't considered positive. Since the corpse's teeth were missing, we can't use dental records. We'll still have to wait on the DNA results."

Christine suddenly felt cold and pulled the blanket higher across the ugly hospital gown. "It's hard to imagine that someone could do something so despicable as to kill someone, mutilate the body, then go on living as if nothing happened."

"Yes, it is." Winter closed his notebook and looked at her pleasantly. "Just a couple more questions. Did your brother or Streak Archer know where you hid the diary?"

"No. Streak had already left and Jeremy was asleep. Jeremy didn't even know we'd read it."

"I see. We'll leave Jeremy out of things for now, but I will need to talk to Mr. Archer. Do you think he'll resist questioning?"

Christine suddenly felt defensive. "Deputy Winter, no matter what you've heard about Streak Archer, he is *not* crazy. After his head injury in the war, his personality changed some. He doesn't like to be around a lot of people. But he's perfectly sane. As a matter of fact, he's brilliant."

"Brilliant enough for Dara Prince to have nicknamed him the Brain?" Winter asked in a coolly challenging voice.

9

1

Christine had launched into her second soap opera of the afternoon, feeling like she should turn to a news channel but unable to drag herself away from the male and female too beautiful to look human discussing how to overturn the corporation of the female's father. "He's had it coming for years," the female said, flashing lip gloss and hair so shiny it looked shellacked. "I haven't an ounce of sympathy for him. He'll sow what he's reaped."

"Is Serena Santarios plotting against her daddy again?"

Christine looked at the doorway to see Bethany Burke standing behind a cart loaded with books and magazines. "Have you decided to become a doctor?" Christine asked.

Bethany smiled, dimples forming in her creamy cheeks. "Yes. I'm starting my training by pushing around this cart. I'll work up to something harder when I feel more confident." She wheeled her cart into the room, glanced up at the television, then at Christine. "Am I interrupting?"

"You're saving me." Christine flipped off the television with the remote control. "In another hour I would have been so hooked I'd have to quit my job so I could stay home to watch this every afternoon."

"You could program your VCR to record it," Bethany said seriously. "That's what I do. I never like to miss Serena Santarios. She's so smart and strong." Bethany's thick chestnut hair hung below her shoulders and her brown eyes were soft and large, like an innocent little girl's. She looked far younger than her thirty-three years. "The hospital is abuzz with the news of your attack."

"I believe I was scared more than hurt, although I look terrible. I have a concussion and got a few stitches in my scalp. I have to stay here tonight."

"It's so hard to believe that someone at the gym could have done this." Bethany shivered. "I was there just yesterday. You didn't see the guy?"

Christine had started to describe the incident when suddenly something within her seemed to jump fearfully away from the memory. A couple of scenes flashed in her mind, then were gone. "I didn't see a thing." Bethany looked taken aback, and Christine realized how sharp she'd sounded. "Sorry. I've just been through it all with the police."

"Oh, I understand. I didn't mean to upset you again."

"You didn't. I haven't seen or talked to you for almost a month. I suppose it's because you've taken this new job."

"Sure." Bethany pulled a face. "It's a very stressful position, works me to a frazzle." She sat down on the vinyl-covered guest chair with a sigh. "Actually, I don't like doing this at all, but Daddy's on the hospital board." Bethany's "Daddy" was on the board of just about everything. Christine suddenly wondered if that's why her friend was so devoted to watching the scheming Serena Santarios, the daughter capable of bringing down her powerful father on the soap opera. Bethany would be terrified of defying her own father. "Daddy thought it would look good for me to do some volunteer work for the hospital. I told him that Jan needs me, but he pointed out that she's in preschool. I can get home before I need to pick her up. He always out-thinks me. But I'm *not* volunteering this summer when she's home all day. After all, next year she'll be in kindergarten—"

"Drinking and carousing, and you'll *never* see her!"

Bethany grinned. "You think I'm silly."

"I think you are an extremely devoted mother to a beautiful little girl. Jeremy is simply enchanted by her. He told me he thinks angels must look like her."

Bethany beamed. "And she thinks he's wonderful. He's so patient with her, going along with all her little games, enduring tea parties. You two are coming to her birthday party, aren't you?"

"I told you we wouldn't miss it. It was sweet of you to invite us."

"Jeremy gets along great with kids and you can help out."

"Me? Help out?" Christine faked a look of horror. "Is that why I got invited? Not for cake and ice cream?"

"You can have all the cake and ice cream you want *after* you help out. Travis is not much good at those things."

"What do you mean? He's one of the favorite professors at Winston University because he's so good with young people. He can even make Biology one-oh-one fun."

Bethany's heart-shaped face took on a wistful look. "You don't have to tell me. I was one of his students. He's great with young people who are over fifteen. Youngsters don't interest him and he doesn't try to hide it."

Christine had met Bethany in an art appreciation class when Bethany had come back to the university a second time to work toward a degree. That time she'd dropped out because of a difficult pregnancy with Jan. Bethany and Christine had remained friends, and over the years, Christine realized that no matter how well things were going for Bethany, she always managed to find a dark side.

"Bethany, I've seen Travis with Jan. He adores her. And he's great with her."

"With her alone, yes. Groups of kids?" Bethany shook her head. "Oh well, here I am going on about trivial problems when you've been through such an ordeal."

"Which has the whole town talking, Chris." Christine and Bethany looked up to see Patricia Prince lounging in the doorway. She was impeccably dressed with her shoulder-length golden brown hair in a chic reproduction of a 1950s movie star's style and a half-smile on her classic lips. "I must say, though, that you don't look half as bad as I'd expected."

Patricia strolled into the room with the proprietary air Christine had always hated. Bethany was immediately intimidated. She jumped up from her chair. "I was just leaving, Patricia. I'm a volunteer now and I have this cart to push around, although no one is much interested in reading, not that I blame them, because everything is so outdated—" Bethany seemed to run out of air.

"Are you enjoying your job?" Patricia asked.

"It's okay. Well, really it's fairly boring."

"Certainly they could find something more interesting for you to do."

"Apparently I'm not qualified for anything else."

"That's ridiculous. You're a wonder with flowers, and those arrangements in the gift shop could certainly use improvement."

"Well, I guess I could suggest it."

"Don't *suggest* it, Bethany," Patricia said impatiently. "Show some spine. *Insist* on it. It isn't as though Hugh Zane's daughter doesn't have any pull around here."

A nervous smile fluttered over Bethany's face. "Well, I'll mention it to someone. I'll be running along now. Hope you feel better, Chris. Good-bye, Patricia."

As soon as Bethany closed the door behind her after crashing her cart into the door frame a couple of times, Christine asked, "Why are you always that way with her?"

Patricia looked genuinely surprised. "What way?"

"Bossy. Annoyed."

"I was only trying to get her to stand up for herself."

"Her father gives her orders constantly. Now you're doing it."

"Oh, for goodness' sake." Patricia shook her head. "I didn't mean to give her orders, but I must admit that trembling-fawn manner of hers drives me crazy. Who would guess she's Hugh Zane's daughter? He's so commanding and—"

"Overbearing."

Patricia laughed. "Yes, I guess he is. But you're allowed to be overbearing when you're loaded with cash. Then it's called self-confident."

"Bethany is trying to be your friend lately, helping you with your garden and all, so it wouldn't kill you to be a little kinder."

"I think you're just finding fault with me because you're a grouchy patient, but I'll humor you. I promise to be *kinder* to Bethany." Patricia sat down on Bethany's abandoned chair, lit a cigarette, blew out the smoke in a swift stream, and smiled at Christine. "Anyway, I'm sure our little Bethany's not so meek with everyone. Travis, for example."

"And what makes you think that?"

"I just do. I know Bethany's type. Meek with others, a bitch to the husband."

"I don't think Bethany could ever be a bitch. And by the way, you're not allowed to smoke in here."

"I know. But I'll get away with it as long as I can." Christine watched her closely and noticed a slight tremor in her long, well-manicured fingers. Patricia caught her gaze and said sharply, "I haven't had one of these for hours. Nicotine withdrawal. Oh, how are you feeling?"

"Thank you for asking. Lousy."

Patricia emitted a husky smoker's laugh. "I'm glad you're not being a martyr. And I'm sure you won't believe it, but I *am* concerned about you."

"Thanks," Christine said, somewhat disconcerted. "You're probably also curious."

"I'm curious as hell, but I was given orders by Ames not to ask you any questions. I don't suppose you'd just volunteer the details of exactly what happened this morning, would you?"

"I suppose I could oblige with a *few* details. I was assaulted by a man who dropped a wet terrycloth robe over my eyes and stuffed a washcloth in my mouth. I was lifting weights. He sat down on my thighs, actually ground his hips into them with these obscene movements, and kept my arms bearing the weights up in the air until my hands were getting sweaty and my arms began to shake. Then he let me lower my arms and he hit me first with his fist, then with a weight, resulting in a concussion and this lovely cut and bruise."

"Good God, Christine!" Patricia looked shocked. "I had no idea it was so . . . foul."

"Foul? I could have been killed."

"A flat-out murder attempt somehow seems *cleaner* than the simulated rape." She shivered.

"Patricia, will you please not spread around the part about the hip grinding? I shouldn't have said anything. The gossips in town would have a field day with that detail."

Patricia's face had gone pale. "I won't say anything to anyone. I promise." She seemed aware that her expression and her voice had become peculiarly sincere and quickly pasted on a smile and retrieved her usual tart tone of voice. "Besides, I don't have any friends in this town to titillate with details. Oh, I've no doubt a few of our nosier neighbors will force themselves to be friendly with me hoping I might slake their curiosity, but I won't give them any satisfaction."

Christine smiled. "I appreciate your silence on the matter, Patricia, whatever your reasons."

Patricia raised her eyebrows. "A thank-you from Christine? I believe my heart will stop. And just to prove I *do* have a heart, my main reason for silence would be the feeling that what happens in your life is none of the town gossips' business. God knows I'm sick of their curiosity about what happens in *my* life. And now the vultures are circling because of Dara. It's a nightmare."

"How's Ames doing, Patricia? He wouldn't say much about himself to me."

"Me neither, I'm afraid. Last night was awful. He was devastated. But it seems the police don't consider his identification conclusive. Something about the ring not being enough proof that the body is Dara's. By this morning, he'd latched on to that fact like a drowning man. He was almost buoyant, convinced the body wasn't Dara's."

"Oh no." Christine shook her head. "You know the body probably *is* Dara's and he's setting himself up for a big fall."

"I know, but I didn't argue with him. Sometimes even false hope is better than nothing. Unfortunately, his mood changed for the worse again after Jeremy blurted out something at lunch about you finding Dara's diary." She raised an eyebrow. "Did you really find her diary?"

"Oh God," Christine groaned. Jeremy and his runaway tongue. "Yes, we did find her diary tucked in a tree down by the creek."

"In a tree! How odd. What made you look there?"

"Rhiannon. She ran up the tree, Jeremy went after her, stuck his hand in a hole, and there it was."

"Sounds like something out of Nancy Drew."

"I know, but in a Nancy Drew book it would have been much more fun. In reality it felt eerie to find it after so long."

"Yes, I can imagine. But Jeremy said you read it and now you're giving it to the police."

"He told Ames that?"

"Yes. Ames just stared at him, then left the table and slammed into his study."

Christine's spirits sank. She remembered that when he'd gone down to bed with Rhiannon before she and Streak read the diary, Jeremy had closed the basement door. But much later, when she realized someone was outside peering in, Rhiannon had been sitting on the dining room table. Obviously, at some time Jeremy had crept up the stairs, opened the door, and heard her and Streak reading the diary and talking about taking it to the police. He wouldn't have meant to hurt Christine by telling Ames, but Jeremy had a strong, if sometimes misguided, conscience. He would have recalled Dara's fervent decree that no one read the diary, which he'd firmly repeated to his sister. He would have felt betrayed by her ignoring his warning and thought it was his duty to report to Dara's father that Christine and Streak not only had read his adored Dara's sacred book but also planned to hand it over to the police.

"Jeremy shouldn't have said anything about the diary, but he was probably angry with me," Christine said. "He said Dara didn't want anyone to read it."

"But you did."

"Yes."

"You *and* Streak."

"Yes."

"What did it say?"

"Not much," Christine hedged, feeling Patricia's gaze sharpen and her tension heighten. The woman knew she was lying and it bothered her. Maybe even frightened her.

"You'd better forget about giving that diary to the police, Chris, and hand it over to Ames."

"It's too late. Deputy Winter has it by now."

"What?" Patricia closed her eyes briefly. "Do you know that all hell will break loose? Ames will go on an absolute rampage."

"I can't imagine Ames on a rampage," Christine said weakly, already dreading her guardian's wrath.

"You can't? Good God, Chris, you don't know him at all."

"I know he'll be mad, but he'll get over it."

"Ha! He'll never get over it. This is Dara we're talking about. His darling, his angel, his—" Patricia broke off and looked at the ceiling. "I'm not going to tell him you've already given it to the police. I'm not fool enough to deliver that piece of news. Honestly, Chris, how could you be so stupid as to give the cops that damned diary?"

"I am not stupid and I gave it to them because they should have it!"

"Even though there was nothing important in it? That's what you said." Patricia's eyes narrowed. Christine suddenly felt like a mouse with a hawk swooping down on it. "But that's not true, is it?" Patricia demanded. "There must have been something significant in the diary or you wouldn't have given it to Winter."

Mercifully, Christine was saved from answering when a nurse poked her head in the door, glaring. "No smoking!" she barked at Patricia. "None. Whatsoever. Nada. Against the rules. Verboten."

"I think I got the message," Patricia said acidly, still holding her cigarette with aplomb.

"You're also shouting."

"Well, you know how crazed we addicts are," Patricia returned.

"Perhaps it's best if you leave now. You're upsetting my patient," the nurse said coldly.

Patricia stood up gracefully and looked down at Christine. "Think you can muddle through the rest of the afternoon and evening in this horrid place with such charming company as your nurse?"

"Sure. I'll be fine," Christine said feebly, still shaken by Patricia's outburst.

"If you can't, I'll come and set a diversionary fire with one of my cigarettes while I break you out of the joint." The nurse shot Patricia a sour look. "Need a lift in the morning?"

"Tess is picking me up."

"Ah, the lovely Tess." Patricia frowned. "If I had a husband seven years younger than I am who looks like hers, you can bet I'd take a little more care of my appearance. What's she put on in the last few months? Twenty pounds?"

"Maybe Rey loves Tess for more than her looks. Besides, she's my best friend."

"Oh. I'm being put in my place for yet another episode of my habitual acerbity." Patricia gave her thick hair a slight toss as if in defiance. "Well, chin up, kid. You look like hell right now, but you should improve in a couple of days. Well, better make that three. And, dear, don't expect a lot of sympathy from Ames after this diary stunt. I'm afraid your good conscience will put you right over the line with him."

"Put out that *cigarette*," the nurse repeated loudly.

Patricia held the woman's gaze as she dropped the cigarette on the floor and slowly ground it out with the toe of her expensive alligator pump. Then she swept past the nurse with a whiff of Chanel No. 5, a swish of the door, and a trail of cigarette smoke floating behind her.

"That woman is outrageous," the nurse muttered venomously. "I wouldn't turn my back on her for a minute, honey.

She's bad news if you ask me. She's the type that might even be *dangerous*."

"Oh God, let's hope not," Christine said as she leaned back against the pillows and closed her eyes, desperately wishing for sleep to obliterate this horrible day.

2

Patricia left the hospital room roiling with frustration. She'd come because she was genuinely concerned about Christine, and she'd ended by verbally attacking her. Of course, finding out that Jeremy hadn't been babbling nonsense about that cursed diary was the cause, she told herself. The consequences of Christine giving the book to the police could be devastating to me, Patricia thought. God only knew what tales that wretched girl had written about her in the diary.

"Patricia Prince! Don't you look lovely today!"

Patricia stopped slowly, gazing at a man exactly her height with thin white hair, bulging pale blue eyes, and a nose turned large and red by acne rosacea. "Thank you, Dr. Holt. It's hard to know what to wear in weather like this—one day cool, the next warm and sunny."

"Camel's hair is always a fine choice. Except in the dead of summer, of course." He snickered at his own feeble joke. "Are you visiting a patient or here on behalf of some of your charitable works?"

Patricia looked at him sharply. She was not involved in any charitable works. Was he insulting her? No. He looked blandly amiable.

"I'm here to see Miss Ireland."

He frowned. "Miss Ireland?" Then light dawned behind the pale blue eyes. "Oh, your ward."

"My husband's former ward."

"Yes. Quite a nasty blow she took to the head. I don't suppose you know the details of what happened?"

Patricia raised an eyebrow. "She didn't tell you?"

"She didn't go into specifics. I'm sure she will when her nerves have settled down. And, of course, I didn't push her for information. I was more concerned with her medical condition." I'll just bet you were, Patricia thought. Holt had a reputation as a gossip. He was fishing for information, the more salacious the better. "A policeman was here," he informed her in a confidential tone. "Not Sheriff Teague. Some flunky deputy."

"I'm certain Christine told him everything anyone needs to know."

"Christine? Oh, Miss Ireland." He reached out and touched the sleeve of her jacket. "Such a stylish cut. Did you get it in New York?"

"Downtown." Patricia tried not to flinch away from the man. She knew he was being friendly because Ames had saved his son from a prison sentence he probably deserved. Holt also fancied himself a ladies' man, although how he could keep up that illusion after one glance in the mirror amazed her. He made her flesh crawl.

Patricia caught a glimpse of Sloane Caldwell coming down the hall. She thought he might stop to talk and rescue her, but he merely smiled, nodded, and headed for Christine's room. Meanwhile, Patricia realized Dr. Holt was staring at her. Years ago, before she'd married Ames, gossip had linked her to this smarmy little man and she'd been appalled.

"How is Mrs. Holt?" Patricia asked.

"Uh, fine. As usual."

"And your sons?"

"Fine, fine. Doing well in their respective colleges."

"That's wonderful," Patricia said sweetly. She couldn't stand Holt, but she didn't need another enemy in this town. After Eve Prince's death from an overdose of sleeping pills, people had said Patricia had been a careless nurse, not keeping track of Eve's medication, letting her hoard pills. Then Patricia had married Ames six months after Eve's death and they'd said even worse about her. Not about Ames, of course. Ames, they said, had acted hastily in a haze of grief.

They'd been right about the reason for Ames's proposal. What they hadn't known was that Patricia had discovered Eve's hoard of pills and taken them away from her two days before her death. Giving in to Eve's desperate pleas, though, Ames had retrieved the pills and helped his wife take the overdose to end her suffering from rampant and agonizing pancreatic cancer. If it hadn't been Patricia's day off, townspeople would probably have said Patricia murdered Eve to get her out of the way. But Ames had let everyone know Patricia hadn't been in the house all day when his wife died. And later he'd confessed to Patricia what he'd done. She'd always kept his secret, and although she was not in love with him—had in fact only married him because of the security he offered her—she would never betray his confidence.

"I take it you have a much better relationship with this Kathleen person than you did with Dara," Dr. Holt was saying.

"It's *Christine*, and yes, I do." That was certainly an exaggeration. Patricia had never argued with Christine as she had with Dara, but she'd resented the intrusion of her and Jeremy into the household because it had made an already tense situation even tenser.

Now, though, Patricia wished she'd been friendlier to Christine over the years, because she needed a confidante. Patricia was not certain what made her sure Christine had good sense and might know how to help her out of the mess she'd gotten herself into lately. Maybe it was because Chris had always seemed older than her years. Maybe it was because she'd always acted so sensibly and responsibly. Or maybe it was because Patricia was just desperate. But it was far too late to mend fences now.

"Christine isn't as high-strung as Dara," Patricia went on to Dr. Holt. "And I'm not her stepmother. Dara never liked the fact that her father remarried."

"Very selfish of her." Holt peered at her. "I've heard about Dara's remains being found. So tragic. Has the family any idea of who is responsible for the poor girl's death?"

"No, and my husband has requested that I not discuss it."

"Certainly that makes sense. Still, the situation must be hard on you." He gave her a fondling look. "Very . . . upsetting."

"Yes." She wanted to scream at the man to stop gazing at her lasciviously, but instead she forced another pleasant smile. "You're so kind. You always have been." She glanced at her watch. "Oh my, look at the time! I'm running late as usual. It's been wonderful seeing you again."

"And you, too, my dear. Perhaps we could get together sometime for coffee. Or better yet, a relaxing drink at some quiet little place—"

"Sounds fabulous," Patricia flung over her shoulder as she hurriedly stepped away from him. "And say hello to your lovely wife and those handsome grown-up sons of yours for me!"

She didn't see Holt's scowl that followed her down the hall.

3

"Good God, Chris, you look dreadful!"

Christine grimaced. "Sloane, if people don't stop telling me how bad I look, I'm going to get a complex."

"Sorry, sweetie." He still called her "sweetie" in spite of their situation. They had remained amicable, if not close, ever since their break-up. "You know I wouldn't deliberately hurt your feelings."

"And I appreciate the sentiment, even if you did just tell me I look dreadful. Are those flowers for me?"

"Yeah. I saw them sitting at the nurses' station and swiped them for you."

"And they just happened to be yellow roses, my favorite!" He laughed and handed the arrangement to her. She sniffed them and sighed in delight. "Thank you, Sloane. A whole dozen. They must have cost the earth."

"Just a small token of my esteem and my extreme gratitude that you're all right." He took the arrangement from her, set it on the bed table, and drew closer to the bed. "I've been instructed by my lord and master Ames Prince not to ask any questions about what happened this morning, although I must tell you that already the Winston rumor mill has you at death's door."

"Far from it, no matter how bad I look. But I guess there's little hope that Jeremy won't hear about it."

"I think he can be kept in the dark at least until tomorrow. And by then you'll be home. Won't you?"

"So they say. I can't wait. I hate hospitals."

"I remember. Not too fond of them myself."

Sloane reached out and gently touched her hair. "Poor girl. What a hell of a thing to happen to you."

There was nothing romantic in his touch—only sympathy—but Christine suddenly felt self-conscious. In her diary, Dara had said one of her lovers was S.C. Christine was convinced S.C. was Sloane. She couldn't help picturing him locked in a wildly sexual embrace with Dara. She felt her face turning red from either anger or embarrassment; she wasn't sure which.

"Chris, you're looking kind of strange. Do you want me to call a nurse?"

"First I look dreadful; now I look strange," she said with an attempt at lightness. "Your visit is cheering me up immensely."

"Sorry. You always said I didn't have the soul of a poet."

"I did not!"

"Yes, you did, one night when you'd had too much wine and insisted on reading someone called William Wadsworth to me."

"Wordsworth. My favorite poet. You were bored senseless. I believe you dozed."

"I never doze. I'm always the life of the party, the one full of loud, pointless stories. The one with the lampshade on my head while I do the jitterbug or burst into a rendition of 'Great Balls of Fire.'"

"You the life of the party?" Christine laughed. "I think not. You're too concerned with making the right impression."

"You make me sound like a colossal dud!"

"Not a dud. Just . . . correct. A gentleman right out of a Henry James novel."

Sloane grinned. "Now you're teasing me, which means you're all right." He bent and kissed her lightly on the forehead. "I'm so happy you're not seriously hurt. When I consider what *might* have happened to you—" He broke off. "Try to get a good night's sleep. I'll give you a call tomorrow."

4

The night seemed interminably long to Christine. Her head hurt, the coarse sheets scratched her legs, her hospital gown kept twisting around her waist, and the nurses seemed unaware that patients were supposed to be getting some sleep. They talked and laughed in normal, or what seemed above normal, voices at the nurses' station. When they weren't talking, they were slipping in to make sure she was sleeping comfortably, their rubber-soled shoes squeaking on the tile floor. By one in the morning, Christine felt like screaming.

Eight more hours of this and I can go home, she thought in near-desperation. I'll be comfortable in my lovely house with music playing and my soft-furred cat following me around, and I'm going to bake a pan of cinnamon rolls to go with my morning gourmet coffee. What flavor shall I choose? Stockholm roast? Kenya? Vanilla nut?

Half an hour later, Christine's body had begun to slow from the sheer strain of the last two days. Her mind drifted from one unfinished thought to another before she heard a ghostly rumbling somewhere deep in the night. Another storm, she thought dismally. More cold water and dreary days.

The sharp ring of the telephone startled Christine from her dreamy dread of the coming storm. As she tried to lift heavy eyelids, she prayed the call was not from Jeremy, who by now had probably heard she was in the hospital.

She slowly lifted the receiver and mumbled, "Christine Ireland."

Silence spun out for a moment. But not complete silence. She detected a faint whirring sound. Mechanical. A sixth sense threw her on instant alert. "Christine Ireland's room."

Abruptly a young woman's voice sounded in her ear. A familiar voice. The hair on Christine's neck rose and she felt as if she were sinking in cold, dank water as she listened, mesmerized, to Dara Prince singing in a weak, lost voice:

> "Everywhere I go
> Dark eyes peer at me.
> I wish they meant me love,
> But I know they desire me harm.
> I want to live long and full,
> But sadly, I am certain that
> All too soon, death waits for me."

10

1

"Miss Ireland, you can't leave until Doctor signs your release papers," a sturdy nurse said for the third time. "If you leave without his approval, your insurance company might not pay your claim."

"Then *I'll* pay it. I just want out of here and you said he won't show up for at least an hour. I cannot *stand* this place for another hour."

"I believe if you'll just take some deep breaths and stop pacing—and by the way, the back of your gown is open—you'll feel calmer."

Christine whipped around to look at her exposed backside. Was making someone wear a hospital gown with only a couple of flimsy strings attached to hold it together in back a special form of torture? She sat down hard on the chair.

"That's good," the nurse said in the soothing voice she might use on a toddler. "Now, don't we feel better?"

"Oh, just peachy!"

The nurse ignored Christine's sarcasm. "And look! We have a lovely breakfast. We'll feel even better when our tummy is full!"

"Maybe you will. I won't."

"Now, now—"

"Now, now, yourself," Christine snarled.

The nurse sighed. "You're such a pretty girl to be such a trial. I'm sure your mother would be embarrassed by your behavior. At least drink your coffee. *Please*."

Christine glowered at her, but the mention of her soft-spoken, ladylike mother pulled her up short. Liv certainly *would* think her daughter was being a complete bitch. After all, it wasn't the nurse's fault Christine had been scared witless last night.

After the phone call, she'd lain stiff with anxiety until dawn. She'd longed to ask for help, but help for what? An anonymous phone call during which someone had played music? Not just music. Music with Dara Prince singing about someone wanting her dead. The remembered sound sent tremors of fear down Christine's back, but she couldn't explain to this definitely earthbound, no-nonsense nurse that a murdered girl had sung to her over the phone last night. The woman would think she was not only a bitch but also crazy. Considering the way Christine's luck had been going lately, she'd end up in the psychiatric ward.

"All right, I'll have some coffee," she said. "I'm sorry I've been so cross, but has anyone ever thought of getting new mattresses for these beds?"

"The bed not as comfy-wumfy as the one at your house?" the nurse asked as she removed the plastic lid from Christine's coffee.

Comfy-wumfy? Did the woman always talk this way? "I have a back problem. I need a good mattress."

"A good mattress is important, but a night spent on one not so luxurious won't be the end of you."

"My mattress isn't luxurious. Just comfortable."

"Yes, well, think of all the people who have no mattress at all." And you should feel ashamed of yourself for complaining, the nurse clearly added silently. With a forced smile, she handed Christine the coffee. "We also have orange juice on the tray. Orange juice will give us energy."

That's all *we* need, Christine thought sourly. Energy. I'll be able to worry more energetically. "You can have my orange juice. I don't want it."

"We nurses are not allowed to eat from the patients' trays."

"I don't know how you can resist," Christine said as she forced down weak lukewarm coffee.

"I am not a finicky eater." The nurse stripped off a wrinkled pillowcase and beat the hapless pillow into a clean one. "I have little patience with finicky eaters. Just think of all the people—"

"Who have no food at all," Christine finished for her, watching the woman grimace with dislike for this ungrateful young woman. "Has my friend Tess called to say what time she'll be here to pick me up?"

"Your friend would call your room, not the nurses' station. We're not receptionists!" she huffed.

Speaking of phone calls sparked an idea for Christine. "Does the switchboard keep a record of phone calls made to patients' rooms?"

"Not that I know of. Why?"

"I received an anonymous call." Christine tried to keep her voice calm. She'd made it this far without mentioning the call, but now she couldn't stop the flow of words. "I'm trying to find out who it was from."

"I wouldn't have any idea."

"It came around one-fifteen A.M."

The nurse had been violently wrestling clean sheets onto the rock of a mattress, but she looked up. "That's impossible."

"Obviously not. I received the call."

"You must have been dreaming. No calls are put through the switchboard to patients' rooms after eleven o'clock."

Christine nearly choked on her awful coffee. "But I wasn't asleep."

"You just thought you weren't."

"I think I know when I'm asleep or awake," Christine bristled. The nurse threw her a glance that said she found this doubtful. "I got a call at one-fifteen."

"Whatever you say, dear. Don't get yourself all worked up about it."

But she was all worked up about it. She was also determined to find out who'd managed to circumvent the switchboard in order to place a call intended to terrify her in the middle of the night.

2

"Thank God you're here," Christine said to Tess when she walked into the hospital room at eight-twenty. "I thought I'd go nuts waiting for you."

"For Pete's sake, Chris, do you know how early it is?" Tess wore jeans washed almost white at the seams and knees and a shapeless gray sweater. She'd had blond streaks put in her brown hair and they'd turned brassy. She'd gained nearly twenty pounds in the last year and had dark, puffy pads under her eyes as if she hadn't slept all night. Tess had never been a beauty, but she was usually stylishly dressed and well groomed. Now she looked sloppy and haggard. Christine wondered how Rey was reacting to the discovery of the body that might be Dara's. If the man Tess adored was devastated by the death of an old love, jealousy and grief might account for her careworn appearance.

"I stopped by your place and got fresh underwear, jeans and a top, and a pair of shoes," Tess said. "Lucky thing I have a key."

"I lock myself out at least twice a year. Someone else needs a spare and it isn't going to be Patricia, who'd no doubt go snooping. You and Bethany are the trusted ones."

"Bethany has one, too?"

"I need backup in case you're not home."

"Good thinking. Now, what's the big rush to get out of here? Was your night that bad?"

"Yes, but not for the reasons you probably think. I'll tell you when we get home."

"Goodness, aren't you the lady of mystery? And not too popular around here. Your nurse stopped me outside and told me in injured tones that you refused to wait for *Doctor* to release you. She said you are a very stubborn young lady."

"I'm sure *stubborn* isn't the adjective she really had in mind. We're not exactly *sympatico*."

Christine had stepped into the bathroom to put on her clothes. Tess had forgotten a bra, but Christine was not voluptuous. She could easily go without one, since the one she'd worn into the hospital yesterday bore dried blood that had soaked through her sweatshirt. Tess had also forgotten socks to go with Christine's oldest pair of running shoes. They were a disgrace, she thought ruefully. She looked like a beaten-up slob with her bruises and crummy clothes. She decided to make her trip through the lobby as fast as possible.

"I'm not waiting on *Doctor*, because I can't stand this place and also because I know you have to open Calliope."

"Not today. All downtown businesses are closed by order of the Army Corps of Engineers. Most able-bodied men are on the riverbank slinging around sandbags."

"Is Rey?"

"Since before dawn."

"I'll bet Jeremy is, too."

"If he is, Rey will look after him. You have to stop worrying about him twenty-four hours a day seven days a week, Chris. It's wearing you out."

And worrying about Rey twenty-four/seven is wearing you out, too, Christine thought, but said nothing. She had too many worries of her own. Like someone attacking her in the gym. Like hearing Dara sing during a phone call in the middle of the night.

"Are you mumbling about Dara singing?" Tess asked, her forehead creased.

"Maybe I was. It's what I'll tell you about later."

"God, I can't wait until later. This secret of yours is killing me."

"Well, don't die until you get me home. Ten more minutes in this place and I'll start howling."

Tess grinned. "*Nurse* will certainly have something to tell *Doctor* then! It would make her whole day. Hell, her whole year!"

"And I won't give her the satisfaction. Let's go."

Half an hour later, after more protesting from the nurse about her hasty flight without release papers, Christine and Tess were headed for home. The day was dry, but the sky was the color of pewter and the streets were littered with debris that collected faster than the street cleaners could collect it.

When they pulled into Christine's driveway, they saw Bethany on the covered porch set a grocery bag and a pot of violets on a heavy redwood bench before rummaging through her purse. She waved and walked toward them as they emerged from the car. "I didn't expect you so early, Chris!"

"She wasn't enjoying her stay at the hospital," Tess muttered. "She has deep, dark reasons, but we're not to be let in on them until she's had a decent cup of coffee."

Bethany looked especially pretty, Christine thought. Her thick chestnut hair fell in soft waves over her shoulders and was held back on the left with a pearl clasp. She wore jeans, but hers were new and crisp and accented by navy trouser socks and expensive navy loafers. Her coral-colored cashmere sweater set made her complexion glow. Christine felt like a bag lady beside her. She could tell Tess felt the same way.

"I hope you don't mind that I was letting myself into your house," Bethany said as she insisted on carrying Christine's purse up the walk. "I stopped by the grocery store early to pick up a few things for you so you could just rest today. I know you never keep much food unless you're expecting Jeremy."

"That was really thoughtful of you, Beth," Christine said as Bethany withdrew a dainty handkerchief from her pocket and wiped her nose. She was the only person Christine knew who carried a handkerchief instead of paper tissues. "Do you have a cold?"

"A slight one. I caught it from Jan. It's going around preschool."

Christine nodded. "I thought your voice sounded deeper at the hospital yesterday. Now you don't feel well and on top of everything else, I've probably thrown off your whole morning schedule."

"I feel fine. I just sound funny. And you haven't thrown off my schedule. Jan's school has been delayed an hour because of the sandbagging operation."

"Are they putting four-year-olds to work sandbagging?" Tess asked seriously.

"You are hilarious and I'm sure some of the four-year-olds would love to be out in that mess," Bethany giggled. "But actually the sandbagging has blocked some of the roads and slowed down traffic. I don't know why they didn't just close the school down for the day. And although Travis's car is on the fritz and I have to take him to the university, his first class isn't until eleven. So you're not inconveniencing me one bit, Chris. Oh, here's my key to your house! No wonder I couldn't find it. I'd put it in the special zipper compartment of my purse where I'd be sure not to lose it. Travis says if I'd just toss things around like everyone else does, I wouldn't spend half my time looking for stuff."

"Men have all the answers," Tess said. "Rey, on the other hand, is always annoyed because I *do* just toss things around. He's the most organized person I've ever met. It drives me nuts."

Bethany unlocked and swung open the front door while Christine picked up the pot of violets. "These are gorgeous! I've never seen any so lush!"

"They're a special kind called Optimara. In the eighties, twenty-five thousand seeds were launched into space and left for six years to orbit on a Long Duration Facility. When the seeds were brought back to earth, they'd undergone a lot of mutations, including multiflorescence, which makes the flowers more abundant. You have perhaps twenty blooming at a time instead of the regular four or five. And unlike regular African violets, they never stop blooming." Tess and Christine stared at her. She blushed. "I'm lecturing. It's just because last week I gave a report on these to the Garden Club."

"Thank goodness," Tess said. "I was afraid you were turning into some kind of intellectual."

"I leave that to my husband," Bethany answered. "He's the professor in the family."

"So these are 'Space Violets,'" Christine said, smiling as she admired the blooms that looked like purple velvet. "Jeremy will be delighted when he sees them. He loves anything having to do with space. I think we've watched every episode of the original *Star Trek* at least twenty times. When Jeremy was young, he worked out a secret password for us. If either of us was in trouble, we were to call the other and say, 'Klingon.'"

"What on earth does *Klingon* mean?" Tess asked.

Bethany and Christine exchanged glances. Bethany said, "The Klingons were the dreaded enemy of the brave and valiant Earthlings. How come you don't know that?"

"How come you do?"

"I'm married to a scientist. Of *course* I know it," Bethany said. "*Star Trek* was the first thing Travis and I ever talked about. I was too shy around him to think of anything else."

"Not even snakes?" Tess asked as she set the bag of groceries on a kitchen counter.

Bethany shuddered. "If I never see another snake in my life, it will be too soon. I thought Travis would outgrow his horrible fascination with them, or at least give up his collection out of respect for my repugnance of them, but *no*." She carefully placed the violets in the center of the kitchen table, where they would receive indirect sunlight. "I think he'd divorce me rather than give up even one of his ghastly creatures."

When they'd entered the house, Rhiannon had not come to greet them. She was shy around strangers, but she knew Tess and Bethany. Christine looked at Tess. "Speaking of creatures, did you see Rhiannon when you stopped by earlier for my clothes?"

"Briefly. She was sitting at the top of the stairs. Then she ran and hid under your bed." Tess frowned. "She acted a little bit scared. She's never run from me before."

"Maybe my being gone last night unnerved her," Christine said. "I never leave her."

"One of these days you'll have to take a vacation," Bethany commented. "This summer Travis and I are taking Jan to San Francisco and Carmel. Actually, he wanted it to be a second honeymoon, but I wouldn't go without Jan."

"I sure wouldn't turn down a second honeymoon with *my* husband," Tess said. "Chris, quit fluttering around the kitchen checking on everything. I assure you I didn't steal the silver when I was here earlier."

"Something just doesn't feel right to me," Christine said vaguely, nervously lifting and setting down a coffee canister. "Nothing is out of place, but something is just *off*."

"Your bad night in the hospital has you acting weird," Tess said. "Why don't you go in the living room, lie down on the couch, and I'll make you some tea?"

"I hate tea."

"Coffee?"

"I already had some and it was so vile, it's ruined my taste for coffee for at least three hours."

"Well, Miss Congeniality, is there anything that *would* please you?"

"Hot chocolate with lots of miniature marshmallows. The chocolate mix and marshmallows are in the cabinet above the microwave."

"Fine. I'll have hot chocolate, too. Very festive on such a drab morning. Bethany, do you have time for a cup?"

"A quick one. Chris, please lie down. You look ready to drop. I brought fresh milk. And wheat bread and cheddar cheese for those grilled cheese sandwiches you like. I also brought a head of lettuce, tomatoes, green peppers, and cucumbers for a salad. You rest now. I'll put everything in the refrigerator while Tess makes the hot chocolate. Oh, I also got some doughnuts fresh from the bakery. I know how you love them."

"Bethany, you are too good to be true," Christine said.

By now her head pounded like a bass drum. Her arm muscles ached from the strain of holding the weights yesterday. She also felt grungy, and her eyes were gritty from lack of sleep. To top it off, her supposedly adoring cat had not shown her face in rapturous greeting. Feeling tired, grumpy, nervous, and defeated, Christine grabbed up the remote control and flipped on a morning news show. Apparently the world was a mess and the stock market was falling after she'd just invested a couple of thousand dollars in a sure thing. She flopped down on the couch with a groan.

That was when Bethany in the kitchen shrieked at the top of her voice.

Christine bolted off the couch and tore into the kitchen. Tess stood frozen in the center of the room, holding a carton of milk. Right hand hovering near her mouth, Bethany was backing away from the refrigerator.

"What is it?" Christine demanded over Bethany's continued screams. "What's *wrong*?"

Bethany raised her left hand and pointed to the open refrigerator. Christine walked to it, feeling the cool air pouring out. She saw nothing unusual on the nearly empty shelves. Then she looked down at the open hydrator drawer.

On the cold white metal lay a filthy, dead, long-haired brown river rat nearly a foot long.

3

"Eat your oatmeal."

"You didn't put raisins in it," Jan Burke said accusingly. "Or cimmaning. I only like it with raisins and cimmaning."

"It's *cinnamon*, not *cinnaming*." Travis rummaged through the kitchen cabinets until he found raisins and cinnamon, then sprinkled both in his four-year-old daughter's bowl of steaming oatmeal. "How's that?"

"Not right. You have to cook the raisins with the oatmeal or they don't get all nice and smooshy."

"Stir them into the hot oatmeal. They'll soften."

"They aren't right."

Travis closed his eyes and counted to ten, then said in an even voice, "Mademoiselle, please eat the oatmeal Daddy made for you. I went to a lot of trouble. It'll hurt my feelings if you don't eat it. All right?"

Jan softened slightly at being called *mademoiselle*, which she knew was a nice name in a beautiful language she would learn someday. She also didn't want to hurt Daddy's feelings. "Oh, okay, I'll eat it," she said magnanimously, then muttered into her bowl, "but it's not right."

Travis Burke loved his daughter more than he'd believed he could ever love another human being, but he didn't know how Bethany managed to treat the little girl with unfailing patience. Jan was a very good girl for her age. Everyone told him so. But even the best four-year-olds were difficult, they added. Unfortunately, Travis had never been even-tempered with humans. Reptiles were another matter.

"I'm going out to check on the snakes before Mommy gets back," he told Jan.

"Ugh. Maybe they'd eat my oatmeal."

"They like a little livelier fare."

"What?"

"Never mind."

"You mean they eat mice. Alive." Jan scrunched up her beautiful little face. "Double ugh! And you'd better hurry. Mommy won't like it if she has to wait for you."

"Mommy shouldn't be so rigid."

"What?"

"Never mind again. I'll be back in ten minutes. And you'd better eat every bite of that oatmeal."

When Travis had first married Bethany, her father, Hugh Zane, had wanted to buy them a large Mediterranean-style house in Winston's most affluent neighborhood, a house not far from his own. Travis had turned down the lavish gift in favor of a ranch-style home less than half the size of the Mediterranean. He'd had two reasons besides not wanting to live under Hugh's watchful eye. The first was that he didn't care to be beholden to Hugh Zane for over $400,000. Hugh would remind him in a hundred little ways how much the house had cost, expecting obedience in return. Second, Travis was determined to live on the outskirts of town, away from close neighbors, where no one would object to his keeping the snakes that had been his passion since he was fourteen.

Now their nearest neighbor lived nearly half a mile away, a retired widower who shared a mild interest in herpetology and dropped by every couple of weeks for a look at "the little guys." Over a mile separated them from other neighbors, who so far had registered no complaints about the snakes, no doubt thinking the odd college professor only kept black, garter, and maybe a couple of small rat snakes.

To Travis's surprise, neither Bethany nor Hugh had ever let up on him about getting rid of the snakes, although before the nuptials he'd been adamant on the subject. Perhaps they'd thought that with enough nagging they could eventually wear away his resolve like water wearing away rock. They'd been wrong, and Travis had been both amazed and unhappy by his seemingly malleable wife's tenacity. Perhaps, he thought later, she was more like her father than she seemed.

The snake house measured thirty by thirty-six feet and was constructed of white-painted concrete blocks with windows made of Lexan, a polycarbonate as clear as glass but nearly unbreakable. Travis removed a ring of keys from his jacket pocket. With the first he unlatched a padlock, with the second a deadbolt, and with the third a regular doorknob lock. He walked inside, swung the metal door shut behind him, and flipped the knob lock shut. He turned on full-spectrum/ultraviolet lights. Water snakes like full-spectrum, while insectivorous species seemed to benefit from ultraviolet. He looked around the well-insulated domain where the heat was carefully maintained at optimum temperatures for the health of the snakes. "Good morning, ladies and gentlemen!"

A series of hisses and rattles greeted his cheerful words. Most people shuddered at the sound. Travis loved it.

After his marriage to a prosperous woman, he no longer had to watch every penny and was able to sink a large portion of his savings into the snake house, whose cages boasted the European-style terraria interiors more natural than most simple American styles. Leaves or sand, sometimes a combination, covered the floors of the cages. Many contained small branches he'd gathered from the woods, some branches placed diagonally in the cages for arboreal snakes. This style of cage made tending the snakes more trouble, but Travis thought the snakes deserved the best.

He glanced in a cage at a bright red-and-orange tree boa, a species highly sought after by hobbyists although generally known to be feisty and to dislike handling. "I'm expecting about ten babies from you this year," Travis said. "You're not going to let me down, are you?" The boa wrapped herself tighter around a branch, turning away her face. "Bitch," Travis murmured, smiling.

He moved on to a common king snake with white markings against black. The snake was plentiful in Appalachia and Travis knew too many people felt no immediate fear of it, not realizing that an untamed one is likely to coil calmly around an arm, then grab and chew with vicious gusto. Travis bore the scars on his right arm to prove the snake's unpleasant trait. This snake was large and torpid, one of his first acquisitions in spite of their less than friendly introduction. Her mate was kept in a separate cage because of the king snake's tendency toward cannibalism.

Travis's tan-and-rust-colored pine snake lay almost invisible in a mass of leaves. He'd found this one in Kentucky and valued it because, of a species known for its belligerence, this was the most aggressive one he'd ever captured. The next cage contained a predominantly gold heavy-bodied ball python. Because of its coloration, this beauty had cost him over $3,000. The species was known to have a lifespan of twenty to forty-seven years. "You'll probably outlive me, buddy," he said to the oblivious snake.

But the snakes holding the greatest fascination for Travis were the vipers, maybe because they were generally the deadliest. Their venom is most dangerous to people because vipers target warm-blooded prey—prey with physiology most like humans. One of Travis's favorites was the large Gaboon viper with its markings of purple and pink. The species had the longest fangs of any venomous snake. He'd carefully measured this one's at one and a half inches each. It also had the intriguing habit of lying still when angered, then inflating and cutting loose with a hissing noise so loud some experts compared it to the sound of a car tire deflating.

His western diamondback rattlesnake seemed to glare at him as he rattled ominously. "Bad mood today, Hugh?" Bethany would be incensed if she knew he'd named the bad-tempered, dangerously venomous snake after her father. Travis moved on to the death adder with its triangular head, the black tiger snake with its large body and tendency to spread its neck when alarmed, the desert horned viper that when annoyed rubbed its scales together to make a loud, rasping sound—

A sharp rap at the steel door made Travis jump and reminded him he'd stayed too long with the snakes. He hurried the length of the snake house, unlocked the steel door, and opened it to face a narrow-eyed Bethany. "It's time to leave. *Past* time."

"Sorry, honey. Hey, why don't you step in and look at the green python? It's beautiful. The color looks especially good today. Maybe it's the light—"

"I do not find *any* snake, no matter how good its color, beautiful. And we're late. Jan has already missed the first fifteen minutes of preschool."

"Oh no," Travis said dramatically. "I wonder how far behind she's fallen in her education? Damn, I hope she can still make it into a good university."

"Don't be sarcastic, Travis. Preschool isn't the nonsense you think."

"All I know is that I got a Ph.D. without one single day of preschool. *Or* kindergarten, for that matter."

"I am not having this discussion again," Bethany announced, glaring. "Lock up your house of horrors and let's get going before we're even later than we are now."

In the car Bethany strapped Jan into the backseat so tightly Travis expected the child to turn blue, then asked if he wanted to drive. Travis declined, although his wife's cautious, creeping, nervous driving style set him wild. Nevertheless, Bethany loved to drive and he hoped concentrating on navigating the car might take the edge off her anger at his tardiness.

They crawled out of the driveway, Bethany peering repeatedly in the rearview and side mirrors and sticking her head out the open window searching for impediments. At last they cleared the driveway and started out at a rip-roaring forty-five miles an hour on open highway.

"So how is Christine?" Travis asked, determined to be sociable, although he could tell Bethany was still sizzling with anger.

"She's not good. Something else happened this morning—" She glanced back at Jan. "I'll tell you about it later, but I'm worried about her. I hope she and Jeremy will be able to come to Jan's birthday party next week."

"Oh yes, let's do hope," Travis said dryly.

Bethany turned to him. "What's with the tone? I thought you liked Christine."

"I like Christine just fine. It's her brother who bothers me."

"Why? He's sweet and gentle—"

"You barely know him, Beth. His kind is unpredictable. I don't like having a big retarded guy around all those little girls."

"Travis!" Bethany gasped.

"I *love* Jeremy," Jan protested loudly. "He's fun like a kid."

"Like an *enormous* kid. I don't want him at the party."

"*I* want him to come, Daddy," Jan said truculently. "It's *my* birthday party and it won't be fun without him!"

"And *un*inviting him would hurt his feelings and insult Christine," Bethany added in an affronted voice. "I can't believe you would even *suggest* such a rude thing!"

"Jeez, what an uproar," Travis muttered. "I think that cold is really getting to you, Beth."

"What does that mean?"

"That you're ridiculously short-tempered."

"I'm short-tempered because we're late!"

"Then drive faster. Everyone is passing us."

Silent with fury, Bethany pushed on the accelerator and they sped up five miles an hour. We're flying now, Travis thought as he gritted his teeth. To take his mind off her maddening driving, he flipped down the sun visor and looked at himself in the mirror on the back. His light brown hair showed a few new gray hairs at the temples. It also seemed his hairline might be receding slightly, a disaster as far as he was concerned. He vowed to buy Rogaine this very afternoon. And some of that subtle dye that gradually darkened the hair. His cheeks also looked a bit pale, maybe even sunken, and his green eyes faintly bloodshot. He hadn't slept well last night.

"You look fine," Bethany said, "although you nicked yourself shaving. There's a little bloody spot on the left side of your chin and one on your throat."

"I hate shaving." Travis licked a finger and rubbed at the dried blood. "Maybe I'll grow a beard."

"Don't you dare. I hate beards. They make men look older." She turned and gave him a hard look. "If you cover up that handsome face with a graying beard, you might not be as attractive to the nineteen-year-olds you favor."

Travis sighed. "I'm not interested in nineteen-year-olds."

"I was nineteen when you started seeing me." Travis flipped up the visor as Bethany braked sharply for a large brown leaf she'd apparently mistaken for a squirrel. The leaf having safely blown to the other side of the road, she accelerated with a lurch. "Dara Prince was nineteen, wasn't she?"

"I have no idea how old Dara Prince was," Travis said tightly.

"Who's Dara Prince?" Jan piped up from the back. "Is she a princess?"

"No, mademoiselle," Travis said. "She was just a student in my class, and a poor one at that."

"You had no interest in Dara Prince?" his wife persisted.

"No, Bethany, I did not."

"Oh really?" She looked over at him with one of her dangerously sweet smiles. "Then why did you say her name twice in your sleep last night?"

11

1

After the discovery of the rat, Christine thought they would have to slap Bethany to stop her screaming. "For God's sake, Beth, it's only a rat!" Tess had shouted above the noise.

"A *big* rat. Dead. In the *refrigerator*!"

"Yeah. Dead. It's not going to hurt anyone. It just looks gross and it stinks."

"I'm going to throw up," Bethany announced.

Christine had suddenly felt calm, almost amused by the uproar caused by a simple rat, repulsive though it was. "Beth, Tess, I think you both need to go home," she said. "Then I'm going to call the police."

"You want us to leave you here with *that*?" Bethany had asked in horror, pointing at the rat.

"I don't think I'm in any danger. You have to drive Jan and Travis to school. Tess, you've been up for hours and you look exhausted. The police might not arrive for an hour or two. I'm going to take a shower and try not to sound like a hysteric when the cops come. I want you two to go about your day and let me take care of myself. I'm not an invalid or a child."

"But you've been through so much—" Bethany protested.

"When Chris says she wants to be alone, she wants to be alone," Tess said gently. "She's the most stubborn woman alive and there's no use arguing with her. But before we leave, we're searching this house. After all, that rat didn't get in here by itself."

"You think there are more rats?" Bethany asked fearfully.

Christine noticed Tess's attempt to control laughter. "No, I don't think this one was brought by his friends. I think the *person* who brought it might still be hiding in here."

"Oh, good heavens, how stupid of me!" Bethany had exclaimed. "I'm not usually this dim-witted, Chris. I'm just—"

"Jumpy. So am I," Christine said. "But I think Tess's idea is a good one."

The three of them toured the whole house, where they found not even a window unlocked. "Then how did someone get in to leave the rat?" Tess had asked.

"I don't know, but the police are better at discovering points of entry than we are," Christine said. "At least we know no one is here now. So you two scram."

After they'd left, Christine ran upstairs and turned on the shower. While she stripped off her running shoes and jeans, Rhiannon appeared.

"At last!" Christine exclaimed. "I thought you'd run back to the Prince house to live with Pom-Pom." The cat stared at her with big golden eyes, then weaved around her legs, rubbing silken fur against the skin. "And how could you let someone get into our house with a *rat*? Oh, because the rat was almost as big as you, you decided not to defend your turf?"

Actually, Christine was vastly relieved to see the cat, whom she'd been afraid had run away in fear or perhaps even been killed and buried by whoever had invaded this house. She hadn't expressed her fears to Tess and Bethany. Bethany probably would have cried, and Tess would have called endlessly for the cat in her loud, rough voice that would send Rhiannon into hiding for the rest of the day.

While Rhiannon sat loyally by the glass door, Christine spent twice as long as usual in the shower. The hot water eased some of the soreness from her arm muscles that had rigidly held the weights so long yesterday, and a bar of glycerin soap softened her dry skin that bore bruises on her thighs from her attacker's grinding hipbones. The memory made her shiver.

She shampooed her hair twice, rubbing easily over the

stitches in her scalp, wondering if she should let her hair grow long. But her short style was so easy to maintain—a little gel, a little blow-drying over a circular brush, and she was done. Five minutes, tops. She had a great complexion, as Tess often commented, and wore only powder, lip gloss, and mascara. She never bothered with jewelry except for a watch. She spent all day handling and showing the stuff. Her only beauty obsession was her nails. Well-manicured nails were a must for modeling rings and bracelets to best effect for customers, and she often felt like she spent an inordinate amount of time applying nail polish.

When she emerged from the bathroom wrapped in a cozy fleece robe, Rhiannon was sitting calmly on the bed having her own bath. "Getting ready for company?" Christine asked. "You've always been vain. But then, I guess I am, too."

She wasn't really concerned with her appearance other than being clean, though. She had taken her time showering because she needed time to regroup, to collect her thoughts, to literally catch her breath before calling the police. She needed not only to calmly discuss finding the rat but also to report the phone call she'd received at the hospital last night.

The shower had calmed her. Breathing was not such an effort now, and she certainly felt more presentable. She slipped on black corduroy jeans and paired them with a copper-colored sweater to give her face more color. She still looked pale, so she added blush on both cheeks and a touch of peach shadow on her eyelids. That was much better, she thought as she looked in the mirror, although the bruise on her temple still showed a glorious blue-purple. "Cheer up," she told her reflection wryly. "In two days the bruise will be an attractive greenish yellow." She slid her feet into black suede loafers, then went downstairs.

Before she called the police, she brewed a pot of coffee and sat down to rest for what seemed like the first time in hours. Had it been only two days ago she'd been working at the store, slightly bored because business was so slow? That was before the body had been washed ashore by the flood, before she was attacked, before the anonymous call to her hospital room, before the rat left in her refrigerator. Really, couldn't whoever was in charge of life give her a break for a while? Maybe just one afternoon, enough time for her head to stop throbbing? Which reminded her, because she'd left the hospital before the doctor signed her release papers, she hadn't gotten a prescription for pain medication. That would teach her to break the rules.

When the coffee was ready, Christine took three bracing sips, then called police headquarters and asked to speak directly to Deputy Winter. Another deputy had wanted to give her the runaround, but she could be forceful when the occasion required, although she didn't think of herself as an aggressive person. "Well, all right," the deputy said in annoyance, "but you just about missed him. Winter, got some woman here on the phone hell-bent on talkin' only to *you*. Must be sweet on you."

"Deputy Winter here," he said in a moment.

"This is Christine Ireland and I wanted to talk to you in particular because you're already familiar with our situation," she explained, embarrassed by the other deputy's accusation. "When I got home from the hospital today, I found a dead rat in my refrigerator."

"A *what?*"

"A rat. Not a mouse. A really big river rat. Dead, thank goodness."

"Nice welcome home gift. Did you throw it out?"

"No. I didn't think I should tamper with a crime scene." How stupid and melodramatic that sounded, she thought. "I mean, I don't think this was a joke. It must be some kind of crime to do this to someone."

"It is. How about I come over and take a look?"

"I would certainly appreciate it."

"I'll be there as soon as possible."

Ten minutes later Christine saw the silver Crown Victoria with the six-pointed gold star painted on the side pull into her driveway. That would make it two days in a row, because he'd been here yesterday looking for the diary. Christine opened the front door and tried for a light tone. "So nice to see you again, Deputy."

He seemed to take his cue from her. He smiled and removed his hat. "And meeting again under such pleasant circumstances is all the nicer. I trust you have a snack for me in the refrigerator."

"I guarantee that no hostess has served you one like it."

Christine didn't know why she felt relieved as soon as she saw him. She had no answers as to who had attacked her, called her, or violated her home, but the edge of terror that had been vibrating under her skin for hours seemed to dull a bit as soon as Michael Winter stepped into her home.

She caught a glimpse of the door across the street opening a crack so the elderly Mrs. Flint could catch as much of the conversation as possible. She probably had her hearing aid turned up as high as it would go, Christine thought, but she still raised her voice: "I've made coffee. A gourmet blend."

"Nothing like gourmet coffee and a river rat to get the circulation going in the morning." The deputy turned his head and called, "Don't you agree, ma'am?"

The door across the street slammed.

"How did you know she was there?" Christine asked.

"Eyes in the back of my head. Comes with the profession. She'll now move to the front windows and peek through a crack in the curtains."

Christine looked. The curtains parted an inch. She began laughing. "I think you have ESP, Deputy Winter."

"No. Just experience." He stood directly opposite her. At five-ten, Christine looked most men in the eyes. She had to look up about three inches into Michael Winter's mahogany gaze. "I can smell the coffee from here," he said.

"Better the coffee than the rat. He's shut up tight in the hydrator drawer of the refrigerator."

"I'll take a look at him first. Then maybe you'll offer me a cup of coffee."

Rhiannon was stationed at the top of the stairs. She peered at the stranger curiously but made no move to run for the bedroom. "That's Rhiannon. She was Dara's cat," Christine said as she saw Winter glance at the animal. "She and Patricia's dog, Pom-Pom, didn't get along, so I took her when I moved out of Ames's house."

"Was Dara really attached to the cat?"

"Extremely."

"And yet Dara's father believes she ran off and left the pet she loved."

"He's come up with several explanations for her abandoning the cat. He's stumped when I ask why Dara never even mentions Rhiannon in her letters."

"Those letters," Winter muttered. "I don't think Mr. Prince can keep them to himself much longer. They need to go to the police lab."

"Good luck with prying them away from him." Christine led Winter into the kitchen and opened the refrigerator door. "The hydrator drawer on the right contains Ricky the Rat. I don't think I can look at him again without getting too queasy for coffee and a doughnut."

"You didn't tell me you had doughnuts," Winter said.

"My friend Bethany brought them. I'm going to wait in the living room."

She listened to the deputy pull out the drawer, then mutter, "You're one hell of a big, rank rat." Then he called out to her, "This one's bigger than most I've seen. Someone went to a lot of trouble to find you a prizewinner!"

"I'm complimented beyond belief," Christine said. "He's probably infested with plague-carrying fleas, too."

"We don't want to get excited over plague on top of everything else. The state lab will let us know if he's sick."

"You're going to send that thing to the lab?"

Winter answered gravely, "We have to make certain this wasn't a homicide, ma'am."

Christine smiled. He was still trying to take the edge off her nerves. It was working. Slightly.

"I have our friend in a plastic bag and I have to pass through the living room to get out to my car," he warned her. "Close your eyes or turn your back. Please don't scream and faint."

"If I scream, Mrs. Flint will be over here in a heartbeat. She can't pass up that kind of excitement."

"I wouldn't be surprised if she turns up even if you don't scream. Not out of curiosity, mind you. Just to make sure you're all right." He walked past her, holding the plastic bag to his side. "I'll be back to look around and see how the intruder entered."

After he'd gone outside, Christine went into the kitchen and pulled the hydrator drawer out of the refrigerator. She'd pour some strong disinfectant in it, then give it a good scrubbing before it went back into the refrigerator. She looked at the refrigerator and for a moment thought recklessly, I'll get a new one that's never been befouled by a rat. Then reason took over. This refrigerator was one year old. She was being silly.

In a minute, Winter returned. "I assume you've searched the house."

"Yes. My friends Bethany and Tess were here when we discovered the rat. They went all over the house with me."

"Would you mind going again? I'd like to do my own search, and I'd be more comfortable if you accompanied me."

"To protect you in case we run across a *live* rat?"

"Well, that of course," he replied in mock seriousness, "but mostly so you'll be certain I'm not taking anything or rifling through underwear drawers."

Christine laughed. "I never for a moment mistook you for a pervert who'd check out my underwear."

"You'd be surprised how many women think that's exactly what I have in mind if a bedroom search is necessary."

"Maybe they're just hoping," she returned, then turned bright red at the inappropriateness of her comment. Michael Winter cocked an eyebrow at her. "I didn't mean that the way it sounded."

"It sounded flattering, but flattery won't get you out of searching the house with me," he said easily. "Let's start upstairs."

"There are three bedrooms upstairs, one of which I've turned into a kind of office, although Rhiannon seems to think it's hers. She'll probably try to glare you to death if you enter. She's extremely territorial."

"My daughter had a cat," Winter said. Abruptly a shadow seemed to fall over his face. Christine knew he was divorced. The daughter probably lived with his ex-wife, but something told her not to ask any questions about the child.

"Pets teach children responsibility," she said lamely. "When Jeremy and I were children, we always had pets. Usually dogs." As they neared the top of the stairs, Rhiannon dashed into Christine's bedroom and hid under the bed. "So much for cats protecting you."

"Once in a while one comes through. I knew a couple who were awakened by their cat sitting on their bed yowling its head off. Turned out their four-year-old child was having a seizure in the next room."

"Good heavens!" Christine was genuinely surprised. "I thought only dogs did that kind of thing."

"Don't let Rhiannon hear you say that. Let's start in this room."

Twenty minutes later, they had worked their way to Jeremy's basement apartment. "This place is great!" Winter exclaimed.

"Do you think so?" Christine asked, pleased. "It sounds awful to say I'm making my brother live in the basement. But I wanted him to have privacy."

"This isn't like any basement I've ever seen," Winter said.

"It was the basement that convinced me to buy this particular house. The land behind it slopes down and the basement opens onto that big, flat expanse with the patio. Jeremy can come and go without having to enter through the upstairs. That will make him feel more independent."

"And so much light comes in through those sliding glass doors, even on a drab day like this. I'll bet he loves it."

"I think he does. I wanted him to move in several months ago, but Ames asked if he could stay through the holidays. I don't know why, though. I don't believe he really pays that much attention to Jeremy, and he annoys Patricia. With everything that's going on now, I'm going to insist Jeremy move in here as soon as possible. The atmosphere at Ames's can't be good for him."

"I agree. But it was good of Jeremy to stay for so long. I'm sure he'd rather be with you." Winter ambled around the big carpeted space, then did a double take when he saw the quilted silver mesh satin bedspread, the huge model of the starship *Enterprise* beside the bed, and a framed poster of Captain Kirk and Mr. Spock looming over the double bed. "Wow," he said simply.

"Jeremy is a die-hard Trekkie," Christine explained.

"I guessed. Where in the world did you find that bedspread?"

"Wilma Archer made it for him. She ordered the material from some place she found on the Internet. Or rather, her son found it."

"Streak Archer?"

"Yes."

"The computer genius."

Christine stiffened. She knew Winter thought Streak might be the Brain to whom Dara referred in her diary. "Streak has always been very kind and patient with Jeremy. He even lets Jeremy come over and mess with his computers. He's a good man."

"He must relate to Jeremy on some level."

"What does that mean?"

"I mean that people see them both as being *different*, and not different in a good way."

"You've heard bad things about my brother?"

"The usual," he said vaguely, clearly wanting to change the subject.

"And you've heard bad things about Streak," Christine pursued.

Winter looked at her with a somber but kind expression. "Miss Ireland, Streak Archer is a recluse who gets hysterical in public places. What do you think a lot of people say about him?"

"Terrible things, especially because he was perfectly *normal*, as they would say, before he went off to serve his country."

"Fighting an unpopular war. I didn't mean to insult you or him. I'm just telling you what I'm sure you already know. People think he's strange."

And he *was* strange, Christine admitted silently. She didn't really know Streak. She had no reason to be so protective. Besides, her defensiveness was probably doing him more harm than good.

"Well, I sure do like that bedspread," Winter said, as if wanting to regain their earlier light tone but not quite knowing how.

"Maybe I can find out where Wilma got the fabric. You might have to quilt it yourself, though."

"Fine. Quilting was on my list of things to learn this summer. That and learning to make my own lye soap."

Winter smiled at her and she relaxed. "I guess this concludes our tour of the house," Christine said.

"And we found no broken or unlocked windows."

"I've only been back a couple of hours. I haven't opened any windows and then relocked them. And the locks on the sliding glass doors are intact. All the other doors were locked when I got home," Christine said as they went upstairs to the kitchen. "I assume whoever put the rat in the refrigerator did so at night. Otherwise Mrs. Flint would have noticed someone strange hanging around the house."

"How do you know she didn't?"

"Did the police get a report of any prowlers around my house?"

"No."

"Then she didn't see anyone. It's Mrs. Flint's dream to be on one of those shows like *Unsolved Mysteries*. She would have been on the horn to police headquarters if she'd noticed anything the least bit peculiar or suspicious."

Winter grinned. "Sometimes that type can be very helpful. Other times they can be a pain. Mostly the problem is that they lose credibility by crying wolf. If she's a habitual caller to headquarters, they might not have taken a report she made too seriously. I'll have to talk to her. Right now, though, I'm going to take a look outside. You don't need to go with me. It's starting to drizzle."

"Fabulous. I'd rather have a regular old steady rain than drizzle. If you come upon any stunning clues, though, will you call me out to see?"

"Certainly," Winter said firmly. "But unlike in books, criminals rarely leave a convenient footprint or matchbook or, best of all, a photo of themselves. They're downright impolite in real life. Never give us cops a chance to show off."

"Let's hope this was an amateur who touched every surface with bare fingers and maybe even dropped his business card."

"That *would* be a blessing. I'll be ready for some of that coffee when I get back."

"I'll have it ready."

While he was outside checking for any sign of the intruder's entrance, Michael thought about his earlier conversation with Christine. Most of it had been serious, but there had been some joking, too. He almost never made jokes on the job, particularly with young, attractive women. Sometimes they took things wrong, thought you were flirting, reported you for sexual harassment. This had never happened to him, though it had happened to some of his friends in LA. But somehow he wasn't worried about Christine Ireland. She didn't seem like the type of person who exaggerated, made something out of nothing, put significant or even malicious spins on casual or innocent statements.

And what makes you think you know her so well? he asked himself as he parted box hedges, looking for depressions in the damp mulch. You've barely met her. And you're acting entirely too lighthearted about all of this. She's scared silly and with good reason, and here you are making jokes about rats and quilting and—

Michael saw a piece of shiny metal lodged in the mulch. He pulled on a latex glove and carefully lifted it, blowing off the dirt to reveal a circular piece of silver with engraving. Jackpot! he thought. Then he read:

Rhiannon
442 Cardinal Way
Winston, WV
304-555-5095

"Oh, hell," he muttered. Miraculous find! The cat's lost tag.

He went back to searching and thinking about Christine. Yes, he was being too casual with her. She probably thought he wasn't taking her case seriously. Besides, he thought with a stab of guilt, he hadn't acted this way around a woman since the death of his daughter and his divorce from Lisa less than a year later. Stacy was dead, his wife still a painful memory. He had no right to feel any happiness, especially with a woman who was going through what Christine Ireland was going through right now. What was wrong with him? Was he going crazy? He was thinking more about making Christine feel calmer than working the case. Well, maybe not more, but too much.

He'd pull himself together, he decided sternly. He would be solemn. He would be earnest. No joking. He'd barely crack a smile until he left.

When he went back inside, Christine looked at him expectantly. "Just as I thought," he said. "No footprints, no signs of anyone having pried at windows with a penknife, not a scratch on a door lock."

"Then obviously it was a ghost," she returned grimly.

He looked at her. She returned his gaze with complete sincerity. Then her aqua eyes seemed to dance and a smile tugged at the right corner of her mouth. He couldn't help himself. Grinning, he said, "You had me worried there for a minute."

"Your face looked like it had turned to granite. You didn't find *anything*?"

He held out Rhiannon's tag. "Just this."

"She lost it about a month ago. I've already had a new one made." She smiled. "Mrs. Flint was watching you the whole time you were in the front yard. I thought she was going to crash through her picture window when you picked up something. She must have thought it was something devastatingly important. How disappointed she'd be to know it was Rhi's tag. Unless she saw for herself."

"How could she have seen something that small?"

"Opera glasses."

"You're kidding!"

"I'm not. I swear as a former Girl Scout."

Winter laughed. "Then I definitely need to ask her a few questions about what she saw going on around here yesterday. She seems fairly observant."

"That's putting it mildly. Ready for some coffee now that the dirty work is done?"

Winter followed Christine into the kitchen, where she set out coffee mugs. She poured cream into a creamer she never bothered with for herself and searched until she found the dainty sugar holder before she remembered that Deputy Winter took his coffee black, just as she did. She left the cream and sugar on the counter and placed doughnuts on a china plate.

"I didn't expect breakfast," he said.

"You don't have to eat. I just thought you might be hungry."

"I am." Winter went to the sink and lathered his hands with antibacterial soap. "And what kind of cop would I be if I turned down doughnuts?"

"Actually, I'm a doughnut junkie. My friend Bethany bought some for me at the bakery this morning. She was here waiting when I got home from the hospital."

Winter looked at her. "Here? In the house?"

"No. She hadn't come in yet, but she does have a key."

"Anyone else have a key?"

"My friend Tess. You met her at the hospital yesterday."

"You mentioned then that she had a key. She's married to

that guy who works for you," he said, drying his hands on a paper towel.

"Reynaldo Cimino. He's a jewelry designer. I met Tess the first week I moved to Winston when I went into her bookstore, Calliope."

"I suppose Ames Prince has a key."

"Well, no," Christine said reluctantly as they sat down at the table. "If he had a key, that would give his wife access to the house, and I've never been comfortable with the idea of Patricia nosing around in here under some imaginary pretext."

"You think she'd do that?"

"I don't really know what she'd do. In spite of our having lived in the same house for years, I don't feel I know her very well."

"But you know her well enough to distrust her."

"To be fair, I'm not sure that distrust is warranted. Patricia and I just never hit it off. I could be suspecting her of doing things she'd never do. I trust Beth and Tess completely, though."

Winter nodded. "I think you should have your locks changed. Just to be safe."

"But I told you I trust the only two people who have keys."

"Did you have the locks changed when you moved in here?"

"No."

"You don't know who the former owners gave keys to. You don't even know how many keys might be floating around out there."

"Oh. I should have thought of that when I bought the house. It never occurred to me."

"It doesn't to a lot of people. But now seems like a good time to correct the oversight."

"A *very* good time. I don't care to have any more wildlife deposited in my refrigerator." She picked up the coffeepot. "You take it black, don't you?"

"How did you know?"

"I'm psychic. I also served you coffee in the store day before yesterday."

He closed his eyes. "God, I was so tired that day I forgot all about the coffee, although it sure hit the spot at the time." He watched as she poured, then said, "Back to the people who have keys to this house. How about your brother?"

"No. Unfortunately, Jeremy has a penchant for losing keys. He tries to hang on to them, but unless you put one on a chain around his neck, which makes him feel dumb . . ." She trailed off, feeling disloyal to say she couldn't even trust her brother with a house key.

Winter smiled. "I understand."

"Most people don't. They think he *is* dumb. And his IQ is a bit low. Around seventy. But he's sweet and so talented in other areas. Jewelry design, for instance—"

"Miss Ireland, you don't have to explain," Winter said gently. "I have a cousin just like Jeremy. We're exactly the same age and were best friends growing up."

"A cousin like Jeremy? Your best friend?" He nodded and she felt surprisingly relieved. Rarely since she'd moved to Winston had she met anyone who really understood Jeremy— his strengths as well as his weaknesses. Many people either avoided him or patronized him. "Are you still close to your cousin?"

"As close as we can be with him in Los Angeles and me in West Virginia. He got married last year."

"Married?"

"Yes. A sweet girl he met in a special school. They both work in a nursery. They love flowers, shrubs, all that stuff that dies if I just look at it, while they make it flourish. They live next door to his parents, who help them out some, but they're really fairly self-sufficient."

"For some reason I'm stunned."

"I can tell. You look like you could use a doughnut to steady your nerves."

"I'm sorry. I didn't even offer you one."

They both reached for the chocolate-covered. "You take it," he said. "Chocolate makes me hyper."

Christine bit into the doughnut, which was light and sweet and tasted as close to heavenly as food came. She hadn't realized how hungry she was. "I guess I just never thought of Jeremy marrying," she said. "Not that he doesn't pay attention to girls. Well, not obsessively, just naturally, like any young man would do. There's nothing abnormal about his interest in women—"

"Miss Ireland, you're doing it again. Making excuses for him. I've told you already I understand."

"And I'm doing him a real disservice by all this overexplaining." She smiled. "And after all we've been through—the rat and all—I think you should call me Christine."

"In honor of the rat, I will call you Christine. Except around other people. Then you'll be Miss Ireland or we'll set the whole town talking. And I'm Michael."

"When we're in private." Which sounded like she planned to spend a lot of private time with Michael Winter. In embarrassment she took another gigantic bite of doughnut and felt chocolate smear across her lips. Honestly, she was acting like a thirteen-year-old, she thought.

"About this key situation," Michael went on smoothly as if he didn't notice her hastily wiping away chocolate, "you say both Tess Cimino and this friend Bethany have keys."

"Yes. Bethany Burke. Her husband, Travis, is a biology professor at the university."

"So that gave four people access to your house while you were in the hospital."

"Four? You mean Rey and Travis? Why on earth would they come here? Tess came very early to get clothes for me to wear home from the hospital. And I suppose if we hadn't arrived when we did, Bethany would have come in to leave the groceries she'd brought. But neither of them would have put a rat in my refrigerator. The idea is absurd. I thought Bethany was going to have a stroke. You should have heard her screaming."

"I'll bet you didn't scream."

"Well, no, I didn't. But why would you assume that?"

"Because you seem to have nerves of steel." He picked his second glazed doughnut off the plate. "Most people would be wrecks after what you've been through, but you're sitting there as calm and collected as the queen at high tea."

"You've been to high tea with the queen, I take it."

"We move in different circles, but I've heard stories."

"I can imagine."

"I mean it. About your being so calm. It's amazing."

"I'm not at all calm."

"Then why don't you show it?"

"Because I can't."

"You mean, you *won't*."

"All right. I spent a lot of years learning to appear strong for my brother's sake. I'm not going to throw all that mental training away now. But I *am* scared." She paused. "You don't know everything that's happened. Last night at the hospital I got a phone call. No one said anything. But Dara was singing."

Michael looked at her expressionlessly. "Dara called you and sang to you?"

"No, of course *Dara* didn't call me. You think I was dreaming, don't you?"

"Well—"

"I wasn't. Someone called and played what was obviously a tape of Dara singing."

"Singing what?"

"I don't know. I've never heard it before. But afterward, I wrote down most of the lyrics I could remember. The paper is in my purse."

She retrieved a piece of paper from her purse on which she'd written the words she'd heard on the phone the night before.

Michael studied them carefully. "I don't recognize this, either."

"The call came around one-fifteen. No one said anything. They just played the song. Then they hung up. This morning a nurse told me the hospital switchboard doesn't put through calls to rooms after eleven o'clock. Someone *did* put through a call, but when I called the switchboard before I left this morning, the operator was adamant about not having put through any calls."

"And this was the same person on duty at one-fifteen?"

"Yes. She works from midnight until eight A.M. After eight, two people operate the board."

"Then the woman you talked to lied," Michael said flatly. "Maybe someone paid her to put through the call."

"I don't know anything about her—how long she's had the job or what she worked at previously. I wrote her name on the paper with the lyrics. She sounded really young and not at all flustered as if she were lying."

"Some people are very good at it, Christine. I'll try to find out more about her. But more important, we need to know who thought you needed a good scare last night. And who would have a tape of Dara singing? Did you know she sang?"

"Oh yes. She thought she was great."

"And she wasn't?"

"I heard someone tell her once she had a 'sweet little voice.' She was furious, but that phrase perfectly described her singing. It wasn't a bad voice, but there was no great range, or timbre, or emotion. She loved to sing, though."

Michael frowned. "I remember something from her diary. She said at the party given by your friend Tess she drank too much and sat on Caldwell's lap and she sang."

"Oh lord," Christine groaned. "Not getting any encouragement from voice coaches didn't put a dent in her ego. That night she sang about five songs. The first couple no one minded. Then she got louder and rowdier. She even climbed up on the coffee table for one unrequested number. Something she'd written. It was pretty bad, but she was carried away with it and herself. I honestly thought she was going to strip or something. She was totally out of control that night."

"How many people were at that party?"

"About twenty to twenty-five."

"So anyone who was around that night knew how obsessive she was about singing."

"Anyone who was around her at all knew she loved to sing. I used to get so annoyed with her in the car because something I loved would come on and she'd drown out a great singer with her own voice. The only person who seemed to really appreciate her was Jeremy. Of course, he thought everything she did was wonderful, but he thought she was a fabulous singer. She just ate up his admiration and sometimes she did him the great honor of letting him sing with her." Christine paused. "I was a total bitch at the hospital this morning and I'm turning into one again. I didn't mean to sound so sarcastic. It's just that—"

"She annoyed the hell out of you."

"Yes, she did."

"And you didn't like that your brother cared so much about her."

Christine drew back. "I'm not sure how you mean that."

"You felt that she used him. Sort of leeched on to him for veneration but had little use for him otherwise."

"Yes," Christine said slowly, relaxing. "That's exactly how I felt. Maybe you should be a psychologist."

"No, I shouldn't. No talent for the field. I just saw a couple of people do the same thing to my cousin. No one else respected these people, but he was eager to like and be liked, and easy to impress. So they used him to feed their egos. Maybe Dara wasn't as secure as you think if she needed that kind of reinforcement all the time."

"Maybe not. And you still sound like a psychologist."

"Thanks. I take that as a compliment. But I'm just a simple cop." He paused. "A cop who would like another doughnut but is embarrassed to wolf down three."

"*Please* have another one. The more you eat, the less I do. And believe me, I would have finished off the entire half-dozen by myself if you hadn't come."

Michael selected a doughnut with sprinkles as Christine refilled his coffee mug. After chewing, sipping coffee, and taking a second bite, he said, "When I came in the store the other day to tell Mr. Prince about the body washing ashore, you told me you never believed Dara had run away. In her file I read that at the time she disappeared you said that things she would have taken with her if she *had* run away were still in her room. What things?"

Christine tapped her fingers on the tabletop, her gaze drifting to the huge fern hanging in front of a kitchen window as she thought. "Well, probably most important, a ring of her mother's was left behind. The ring was hematite. It's an inexpensive metal, really the mineral iron oxide. It used to be called blood-stone. It's important to a lot of people who practice the Craft because it's considered close to the earth."

"The Craft?"

"Wicca. Witchcraft." Michael's expression suddenly turned wary. "Are you going to bolt?" Christine laughed.

"No. I just had a flashback of my childhood terror of witches."

"You know Dara's mother, Eve, died before Jeremy and I came to live at the Prince home, but Eve dabbled in Wicca. She dabbled in a lot of things, so I don't know how serious she was about it. Ames didn't really approve, but from what I've heard, Eve did as she pleased. Apparently her interest in Wicca became much stronger after she got sick. I guess that's understandable. She thought she could heal herself."

"May I interrupt for a second?" Michael looked at her closely. "Are you into witchcraft?"

Christine smiled. "No, but I think it's interesting. And you must know we're talking about white witchcraft. It teaches harmony with nature and doing no harm to others because if you do, that harm can act like a boomerang. What you send out returns times three."

"Okay. I'll try to rid myself of the image of the Wicked Witch from *The Wizard of Oz*. Back to the hematite ring."

"Eve had large hands and she wore the ring on her middle finger. Naturally, she left the ring to Dara. Dara had small hands, but she never wanted to have the ring cut down to fit because she thought cutting might lessen its power or something, so she wore it on a chain around her neck. I found it on her dresser after she supposedly ran away. But I don't believe she would have left it behind."

"Unless she was in a hurry and just forgot it. Or maybe dropped it."

"Dropped it off her neck?" Christine frowned. "The clasp on the chain wasn't broken. She certainly wouldn't have taken it off, put it on her dresser, then left it."

"I see what you mean. Anything else?"

"On her dresser Dara kept a five-by-seven framed picture of her with Eve. It was taken just months before Eve got sick, and she was still beautiful. Dara cherished that photo and kept it in an ornate silver frame. She wouldn't have left it."

"The frame would have been too heavy or cumbersome to lug around with her if she was traveling light."

"So why wouldn't she just take the photo out of the frame?" Christine countered. "Finally, Dara had certain outfits, pieces of clothing she always wore together. She was fanatic about it. For instance, a pair of black wool slacks she paired with a gray cashmere turtleneck sweater. The pants were gone, but the sweater was still in the closet. She also had a tan suede jacket she adored. The weather was cool, but we found the jacket flung on the back of a chair in her bedroom." Christine paused. "There were a couple more things left behind that made me doubt she'd done her own packing—favorite lip glosses, earrings, a few other small items—but I've given you a sample."

Michael stared off, rubbing a finger up and down beneath his chin as he thought. Finally, he said, "I'll grant you it seems pretty odd she'd leave those things behind, but not impossible if she was in a hurry."

"Maybe, but there's one other thing that has always had me stumped. Dara's mother had a crystal ball. Real crystal. It was about the size of a large grapefruit and it must have weighed close to twenty pounds. It was missing. Now I wonder why she didn't take the ring or the photo, but she took the heavy crystal ball."

"You're sure she didn't just lose it?"

"Lose it? You would have thought it was the Hope Diamond to her."

"Maybe she kept it at the creek like her diary."

"No way. It could have gotten broken. She kept it in her bedroom in a black velvet bag. I saw her lying on her bed and holding it up to the light coming from the window the day before she disappeared."

"Well, now that *is* a puzzler," Michael said thoughtfully. "You know, it would have been the perfect thing to help weigh down a corpse, but no crystal ball was found with the body."

"But the plastic was torn. It could have fallen out. And speaking of things found in the plastic, there's another thing bothering me. The killer bashed out all her teeth and cut off her fingertips, clearly so that if the body surfaced, it couldn't be identified. But why go to all that trouble, then leave her ruby ring wrapped up with her in the plastic? A ring especially made for her with her initials, for God's sake!"

"I don't understand that," Michael said. "At the stage when the body was retrieved, fingerprints would no longer be a problem. Not even the heel print that's recorded on her birth certificate. The teeth *would* have identified her, even three years later. But our killer thought of that. But the presence of Dara's ring baffles me."

"Unless the body isn't Dara's. Maybe someone wanted to throw off the police, have them identify the body as Dara's because of the ring."

"If someone thought that, they wouldn't know much about formal identification procedures," Michael said. "A body is identified by the body itself, not by a button or piece of jewelry or something else found *with* the body."

"So the killer wasn't knowledgeable about identification."

"Either that, or he was careless," Michael said. "I vote for careless."

Christine looked at him closely. "You have no doubt that the body is Dara's, do you?"

Michael hesitated, then shook his head. "No, I don't. But

please don't quote me on that. I'm not supposed to say anything until the official identification has been made."

"I won't say anything, but I'm sure it's Dara, too. She wouldn't just vanish for three years. She was too pampered, too dependent on her father's money and influence. No matter how mad she got, no matter what was bothering her, she wasn't the type to go knocking around in the big, bad world for three years. She just couldn't have taken it."

"And suicides don't swathe themselves in plastic and seal it before jumping into a creek," Michael said. "This was a murder. And the murderer is still out there, Christine, only now he has you in his sights because of that diary. He's already attacked you once. We don't know when he might do it again. And worst of all, so far we don't have one clue about who he is."

2

Reynaldo Cimino shoveled sand into a burlap bag. A man with salt-and-pepper hair glanced at him and grinned. "I'm old enough to be your father, Cimino, but I can shovel twice as fast as you."

"Maybe that's because I've been here since five this morning. You got here half an hour ago."

"Forty-five minutes, but who's counting? Why don't you take a break?"

"I don't need a break," Rey said, although his black hair hung wet with sweat over his forehead and his arms had begun to tremble from hours of shoveling heavy sand. "I'm good for at least another hour."

The older man looked up. "Your wife might have something to say about that. Here she comes."

Rey halted the shovel in midair and spun around. Tess marched through mud and debris with a resolute air and eyes focused intently on him. He was the only person in the world, her gaze said, and he wanted to cringe. Tess was a wonderful woman—intelligent, funny, selfless—and utterly, wildly, possessively in love with him. Sometimes he felt as if he were smothering to death in that love. At other times, like now, he felt as if he were being stalked, never allowed more than a few hours to himself before she came to hover, comfort, dote, nag, and generally mortify him with her lack of pride and decorum.

"Sweetheart, I've been searching for you for nearly an hour! You look exhausted!" she exclaimed loudly, wrapping an arm around his shoulders and planting a smackingly loud kiss on his dirty, sweaty cheek. "I insist that you come home this minute."

Rey glanced at his friend, who directed extreme concentration on his work. "I want to work at least another hour."

"Why? There are tons of people here. You won't be missed."

"Thank you, *cara mia*. It's nice to know my efforts amount to so little."

"Oh, you know what I mean." Tess's sharp gaze sliced to the right. "Is that Jeremy over there?"

"Yes. He's been working for hours and doesn't seem at all tired."

"Is that Danny Torrance from the fitness center with him?" She didn't wait for an answer. "Who's that other guy with the white hair?"

"I don't know," Rey said, stabbing his shovel into the sand.

His friend looked up. "It's Streak Archer."

"Streak *Archer*!" Tess blared. Reynaldo shuddered. Had her voice gotten louder and harsher since their marriage, or did it only bother him more now than two years ago? "I thought he never went out in daylight!"

"Guess he made an exception for an emergency," the man said. "He's a good guy, Mrs. Cimino. Just a little odd."

"That's what Christine Ireland says, but I have my doubts about him."

"Which you've just announced to everyone within a fifty-foot radius," Rey muttered.

"Don't be silly. No one is paying any attention to me." If only that were true, Rey thought. "Come home, Rey. You didn't feel well yesterday and you're going to catch cold out here. I'll fix you some coffee and rub your poor, tired feet."

Rey's face flamed. "Rub my feet!" His friend ducked his head too late to hide a burst of amusement. "Tess, I do not need to have my feet rubbed. God!"

"What's wrong with you?"

"I'm tired."

"Then come home. You've barely slept for two days and now you're out here working yourself to a frazzle." She took his arm and tugged. "Don't be so stubborn!"

Rey jerked his arm free, his simmering anger turning into overwhelming fury at her for embarrassing him. "Tess, stop it and leave," he said with deadly quiet.

She drew back slightly, blinked through hurt feelings, drew herself up, and announced, "When I brought Christine home from the hospital this morning, we found a dead rat in her refrigerator!"

"You found *what*?"

Tess's face lit up. She now had his full attention. "A rat. A *big* rat. It was in her hydrator. I've never seen anything so gross. It'd been dead a couple of days and stank to high heaven in spite of the cold air."

Rey put down his shovel. "I have to go check on her."

"Check on Christine?" Tess frowned. "Why?"

"To see if she's all right. Someone might still be in her house."

"Bethany was there, too. The three of us checked every room, every closet. There was no one."

"I still think I should go."

Tess put her hands on her hips. "I ask you to stop this ridiculous shoveling and come home with me and you say no. You hear some little thing's gone wrong at Chris's and you're ready to fly to her rescue."

"I don't call someone breaking into her house and putting a rat in the refrigerator a little thing, especially after she was attacked yesterday."

"But she's all right. I told you that. Besides, she was going to call the police. They've probably already been there and gone."

She gave him a close look. "Why are you so concerned about Chris?"

"Because she's my friend. *And* yours." Tess's eyes narrowed. "Oh, for God's sake, you're not going to get jealous over Christine, are you? Can't I show simple friendship to a woman without you going nuts?"

"I am not going nuts." Each word came out slowly, like the toll of a doleful bell. "I just don't understand your hysteria over Christine."

"Hysteria?" By now Rey's friend was wandering away, looking for any constructive activity that would remove him from the quarreling couple. "You're the one prone to hysteria, not me," Rey said coldly.

Tess's cell phone rang and she jerked it from the pocket of her jacket. "Yeah, what is it?" Her face went still. "Sorry, Mom. I'm a little out of sorts this morning. What do you need?"

While Tess listened, tapping her foot and chewing on a thumbnail, Rey went back to shoveling. "Well, why can't Tom help?" Tess finally asked, referring to her brother. More tapping. More chewing. Then a grimace. "Oh, okay. I'll be there as soon as possible. And calm down. Have a drink or take a tranquilizer—"Tess closed her eyes. "I was joking, Mom. I'll be there in fifteen minutes."

She jammed the phone back in her pocket. "Mom's basement is flooding. She needs someone to help her move stuff upstairs and Tom, as usual, is busy. Working on his sermon for Sunday service, he says. Can't be torn away! Anyway, I want you to come and help me, Rey."

Rey sighed. "First you claim I'm exhausted and you want me to quit working here, then you want me to spend hours at your mother's rearranging her basement. Even if I had the energy, you know she can't stand me."

"You're Catholic. She doesn't trust Catholics. And you're an artist. She thinks all artists are gay."

"And I married you to hide my shameful secret, something a shifty Catholic would do. Such a warm and accepting soul your religious mother has. Anyway, I won't be able to do anything to suit her, and then you two will get in a fight because she won't stop griping at me." Rey tried to make his voice less resentful: "Tess, dear, I'll work here just a little longer, then go home, take a shower, and get some rest like you wanted me to. If you call Tom, you can intimidate him into giving you a hand with your mother. *You* can intimidate him into anything." Tess smiled, taking this as a compliment as he knew she would. "Okay, *cara mia*?"

Tess put her hand firmly on his arm. "Okay, but promise me you won't stay here much longer. An hour, tops."

"I promise."

"I'm going to call home in an hour and a half to make sure you kept that promise."

"I told you I'm going to try to get some sleep. How am I supposed to do that with you calling me?"

She frowned. "Okay. I guess you're on your honor." Reynaldo felt vastly relieved his friend hadn't heard this last remark, which would have been more appropriately made to an eight-year-old.

She pulled Rey toward her and kissed him full on the lips, then plodded off through the mud. For the first time in years, Rey felt like hugging his harridan of a mother-in-law. Because she was dragging Tess away from him and would keep her busy for hours, he could quit shoveling, leave the riverbank, and have the whole afternoon without Tess breathing down his neck. And he had plans.

3

Patricia brushed her long hair, touched up her bisque eyeshadow, and applied a layer of lipstick called Nude Blush. The makeup looked so subtle she appeared to be wearing no makeup at all. Actually, the artificial enhancement made her look twice as good as she did without it, and looking good was of utmost importance to her this afternoon.

She withdrew the note from her lacy bra and looked at it for the fifth time:

Meet me at the barn at 1:00 Thursday. Romance among the horses!

The note looked worn. He must have carried it around a day or two before finding a chance to place it under the statue in Eve's "magic" garden. When Patricia had first visited the garden while Eve was still alive, she'd admired the statue of Venus. Her companion, a haughty twelve-year-old Dara, had informed her the statue was of Persephone in a tone that said Patricia must be a complete idiot not to know Greek mythology, so Patricia had not asked the identity of Persephone but waited and looked her up in a book of myths. Even years later, she never looked at the statue without remembering the disdain in Dara's voice and eyes. She'd come to dislike the statue until he'd whispered to her one night that he'd left a note for her under it. Notes left beneath the statue had become a ritual now.

Patricia went to her bedroom window, once Eve's bedroom window, and looked down at the garden. It looked rather pathetic now, but within a month it would be beautiful. After Eve's death, Dara had looked after it. Then Dara vanished, and within six months the place had fallen into neglect.

To her surprise, Patricia had decided she couldn't let the garden destroy itself. Bethany, whom she'd met through Christine, had come to her rescue. Patricia knew Bethany felt no particular affection for her, but she didn't want to see the garden ruined. She'd told Patricia she'd help restore the garden, although she knew little about the herbs Eve had grown there for use in her Wiccan rituals. "We'll just let those die," Bethany had said. "I get scared even thinking about witchcraft, much less growing stuff to use in spells." That had been fine with Patricia, not only because she thought Wicca was ridiculous but also because the death of the herbs made the lovely garden seem more hers than Eve's.

Last fall Bethany had helped her select over 200 new bulbs

for the garden. They would begin blooming soon. Patricia hoped the mischievous Pom-Pom wouldn't decide the garden was an excellent place for digging. At age eleven he'd suddenly developed a voracious curiosity and started digging and burrowing and nosing into every space that was unfamiliar to him. Patricia loved the little dog beyond reason, but she regretted his new inquisitiveness, regretted it deeply, especially after what had happened two weeks ago.

Her hands began to tremble a bit at the memory. She pushed an image from her mind and flipped her thick hair over her shoulder, then went back to the mirror, inspecting herself closely. Yes, she could easily pass for twenty-nine, she thought. But did it really matter to *him* that she wasn't twenty-nine? How many men were romantic enough to consistently place notes in "magic" gardens? He was fun and smart and sexy, and she knew he thought of her as fun and smart and sexy. And young. "You seem so much younger than your years," he always said admiringly. "How could a dried-up prune like Ames Prince ever appreciate you?" And wasn't he proving how desirable he found her by taking such risks to see her? After all, it wasn't as if he didn't have anything to lose.

How lucky she was to have days to herself, she mused. A woman came in to clean twice a week, but that was Patricia's only interruption since Jeremy went to work at Prince Jewelry almost a year ago. She'd been relieved to not have him underfoot constantly. Not that he'd been particularly bothersome. He'd spent most of his time in the basement recreation room watching television, practicing pool, that he could never come close to really playing, listening to music, singing his heart out into his karaoke machine. That last activity he'd shared with Dara.

Patricia used to resent all the fun they'd seemed to be having, singing along with records, taping each other, making up songs—although Jeremy's were always simple and repetitive. That was when Patricia had begun to think of how much better her life could be if Dara should die. Then, after Dara mercifully had exited their lives, one day he'd asked Patricia to join him. She'd already indulged in two scotches on the rocks and was feeling warm and generous, so she'd agreed. Her voice had jumped and cracked. Her mother had always told her she had the voice of a baby crow. Jeremy had told her she had a pretty voice. She knew it wasn't true, but he'd wanted to please her and she'd been so touched she'd joined him a few other times.

No, Jeremy's presence hadn't bothered Patricia nearly as much as she'd pretended. But she'd needed her privacy. Under the best of circumstances, extramarital affairs were tricky business. They were even harder to manage with someone like a curious Jeremy wandering around constantly, inadvertently stumbling onto knowledge he shouldn't have. Knowledge that was dangerous to her.

Patricia checked her clothes in the full-length mirror across from her bed. A blue silk turtleneck sweater, tight khaki pants, low-heeled leather boots, a casual denim barn jacket. Just in case she had an unknown observer, she wanted to look as if she were merely going to the barn to spend time with the horses, Sultan and Fatima.

Pom-Pom was nowhere to be found, so she couldn't shut him in a room so he wouldn't follow her. Maybe he was sleeping in a hiding place like Dara's cat, Rhiannon, used to do. Patricia glanced at her watch and saw she had no more time to look for him. She'd be a couple of minutes late as it was.

Outside no rain fell, but the air felt heavy, wet, and chilly. Patricia hated this weather. Some people said there was beauty in all God's seasons. She didn't believe it. She didn't believe in God, either, although her mother had insisted on regular church attendance and Patricia had suffered through more boisterous revival meetings than she cared to remember.

But being a woman of faith had not helped her mother hold on to a husband who'd absconded with all their savings and another woman. It hadn't protected her mother's adored son from dying of leukemia at ten or her elder daughter from death by a heroin overdose when she was twenty. Nor had faith given her peace, health, or happiness. Patricia's mother was a bitter, depressed, hopeless woman with congestive heart failure and rheumatoid arthritis and a remaining child she didn't like. Patricia only visited her mother when the woman was in particularly bad shape, and even then she knew her presence was neither really wanted nor appreciated, just grudgingly endured.

And Ames doesn't want me, either, she thought as she strode across the lawn. He hadn't touched her sexually for years, and even those first encounters after their marriage had been quick and passionless. She'd known when she married him he didn't love her, but she'd thought his long abstinence because of Eve's illness, coupled with her own lovely face and body, would evoke his ardor. They hadn't. And after Dara disappeared, he'd dropped all pretense of sexual attraction to Patricia. That was when loneliness and a shriveling ego had driven her to take lovers.

But now she didn't have just a lover—she had actually found love, and it felt wonderful. She thought of her lover constantly and dreamed of him frequently, awakening drenched in perspiration. She fantasized about when they would really be together, because that was what they both wanted. Their eventual union would be tricky. It would cause embarrassment, scandal, and maybe even reprisals, but it *would* happen. She knew it.

Patricia didn't feel like worrying about any ugly details now, though. She wanted to look forward to her afternoon and forget last night when that good-looking deputy had come to the house. Ames had sent Patricia from his study like a child while he talked with Michael Winter, but she'd listened outside the door. Ames had been chilly as an autumn frost in the deputy's presence, even when Winter asked him for the letters supposedly from Dara, even when Winter told him about being in possession of Dara's diary. Ames had already known about the diary thanks to Jeremy. He demanded that the deputy return it. Winter had refused, claiming the diary was evidence, which Ames well knew. Ames, in turn, had coldly refused to give up Dara's letters or even let Winter look at them. He'd bade the deputy a stony goodnight at the door and shut it quietly.

Within half an hour, though, Ames had drunk two glasses of brandy and turned into a different man. He'd spent most of the night pacing, talking to himself, and drinking. Ames rarely took so much as a glass of wine, and the strong brandy had a frightening effect on him. He'd cursed Christine as a traitor for giving the diary to the police. He'd yelled until Pom-Pom shivered. He'd dashed an expensive crystal ashtray into a fireplace. Patricia had taken refuge in her room, clutching the terrified Pom-Pom, knowing this was one night when she wouldn't sleep. Ames's ranting, threats against Christine, and eventual stormy sobbing over his lost daughter had made Patricia wonder if he was having a nervous breakdown. In the ten years since she'd met Ames, she'd never guessed he could be so fierce or so vengeful, and for the first time, she felt fear of him.

A bright red cardinal sitting on a fence post caught her eye. He cocked his head at her, and suddenly thoughts of Ames flew from her mind. In the summer, cardinals would flock to the garden feeders. Jewel-colored hummingbirds and gentle doves and obstreperous blue jays and melodious warblers would come. It would be lovely. And it would now be Patricia's garden, no longer Eve's.

As she walked the long path to the barn, which sat about a hundred yards from the house and was partially hidden from it by a stand of evergreens, Patricia was still careful not to look back. Ames had left hours ago and said he wouldn't return until dark, but if for some reason he'd decided to come home early and spotted her headed to the barn while repeatedly looking over her shoulder, he might get suspicious. But she had no qualms about him coming to the barn without a good reason. Ames didn't like horses, couldn't even stand the smell of them. He'd probably only been in the barn a few times since it was built fifteen years ago. And Jeremy would be completely obsessed with the sandbagging operation. She didn't have to worry about him following her like a faithful pet. No, all she really had to think about was seeing *him*. It had been almost two weeks and she longed for his touch, his smell, the aura of romance he created even more than she longed for the sex.

The dark red barn loomed in front of her. She hated the Pennsylvania Dutch hex symbols that decorated the outside. She thought they looked garish, but they had been Eve's touch, so naturally Ames would not allow them to be removed. One looked like it was in danger of falling off. Good, Patricia thought. Maybe within the next couple of years they'd all drop to the ground, and Ames would never replace them. Of course, she wouldn't be living here then, but she'd still like to see them all buried in the mud.

Abruptly the sun appeared through the low cloud layer and the landscape turned surprisingly bright. And cheerful. Patricia smiled. It's shining for us, she thought, not caring that she was being silly and romantic. He made her feel silly and romantic, and she had no trouble believing the sun had emerged just for them.

Rather than opening the big main doors of the barn, Patricia entered the side door. The smell of hay and horses washed over her, and she breathed deeply. Unlike Ames, she loved the scent of horses, and the boy they'd hired to tend to the animals kept the stalls scrupulously clean. A sophisticated ventilation system also prevented the unpleasant damp mustiness that could spoil hay. The barn was large, with a vaulted roof and a concrete floor. It was at least ten degrees cooler in here than outside, and she drew her barn jacket tighter around her.

Patricia saw no sign of her lover, yet, so she stopped to admire the horses, who'd neighed greetings as soon as she entered. She went first to her own horse, Sultan. He was gray, approximately fifteen hands, or sixty inches, tall, and weighed around nine hundred pounds. Patricia loved the Arabian, which research had taught her was the oldest recognized breed, similar to horses of Assyria and Egypt written about as early as 1,000 B.C. The lineage was impressive, but what she loved most about the Arabians was their intelligence and good nature. "Hello, my Sultan," she crooned. "Have you missed me? The weather has just been too horrid for riding. Wait until the rain stops and the ground dries. Then we'll fly like the wind."

Sultan looked from side to side, pawed the floor of his stall, and nudged at her hand, blowing air out of his mouth and making his lips flap. As he'd expected, she brought out an apple from her pocket. "Not too many of these, my lad," she said, "or you'll be getting soft teeth."

Next she moved to Fatima. Unlike Sultan, the smaller brown Fatima seemed downright nervous, looking around constantly. "What's wrong, girl? Weather getting you down?" Patricia made a point of riding Fatima as much as she did Sultan because Dara was no longer here to care for her horse. Patricia knew she should have offered to let Christine ride Fatima, but she never had, not out of pettiness but out of convenience. Letting Christine ride the horses might encourage her to drop by during the day to ride, and Patricia needed her solitude. *Maybe this summer I'll invite her*, Patricia thought, although that would be problematic if the barn was still being used as a rendezvous point for her and her lover. She hoped he would have his own place by then, a place she would be sharing with him in the next year.

Fatima kicked the side of her stall and snorted. "Okay. I guess my very presence isn't enough to satisfy you." Fatima snorted again, then pulled back her lips and showed her teeth. "It's an apple you want." Patricia pulled a second apple from her other pocket. "And an apple you shall have—"

The wood overhead creaked and Patricia looked up. A low inside ceiling created an upper room that was the loft, one end of which was neatly stacked with bales of hay. The other remained empty, a cool and private spot for meetings with her lover. A large, square hole in the center of the ceiling, several feet away from the stalls, allowed for hay to be pitched down for the horses. A sturdy ladder led up to it.

"Darling?" she called, her heart beating harder.

For a moment, nothing except silence answered her. Sultan blew air, flapping his lips and tossing his head. Patricia glanced at him. "You want another apple, but no more." He snorted again at the sound of wood popping and kicked the side of his stall. "Darling?" Patricia called again, looking up.

Suddenly music floated down to her. Music from Prokofiev's ballet *Romeo and Juliet*. A thrill rushed over Patricia. How she loved ballet. How she loved this music. How she loved this man who could make a secret meeting in a horse barn romantic. "Thank you for him, God," she whispered, temporarily forgetting that she didn't believe in God.

In an instant, the horses she cared for so deeply were forgotten. She strode toward the ladder leading up to the opening in the loft, then took a deep breath, bracing herself. This was the only part of the rendezvous she didn't like. Heights bothered her. Not to the point where she couldn't brave the ladder if her motivation was strong enough, but she was always relieved to reach the top or the bottom. She let out her breath and started up. One step. Two steps. He would have brought liquor, she thought. He always did. And something to snack on. One time expensive caviar, another time oysters. She'd tasted the food in her mouth for hours and imagined she smelled it for days.

"And what are we having today, darling?" she called. "Festive champagne? Pale, golden sherry? Or are you going to lead me into the depths of sin with absinthe?"

"Something better!" he called, his voice muffled by the music.

Another step and another as she tightly grasped the sides of the steep ladder. "I can already smell something delicious!"

"Vanilla candle wax."

"Aside from that, silly!"

"Hurry!"

"I am. We need an elevator in here. Exactly how many steps are on this blasted ladder?"

"Too many."

Slightly out of breath from climbing twenty feet, Patricia was blinded as she stepped into the loft. Dust motes swam in the light streaming through two windows in the roof. The light of candles flickered at the eastern end of the barn, away from the hay bales. The floating hay dust, candlelight mixed with the strangely bright sunlight, and the smell of vanilla tinged with that of straw gave the scene a surreal quality. Patricia stood still for a moment, trying to adjust. "Well, here I am. Where are you?"

"Stand still and close your eyes. I have a surprise for you."

"Close my eyes? I really ..." Patricia was embarrassed for abruptly feeling old and tottering as she stood beside the hole in the loft. "I have to close my eyes? I ... well ... I feel slightly dizzy."

"Trust me."

"Okay," she sighed. "Anything for you."

Patricia closed her eyes. She heard the whisper of footsteps coming across the wooden floor. She heard one of the horses whinny. She felt the strong hands clamp on to her shoulders—

The fall seemed to go on forever. One minute her boot-encased feet stood firmly by the opening in the loft. The next she was plummeting down, hitting the ladder a couple of times with a force that sent excruciating pain up her arm as a bone snapped. Then she slammed against the concrete barn floor, her head angled oddly to the left, and all pain ceased. She saw a long-legged spider creeping through a tiny shaft of sunlight. She heard one of the horses kick the side of its stall. She smelled a faint mustiness seeping up from the cold concrete. But she felt nothing. Absolutely nothing. Physically. Mentally, her mind spiraled into a black pit of shock and panic.

The rungs of the ladder creaked. A horse kicked again and Sultan whinnied. She knew Sultan's sound. Human knees popped as ligaments snapped over bone, and someone knelt beside her.

"Still alive? My God, you *do* have stamina." Patricia tried to open her mouth, but the effort was too much. She lay crushed, bleeding, and barely breathing as her vision darkened. "You're turning blue, you know. You've broken your pretty neck." A long sigh. "I'd hoped the fall would kill you instantly, but do you want to know something? This is even better. Now I get to *watch* you

die. I guess it's true that all good things come to those who wait."
A flutter of movement near her forehead, maybe a kiss. "Good
night, *darling*."

Patricia heard one last frightened neigh from Sultan. Then a
fantastic thought popped into her dimming mind. She'd found
the note asking for this meeting in Eve's "magic" garden, under
the statue of Persephone. Persephone, who in Greek myth had
been carried away to the underworld by the lord of the dead.

12

1

Christine had known that Jeremy had told Ames about their finding Dara's diary. From Michael she had learned that Ames now knew the diary was in the possession of the police. The deputy's description of Ames's behavior let her know he was enraged.

What did I expect? Christine thought. She'd known he'd be angry if she gave Dara's diary to the police. But being honest with herself, she had to admit she'd thought the attack on her would elicit some sympathy that would dissipate his wrath, or at least weaken it. She now knew that she'd been fooling herself. Ames cared about her, but he'd adored his daughter. Anyone who hurt her, or her reputation if she was dead, would suffer Ames's everlasting ire.

The thought hurt. Ames had been so good to take in her and Jeremy. It wasn't as if he and her father had been close in the years right before the deaths of her parents. Christmas cards and an occasional phone call were all that remained of the old law school friendship. But Ames had honored the promise he'd made to her father right after the birth of Jeremy—that if anything happened to him, Ames would step in. He had. And although he hadn't been able to show her and Jeremy love, he'd provided a home and unfailing consideration. And what had she given him in return?

After Michael left, she had time alone to brood on the matter. By afternoon, she was miserable. Restless, she started to watch television, tried to take a nap, wandered around her house like an uncomfortable visitor, and finally ended up listening to music while absently downing the last, lonely doughnut as her mind churned. She should give Ames time to calm down, she told herself. She should just leave the situation alone for a couple of days, maybe even a week . . .

Patience had never been one of Christine's virtues. She rose from the table and went for the phone. Without thinking, she called the law office, because it was a weekday afternoon. The receptionist told her Mr. Prince had come in for an hour, then left saying he wouldn't return for the rest of the day. Christine wondered if Sloane could give her a reading on Ames's mood, but when she asked to talk to him, the receptionist said he was out on a deposition. Frustrated, Christine hung up and wondered what to do next. Ames had already taken one bad blow when the body was found. Now he'd suffered another. She felt desperate to talk to him, to explain why she had turned over the diary to the police.

Perhaps he was at home, she thought. If not at home, then maybe at Streak's. She called the Prince home first. She listened to the answering machine message, which did not mean Ames wasn't around. He could just be screening calls. She felt compelled to drive to his house first. If she didn't find him there, she would try Streak's.

The drizzle had stopped just as Michael left. A short while later two men arrived in separate vehicles—a pickup truck and a car. The car was a rental from the garage where her Dodge Neon was being repaired, they told her. Ames had arranged the rental for her yesterday. Ames thought of everything, she thought. Her eyes filled with tears. She felt lower than low.

Right after the men drove away in the truck, a blazing sun had mysteriously appeared, then vanished half an hour later, leaving the day gray and dismal. She had the doleful feeling that she'd seen the sun's last gasp. It would never shine again. At least it would never shine so brightly as in the past. But she was being maudlin. She was being scared. She'd never realized until this day how much Ames's good opinion of her meant.

Ames's silver Mercedes was not in the driveway, but the windowless doors of the three-car garage were shut. The car could be in there. Christine went to the front door and rang the bell. Nothing. Of course Ames could merely look out a window, see it was her, and decide not to answer the door. And she had no idea whether or not Patricia was home. Even if she was, he could order her not to answer the door, either. But perhaps she was making the scene more dramatic than it was. Maybe Ames or Patricia was merely behind the house in Eve's garden. Although this didn't seem likely on such a dreary day when nothing bloomed except a few misguided crocuses, it was worth a try.

But her instinct had been right. The garden looked sad and dingy, although not neglected. Bethany had been helping Patricia tend to it simply because she couldn't bear to see what had been such a lovely garden fall to ruin, not because Bethany had any special desire to please Patricia. The statue of Persephone looked especially sad today, Christine thought. According to the Greek myth, the lord of the underworld had drawn her down into a chasm in a chariot pulled by four black steeds. Her mother, Demeter, the goddess of corn, in her grief turned the world bleak, killing all vegetation. At last Zeus decreed Persephone could return to her mother four months a year, and during these four months Demeter allowed the earth to bloom into summer.

"Apparently you're still in the underworld," Christine muttered inanely to the statue, which needed a good bath of bleach to remove mildew and the stains of winter. "I hope you come back soon. This garden is too dismal to bear."

She jumped in surprise when something stung her ankle. A snake at this time of year? Christine looked down and was shocked to see a wet, mud-covered Pom-Pom dancing around her legs. He tried to nip her again, but she backed away too soon.

"What on earth are you doing out here?" she demanded as if the dog could answer. Patricia always kept Pom-Pom on a leash when she brought him outside. And she never allowed him to get dirty, although even fresh from a trip to the dog groomer he looked like a ragamuffin. Christine was convinced no one with mere earthly talents could improve Pom-Pom's appearance.

She stooped and touched the top of his matted head. Even his fancy rhinestone collar was caked with mud. "Where's your mistress, boy?" The dog panted, then turned in a jittery circle. "Where's Patricia? I've never seen you outside without her. Did you manage to break free of her?"

Pom-Pom yipped three times and turned in that frantic circle again. Christine looked at him. Pom-Pom seemed to adore Patricia as she did him. Even if he'd broken free of his leash, which Christine had never known him to do, he wouldn't have run far from Patricia. He was a colossal yipping, snapping ankle biter, but he displayed such ferocity only around his mistress. He seemed to feel safe and strong only in her presence. He wouldn't have left her far behind.

Christine stood up and looked at the French doors at the back of the house. She hadn't noticed earlier, but one of them stood slightly ajar. Could Pom-Pom have simply escaped and, not being the smartest canine in the country, not been able to find his way back inside? That would be fairly dumb, even for Pom-Pom.

Christine walked toward the house and pushed the door open farther. "Patricia?" she called. "Ames?" No one answered and she stepped inside. Although she had once lived in this house, she had never thought of it as home, had never entered uninvited since she moved away. Pom-Pom followed her, breathing noisily, his muddy paws leaving tracks on the pale carpet. "Patricia? It's Christine! Are you here?"

Complete silence. Pom-Pom stood beside her, not running in search of his mistress. He had never shown the slightest affection for Christine, so she was certain devotion didn't rule his actions. The dog simply knew Patricia wasn't in the house. And neither was Ames. Although he might be angry with Christine, he wouldn't have let her stand at the door bellowing for him. He would have come to confront her. The house was empty. The cherished, overprotected nitwit of a dog who didn't know to avoid speeding cars was on the loose. Something was wrong.

They walked back outside. "Okay, Pom-Pom," Christine said, looking down at the panting, shivering dog. "I know heroics aren't your forte, but you're all I have right now. I'm going to follow you. Take me to Patricia."

Pom-Pom cocked his head, gazing at her with the beady eyes of a crow. "Come on, Pom-Pom, act like the dogs on television and take me to your mistress. I know she's around here somewhere and I know something isn't right or you wouldn't be such a wreck. So do that wonderful thing dogs do—track a person. *Please*."

Pom-Pom looked confused, then lifted his leg and drenched a budding purple crocus. Christine closed her eyes, determined not to yell at him. When she'd taken a couple of deep breaths, she focused on him again. This time he turned around twice, yipped shatteringly, then tore away from the house and headed for the acres of damp field lying beyond.

"Great," Christine muttered. "This just couldn't be easy, could it?"

She thought about following the dog in the car, then decided that method might completely confuse the less-than-brilliant Pom-Pom. So she tramped after him, wishing she were wearing boots instead of her best black loafers. Halfway between the house and barn, Pom-Pom stopped running and began spinning in agitated circles. Then he dashed back and nipped her ankle.

"Dammit, Pom-Pom!" Christine exploded. "We're on a mission. Or are we? Did Patricia just go someplace, you managed to get out of the house, and now you're trying to impress me? Well, all you've done is piss me off after that last ankle bite." She paused, looking at the usually cosseted dog, now quivering and covered with drying mud. He looked twice as bad as usual, and usual was bad enough. He suddenly struck her as pathetic, and she asked in a kinder voice, "Are you really so scared you don't know what you're doing?"

He appeared to be mulling this over behind his tiny, undog-
like eyes; then he was off again, running at top speed for the
barn and managing to hit every water puddle along the way. If
he's just having fun with me, I'll kill him, Christine thought as
she felt water seeping into her shoes.

As they neared the barn, Christine could have sworn she
heard music. Maybe I'm flashing back to yesterday morning
and the attack, she thought as a chill rushed over her at the
memory. But she wasn't hearing anything that sounded faintly
like the pounding "Relax." Pom-Pom stopped. He ran back to
her and whined. Christine ignored him and walked forward,
intent on the music. It was something classical, now growing
louder, the sound soaring. And the horses were kicking their
stalls. Hard. Continuously.

I'm going right back to the house, she thought in a panic. I
am going into the house and shut the door and not even look at
what's going on in that barn.

As the thought repeated itself, she looked at the securely padlocked
double doors. Go back, her mind said. Go back. She stood frozen
with indecision until Pom-Pom whined again and shuddered.

Go back! her mind screamed as her body seemed to move
without directions from her brain around the corner of the barn
to the narrow side door, which stood open. She paused before
the open door. *Go back.* She entered.

The music swelled around her. Although the barn sat far
from the house, the music could not long have gone unnoticed.
At least five cars passed near the barn each day. Unless their
radios were blasting, passengers would have heard the music
through the open door. It had undoubtedly drawn Pom-Pom to
the spot. It was setting the horses wild.

Christine walked slowly into the dim, cool barn interior, her
hand closing over a pen lying in the bottom of her jacket pocket.
Consciously she did not consider the pen a weapon. Without
thought, though, she snapped off the plastic top to expose the
sharp point. A pen was a pathetic weapon, but she might slow
down someone with it if she aimed carefully.

A weapon? Slow down someone? She was being crazy. She needed to get back to the safety of the house, away from the awful thing she knew awaited her in the barn. But she couldn't stop herself.

Christine took three more hesitant steps into the barn and looked up. The music came from the loft. She glanced at the kicking, rolling-eyed horses. "Settle down, you two," she said gently, more to bolster herself than to calm them. "I'm here. Everything is all right now."

Her apprehensive gaze shot around the dim first floor interior. Gray light fought its way inside, almost tunneling through the gloom to fall on a heap of clothes at the foot of the ladder—

Christine squinted in the light, which seemed to grow brighter as she focused on the clothes. But they weren't just clothes.

Patricia lay huddled and broken at the foot of the ladder on the cold concrete floor. In one terrible glance that would imprint itself on her mind forever, Christine saw her bluish face, her blood drying in a little streak running from her mouth, and her blue eyes staring blindly at the horses.

Christine felt as if her heart were plunging to her feet, leaving her weak and light-headed and clinging to consciousness. She closed her eyes, fighting not to faint. "I lied," she said softly to the horses. "Everything isn't all right now."

2

Later Christine barely remembered the next few minutes. She recalled kneeling by Patricia, feeling for a pulse, making a clumsy and futile attempt at resuscitation, noting with horror that her skin was still warm. Next came a mad run back to the house, Pom-Pom galloping along behind her, abandoning the mistress who'd loved him so dearly. She'd hit the French doors with a bang, so breathless she was on the verge of passing out, cursing herself for leaving her cell phone in the car. Then a call to 911. Then she sat down on an elegant Queen Anne chair, put her head between her knees, and drew in deep breaths while the wet dog lay on her wet feet, shaking, terrified, and confused.

For many years Christine had been complimented on her cool handling of rough situations. Christine was the strong one, people said. Christine was the capable one. Sometimes they made her sound ten feet tall instead of five-ten. But the last two days had been too much. First the attack on her in the gym, then the phone call, then the rat, and now Patricia dead in the horse barn.

And she didn't fall, a voice from far off said. She *didn't* fall.

Christine's head jerked up. She expected to see someone standing in front of her speaking. Instead, she saw only an empty room. Her own thoughts seemed to be shouting into her ears.

Patricia did not fall!

"Of course she fell," she said aloud. Pom-Pom looked up, beady eyes fastened on her face as he tensed. "Why do I keep thinking she didn't fall? She just went to the barn and . . ."

She frowned. And what? Went up into the loft, put on music, then went back to the loft entrance and stumbled, hurtling down twenty feet?

Yes, Patricia loved the horses. Yes, she visited them nearly every day even if she didn't ride.

But in all the years Christine had lived in the house, she'd never known of Patricia climbing the ladder into the loft. For one thing, nothing was in the loft except hay, and a hired boy fed the horses. More important, Patricia didn't like heights. She avoided them unless it was necessary. She wouldn't have chosen the loft as a place to be alone, much less climbed the ladder while carrying a boom box from which the music must have been coming.

Patricia had not been alone. Christine was sure of it. She'd gone up to the loft to be with someone who'd brought the boom box, someone she desired to be with enough to swallow her fear of heights and climb that steep ladder.

Filled with anxiety, Christine jumped from her chair and strode to the front door, Pom-Pom at her heels. She saw no police cars or EMS van. She knew traffic was tangled because of the flood, but it seemed she'd called 911 twenty minutes ago. Half of that time was more like it. Against her better judgment, she called Tess's cell phone number. She felt a desperate need to hear a familiar human voice but got no answer. Just as well, Christine thought. Tess might have insisted on coming over, then gotten in everyone's way. Finesse was not Tess's strong point.

Just as she hung up the phone, Christine heard a siren. Pom-Pom went wild, yipping uncontrollably, then dashing up the stairs to the second floor. Christine was glad to see him go. The last thing everyone needed was Pom-Pom underfoot. The EMS van slowed in front of the house, but before it had time to stop, Christine ran outside and called to the driver, "Take Crescent Creek Lane down to the barn. Someone is hurt inside. The side door is open."

The van sped over the hill without the siren but with lights still flashing. Christine wanted to shut the door, to let the EMS technicians handle everything, to hide inside the house from the ugliness that lay in the barn. But she knew she couldn't. She wasn't a child. There would be questions, and she was the only person here to answer them.

She got in her rental car and slowly drove to the barn. A uniformed man and woman were dashing through the barn's side door. Christine stopped her car, then sat behind the wheel for a few minutes. She rolled down her window but heard no beautiful music flowing from the barn. The CD had ended, thank God. The horses still kicked in their stalls, though.

Christine glanced in the rearview mirror to see a patrol car pull up behind her. Michael Winter got out and came to the side of her car. She got out.

"I picked up on the nine-one-one call from you," he said. "Saw the EMS lights down here."

She nodded. "Patricia's in the barn. She's dead."

He raised his dark eyebrows. "You're sure."

"Her face was blue. There was no breath, no pulse."

"You touched the body?"

"I only tilted her head slightly so I could try mouth-to-mouth resuscitation. Her lips were still warm . . ." Christine swallowed hard. "I know I shouldn't have touched her."

"You were giving her a chance at life. It's all right as long as you didn't move her."

Christine desperately did not want to enter the barn again, but Michael seemed to expect it. He led the way with her almost dragging her feet behind him. When they got inside, the female paramedic remained kneeling beside Patricia, but the male stood up. "She's dead," he said without feeling. "Neck is broken and I'd say a hell of a lot more than that is shattered. Looks like she fell from the loft." Everyone automatically looked up. "But if it was a simple fall," the paramedic went on, "I don't know how she got all this hay on her body."

"There's hay in the loft," Christine said.

The paramedic shook his head. "I'm not a crime scene expert, but there's something funny about the hay. It doesn't look like it just tumbled down on her. It looks like it's been carefully placed on her. Sort of like a blanket." He shrugged. "I guess that sounds lame."

Michael looked at the body closely. "You're right." He glanced at Christine. "Is this how it looked when you were here earlier?"

"I didn't notice," she said in a small voice. "I was so shocked, I didn't really look at anything except her face."

"But you didn't rearrange the hay?"

"No." Christine's voice grew a bit stronger. "Of course not."

"Maybe by accident?"

"No, Deputy Winter. I didn't touch her body. Only her head." Christine felt all over again the cooling blood that had seeped into Patricia's beautiful hair from some kind of head wound. She looked at her hand, which was stained dull red. She hadn't even noticed her own hand. "Only her head," she said again.

None of them had heard another car drive up, but suddenly

Ames Prince stood in the barn a few feet away from them. His thin body was rigid. He stared at Patricia's body for nearly ten seconds, his angular face expressionless. Then he turned his cool gray eyes on Christine and said in a venomous voice, "My God, girl, what have you done now?"

13

1

Later Christine could only replay that afternoon in her mind as she would a nightmare, not a real event, because she couldn't bear the reality of Ames's frigid gaze or the lash of his voice. She'd been so shocked she hadn't realized for a few seconds that the paramedics and Michael Winter were all staring at her.

Michael broke the silence: "Mr. Prince, we're not certain what happened here—"

"Patricia died, that's what happened here," Ames snapped. "Anyone can see she's dead. She died suddenly and violently and—" He broke off, made a sound between a gag and a cough, turned quickly, and strode out of the barn.

Christine ran after him. "Ames, slow down. Ames, please . . ."

He whirled on her. "What on earth could you *possibly* have to say to me?"

"That I'm sorry about Patricia. That I don't know what happened."

"That you're not trying to tear apart what's left of my family? That you didn't mean to give my daughter's private, deeply personal diary to the police for everyone to read and snicker over? That my daughter didn't disappear just a week after you blamed her for the calling off of your engagement? That I just saw my wife, whom you detested, lying dead on a concrete barn floor with you standing over her? That—"

"Mr. Prince, you're upset," Michael Winter's commanding voice cut him off. Ames's head snapped toward the deputy. "I think it would be wise for you to not make accusations, especially to Miss Ireland, that you will later regret."

"I haven't said anything I'll regret. And I would suggest, Deputy, that your efforts would be better spent on investigating my wife's murder than playing white knight to Miss Ireland. I assure you that she's a master at taking care of herself."

Abruptly Ames turned, got in his Mercedes, and flung gravel as he sped away from the barn. Christine stood with her face slack, hating the burning tears she felt welling in her eyes. "Does he think I killed Patricia?" she whispered in disbelief.

Michael stared as the Mercedes reached the house and turned in the driveway. "He's furious because you gave me Dara's diary. As for Patricia, maybe he's just lashing out."

She looked at him. "Maybe? Do you mean *you* think I did something to her?"

"No, I meant—" He broke off and Christine could almost feel him wrap himself in a cloak of professionalism. "We don't know what happened here yet. I need to call in and get some crime scene people out here. You should wait up at the house."

"*Ames's* house? He wouldn't let me in the door."

"You're probably right. It's not a good idea for you to be around him right now anyway. He's too angry. Go home for now. And stay there. I'll need to question you in a little while." Michael started back inside the barn.

"Deputy, I don't want Jeremy to see any of this or to be around Ames, either," she said. "He's working at the sandbagging operation, but he could come back any minute. May I go look for him so *I* can tell him what's happened? I'll take him straight to my house and I won't go anywhere the rest of the day until you've come to question me."

Michael looked at her, clearly mulling over the possibility that she would simply take off, leaving town to escape any police interrogation. The idea that he doubted her inexplicably stung her feelings. Then good sense stepped in. He barely knew her. Why should he trust her?

"Okay," he said finally. "Go find Jeremy. You're right—he shouldn't be involved in this. I'll come by your house later."

He turned and walked back inside the barn without a good-bye or even a hint of a smile, but Christine felt remarkably better considering the circumstances. He'd clearly made a decision about her character—a favorable one. Now all she had to do was find Jeremy and break the news.

2

Streak Archer's sweaty, shaking hand dropped his key twice before he was able to unlock the door. When it swung open, he nearly fell inside his house, slamming the door shut behind him, leaning against it, and trying desperately to draw breath into lungs that seemed to have shrunk beyond life-sustaining capacity. Rivulets of perspiration ran down his dirty face and his shirt was soaked, clinging to his chest and back like a wetsuit.

How long ago had he left the sanctity of his home? It seemed like days. But the clock said it was two in the afternoon. What a risk he'd taken. He could be rolled up in a ball shaking and spinning totally out of control right now. That would have been a hell of a note. But he'd taken the risk. And he'd beaten his demons. Sort of. He'd had no choice.

Streak went straight for the kitchen, ran water into a Dixie cup, fumbled among a number of prescription bottles in a cabinet, and withdrew the Valium. He gulped a ten-milligram, refilled his cup, and took a second. He hated his dependence on antidepressants and tranquilizers, but he didn't think he could function without them. His psychiatrist agreed. And who cared if he was addicted? He wasn't exactly a role model for any young people.

He sat down at his chrome-topped kitchen table and glanced around the room. From the outside, his house looked like a quaint country stone cottage. The inside was a tribute to modernistic minimalism. His mother hated all the white and black and chrome. Ames never actually said anything, but his facial expression conveyed volumes of distaste. Only Jeremy liked the place. He said it looked like the inside of a spaceship. Streak smiled wryly. Jeremy was right. For Streak, the house was an escape from the day-to-day reality in which he had so much trouble existing. In here, he had created a comfortable virtual reality.

Streak needed his stark lair now more than he had for a decade. He'd been experimenting too much with the outside world lately. It hadn't worked. Not three years ago. Not now.

Someone knocked on his front door and he had a wild urge to crawl under the table and wait until she went away. But he knew that knock. It was his mother, and she would stand out there knocking until her knuckles bled.

He opened the door and Wilma Archer looked at him as if he'd turned green. "What's wrong with you? Are you in a bad way? I'm taking you to the emergency room!"

"No, Mom, please," Streak said quickly, panicked at the mere thought of going out again today. "I'll be fine. Just come in. The light outside is blinding."

Wilma looked up at the overcast sky. "You have a migraine. I still think we should go—"

"I'm not going *anywhere!*" Wilma drew back. "I'm sorry. Just please come in. I need to lie down. I'll be okay in half an hour."

Wilma stepped inside and closed the door behind her. "Go stretch out on that white board you call a couch and I'll fix you some orange juice."

"I don't want juice."

"A soft drink. Milk."

"Coffee," Streak said. He didn't want coffee, but he knew his mother wouldn't let up. Wilma Archer was at least fifty pounds overweight because she believed food and beverage could cure all ills. "I'll lie down. You make the coffee, Mom. You know where I keep everything."

"Your father and I have been worried sick about you!" Wilma called from the kitchen as Streak lay down on the "board" of a couch with no pillow under his head. "You haven't called for ages."

"Mom, you talked to me the day the body was pulled out of the river."

"I called you. You didn't call me."

"I didn't know we were keeping track of who called whom."

"I keep track. I'm your mother."

"All right. I'm sorry. I just don't like talking on the phone."

"No, all you want to do is fiddle with your computers and play on the Interstate."

"Internet, Mom, although at the moment playing on the interstate doesn't sound so bad. Maybe I'd get run over and my head would stop hurting." Streak did not have a migraine, but for some reason, his mother understood headaches better than anxiety attacks. "I need rest. Quiet."

Wilma marched into the living room and stood peering down at him, her hands on her hips. "I still say you need to go to the emergency room."

"Where I can sit in misery in a waiting room full of people for at least an hour until someone gets around to seeing me, pronounces I have a migraine, prescribes a couple of pills that will not help in the least, and then sends me home with a huge bill?"

"You have insurance."

"I have pain. You're making it worse. Mom, for the love of God, sit down, calm down, and speak softly. Quit nagging."

Wilma sighed. "I'm going to check on that coffee."

"Please do."

Streak loved his mother. He thought she probably had more capacity for love, kindness, and generosity than four-fifths of the population of the world. But he could not bear hovering, and Wilma Archer had a gold medal in hovering.

While she was in the kitchen, Streak listened with comfort to the sound of his humming computers. He had a computer in every room except the bathroom, where he kept a laptop. Three computers sat in the living room, all connected to a server, and four more computers in an upstairs room that had once been two large bedrooms, until he'd had the dividing wall torn down.

Throughout the house he had five televisions, the one in the living room being a thirty-six-inch flat-panel high-definition television monitor mounted on the wall. Accompanying it was a state-of-the-art stereo system with four towering speakers Christine once said made her feel as if she were in a temple with pillars erected to exotic gods. Of course, Christine had been in his house exactly twice. Streak did not encourage visitors, and most people respected his desire for complete privacy. Most people.

Wilma tramped back into the living room holding a gigantic thermal mug of coffee with an elbow straw bobbing around the top.

"What's with the straw?" Streak asked.

"I don't want you to spill this down the front of you and burn your chest."

"Gee, maybe you should get me a bib, too."

"I'm going to ignore that remark because you feel so bad. But one cranky remark is your limit. You're not too big for me to—"

"To what?" Streak interrupted, suddenly amused. "Turn me over your knee?"

"Don't get too sure of yourself, mister. I have substantial knees. Now tell me what's set you off like this."

Streak's amusement faded. "You know nothing has to *set me off*, as you put it. I get these anxiety attacks and headaches out of nowhere."

"No. Not anymore. When you first came home from the war, yes. For years after that, yes. But not for a long time. There has to be a trigger. Now tell me what happened and you'll feel better."

Streak glanced at one of his computers. The screen blanker showed a house at night where lights came on in various windows, a moon sailed overhead, a black cat crept across the lawn, bats flew blithely against the dark sky. My head, he thought. That's the inside of my head.

"I went down and helped with the sandbagging operation," he said.

"You did *what*?"

"We're having a flood. I helped put sandbags in place. I did my civic duty."

Wilma looked appalled. "But you don't do that kind of thing!"

"My civic duty?"

"Not with all those people around. You know better than to try something like that."

"I do now. I thought maybe things had changed for me during all these years. Maybe I could be around more than four people at a time without freaking out. Guess I was wrong."

"Well . . ." Wilma twisted her wedding ring. "There wasn't . . . I mean, you didn't . . . well . . ."

"Cause a scene? Make a spectacle of myself? No, Mom. I went down this morning and helped for a while. Then I left like a normal person. At least, I think I *looked* normal."

"This morning? But it's afternoon. How many hours did you spend at the river?"

"I don't know. A couple, maybe three—"

"Three? You made it through *three* hours?"

"Maybe it only seemed like three. I didn't keep track of time. I just worked alongside Jeremy for a while and a couple of other guys I used to know real well and—" Streak's hands started jittering again. He shivered, set his coffee mug on the floor beside the couch, and closed his eyes. "Mom, I appreciate you coming by and making coffee and all, but I don't think I can keep talking. I have to try to sleep off this headache. Do you mind?"

"You're cold. You need a blanket over you. Where's that afghan I knitted for you?"

The one in neon colors she said looked cheerful, Streak thought. "Upstairs somewhere," he said vaguely. "I don't want a cover over me. I'm sweating. I just want to sleep."

"Can't you sleep with me here? I'll be quiet as a mouse."

"That'll be the day," Streak said dryly.

Wilma laughed softly. "My boy. You know me too well." She bent and kissed him directly on the scar on his forehead, the place where a bullet had entered his skull and figuratively, if not literally, taken over his life thirty years ago. "You call me if you need me. Sleep tight."

"And don't let the bedbugs bite," he murmured, closing his eyes.

Wilma tiptoed out of the room and shut the front door softly behind her. As soon as Streak heard her car start and back out of his driveway, he rose from the couch and went to his stereo. He sorted through some CDs, put one in the player, and lay down again. In a few moments, the strains of Prokofiev's *Romeo and Juliet* washed over him as he shivered uncontrollably and rolled himself into a tight, protective ball.

3

Christine tried to put the image of Patricia out of her mind as she drove downtown to look for Jeremy. To her surprise, that was easier for her to do than to wipe out the memory of Ames's eyes. She'd always thought of him as a starkly handsome, intelligent, kind, but basically bland gentleman, like some cardboard figure out of a bad Victorian novel. This afternoon he'd shown her he was anything except bland. He was a man who'd masterfully kept his passions repressed until the last couple of days. Now that they had been unleashed, Christine didn't know if he could ever again get them in check.

As she drove into town, Christine realized she didn't have a clue about where to look for Jeremy. Prince Jewelry was located two streets over from the riverbank, so he wouldn't be near the store. She parked the car and walked back to the area between the stores and the river, which had become a beehive of activity with people piling sandbags against the rising water. So far, they were winning the battle. A few looked at her reproachfully, clearly thinking she should be helping. Normally she would have been, but not on this awful day.

Christine glanced up at the back of the old Duvoy Hotel, a jewel over a century ago but now a warren of tiny cheap offices and apartments. She saw a lot of people working, but no Jeremy. She strode on, coming to Hadden's Department Store. On the huge brick back of the building someone had painted a scene of a cream-colored structure with an exterior winding staircase edged with a lacy wrought-iron railing from which hung lush red and purple flowers. Christine knew the owner of Hadden's had let his seventeen-year-old grandson use the store as a giant canvas for what some people in town called graffiti. If it were graffiti, she thought, it was certainly beautiful and probably inspired by the grandson's last vacation with the family in New Orleans.

Christine looked out over the river, which ran high, murky, and littered with debris. An aluminum lawn chair floated lazily by, and not far behind bobbed pieces of white wood, the remnants of a flimsy structure decimated by the force of rising, rushing water. After the flood, the riverbank would be the ugly site of filth, junk, and dead animals. And another dead girl wrapped in plastic? Christine shivered at the thought of what further horrible secrets the flood might reveal.

After half an hour of walking and inquiries, Christine finally located Jeremy working with Danny Torrance from the fitness center. They were behind the old Starlight Theater, which had been in business for almost seventy years, and they both looked exhausted.

"Jeremy, I've been looking for you for twenty minutes," Christine said. "Hi, Danny."

"How're you feeling, Chris?" Danny asked.

"Okay."

"Okay?" Jeremy burst out, alarmed. "Your face is all bruised. What happened?"

Danny looked abashed, realizing his gaffe. She'd told him she didn't want Jeremy to know what had happened to her. It would frighten him.

"I fell down the basement steps." Christine rarely lied to her brother. Lies made her uncomfortable. Besides, he usually found out the truth anyway. But she didn't want him to know the truth just yet. "I tripped over Rhiannon."

"You didn't fall on her, did you?" Jeremy asked worriedly. "You're big enough to squash her."

"Thank you," Christine said dryly. "Rhi's fine. Not a mark on her."

"Well, you sure don't look so good," Jeremy persisted.

The memory of finding Patricia lying on the floor with her staring eyes jumped to life in Christine's mind. "I didn't get a lot of sleep last night, but I'm great. Really. And now I'd like to take you home. I may look bad, but *you* look worn out."

"Yeah, Jeremy, you look tired enough to fall right into the river," Danny said. "Go with your sister."

Jeremy clung stubbornly to a sandbag. "I'm not tired. But I am kind of hungry. Did you bring food, Christy?"

"No. I want you to come home. And, Danny, you look as tired as Jeremy. I'll be glad to drop you anywhere you want."

He shook his head. "Marti's supposed to come by about now." Marti, the pretty fitness trainer who possessed amazing strength for a small woman. Christine wondered why she wasn't working alongside Danny. "You're right, Chris—I've reached my limit. And so has Jeremy, if he'd only admit it." He nudged her brother. "Haven't you, guy?"

"No." A note of petulance. Oh no, she thought. She didn't feel like standing out here cajoling Jeremy for twenty minutes. "I'm not *tired,*" Jeremy announced loudly.

"You're hungry," Danny continued. "I heard your stomach growl three times. Really loud. Scared me half to death. I thought the flood had carried a lion all the way here from Africa." Jeremy's lips twitched. "I'll bet if you go with Chris, she'll take you to McDonald's."

"I sure will," Christine said. "I could use some food myself. All I've had today is doughnuts."

"Doughnuts?" Jeremy echoed. "Gosh, I love doughnuts."

"You love everything. You should weigh three hundred pounds the way you eat." Danny actually grinned. "Little brother, if you don't come with me, I'll still go to McDonald's and you'll miss out on all that good food. Just think of it. Big Macs, fries—"

Jeremy dropped his sandbag. "I gotta go, Danny. Will you be okay here without me?"

"Sure, buddy. I had fun working with you."

"Me, too. With you. Bye."

After they'd made their way back to the car, Christine said, "I'd really like to pick up the food and take it home to eat. Is that okay with you?"

"Back to your, I mean *our*, house?" She nodded. "What about Ames and Patricia? They'll be waiting for me. Should I call them or should we get them some food, too, and eat it at their house?"

Oh yes, Ames would love to share a late lunch with me, Christine thought. And Patricia. She could now stop rigorously maintaining her slender figure. "They called," she lied again for the second time in half an hour. "They're going out tonight and want you to stay with me."

Jeremy instantly brightened. "Good. It's awful sad at that house. I try not to make any noise or get in anyone's way, but I can't always be quiet."

"Well, you don't have to be quiet at our house. And Rhiannon will be *so* happy to see you."

"She can tell me all about you falling over her. Christy, could you drive faster? I'm *starving*!"

Fifteen minutes later it seemed that half the town couldn't wait to have something from McDonald's. They sat in a long line, inching their way toward the speaker, where Jeremy ordered two Big Macs, a double serving of fries, and a fudge sundae. Christine settled on a cheeseburger, and Jeremy insisted on an order of Chicken McNuggets for Rhiannon. While they again crept forward toward the pickup window, Jeremy sang an a cappella version of "Fly Away" because the Lenny Kravitz CD was in her car. The mechanics had said it would be finished by tomorrow, because there was no bodywork or painting to be done. Just a window would be replaced and the carpet reattached.

When they got home, Christine insisted Jeremy take a quick

shower before they ate. "I'll put your sundae in the freezer, and as soon as you're done, we'll get the food piping hot again in the microwave. Now scoot. You're filthy."

Jeremy did not have to be told twice. The faster he cleaned up, the quicker he could eat. Christine put his sundae in the freezer, her mind flashing again on the rat in the hydrator, and placed the bags of food on the counter, where Rhiannon had the good manners not to venture.

As Christine walked through the living room to flip on the television for Jeremy's amusement, she saw the red light on her telephone answering machine blinking. She pressed the PLAY button and froze as she heard a deep, raspy mechanical voice say tonelessly, "Poor Patricia. See what happens when you find out too much?"

14

1

Christine stood motionlessly by the answering machine for a few moments. She pressed the PLAY button again. The message—cold, mechanical, terrifying. The machine announced that the call had come at three-fifteen, after the body had been discovered and taken to the hospital, although it was obvious to all who'd been present that she was dead.

The shower water stopped. Jeremy would be back in a couple of minutes. Should she erase the message? No. Michael Winter should hear it. Maybe it could be traced. She turned off the answering machine so the blinking light wouldn't draw Jeremy's attention.

"Be right there!" Jeremy called as he pounded up the basement stairs to the kitchen. Christine knew Rhiannon would be zipping along beside him, trying to beat him to the top of the stairs. She went back into the kitchen and withdrew food from the foil wrappers, placing it on plates to slip into the microwave for a quick reheating. "Big Macs and fries piping hot in one minute," she announced.

"I need ketchup for my fries."

"Coming right up." Christine made a great fuss over pouring ketchup, opening salt packets, sticking straws in soft drinks, tearing Chicken McNuggets into bits for Rhiannon. She knew she was stalling, delaying the time when she must tell Jeremy about Patricia's death. Maybe she'd wait until after he'd eaten, not during his meal. Maybe even after a television show. She'd downplay it. Say it was definitely just a fall. Not mention anything about music coming from the loft or the strange placement of hay over Patricia's body.

"You're muttering to yourself," Jeremy said suddenly as she dropped the last morsels of McNuggets into Rhiannon's dish. "What's wrong?"

"I was singing."

"It didn't sound like a song."

"I don't have a good voice like you do."

"I've got an okay voice. Not good. Did I tell you I'm gonna work on learning the words to 'Smooth' by Santana?"

"Going Latino on me, are you?"

"What's Latino?"

"In this case, a style of music. I love that song. Maybe we can salsa dance together."

"What's salsa dancing?"

"It's a style of dancing. You remember—we watched the salsa dancing competition last year on TV. The girls all wore the sparkly dresses and looked like they were double-jointed."

"I don't know what *double-jointed* means, but they were cool. I'm not a very good dancer, though."

"That makes two of us. But we can have fun trying."

"I'll step on your toes."

"I'll wear big steel-toed boots with my beautiful sparkly dress."

This sent Jeremy into hysterics. Meanwhile, Rhiannon nosed Christine's hand away from her dish, impatient with the human hilarity keeping her from the McNuggets. "I'm sorry to be such a slowpoke," Christine said to the cat. "I know you're about to drop dead from starvation."

Christine went to the sink to wash the grease from her fingers and Jeremy said suddenly, "Christy, I don't believe you really tripped over Rhiannon and banged up your face. I can always tell when you're fibbing to me."

And he could. He'd been able to detect any falsehood she told him since he was a child. Maybe it was because he knew her so well or maybe he'd just developed a radar over the years for when people were trying to shield him from truths they thought he couldn't handle.

Christine sat down at the table. "Jeremy, remember when I went to the gym?"

"Sure. It was only two days ago."

"Well, someone tried to hurt me there. He hit me on the head with one of the weights."

Jeremy's lips parted, his face flushed, and one of his large hands immediately fisted. "Who? I'll knock his block off! I'll—"

"Jeremy, settle down. He covered my face first. I didn't see who it was. But I'm all right and Deputy Winter is looking for the man. You trust Deputy Winter, don't you?" Jeremy nodded slowly. "Then leave this to him."

"Maybe I could help him."

"I don't think the police want civilians doing their work. They're trained. And Deputy Winter could arrest him. You don't have that authority."

Jeremy looked down at his French fries drowning in ketchup. "Okay. I'll let him handle it. But I don't like for *anyone* to hurt you, Christy. Not even a little bit. I'd never let it happen if I was there, even if I don't have authority to arrest someone."

"I know. And I appreciate that, Jeremy. You've always been the best brother any girl could have."

He looked up and gave her a weak smile. "How long is your face gonna look that way?"

"I don't know. Maybe a couple more days. Is it so bad?"

"Well, it's weird. But not awful. You could put makeup on it. Patricia wears this skin-colored liquid stuff that comes in a bottle. Maybe she'd let you use a little."

"I can buy some for myself," Christine said vaguely. She took a small bite of her cheeseburger and chewed slowly, feeling as if she couldn't swallow.

Jeremy sat silently staring at her; then finally he said, "I think something else is wrong. Something besides you getting hurt."

Christine took a deep breath. "You amaze me, Jeremy. I can't hide anything from you."

"You've been my sister a long time," he said solemnly. "I'm not as smart as you, but we've been best friends. And I'm not a little boy. I understand lots of things and I feel better when people tell me the truth."

Christine looked at him, thinking how foolish she'd been for so long. She'd always known Jeremy was perceptive. Of course he sensed when trouble existed, but so often she and the family had tried to shield him from anything they thought might upset him. She'd never thought that perhaps keeping Jeremy in the dark caused him more anxiety than simply telling him the truth.

"Jeremy, something terrible happened today," Christine began. "Patricia . . . died."

"Died?" Jeremy repeated blankly. "But she wasn't sick. Was she in some kind of crash like Mom and Dad?"

"Not a crash but probably an accident. It looks like she fell from the loft in the barn." Christine added details to make Jeremy feel better. "She broke her neck and died instantly, so she never felt a thing. No fear and no pain."

"She was in the barn?"

Christine nodded. "She must have gone out to see Sultan and Fatima and—" She broke off. "Why are you looking at me like that? Why are you shaking your head?"

"You said she fell out of the loft. Patricia wouldn't go up in the loft if she went to visit Sultan and Fatima."

"She might have. Maybe she thought they needed more hay."

Jeremy shook his head even more vehemently. "She doesn't feed the horses. And I don't think she walked across the muddy field just to visit the horses."

"Then why would she have gone?"

Jeremy stared at her for a moment, his cheeks growing flushed. "Well, I know I'm not s'posed to tell this. I'm not even s'posed to know it. But the barn is where Patricia always went to meet her boyfriend."

2

Sloane Caldwell entered his house, threw his trench coat over a chair, and headed straight for the small bar area set up in his living room. He poured a double scotch neat and dropped down with a groan on his brown leather couch.

He'd expected the day to be nerve-straining, but it had been downright grueling, even for a man with his mental stamina. At least he'd accrued seven billable hours, which should please Ames Prince, but they'd been seven hours of living hell.

Enoch Tate's insurance company was balking at paying for medical treatment after Tate's car accident four months ago. Today his deposition had been taken. Tate himself was a delight—eighty-five, half-deaf, dyspeptic, cantankerous, and suffering early stages of Alzheimer's. The very sight of the old man caused Sloane to shudder when he stopped by Sloane's office at least twice a week to see how his case was progressing and harangue about the miserable state of the modern world.

Enoch Tate had begun the proceedings by demanding iced tea, whose sugar content had to be adjusted three times until it met his standards. Every half an hour he wanted more tea, wasting time while with infuriating slowness he varied the amount of artificial sweetener, refusing to continue until the drink was perfect.

To make matters worse, the insurance company's lawyer had been sharp, asking each question in a slightly different way at least five times so Sloane couldn't object by saying, "Asked and answered," to speed things along. Tate had been enraged but helpless in the face of the legal maneuver. Every time he answered, he got louder and more verbose. He'd ended up bellowing and burping all through the last half of the exhausting session, both his temper and his indigestion worse after their lunch break than in the morning. Sloane could not believe one shriveled little man could harbor so much gas.

But this day Sloane had dreaded for weeks was finally over. It had been hectic and he felt drained, but he'd managed to successfully handle everything and now he could reap the benefits—an evening with Monique Lawson, an associate at the law firm. They hadn't been seeing each other for long. Sloane found Monique a bit too direct in her speech, and both her manners and her general demeanor were in need of polish, but she was beautiful and smart, and he felt the relationship had potential.

He'd taken his second sip of scotch and decided to put a relaxing CD selection on the stereo when the doorbell rang. Monique was meeting him here, but it was too early for her. He had few visitors, although he'd decorated his house with care and hired a cleaning lady to come by twice a week to keep it spotless. Unfortunately, he wasn't home much. He was determined to take Ames Prince's place someday, and he worked long hours at the office to prove he was worthy of the position.

He set his drink on a coaster on the oversize oak coffee table and went to the door. Outside stood a tall, slender man with dark hair and eyes. His coat hung open to reveal a police uniform.

"Mr. Caldwell, I'm Deputy Sheriff Michael Winter," he said in a deep, pleasantly resonant voice. "I'm sorry to interrupt your evening, but I haven't been able to reach you all day. I wonder if you have a few minutes to talk to me."

Sloane cursed inwardly. He was tired. His nerves were strung so tight his neck hurt. Monique would be here within the hour. The last thing he wanted was a police interview. But it was better to get it over with now than to try to arrange something for tomorrow, which Sloane expected to be another busy day.

"Certainly I'll speak with you, Deputy Winter, but I only have about an hour." Sloane opened the door wider.

"Oh, I won't take up that much of your time, sir." Michael Winter wiped his feet on the rough-woven WELCOME mat and stepped inside. "As I said, I wouldn't be bothering you at this hour if I could have reached you earlier."

"I won't even try to describe the endless and tedious deposition that took up some of the morning and all of the afternoon," Sloane explained. "Sometimes I *hate* my job, and this was one of those times." He smiled. "Don't mind me. I can gripe along with the best of them. Let me take your coat and come into the living room, where we can be comfortable and I can put my feet up."

Sloane hung Michael's raincoat on the hall coat tree, then led him into the big living room done in shades of cream, brown, and forest green. Indian print rugs lay on hardwood floors and oil paintings of deer, bears, and moose hung everywhere. Carvings of ducks sat on end tables and a mantel. "Comfortable room," Michael said, at a loss for a more flattering description.

"I decorated it myself." Sloane frowned. "I worked really hard on it, but I've been told a couple of times it looks like a hunting lodge. That wasn't the look I was going for. Guess I should have hired a professional decorator."

"What's important is that *you* like it, not what anyone else thinks."

"So true," Sloane said, but Michael heard the doubt in his voice and immediately knew other people's opinion mattered a great deal to this man. "I was having a scotch. A double." Sloane grinned. "I earned it today. How about you? Care for something alcoholic, or are you on duty?"

"On duty for another half hour," Michael said. "But I could use a soft drink. Anything will do."

While Sloane went behind the small bar and removed a Coke can from the refrigerator, Michael took another glance around the room. The walls were paneled in knotty pine. In the corner sat a curio cabinet filled with what looked like sports trophies. "Did you play sports in college?" he asked.

"Football in high school in New Orleans and college in Massachusetts."

"How did you end up in Winston?"

Sloane shrugged, handing him a Coke over ice in a tall glass. "I didn't like the winters up north. I like heat, but I didn't want to go back to New Orleans. My parents and younger sister were killed in a car wreck when I was a junior in college. I just couldn't live down there anymore. Too many memories."

"I'm sorry about your family. And I know what you mean about needing to leave places with memories," Michael said, hearing the bleakness creep into his own voice. "Sometimes when you've suffered a great loss, a change of scene is the only thing that even begins to help you heal."

Sloane studied him closely, seemed on the verge of asking what his "great loss" had been, then thought better of it. "I'm being a terrible host. Have a seat, Deputy, and tell me why you've come to see me. I assume it has something to do with Dara Prince."

"What makes you think that?" Michael asked, settling down on a dark green recliner. The chair looked like a lump, totally without style, but it was heavily padded and Michael was so tired, he felt like he'd landed on a cloud.

"What makes me think you're here about Dara, Deputy?" Sloane looked intently at Michael as he took a seat on the sofa and sipped his drink. "Because of all the uproar over her diary Christine gave you. I've never seen Ames Prince in such a state."

"He discussed it with you?"

"God, no. It's family business. But I stopped by the house yesterday. Jeremy let me in and I heard Ames ranting to Patricia about it. Jeremy whispered to me what Ames was mad about. Poor guy looked terrified and guilty as hell. By then, Ames was threatening to take some kind of legal action against Christine. Patricia was trying to calm him down, but she's never been much good at that. The only person who ever had any influence over him was Dara. And from what I've heard, his late wife, Eve. Anyway, I overheard Ames say Dara had written about one of her boyfriends. Lovers, rather. Said his initials were *S.C.* He said Christine and Streak Archer were certain that was me and wanted to know if Patricia knew anything about it, which of course she didn't because it wasn't true."

"Did Prince ask you if you were S.C.?"

Sloane shook his head while taking another sip of scotch. "I think he started to, then reason began seeping back in his overheated brain. He knows I'm not stupid, and dating his nineteen-year-old daughter when I was relatively new at the firm would have been extremely stupid."

"You think he would have fired you for seeing her?"

"Damned right he would have."

"But he approved of Reynaldo Cimino?"

"Not on your life, but I don't think he took the relationship seriously. He thought—he *knew*—Dara would move on. Ames wanted her with someone rich, influential, maybe a potential political candidate. A governor's or senator's wife. Or even better. The modern-day Jackie Kennedy."

"From what I've heard, she didn't strike me as the Jacqueline Kennedy type."

Sloane laughed. "I'll say she wasn't, but parents see their children with some kind of special vision. Anyway, even though I was a lawyer and my family left me quite comfortable, I'm not rich and I have no political aspirations. So Ames considered me out of the running for his prize. Anyway, aside from being a new guy at the firm who had better sense than to mess around with his teenage daughter, I was engaged to Christine Ireland at the time."

"Who was all of twenty when you proposed?"

"Almost twenty-one." Sloane grinned. "I know it sounds like I was robbing the cradle, but you don't know Christine. She seemed a lot older. And she's beautiful and intelligent. And *settled*, which Dara certainly wasn't. At the time she struck me as the perfect wife for a rising young lawyer."

"Even with a mentally disabled brother?"

"Hey, Jeremy's great. He's accomplished a lot for someone with his disadvantages, not to mention that he's just a damned likable guy. I would have been glad to have him for a brother-in-law."

"So what happened to the engagement?"

Sloane frowned. "According to Christine, Dara happened. Dara flirted with me a lot. I don't know why. Maybe because she flirted with *all* men. Maybe because she particularly wanted to make Chris mad. Dara really hated that her father had taken in Christine and Jeremy."

"But according to Miss Ireland, you did nothing to discourage Dara's attentions to you."

Sloane looked at him narrowly. "So you've discussed this with Miss Ireland?"

"She brought it up, sir," Winter said firmly, although he couldn't really remember whether she had or not.

"I see. Well, it's old news. At least to me." He shook his head, smiling. "Women have amazing egos, though. I guess Christine still hasn't gotten over how much Dara came on to me."

She didn't sound to me like she gave a damn anymore, Winter thought, suddenly feeling indignant for Christine's sake, although he wasn't certain why. He hardly knew her. Why should he care? Still, it was an effort to say nothing sarcastic and to keep his expression neutral.

Sloane drained his glass and rattled ice cubes around the bottom. "Our past troubles aside, Chris and I have remained friends. I was appalled when I heard about the attack on her at the gym. Any leads on who did it?"

"I'm afraid not, sir. Sheriff Teague has pulled in the usual suspects, as he calls them, but none of them strike me as having the intelligence to pull off that attack."

"The intelligence? Chris wouldn't describe it to me. What took brains to smack a woman in the head with a metal weight?"

"Someone came to that gym well prepared. Razor to cut a hole in a window, suction cup to attach to the glass so it wouldn't crash to the ground and draw attention. He used very swift, powerful movements to silence and restrain Miss Ireland."

Sloane looked slightly ill. "Good God, I didn't know all that. She could have been killed."

"Yes, sir."

"I feel like strangling the bastard who did that to her."

"If we find him, I wouldn't recommend strangling him. You'd end up in jail yourself."

"It would almost be worth it."

Michael tilted his head. "You still seem to be extremely fond of Miss Ireland."

"It's hard not to be. She's a fine woman."

"No hard feelings over the broken engagement?"

"Deputy, your less-than-subtle inquisition isn't necessary. I did not attack Christine Ireland." He smiled. "However, I don't mind talking about her. Looking back to when we were planning to marry, I realize Chris and I cared a lot for each other, but we weren't in love. I think she was desperate to get out of the Prince home and didn't trust herself enough to take care of Jeremy all alone. And I thought she was a great catch. I know how mercenary that sounds, but I was younger then. A little more selfish. I hope the years have deepened my sensitivity. Anyway, it was better for both of us that the engagement ended."

"Because of Dara."

"It didn't end because of Dara. Chris used Dara as an excuse. I knew it at the time, but I didn't tell Chris I knew. I just let her take control of the situation and end it. It seemed more sporting that way—to let the girl break the engagement."

"And smarter. She was your boss's ward."

Sloane grinned. "You've got me there. But even if Chris hadn't ended it, I would have. My heart wasn't really in it. We wouldn't have been happy together. The marriage would have ended in divorce after a few bad years when we might have come to actually dislike each other. And to have hurt Jeremy. Emotionally, I mean. No, Deputy, our marriage just wasn't meant to be."

"So what was there between you and Dara?"

Sloane was beginning to look a bit impatient. "Nothing, Deputy. In the weeks before she vanished, or was killed, she was acting pretty wild, even for her. Something was going on with her, but I wouldn't have any way of knowing what it was. I barely knew her."

"But even *you* admitted she was flirting with you."

"Yes. I told you her behavior was strange, although flirting with men was second nature with Dara. She did seem to be focusing on me, though. Maybe it was to piss off Chris."

"And according to Miss Ireland, you didn't discourage her."

Sloane glanced at his watch. "Deputy, I'm expecting a guest. I only have a few more minutes to talk to you. But I will tell you that Dara was Ames Prince's daughter. *Teenage* daughter. I'd only been with the Prince firm for a year. Do you think I wanted to offend the child who had my boss wrapped around her little finger? I would have been out of Prince Law in a heartbeat if she'd complained to Daddy Ames about me. So I *endured* her because I felt I had to." He swirled the melting ice cubes around his glass. "In fact, I was pretty damned mad at Dara at the time. She was putting me between the proverbial rock and a hard place, jeopardizing my job and my relationship with Christine. And she didn't care how much trouble she was causing me. She thought it was funny."

"You don't sound like you cared much for Dara."

"From what I knew of her, I didn't like her at all. She was beautiful, sure, but she was also completely self-centered and a troublemaker. That's what all the flirting with me was about— causing trouble. But before you get the wrong idea, I didn't dislike her enough to kill her."

"Killing her for flirting with you would be a bit extreme," Michael said solemnly.

Sloane looked at him closely for a moment, then threw back his head and guffawed. The sound echoed around the big, badly decorated room. "You're all right, Winter."

Michael smiled back. "Thanks. But I take it you *do* think she's dead."

Sloane glanced at him in surprise. "Well, of course. I know the cops don't consider Ames's identification of the body official, but it's her. Right height, hair, the presence of her ring. Why? Do you think there's some doubt?"

"No, sir, I don't. But I wouldn't want you to repeat that to Mr. Prince."

"Believe me, I don't say one word to Ames Prince about Dara. If he wants to believe it wasn't her body found on the riverbank, that she's off someplace having a high old time and sending home a letter every few months, that's fine with me. It makes him happy and that makes everything easier for his family and his staff at the law firm." He glanced at his watch again. "Deputy, I hate to be rude—"

"One more question, sir. Do you know who Dara called the Brain?"

"The Brain? I don't know. Christine? She was a straight-A student and I think that bothered Dara, although she claimed she didn't give a damn about grades."

"This would have been a man she was involved with. Someone she mentioned in her diary. Do you think it could have been Streak Archer?"

Sloane Caldwell looked stunned. "Streak *Archer*? My God, the guy's a hermit!"

"And a genius."

"Maybe. With computers, for what that's worth. He's also unbalanced."

"And good-looking."

Sloane raised an eyebrow. "You think so? Well, I'm not attracted to men, so I wouldn't know."

Michael acted as if he'd missed the faint innuendo: "But you must realize Streak Archer would be appealing to a lot of women. The handsome wounded war hero. And Dara mentioned him by name in her diary. She said she liked him. A *lot*."

"Well . . ." Sloane shook his head as if baffled and amused at the same time. "Well, I'll be damned. Dara and Streak Archer friends? That's a shocker."

"She said she was having an affair with the Brain."

"Then I *know* Streak Archer can't be the Brain. I don't think he has anything to do with women. I've never heard that he's gay; he's just . . . I don't know. Too strange. I mean, what woman wants a guy who throws some kind of nervous fit every time he goes out in public?"

"Does he?"

"From what I've heard, yes. I feel sorry for the guy, but come on. Streak a love interest? For *Dara*?"

"I guess it was a fairly big reach to think the Brain could be Archer," Michael said affably.

"I'll say." Sloane looked at his watch for the third time. "Deputy, I want to be helpful, but I barely knew Dara and frankly, I'm not all that concerned about her love life. I am concerned about *mine*. I have a lady arriving here in about half an hour. We're having dinner with Travis Burke and his wife, Bethany, and I haven't even had time to shower."

"You're friends with the Burkes?"

"I'm very good friends with Travis. I don't know Bethany as well." Sloane's smile was becoming strained. "I really can't tell you anything else about Dara, but I do have to get ready for dinner."

Michael stood. "Sorry to have taken up so much of your time, Mr. Caldwell. I'm a dog with a bone about a mystery, and untangling all these nicknames I've found in Dara's diary is driving me wild."

"I guess it could be fascinating," Sloane mumbled, although his tone said it could only be fascinating if you didn't have a whole lot else on your mind. "I'm sorry to rush you off, Winter, but as I said—"

"Young lady coming. I understand." Suddenly Michael felt unreasonably angry with the man's heartiness, the dismissive way he'd said his heart wasn't in his engagement to Christine Ireland, his smugness over the "fact" that Christine still brooded over Dara's attentions to her ex-fiancé. The guy had a big ego. So what? Still, Michael decided he didn't like Sloane Caldwell. Not at all. Perversely, he lingered, talking. "I'm divorced myself. My ex-wife, Lisa, lives in Los Angeles."

"Really?" Sloane began edging Michael toward the door. "Has she remarried?"

"No. She's an actress. Or a want-to-be actress. Right now she's in a fabric softener commercial. You might have seen her on TV. She has these great big green eyes and gorgeous auburn hair halfway down her back. They have her running through a meadow waving her fabric softener sheet."

"Auburn hair running through a meadow. Umm, sounds lovely. I'll have to look for it, although I don't watch much television." Sloane almost bumped into Michael as he tried to hasten him along to the front door. Michael heard a car door slamming outside. The date had arrived early, and Sloane didn't want this deputy intruding on his evening, blathering on about a dead girl's lovers. That would certainly put a chill on the evening, Michael thought, almost smiling. Caldwell wanted him out. *Now.*

Too late. The doorbell rang. Sloane opened it. Michael peered past him to see a woman wearing a smile and a beautiful cashmere coat. "I'm early, but I saw the police car," she said lightly to Sloane. "I thought you might need a lawyer."

"I don't think things are that dire," Sloane said. He ushered her in. "Monique Lawson, Deputy Sheriff Winter. I'm sorry. I don't remember your first name."

"Michael," he nearly choked out. Monique Lawson looked enough like his ex-wife, Lisa, to be her older sister. "How do you do, Miss Lawson?"

"I prefer Ms." She extended her hand. It was surprisingly large and strong and her gaze direct to the point of being unpleasantly searing. "Michael Winter. You moved into your grandparents' house."

"Yes. My grandfather left it to me when he passed away last year."

"And you decided to abandon Los Angeles for Winston? Why?"

Sloane looked uncomfortable. "Monique, I really don't think that's any of our business."

"I'm curious, that's all."

"I wanted a change of scene," Michael said tersely. The woman's intrusive manner immediately put him off.

She gave Michael a penetrating look. "I hope there's no trouble here."

"None whatsoever," Michael said. "I just had a couple of questions for Mr. Caldwell."

"But you're done now?"

"Yes."

"Good," Monique said emphatically. "We have a lovely evening planned with friends at the Tudor Rose Restaurant. Ever been there, Deputy Winter?"

"No."

"You should go. It's one of the best restaurants in the state."

Sloane Caldwell gave him a meaningful look. "I hope I was of some help, Deputy Winter, but we are running late. It was a pleasure meeting you. Good evening."

And get lost, his tone said. Michael bristled inside at the dismissal. He couldn't resist adding, "Oh, Mr. Caldwell, there's something I meant to tell you earlier."

"What is it?" Sloane snapped, nearly pushing him out the door.

"Patricia Prince was found dead this afternoon. We think she was murdered."

3

Christine stared at her brother openmouthed for a full five seconds before she managed, "Patricia had a boyfriend she met in the barn?"

"Yeah." Jeremy's face reddened. "I knew I shouldn't tell anyone, but I guess it doesn't matter now if I tell you. But you shouldn't tell anyone else."

Christine leaned back in her chair. "Jeremy, what makes you think Patricia had a boyfriend she saw in the barn?"

"One afternoon I came home early. You remember that day I had the upset stomach? Anyway, I saw Patricia going down to the barn. I thought she was going to ride Sultan and I stayed at the window awhile to see her riding him, but she didn't come out. A long time later, a guy came out of the barn. I couldn't really see his face. He acted sort of sneaky. He went away from the barn toward the river without ever looking back. Then a little while later, Patricia came out. When she got to the house and found me there, she said the vet had been in to look at the horses, but she was all nervous and stuttering and guilty-looking."

"Well, that doesn't mean the man in the barn was her boyfriend."

"Her hair was messed up and her makeup was gone and her blouse was buttoned up all wrong."

"Oh. Did you get any sense of what the man you saw leaving the barn looked like?"

"No. He had on a jacket with a hood. It was beginning to rain a little. Anyway, one Sunday Ames went somewhere and I was supposed to go with him, but I changed my mind right before he left. Patricia wasn't in the house and I went down to visit the horses. I went in the barn and I heard music coming from up in the loft. And I heard, well, noises." His face grew redder. "Moaning and stuff. And I heard Patricia say, 'I love you,' and I heard a man's voice. I sort of recognized it, but not exactly, 'cause the music got louder. I guess I should've yelled to them that I was there, but I was too embarrassed and I knew Patricia would get really mad at me, so I just took off."

"Jeremy, how long ago was that?"

He frowned ferociously. "Around Valentine's Day. I remember 'cause Danny Torrance's little sister sent me a valentine. She's only nine, but she says she wants to marry me. She's so funny. That's how I remember."

"So that was almost two months ago."

"I guess."

"Jeremy, are you *sure* you have no idea who Patricia was meeting in the barn?"

"I don't know. Well, maybe I do, but I just can't *get* it. You know what I mean? When you think you know something, but it won't come, no matter how hard you think?"

"Yes, I know that feeling."

"But since she met her boyfriend in the barn and she died in the barn, maybe it's real important that I *make* it come to my mind, that I *make* myself think of who it was."

He rubbed a hand across his forehead. He got headaches when he was upset. Christine could tell one was coming on, and she wasn't going to push him further. "Sometimes when I can't think of something, I just try to put it completely out of my mind for a while. Then, at the oddest time, up it pops!"

"Really? You think maybe that would work for me?"

"I'm sure of it. Just stop thinking about Patricia."

"I'll try." He sighed. "But, Christy, there's something else. I think maybe Patricia knew I knew about her boyfriend and didn't want me to tell, because she got a lot nicer to me after I was in the barn that time. She even sang on the karaoke machine with me, even though I'd asked her to a hundred times and she'd always said no."

"She sang with you?"

"Yeah. She tried to sing like Jewel. She was pretty bad, but I told her she was good anyway."

"You always tell me I'm good, too."

"Yeah, but you aren't as bad as Patricia."

"Thank you, kind sir."

"Hey, I didn't mean to hurt your feelings. It's not that you're not good—"

"It doesn't matter, Jeremy. I'm *not* a good singer." Christine paused. "Not like Dara was."

"Yeah, Dara was *real* good. I even made tapes of her singing."

"Tapes?" Christine repeated, a shock going through her. "You made cassette tapes of Dara singing?"

"Yeah. Sure." Jeremy suddenly looked alarmed. "There's nothing wrong with that, is there?"

"No, of course not."

"Her favorite thing to sing was 'Rhiannon.' And she sang a couple of songs called 'These Dreams' and 'Walkin' After Midnight.' I can't remember who they're by."

"The group Heart and Patsy Cline. But I want to know about a particular song she sang."

"Which song?"

"I don't know it. I never heard it before, but I have the words." Christine dashed to the desk where she'd placed the paper on which she'd written the words to the song someone had played over the phone the night she was in the hospital. She rushed back to the table. "I'll read the lyrics and you tell me if you recognize them." Jeremy gave her that wide-eyed look that said he was afraid he was in trouble, but she had his full attention. "I can't remember the melody. I just wrote down the words."

"Yeah, okay, say them already. You're creepin' me out." Christine read slowly:

> "'Everywhere I go
> Dark eyes peer at me.
> I wish they meant me love,
> But I know they desire me harm.
> I want to live long and full,
> But sadly, I am certain that
> All too soon, death waits for me.'"

Christine looked up at Jeremy. "Well? Do you recognize them?"

Jeremy's face had paled and his eyes widened. He nodded. "I think it was the last song Dara ever sang on my karaoke machine. She wrote it. It was so sad—not like her other songs."

"But you taped it?"

He nodded again. "Yeah. I didn't really want to 'cause like I said, it was so sad. But she made me tape it. Twice."

"You mean she didn't like the first version and taped over it a second time?"

"Nooo." Jeremy was looking more and more frightened. "She asked me to make two tapes. I kept one. She took the other one." His forehead puckered. "Are you sure I'm not in trouble? I didn't mean to do anything wrong."

Christine reached over and touched his hand, smiling. "No, honey. You didn't do anything wrong. I just got excited because this is important. What happened to the tapes?"

Jeremy looked down. "I . . . I don't remember. It was a long time ago. And right after she sang the song, she went away. Everybody was all to pieces and the days after sort of seem like a dream or something."

"But you keep the tapes you make in a special place."

He nodded. "Uh-huh. But Dara took one of them, like I said."

"Jeremy, I want you to look for your copy of the tape."

His voice rose. "Why? I don't get why you care so much about that song."

"I just do. But not because of anything you did wrong, understand? Just because I want to hear the tape again."

"Again? When did you hear it? Dara never let you listen to her music and I didn't play it for you."

Christine looked at her fearful brother. She didn't want to tell him the truth, but he could always tell when she was lying, and at this point a lie would scare him more than the facts. "Someone called me late at night. They didn't say anything. They just played the tape of Dara singing this song. Then they hung up."

Jeremy's mouth slackened. "Really and truly? You didn't dream it?"

"How could I dream about a song I'd never heard?"

"Oh gosh," Jeremy fretted. "Oh golly. It would be just like Dara, singing to you in the night. Christy, this is too creepy."

"It sure is. That's why I want to find out who could have that tape and played it to scare me. I want you to look for your copy of the tape."

His gaze grew even more miserable. "I already did. After they found that body and Ames said it was Dara, because I wanted to hear her sing again."

"And?"

"And all the tapes of her singing were gone. I didn't lose them, Christy, honest," Jeremy assured her fervently. "I'm real careful with my tapes. But they weren't there. Maybe she took them when she left. Only I guess she didn't really leave. So maybe someone else took them. They weren't a big secret or anything. Patricia heard us singing on the karaoke machine. And Ames. Maybe other people. I just can't remember the last time I saw the tapes. I'm real sorry, Christy."

He sounded completely sincere, and it wasn't like Jeremy to lie. But he could be forgetful. He'd made the tapes three years ago. He could have misplaced them in all that time, no matter how much he cherished them. That's the best spin she could put on the situation. At least it was the least frightening. Jeremy was looking at her warily. "It's okay, Jeremy. The tapes aren't that important."

His fingers twisted together as trouble churned in the beautiful blue of his eyes. "Hey, Christy?"

"Yes?"

"I think maybe the tapes *are* important. Could the person who played you the tape on the phone have killed Dara and taken her tape away from her?"

"I suppose that's possible," she said reluctantly.

"Then why would he play the tape to you on the phone late at night?"

"Maybe to play a joke."

"What kind of joke is that?" Jeremy demanded. "It's not one bit funny." He paused. "Christy, I think maybe he did it to scare you. But why would somebody want to scare you?"

To get me to stop nosing into Dara's death, Christine thought grimly. To get me to back off, stop searching for a killer, so that most people in town would go on thinking that you, my darling brother, murdered Dara Prince.

15

1

Christine felt as if she were struggling up from deep water. Pressure. Coldness. Dark. Then her world grew lighter, lighter, and lighter until she opened her eyes and realized she'd been asleep and it was morning. Nine-thirty, to be exact. She hadn't slept this late for months.

For a few minutes she lay still, staring at the ceiling. She thought about Patricia. Yesterday at this time she'd been alive, maybe excited about seeing a man she loved. Now she lay cold and stiff in a morgue. And Christine thought about the message on her answering machine saying tonelessly, "Poor Patricia. See what happens when you find out too much?" What had Patricia found out? Who killed Dara? Exactly the same thing Christine was trying to find out? And if she did, would her fate be the same as Patricia's?

At last the sound of the television penetrated her consciousness and she remembered that Jeremy had spent the night. She'd told him she thought now was the time for him to move in with her permanently, and although he'd demurred weakly, saying maybe Ames would need him now that Patricia was dead, Christine was certain he'd seemed relieved. He couldn't have relished the idea of living with an even gloomier Ames in that large, somber house.

When she went downstairs, she found Jeremy sprawled on the floor in front of the television. Rhiannon sat on his back tangling a delicate black paw in his blond hair. "What are you watching?" she asked.

"News."

"Since when do you watch the news instead of cartoons in the morning?"

"Since we got a flood. The weatherman says the river crested last night. That means the water went as far up as it's gonna go. Now it's on its way back down. The flood's over and we don't need to pile up any more sandbags."

"Hallelujah."

"Think maybe we can open the store now?"

"Not until after Patricia's funeral, Jeremy. It wouldn't be proper."

He looked slightly downcast. Christine was not sure whether his fallen mood was caused by a reminder of Patricia's death or the knowledge that the store wouldn't open for a few days. "Have we lost too much business at the store?" he asked. "Are we going to the poorhouse?"

"It would take a lot more than a few days of lost business to put Prince Jewelry into bankruptcy." Jeremy frowned, not understanding. "We're not going to the poorhouse. Where did you hear about the poorhouse, anyway?"

"Wilma. She's always saying to Streak's brother, 'You'd better stop spending all your money. The poorhouse is right around the corner, Mr. Big Shot.' He gets mad when she says that. Anyway, I'm glad Prince Jewelry isn't losing all its money, 'cause I don't want to lose my job. I *love* my job." Jeremy smiled. "I made coffee!"

"I know." As Christine walked into the kitchen, the smell alone burned the inside of her nose. One cup of Jeremy's coffee could set you jittering for at least two hours. She didn't want to hurt his feelings by emptying the pot and fixing a fresh one, so she mixed equal parts of milk and coffee like espresso. The result tasted nothing like espresso. She shuddered as she forced down a second sip. At least the strong brew was eye-opening.

Jeremy came into the kitchen. "Maybe I should go tell Ames I'm gonna move in here with you now."

"I think I should be the one to do that," Christine answered quickly. She did not want Ames's bitterness at her spilling over onto Jeremy. She also feared the slim chance that Ames might plead with Jeremy to remain in his house, either out of genuine loneliness or possibly out of a desire to hurt Christine. Two days ago she would not have considered Ames capable of such petty cruelty. Now she didn't know what to expect of him. "If you do it, he might think you're not happy living with him."

"Well, I'm not really happy living there," Jeremy said meekly.

"I know, but we don't want to hurt his feelings. I'll make it sound like it's all my idea and I just *insist* that you move in with me now. After all, you're my brother and I've fixed up a room for you and Rhiannon is here. He knows how much you love Rhiannon."

"That all sounds real good," Jeremy agreed. "And it's true."

"Yes. I won't be lying. I don't know how things will be at the house today because of Patricia's death, but I still think I should talk to him about your moving no later than this afternoon. You can hang out here with Rhi."

"Christy, I'd rather go to the store."

"The store is closed today."

"I know, but there's something I want to work on."

"Jeremy, you sound like you did the other morning when you were so determined to go in early. You're working on something secret, aren't you?"

Jeremy's gaze shifted. "Okay. It's a secret. But it's nothing bad."

"I didn't think it was."

"It's just something special that I wanted to do all by myself without Rey helping me. So will you let me go to the store alone like the other day? I won't lose the key, I *promise*." He crossed his heart. "I'll guard it with my life—"

"All right. Let's have some breakfast, then get dressed, and I'll take you to the store while I go to Ames's house." She tried to sound chagrined. "Oh gosh, we've drunk all the coffee! I'll have to make a fresh pot."

"I know you poured some of the coffee down the sink. It's okay. I think the stuff I made was maybe too strong."

"Then fresh coffee and pancakes coming up."

About an hour later, when Jeremy had consumed even more pancakes than Christine thought a guy of his size could possibly hold, they loaded into her rental car and headed out.

"Hey, look at the sky!" Jeremy exclaimed.

Christine was so used to looking at a low gray sky she hadn't paid any attention to it this morning. But a glance upward through the windshield showed her a beautiful day of powder blue tinged with pink and yellow where the sun was breaking through. Maybe it was a good omen, Christine thought. Maybe only shock had made Ames strike out at her yesterday. Maybe during the night Ames had had time to calm down, to realize how brutal and unjust he'd been to insinuate she'd had anything to do with Patricia's death.

Her hope was short-lived. After dropping off Jeremy at the store with more warnings not to lose the back door key, she drove to the Prince home. Wilma Archer's car sat in the driveway. Good, Christine thought. If Ames was still being unreasonable, Wilma could arbitrate. She had a way with Ames no one else could equal.

Christine rang the doorbell. Wilma opened the door and promptly threw her plump arms around Christine. "Oh, honey, I'm so glad you stopped by. Isn't this just the worst thing? I can't believe it! Patricia seemed like one of those women who would live to be a hundred. And some people are saying her death wasn't an accident! I'm telling you, I just don't know how much more poor Ames can take."

Through the whole spiel, Wilma patted Christine's back with such force Christine was certain she'd have a bruise tomorrow. She drew back and looked at Wilma. Her eyes were dry and unswollen. Not even she had been able to work up tears for Patricia, even though Christine knew the woman genuinely regretted the death of Ames's wife. The second wife, the second death. And this only three years after the disappearance, the certain murder, of Ames's only child. Wilma was right. It did seem like too much for one man to endure.

Before Christine had a chance to say anything, though, Ames walked out of his study. He stopped and stared at her, his gaze cold.

"Ames," she said gently, pulling away from Wilma and heading toward him. "I just wanted to tell you how sorry—"

He held out his arm, the palm of his hand raised in the traditional *stop* signal. "Don't come any closer. And don't spout any false sympathy for Patricia. You have repaid my kindness to you and your brother with treachery. I don't forgive that kind of thing. Not ever. You are no longer welcome in this house. Or in the store, for that matter. I never want to see you again."

"Ames!" Wilma gasped. "You don't know what you're saying. This is Christine!"

"I know exactly what I'm saying and to whom. Get out of my house, Christine. *Now!*"

With that he turned, walked stiffly back into his study, and slammed the door.

2

Michael Winter walked up to the double doors of the Prince home and rang the bell. In a moment a plump, flustered-looking woman opened the door, her eyes widening at the sight of his uniform. "Oh lord! What now?" she almost wailed.

How great to be greeted this way half the time, Michael thought. But then, not many people welcomed the sight of a cop at the door. "I'm Deputy Michael Winter," he said. "I'd like to speak to Mr. Prince."

"He's too upset. You'll have to come back."

She started to shut the door, but Michael stepped forward. He remembered this woman from the jewelry store. "Mrs. Archer, isn't it?" She nodded. "Ma'am, I'm sure Mr. Prince is upset and I'm sorry to intrude at such a time, but I just have a couple of questions for him." He gave her his half-winning, half-pathetic smile. "If I don't ask the questions now, the sheriff will keep sending me back until I get answers. Or maybe he'll even come himself." Winter had already been told Ames Prince couldn't stand-Sheriff Teague. "I sure don't want Mr. Prince harassed at a time like this. So please ask if he'll see me for a few minutes and I'll be out of his hair as soon as possible."

She hesitated, then closed her eyes and shook her head. "Oh, all right. I guess there's nothing else to do. Come on in."

"Thank you, ma'am. I sure appreciate this." Michael stepped into the entrance hall and saw Christine Ireland. She stood rigidly, as if she were trying to control trembling, and her face was parchment pale. "Hello, Miss Ireland."

"Deputy," she answered in a shaky voice. "I was just leaving, but I need to talk to you later today if you don't mind."

"Of course I don't mind."

"Does this have something to do with Patricia's death?" Wilma asked.

"I'm sure Miss Ireland would rather not go into it now, Mrs. Archer," Michael said, although his curiosity was running wild. Christine looked awful and she had something to tell him she didn't want to say in this house. "I'll drop by your place later on this afternoon, if that's all right."

"That would be fine." Christine turned to Wilma Archer. "I'll talk to you soon, Wilma."

"Honey, I don't think you should run off this way. Ames is just ruffled. He'll settle down in a little while, and you don't need to be driving, as upset as you are. Come in the kitchen and have a cup of tea before you leave."

"I think I need more than tea to calm me down. Besides, I've been asked by the master of the house to leave. Don't worry— I'll be fine." She looked at Michael. "See you later, Deputy Winter."

"Yes. Later." Michael touched his hat as she fled past him and out the front door. Wilma Archer looked at him helplessly. "Trouble here?" he asked lightly.

"Yes. With Ames. He's being ..." She floundered. "He's being a complete jackass." Michael almost burst out laughing at her language. "I'm sorry for him, but I could just smack him at the same time. He's a very difficult man. So are my sons. Robert—Streak, everyone calls him—in one way, but then, he's had a hard go of it, the war and all, and the other one thinks he's a Rockefeller or something, the way he throws money around. Oh, listen to me. I'm just babbling. I do that when I get flustered."

"I think we all do, ma'am."

"You're very polite. More than I can say for *some* people in this house." She glared at a closed door. "I'll tell Ames you're here, but don't expect him to be cordial."

"I won't, ma'am. I'll just be grateful if he'll see me."

"Oh, he'll see you," Wilma Archer said with determination, "or he'll have me to deal with. Grief or no grief, I've had just about enough of his nonsense for one day."

Michael stood in the entrance hall. Wilma Archer went into a room and closed a door behind her. After a few moments, he heard raised voices. Prince was putting up a fight about seeing him. He'd probably have to make another trip back here, dammit. Or suggest that Prince might prefer to be questioned at the station. The guy had to know he couldn't get out of this, but he could make it difficult.

Michael was just planning his next method of approach when Wilma Archer opened the door and said tightly, "Mr. Prince will see you now, Deputy." Her cheeks were flushed and her eyes snapped. Michael smothered a smile, knowing Ames Prince had just been put down a peg by this feisty woman.

Prince sat behind a massive desk looking as if he were carved out of stone. His gaunt face was haggard, his eyes bloodshot, and he held his hands tightly together, perhaps to stop them from trembling. He looked at Michael challengingly.

"Hello, Mr. Prince," Michael said easily. "You took off on us yesterday." Ames continued to stare at him. "You know you should have stayed around for questioning."

"Why? I wasn't present when my wife . . . died."

"Let's not play games." Michael sat down on a leather chair opposite Ames's desk although he'd not been invited to sit. "I don't need to tell you the police had questions for you."

"I was upset, naturally. I went for a drive."

"I see." Michael withdrew a notebook from his pocket. "And where were you at the time of your wife's death?"

"I don't know the precise time of my wife's death."

Michael gave him a hard look. "I asked you not to play games. As a lawyer, you know it's not in your best interest. According to your receptionist, you stopped in the office around ten A.M, checked your mail, left within fifteen minutes, and did not return. I saw you here a little before two in the afternoon. Where were you in the meantime?"

Ames glowered at him for a moment, then sighed. "Oh, what does it matter? I was at my wife's mother's apartment."

Michael looked at him steadily. "Patricia's mother lives in Florida."

"My *first* wife. Eve. Her mother lives in Charleston. I knew she would be upset about the body that was dragged out of the river. She would jump to the conclusion that it was definitely Dara. I wanted to calm her, to reassure her that we have every reason to believe Dara is still alive."

"Sir, that body was found days ago. Why did you wait until yesterday to visit Dara's grandmother?"

"Frankly, I didn't think of it. I was too shaken. Besides, the woman is an invalid and doesn't watch much television or read the newspapers. But you can't keep bad news a secret for too long. One of her friends would tell her, or perhaps the woman who lives with and takes care of her. So I decided I needed to check on her for myself."

"Instead of just calling."

"I thought a personal visit would be more effective. She is Dara's *grandmother*, after all. Not some distant relative."

"I see." Michael looked at the notebook he routinely withdrew from his pocket whether he intended to make notes or not.

"It takes around an hour to get to Charleston from here. An hour's drive back accounts for two hours. You spent only an hour with Dara's grandmother?"

"Yes. She's in very bad shape. Tires easily. I didn't want to tax her strength."

"I would like to have her name and address."

"I will not have you badgering her, Deputy."

"I don't intend to badger her, Mr. Prince. I just have to verify your presence at her apartment. You know I do. It won't take more than five minutes."

Ames Prince drew another deep breath. When he let it out, he looked smaller, almost shrunken behind his big desk. He gave the woman's name, address, and phone number. "And after this, I expect to be left alone," he said firmly.

"Believe me, sir, I'd like to leave things at this, but I can't. I have to ask you for the notes you received presumably from Dara."

"What!" Ames exploded.

"For fingerprints, sir. I know you've never had them fingerprinted."

"Ah, Christine's work again. She just can't stop chattering to you, can she, Deputy? Tell me, has she lured you into a romantic involvement?"

The door to the study flew open and Wilma Archer stepped in, her face red with fury. "Ames Prince, you stop that kind of talk right this minute! Christine is a wonderful girl. I cannot—I *will* not—allow you to keep slandering her!"

"Wilma, this is none of your concern—"

"Be quiet, Ames." Michael watched in amazement as Ames Prince blinked at her, then shut his mouth. "If the deputy needs those letters, you give them to him. He's the police, for heaven's sake. He's trying to *help* you!"

"He is not trying to help me. He is trying to prove my daughter has been dead for three years."

"And maybe she has been!" Wilma's face crumpled. "Maybe she has been, but if so, isn't it better to know?"

Ames looked at his thin hands folded on top of his desk. "No, Wilma, it is not better."

"Give him the letters."

"I don't have them."

Michael could see that Wilma was both exhausted and crushed. He immediately stepped back into the fray she'd taken up on his behalf. "Mr. Prince, the letters are very important. If your daughter's fingerprints are on them, we'll know she did send them to you."

"Who else would send them?"

"Someone who wanted you to think she'd simply run away and short-circuit a murder investigation."

"I don't have the letters."

"Mr. Prince, I don't like to threaten you, but you know I can easily get a search warrant for them."

"They do not exist any longer." Ames's voice was flat, completely absent of emotion. "Now, I believe we are finished here, unless you plan to charge me with something, in which case I will of course retain counsel. Understood?"

"You'll have to take that up with Sheriff Teague," Michael said coolly. "But the sheriff will want to know what happened to those letters. You say they don't exist anymore. If you destroyed them recently to keep them from the police, that's obstruction of justice."

"I do not need you to lecture me on the law, young man."

"Also, I'm sure the sheriff will be as curious as I am about why you were so reluctant to reveal your movements yesterday at the time of your wife's death and why you vanished for hours after her body was found. Makes you sound guilty, you know?"

"And your obvious baiting of me makes you sound clumsy and stupid, Deputy." Ames looked down at a sheaf of papers on his desk. "We are through here. I'm certain you can find your way out."

"Yes, sir. I'm certainly not too stupid and clumsy to find the front door." Michael rose and added casually, "And by the way, I'm sorry for your loss. I can tell how distressed you are about your wife's death by the fact that you haven't asked me a single question about how the investigation is going." Ames's gaze shot up and Michael nodded solemnly. "Good-bye for now, Mr. Prince."

16

1

Christine Ireland opened the door holding a glass of wine. "Come in, Deputy Winter. I'm watching a movie and having white wine. It's a lovely way to wind down from a distressing morning."

"I thought I was going to be Michael, not Deputy," he said, looking at her closely. Either this was not her first glass of wine or she'd been crying. Possibly both.

"Yes. I remember. When other people aren't lurking around and we can be informal. Michael. Do you know your name is of Hebrew origin? It means 'who is like God.'"

"Then I was inaptly named. I'm not like God. In fact, my mother named me after the character of Michael Corleone in *The Godfather*."

"A Mafioso?"

"Yeah. I believe she thought his good looks redeemed the character from all wrongdoings."

"A policeman named after a Mafia godfather."

Michael shrugged. "What's in a name, anyway? May I come in?"

She bowed slightly at the waist. "Enter." He stepped inside and she waved her glass at him. "I know you're on duty and can't join me in a glass of wine. How about coffee? Or a soft drink? Hot chocolate? I *love* hot chocolate."

"Maybe we should both have coffee."

"No caffeine for me. But I'll make coffee for you."

"Never mind. I only want ice water. I'll get it," Michael said. "I see you're watching a movie. What is it?"

"*The English Patient*." Christine thumped down on the couch and her voice wavered. "I *love* this movie. Have you ever seen it?"

"Parts of it." Actually, he had sat mesmerized through it three times, but he didn't want her to think he was a romantic sap. "Great scenery."

"Beautiful. Just beautiful," she quavered. "It's just so damned beautiful."

Oh boy, Michael thought as he put ice in a glass and poured spring water over it. Miss Pulled-Together, Handle-Any-Situation Christine Ireland was not only heartbroken but also looped. He walked back into the living room. The movie played on a surround-sound DVD system with the volume turned loud. Christine made no move to turn it down, and he hated to ask her to, because she seemed so involved in the movie.

"Are you sure you only want ice water?" she asked loudly. "I have some cookies. Store-bought. I'm not great with the baking."

"I'm not hungry anyway."

"Don't tell me. Ames served you a lovely lunch."

Michael laughed. "Ames told me I seemed clumsy and stupid."

"Wow. He's not generally so blunt. Or wrong."

"Thanks."

Both living room chairs were loaded with books. "I thought I'd rearrange the bookshelves. I pulled out all of them, then lost interest in the job," Christine said. "You can sit on the couch with Rhi and me."

The cat huddled on Christine's lap, watching him with huge golden eyes as her mistress stroked her with long, gentle fingers. He figured she would spring away when he sat down, but Rhiannon held steady, as if protecting her mistress. Christine rubbed gently under the cat's triangular chin. "Want to tell me what went on at Ames's house earlier with you?" Michael asked.

"He called me treacherous. Then he fired me."

"He *fired* you! From the store?"

"Where else?"

"He's right. I do sound stupid." Michael gulped icy water. "Christine, he's a mess. He doesn't know what he's saying."

"I'm not sure whether he does or not." She never took her eyes from the television. "And I don't care if he's completely rational or not. My immediate concern is that I'm out of a job."

Michael worded the next question carefully. "I know you bought this house not too long ago. Are you in . . . well, it's none of my business, but are you in financial straits?"

"No, I'm fine. My parents left us very secure. We can coast for a while. I'm not worried about money. And I'm not even devastated over my job. It was okay, although managing some-one else's store didn't set me ablaze with excitement. But I am devastated about *Jeremy's* job. I'm not sure if Ames was firing him, too, but even if he wasn't, Jeremy would never stay without me at the store. It would be a point of honor with him. He's fiercely loyal to me even if sometimes he blabs information I'd rather he kept to himself. Anyway, he'll just be emotionally flat-tened. You don't know what working at Prince Jewelry has meant to him. He seems so much happier and more confident than he did a year ago." Her incredible aqua eyes filled with tears. "And I ruined it for him."

The wave of tenderness Michael felt for Christine was so strong, he was hardly aware of leaning toward her and gently caressing her cheek. A warm tear rolled down over his finger as his gaze held hers. Slowly their faces neared, then touched. Their lips met.

They didn't sink into a rapturous embrace as the music from the movie soared. The kiss remained soft, tenuous, almost what Michael's grandmother used to call a butterfly kiss, when lashes brushed cheeks like vibrating butterfly wings with just enough force to set each being tingling from the fragile contact.

Michael felt as if time stopped, or at least slowed considerably. The television music softened and Michael could hear the ring-ing of the wind chimes in front of an open window facing the street—perfectly tuned, resonant chimes, tinkling hauntingly.

They pulled back and looked at each other. Michael knew he

should feel embarrassed, but he didn't. And Christine did not look uncomfortable or regretful. The kiss had felt natural, inevitable. And calming, he realized. For the first time in years, his world seemed to regain color and to slowly ease from pain into a tranquil peace where none of the devastating things that had happened to him in Los Angeles jabbed constantly at his psyche.

Michael looked at Christine solemnly. "I should have asked—"

She put her fingertip to his lips. "No. You knew it's what I wanted."

"It's what *I* wanted. Maybe what I've wanted since I first walked into Prince Jewelry. Behind the counter, you seemed so strong, so sure of yourself. But when you served me coffee and sat at the table talking with me about Dara, I could see the vulnerability in your eyes. Strength and vulnerability in one gorgeous package. You don't give a guy a chance, Christine Ireland."

Christine smiled, ducking her head a bit. "You must see me in a different light than most men do." She smiled. "I believe I usually come off as big and bossy."

"Maybe you do, to people who are intimidated by you." He put his arm around her shoulder without asking himself if it was proper. He thought Rhiannon would leap away for safety, but she only shifted position and burrowed further into Christine's lap. Christine sighed and leaned against him. "I hadn't realized how tired I was."

"Mental turmoil can exhaust you faster than physical activity."

"I guess." Her head rested against his shoulder, her blond hair gleaming and soft. Her gaze was fixed on the television.

"I'm sorry for the spectacle I've made of myself, Michael. I'm not usually so whiny. And I'm not usually drunk at two in the afternoon."

"You haven't been in the least bit whiny. If you had, I would have given you a sharp rap across the knuckles to bring you back to your senses."

"You're a hard taskmaster."

"And as for the drinking . . ." She drew back, looking at him intently. "You're extremely cute when your guard is down."

"Oh, it's down," she said with a rueful smile. "In spite of the wine, I feel like someone kicked me."

"Ames was a bastard to you. You certainly don't deserve that kind of treatment."

"I'd like to think that, but I know how much I've hurt him by giving you the diary."

"You didn't give it to me to hurt him. This isn't about *him*. That's what he has to get through his head. This is about *Dara*. You are trying to help figure out who killed her."

She nodded silently, with a trace of guilt. She wanted to know who had murdered Dara. But mostly she wanted to clear her brother of any suspicion. "Michael, I didn't mention this before, but if you read the whole diary, you know she was pregnant."

"Yes."

"They must have done an autopsy on the corpse by now. Was there a fetus?"

Michael hesitated. "I'm afraid that's one of those things I'm not allowed to discuss with civilians."

"You're dodging the question, which means they *did* find a fetus," Christine said dully. "Poor Dara. I wonder what she planned to do about it? She says she was afraid of abortion and I remember her telling me about a friend of hers who'd hemorrhaged to death after having one done by some amateur, then not going to the hospital when the bleeding started. Dara usually wasn't the most empathetic or compassionate person in the world, but both Dara and the other girl were only fourteen when it happened. Her death seemed to have made a really lasting, horrifying impression on Dara. I *know* she feared abortion. So did she think she'd marry the father and have the baby? Or have it even if she didn't marry the father?"

"That would probably have depended on who the father was. She doesn't give any clues in the diary. We also don't know how her lovers would have felt about it. One might have wanted it if it was his; another would have wanted her to get rid of it."

"Maybe that's what got her killed," Michael said. "Maybe the lover insisted she have an abortion, she wouldn't cooperate, and he had too much to lose if the truth came out."

"And maybe she told a man who loved her she was pregnant with another man's child."

"We can speculate for hours, but at this point, we don't know anything." Michael stroked her hair. "I want you to put all of this out of your head for now. I want you to relax, to think pleasant thoughts if you can, and to give yourself up to the movie. It's a beautiful and tragic love story. The kind all you girls like."

Christine looked into Rhiannon's face. "Hear that? Mr. Stone Age thinks only *women* like beautiful and tragic love stories."

"Well, not only women—" Michael began.

"Too late and no harm done." She turned her head and gave him a quick, shy kiss on the cheek. "Go catch some bad guys."

Michael paused at the door and looked back. Christine was watching the movie closely as Count Almásy carefully wrapped the body of his love, Katharine Clifton, in a parachute and carried her down from the Cave of Fishes to a small open plane long buried in the sand. He placed her in the back of the half-rotten plane and began the doomed flight meant to begin Katharine's journey to England for her final rest.

Michael saw Christine's eyes fill with tears as the tiny plane took off and soared over an endless, rippling sea of camel-colored desert while Katharine's golden hair, slender arm, and canvas shroud fluttered gracefully against the tranquility of an exotic turquoise sky.

2

An hour later someone knocked at Christine's door. She'd dried her eyes after her movie, drunk two cups of coffee, and tried to concentrate on a book she'd been reading for the past two weeks but couldn't get past the third chapter. When the knocking started, she gratefully tossed the book aside, deciding to give up on it for good, and opened her door to find Rey Cimino.

"Hey there," he said, smiling. "Decide to quit answering your phone?"

"What? No."

"Jeremy has called. I've called."

"Is something wrong with Jeremy?" she asked anxiously. "He's at the store."

"I know he's at the store. He called me. He wants both of us to come there."

Christine rushed to her phone and picked it up. No dial tone. She checked the cord and found it disconnected from the wall. She whirled on Rhiannon. "Rhi, have you been playing with this again?" The cat fled from the room. "Guilty, obviously. And I had the television on too loud to hear the upstairs phone. Why didn't you call my cell phone?"

"I did. But when I got here, I saw it lying in your car."

Christine closed her eyes. She'd been so upset when she left Ames's house after he'd fired her, she hadn't closed her purse after removing her car keys. The cell phone had fallen out and she hadn't even noticed it.

"God, anything could have happened to Jeremy and I wouldn't have noticed!"

"Relax, Chris; he's fine. But excited. He said he wants both of us to come to the store because he has a surprise. It's something he's been working on for a while."

Christine raised her eyebrows. "The mysterious something that's been compelling him to go in early, when he can work without you watching him?"

"I guess so. Get your things. We're on a mission!"

Christine was still chastising herself for her carelessness with the cell phone, as well as thinking up ways to keep Rhiannon away from the house phone's wall connection, when they reached the store.

Ginger waited with Jeremy inside. "I just happened to be down here looking at the flood damage and I saw this character in here," she said, nudging Jeremy, who smiled. "I hope you don't care that I invaded the place!"

"It doesn't look like you've done too much damage," Christine said in a weak attempt at a joke. She was no longer the manager of this store. What happened here really wasn't her business, but she couldn't force herself to tell everyone. Certainly she couldn't tell Rey and Ginger before she told Jeremy. "So, little brother, what's the big deal?"

"I wanted to show everybody what I've been working on," Jeremy said excitedly. "Only I hoped Tess would be here, too."

"She was supposed to stop by Chris's earlier," Rey said. "I guess she changed her mind, though. But let's not wait for her. What is it, Jeremy?"

"Well, before I've designed jewelry, but I never made any," Jeremy told everyone. "Rey did the making. But I came in the store at times when Rey wouldn't be here so I could make something all by myself. Only I wanted him to see it to make sure it was okay before I showed it to Ames. And you, too, Christy."

Jeremy held out a little black jewelry box in which nestled a beautiful pin. At the center was a perfect rosebud carved from coral. Surrounding the rose were intricately etched silver leaves.

"I'm calling it the Dara Pin," Jeremy explained slowly. "Everything in it means something to her. Like, she thought maybe these really old Indians called the Incas lived on the land across from Crescent Creek and built the mounds. Rey told me the Incas called silver 'tears of the moon.' Dara would like that. And I read in one of my jewelry books that there's this real old belief that coral keeps evil away. She would like that, too. And I carved the coral into the shape of a rose like the ones that grow in her mother's garden in the summer." Jeremy paused and looked at Christine hopefully. "Do you like it?"

Christine's throat had been tightening the whole time Jeremy talked. What a Herculean effort he had put into thinking out the design of this pin, dredging up what Dara and Rey had told him, plowing in his slow way through jewelry books to find a stone that would be meaningful to Dara, deciding on the design of a rose that would charm her because she associated it with her mother. And he wanted Christine's approval before he showed it to Ames, whom he hoped to please. But most of all, he wanted to please Dara—Dara, who Christine was certain was dead, but who Jeremy so desperately wanted to believe would someday come home.

"I think it's beautiful," Christine said softly, hearing the quaver in her voice. *Please* don't let me cry in front of everyone, she thought. Reynaldo and Ginger would know she wasn't just crying over the beauty of the pin Jeremy had designed and crafted. They would know something else was wrong, and she couldn't discuss her dismissal from the store now. Not until she had told Jeremy. "You put so much work into this!"

"It was fun," Jeremy said proudly. "And I didn't use expensive stuff, in case I messed up. You know, like eighteen-karat gold and a ruby or something."

"I think this is lovelier," Christine answered. "There's a bush in Eve's garden that bears a rose exactly the color of this coral. That makes it extra-special."

"That rosebush was Dara's favorite!" Jeremy exclaimed.

He beamed as Rey and Ginger stepped closer to look at the pin. Ginger immediately gushed. Rey studied the pin, then gave Jeremy a slow smile. "You did a wonderful job, Jeremy," he said at last. "I don't think I could have done as well. Dara would love this. So will Ames."

Oh God, Christine thought. Should she risk letting Jeremy present the pin to Ames? The man was behaving so erratically he could throw down the ring and stomp on it for all she knew. She wasn't about to let Ames's anger with her crush Jeremy's ego. She would have to think this out, maybe talk over a solution with Streak and Wilma.

Rey draped an arm over her shoulder and looked into her face. "What's wrong, Chris? You look like you're going to cry."

"I'm just so touched by what Jeremy has done. I didn't even know he'd come this far in his craftsmanship."

"Frankly, neither did I," Rey said. "Jeremy, you've been holding out on me. Were you afraid I'd get jealous, afraid you were going to steal my job?"

"Oh, I could never take over from you," Jeremy assured him sincerely. "This is just one piece and it took me *forever*."

"Oh, but it was worth it!" Ginger enthused. "I wish I had a pin like that!"

"I think it's one of a kind," Rey told her. "Isn't it, Jeremy?"

"Yeah. Just for Dara. But maybe I could make you something else for Christmas, Ginger."

"That would be so cool, Jeremy!" Ginger's pixie face was all freckles and animation. "A Jeremy Ireland original!"

"Well, don't we look cozy!"

Everyone looked up to see Tess standing in the doorway. Her gaze was leveled at Rey and Christine. Rey quickly lowered his arm from Christine's shoulder, but accusation burned in Tess's eyes. "Am I interrupting a private party?"

"Don't be silly," Christine said. "Come look what Jeremy made."

Tess looked at the pin. Christine could see her drawing herself together for Jeremy's sake in order to force a smile. "Jeremy, that is beautiful," she said. "And you made it all by yourself?"

"Yes," he said, eyes still glowing. "For Dara. She can wear it when she comes home." He paused before saying sadly, "I guess I mean *if* she comes home."

Christine broke in. "Isn't the carving exquisite, Tess? I had no idea Jeremy's skills had developed to this extent."

"Yes, exquisite," Tess repeated. She looked at Rey. "Sure you didn't help?"

"No, I did not," Rey said firmly. "I didn't know anything about it. This was a surprise to all of us. A wonderful surprise, Jeremy!"

"Can we go show it to Ames now, Christy?" Jeremy asked.

"Oh, it's getting pretty late and I think he's busy with arrangements for Patricia's funeral. I don't believe this would be the best time."

"Oh. Patricia. Gosh, I forgot. That was really bad of me."

"Not bad. You were just excited over the pin. You can show it to him in a few days." Christine glanced at her watch. "I think we should go home now, Jeremy. Only I didn't drive down here. Rey brought me."

"Rey brought you?" Tess asked sharply.

"Yes. Rhiannon had unplugged my phone and my cell was in the car. Jeremy couldn't reach me, but he got Rey, so he stopped by for me. Rey, would you mind taking Jeremy and me home?"

"*I'll* take you home," Tess said adamantly. "Rey, I'll see you at our house later."

And that was the first inkling Christine had that along with all other halfway attractive women, Tess saw her as a rival for her husband's affections. Christine felt slightly sick inside, both for the damage Tess's doubts would do to their relationship, but also because she realized her friend's jealousy where Rey was concerned had reached the stage of destructive paranoia.

Or had it always been that way?

3

Rey stared at the television. Prosecutor Jack McCoy jumped to his feet and in his resonant voice tossed a violent objection into the arena of the courtroom. The judge overruled him and he sat down, frustration etched all over his craggy, handsome face.

Tess walked into the room swathed in her old flannel robe, an even older discolored towel thrown over her shoulders and her hair slicked flat with a smelly dark concoction. Rey wrinkled his nose. "What is on your hair?"

"Honeyed Almond Number Thirty-five," she said, touching her hair with a plastic-gloved hand. "You said you hated the blond streaks."

"They didn't look like any shade of blond I've seen in nature," he returned, craning his neck to look past her at the television. Jack McCoy was objecting again.

"You mean my hair didn't look like Christine's."

"I meant your hair looked better its natural color."

Tess sighed. "How many times have you seen this rerun of *Law and Order*?"

"Fifty-two. Fifty-two and three-fourths counting tonight. Please move. You're blocking the screen."

"You could recite the dialogue from memory."

"Yes, but McCoy's delivery is better than mine. No accent."

"I love your accent."

"Thanks. Move."

Tess sighed again and moved to the couch, sitting down near Rey's chair. She looked at the television. A weeping woman told of her heartbreak over having her son slain by a vicious killer. "Why are you so hung up on all this murder stuff?" Tess asked. "It's not natural."

"I like the mystery. And judging by the popularity of the show, I must not be too unnatural."

"I think it's unnatural to watch the same show over and over."

"You're in a bad mood, Tess. You've been in a bad mood ever since you walked into Prince Jewelry today."

"And found you holding Christine in your arms."

Rey looked at her incredulously. "I had my arm around her shoulder. She looked upset. I don't know what's wrong, but something is. It seems to me you'd be concerned about her, too, after all she's been through."

"I am, but I don't find it necessary to embrace her in front of a lot of people. Don't you know how embarrassing that is to me, your wife?"

"Embrace her? Throwing my arm around her shoulder is embracing her?" He shook his head and looked back at the television. "I think that hair color has seeped through to your brain."

"And now you insult me!"

Rey didn't answer and Tess felt a surge of fury toward him. He wouldn't even take his gaze from a rerun he'd seen countless times to look at her when she talked. "If you're so fond of murder mysteries," she began in a waspish voice she couldn't stop, "then why don't you solve the mystery of who murdered your precious Dara and tossed her in the river to rot?"

Rey's dark eyes slashed to her. She saw his hands—his beautiful but strong artist's hands—tighten on the arms of his chair. "Don't start, Tess. Just don't start on Dara."

"Oh? Because you can't solve the mystery? Or because you can't bear to even think about your lost love? Your one and *only* love."

"Tess—"

"The beautiful girl you adored. The girl you put on a pedestal. The girl you remain faithful to in your heart even though you're married to me. Well, let me tell you something, Reynaldo. Your precious Dara was pregnant when she died!"

Now she had his attention. He glared at her. "That is impossible," he said in a slow, deadly voice.

"Why? Because you always used a condom when you were with her? To protect her? To protect your darling from unwanted pregnancy? You told me that once, you know, before we were married, when you'd had way too much to drink. You told me how careful you always were with her."

"I can't believe I ever confided that to you, no matter how drunk I got!" Rey shouted. "But I was careful with her. Always!"

"Well, my darling, someone wasn't, because she wrote in her diary that she was pregnant. I stopped by your new interest Christine's today like I planned, but she was inside with her precious deputy. The window was open and I heard them talking about Dara writing in her diary that she was pregnant. And to prove my point, the corpse you're certain was your Dara was carrying a fetus. A baby that *wasn't* yours!"

Rey jumped up from his chair. He loomed over her, and for a moment Tess was certain he was going to strike her. Hard. The rage in his eyes surpassed anything she'd ever seen in him, anything of which she'd thought him capable. His whole body trembled. Then, with a few guttural words, almost hissed, in Italian, he turned and slammed out of the house.

Oh, my God, Tess thought, trembling. What have I done?

4

"Gosh, what was wrong with Tess?" Jeremy had asked after she'd driven over the speed limit to get them home, refused to come in the house, and barely said good-bye before whizzing out of their driveway. "Do you think she didn't like the Dara Pin?"

"There's no way she couldn't have thought the pin was spectacular," Christine had said. "But you know Rey was Dara's boyfriend. Maybe she felt a little jealous."

"Oh. I didn't even think of that. Rey sure did love Dara. I guess I shouldn't have showed the pin to Tess."

"You didn't have any choice." Christine had fished in her purse for the house keys as they walked up the front porch steps. "She just burst into the store."

"Looking mad," Jeremy had sighed. "Could we have pizza for dinner? I've been thinking about pizza all day."

"Then pizza it is," Christine had said. "Only let's get delivery. I really don't feel like going out to a noisy pizza place tonight."

An hour later a huge pizza sat on the coffee table. They shared slices while watching television, Christine seated on the couch, Jeremy on the floor with Rhiannon beside him, waiting for bits of pepperoni, which she took gracefully between her sharp little teeth. The television blared out a horror movie Christine was definitely not in the mood for, but that had managed to entrance Jeremy, who'd insisted it be played on the VCR.

"Are you sure you wouldn't rather see a comedy?" she asked as someone crept through dark halls wielding an ax.

"Nope. You're supposed to watch scary movies when you eat pizza!"

"And where did you hear that rule?"

"From Danny Torrance. When he lived next door to Ames, we used to watch scary movies in his basement when he ordered a pizza. He said scary movies and pizza were a sacred ritual."

"I had no idea Danny was so wise," Christine said dryly. "How old was he when he made up this sacred ritual?"

"He didn't make it up, Christy. It's a true thing."

"Oh. Forgive me my lack of education." She finished her second slice of pizza and drained her soft drink. Jeremy's glass was empty, too. "Ready for more Coke?"

"Yeah, please. Only this time can I have Cherry Coke? It's my favorite."

"Cherry Coke and pizza. Jeremy, you're a true gourmet."

"Okay, whatever that means."

Christine carried both glasses into the kitchen. She got out the ice trays and put four cubes in each glass, then reached for a regular Coke for herself, a Cherry Coke for Jeremy. She was just filling his glass when he let out something between a shout and a scream.

Christine nearly dropped the Coke can. She righted it on the counter, then ran into the living room. Jeremy sat rigid on the floor staring at the television, a look of stark terror on his face. "My dream," he said in a chilling, almost disembodied voice. "My dream, my dream, my dream, my dream, my—"

Christine rushed to his side and took his face in her hands. "Jeremy, stop it!"

"My dream, my dream, my—"

She smacked his cheek. She cringed; he blinked; then his blue eyes finally focused on her. "Ouch."

"I'm sorry," she said, still holding his face, but with gentle hands. "What is it, Jeremy? What frightened you?"

He looked into her eyes, then at Rhiannon, who stood a foot away from him, back raised in alarm, then at the television. Jeremy pointed. "The movie! It's my dream, Christy. My dream about being thrown in the water and not being able to see or breathe!"

He picked up the remote control and hit REWIND. In a moment, he replayed the scene that had frightened him. A man carried the limp body of a young woman with long, dark hair to the bank of a river. He laid down the body, which bore a bloody gash at the temple, on a carpet and began to slowly, methodically roll her over and over until she was completely encased in the heavy fabric. "Goodbye, Juliet," he said softly, strange eyes burning in his blood-streaked face. "May you rest in peace." And then he shoved her into the river.

The camera followed the roll of carpet down, down, down into the water. It invaded the carpet for a closer look at the body of Juliet. Then her dark eyes snapped open. She fought to raise arms trapped in their tight wrappings. She opened her mouth. Tiny, pitiful sounds emerged, but she was helpless, sinking to the bottom of the river, bound and doomed like a living mummy.

"She was alive!" Jeremy cried. "He threw her in the water and she was alive!"

"Jeremy, it's only a movie," Christine soothed as he buried his head in her shoulder, sobbing. "I told you we shouldn't have watched this. It's scary. But you usually don't get *this* upset over a scary movie."

"That's because I saw this movie before," Jeremy sniffled. "I forgot until now. I saw it the night I was at Danny's party—the night Dara went away." He pulled back and looked at her earnestly. "Just like the girl in the movie, Christy. That's what happened to Dara! I *know* it!"

It took Jeremy almost two hours to completely calm down after the movie. When at last he got his nerves under control, with much comforting and reassuring from Christine, he seemed to deflate like a punctured balloon. "Christy, I'm awful sleepy," he announced at nine o'clock. "I know it's way before my bedtime, but I think I gotta say goodnight."

"You need a good night's sleep," Christine told him. "Take Rhiannon down and let her cuddle you. She always makes you feel better. And in the morning, you'll be a new man."

"Who'll I be?" he asked, in an encouraging attempt at a joke.

"Zorro. I'll make you a cape tonight."

"I'll need a sword, too," he said as Christine kissed his cheek. "And a mask."

"I'll get right on it. You and Rhi sleep tight."

When he'd gone to his room, Christine sat down on the couch, feeling worn out from tension and fright. She'd never seen Jeremy react so violently to a movie or television show. But this movie had special meaning for him. He'd seen it the night Dara disappeared. And he'd known she was going to Crescent Creek. "That's why he was so sure she vanished from there," she said aloud. "That's why he's had all the dreams about her being trapped in the water. He blended the movie with her disappearance."

At least that was one mystery solved, she thought. And for her, it was an important solution. For days she'd worried about Jeremy's dream, his certainty that Dara had lain trapped underwater, especially after Dara's body wrapped in plastic had surfaced. Jeremy hadn't *known* she was in the water. He'd only *imagined* she was because of the confluence of the movie and Dara's disappearance. For Christine the answer made perfect sense. But what about for other people, people like Sheriff Teague? No, it wasn't enough. Her brother's innocence still had not been proved.

She wasn't certain how long she'd sat on the couch thinking before she remembered she hadn't collected the day's mail. She flipped on the porch light, unchained the front door, and looked outside at her heaping mailbox. "Please tell me those aren't all bills," she said aloud.

Christine unloaded the box and carried everything inside to sort. This week's *People* magazine. A catalog from a clothing company. An Avon circular. Four pieces of mail marked: "Occupant." The electric bill. The cable bill. A credit card bill. The phone bill. And a card in a pink envelope. Her fingers seemed to tingle when they touched that envelope, and instinctively she knew it was not as harmless as her other mail.

She sat down on the couch again, staring warily at the pink envelope. Her name and address had been typed, but the envelope bore no return address. Slowly she opened it and withdrew a card. On the front of the card was a picture of a beautiful little girl with blond hair the shade of Christine's.

When she opened the card, three photos fell onto her lap and she gasped. One was a Polaroid shot of Dara. She wore jeans and the suede jacket she'd favored. Her long black hair blew out behind her, and she looked worried as she strode along a brick walkway Christine recognized from Winston University. Clearly Dara had not known someone was photographing her.

The second photo was of Patricia. She, too, wore jeans and a denim jacket, the one she'd had on when Christine found her body. Her brown hair was tied back with a bright yellow ribbon, and she smiled as she reached for the knob on the door at the side of the red barn.

Christine was the subject of the third Polaroid photo. The light was dim and she was kneeling in her backyard, picking up Rhiannon, who was crouching under a lawn chair. She knew from her outfit and Rhiannon's position that the photo had been taken on the day Christine returned from the hospital, the day after someone had attacked her in the gym.

With trembling hands, she finally opened the card. A piece of paper was taped over the card's original verse. On the paper had been typed two lines:

Pretty maids all in a row,
Who will be the next to go?

17

1

An autopsy revealed Patricia had died of a broken neck. No bruises or lacerations appeared on her body that were not consistent with the fall from the loft. Sheriff Teague would have been happy to conclude this was not a homicide, but according to Michael Winter, not even Teague could ignore the carefully strewn hay over the body. They had also found a portable CD player in the loft along with burning candles, although the family insisted Patricia Prince feared heights and would not have chosen the loft as a place of solitude. So the investigation into Patricia's death would continue, although her funeral was being held less than seventy-two hours after Christine had found her.

The day was beautiful. How sad, Christine thought as she and Jeremy drove to the church. Patricia didn't live to see the terrible gray days and the cold rain end. She didn't get to see the sun hanging lemon yellow in the sky again, warming the air, drying the saturated ground, coaxing the spring flowers to bud in glorious color. She'd missed it all.

Christine had told Jeremy that perhaps it was better if he didn't show Ames the Dara Pin on this day. "He'll already be sad enough about Patricia," she said. "Reminding him of Dara might be too much. Let's wait awhile. In fact, let's just steer clear of him today."

"Steer clear of him?" Jeremy had repeated, looking incredibly handsome in a charcoal gray suit. "Doesn't he need us today?"

"Maybe he needs Wilma more. We might just upset him."

"I don't understand."

No, he wouldn't understand, Christine thought. She still hadn't said anything about being fired or Ames's antagonism toward her, which she feared might show itself in hostility toward Jeremy as well. Jeremy would be baffled and hurt, and the only way she could think of to avoid it was to keep him away from Ames.

"Will you just accept what I say on this one day without my going into a big explanation?" Christine had asked. "Just this once?"

Jeremy had shaken his head. "I don't get why you want me not to talk to Ames, but I'll do what you say. I'll steer clear. I won't go up and hug him. But I can just say hello, can't I?"

"Sure. But he'll have his mind on other things. Don't be upset if he doesn't say anything back."

When they reached the church, which Patricia had formally been a member of, but rarely attended, Christine was amazed by the number of cars lining either side of the street. Patricia had not been liked in Winston. Ames, however, was highly respected. And Wilma had a hundred friends, all of whom knew how close her family was to Ames. Probably only a handful of people had actually come here for Patricia's sake, if that many. Christine wondered if Patricia would have cared.

The interior of the church was somber, almost tomblike. Christine had never liked it and knew Patricia had only joined because some of whom she considered Winston's "best" families belonged. Christine's impulse was to slide unobtrusively into a pew at the back of the church, but she knew that action would be noted and commented on at length when the funeral ended. After all, she and Jeremy had been Ames's wards. They were almost family. They had to sit near the front, where she saw Ames already seated stiff and tall, Wilma beside him. She and Jeremy slid into a pew behind them. Wilma turned and smiled. Ames caught Jeremy's eye and had the good grace to nod at him. Christine he ignored completely.

To Christine, the minister seemed to drone for hours. She attributed her feeling to nerves until she saw Wilma squirming uncomfortably. He *must* be droning if she's restless, Christine thought. Maybe he was carried away by the packed church and couldn't tear himself away from the podium. Next he'd tell a couple of jokes, then burst into a rendition of "Feelings" or some other ballad . . .

Stop thinking like someone having a nervous breakdown, she told herself sternly. She had to get through this excruciating situation although she felt giddy from apprehension and lack of sleep since the arrival of the card and the photographs, which she'd dutifully reported to Michael. But no matter how agitated she felt, she had to keep control of herself because she had to look out for Jeremy. She didn't want him crossing Ames's path. And surely this minister who didn't even know Patricia couldn't think of much more to say about her.

Suddenly everyone was rising and a relieved murmur surged behind her. The service was finally over. Ames turned and headed up the aisle, not looking at her and Jeremy. Wilma followed with a bracing smile for both of them. Behind Wilma was her husband—a small, quiet man who looked like he'd been weathered like an old piece of leather. Then came Streak, perspiring and tight-faced. Other members of the Archer family followed. Patricia's mother had claimed she was too ill to attend the funeral, which Christine had learned from Wilma. Wilma didn't believe the woman. "She didn't even sound upset when I talked to her right after Ames did," she'd said huffily. "I thought maybe I could talk some sense into her. Patricia was her only living child. But no. Cold as ice, that woman. Maybe she's the reason Patricia was so hard inside."

Christine and Jeremy followed the Archers out of the church and Christine rushed Jeremy to her newly repaired and returned Dodge Neon, not allowing him time to go near Ames. "You're acting weird, Christy," Jeremy complained. "I wish you'd tell me what's wrong."

"I will. Later. Just follow my lead."

"I don't know what you mean."

"Stay right by my side. Don't try to force yourself on Ames."

Jeremy sighed loudly. "You already told me not to talk to him because he's too upset. I don't know why talking to me would make him more upset. I still think you're just being weird."

"Okay, I'm weird. But I'm your big sister, so do what I tell you."

The Prince family plots lay in a cemetery only a mile from the church. After they'd parked the car and walked down a grassy slope to the spot, Christine was surprised to see that the hole for Patricia's coffin had been dug an insulting two plots away from the one she knew Ames had reserved for himself right beside Eve's. People would talk about this affront that equaled a slap in the face to Patricia, just like the lack of a visitation the night before the funeral and skipping a reception at the Prince home after the service. People would want to know why Ames had decided to demean his second wife at the time of her death. Christine was certain Wilma had tried to bully him into maintaining a respectful ceremony. Clearly, she had failed.

Christine saw with dread that the garrulous minister had followed them to the cemetery. She hoped he'd keep the graveside service short, although he looked alarmingly energetic. The murmur she'd heard in the church rose again as people gathered, almost tiptoeing in their desire not to tread on any graves. Christine wondered if a person could really feel someone walking on his grave. She doubted it. She wanted to believe the dead moved on to a different plane where they didn't feel the sharp edges of this world, especially when she thought of her parents.

The minister started out with gusto, and Christine felt a stab of annoyance that almost emerged as a groan. She diverted herself by looking around. Directly across from her stood Tess and Reynaldo. Neither had any love for Patricia, but Rey was Ames's employee and therefore expected to attend. He looked distant, as if mentally he'd gone someplace else. Tess clung possessively to his arm. She'd done away with the brassy streaks in her hair, returning it to a soft, flattering brown. Her navy blue dress complimented her figure, and her makeup was skillfully applied to bring out the contours of her face. Except for a tiredness around the eyes, she looked prettier than she had for months. But she still doesn't have Rey's attention, Christine thought sadly. Had she ever really possessed his attention?

Ginger stood near Rey and Tess. When she saw Christine looking at her, she started to wave, then caught herself. Christine gave her a brief smile and shifted her gaze to discourage further inappropriate gestures. Streak stood between Ames and Wilma. Christine could only see his back, but that was enough to reveal a perspiring neck. His silver hair was dampened by the sweat, and small tremors rippled beneath the shoulders of his suit jacket. What an ordeal this must be for him, Christine thought. She hoped Ames appreciated Streak's effort.

Just a couple of feet away from her stood Sloane Caldwell. He was impeccably dressed, as always, and looked tall and solid, although she noticed slight pockets under his hazel eyes, as if he were tired. He was extremely good-looking in a rough-hewn way, but she realized with a start that she far preferred the slender, high-planed face of Michael Winter. She'd once believed Sloane to be the handsomest man she knew. And they'd been so close. Now it seemed impossible that she and Sloane had ever been loving, shared secrets, planned a wedding and a future. It seemed as if he'd always just been her very good friend.

Beside Sloane stood a striking woman with auburn hair Christine recognized as the newest lawyer in Ames's firm, Monique Lawson. She wondered how serious Sloane was about Monique. Christine really had nothing to go on, but something about Monique struck her as grasping. She wouldn't be surprised if Sloane's main attraction for Monique was his blue-blood background, the family that had owned a magnificent house on the River Road outside of New Orleans, the teenage years spent in expensive prep schools, the friendships with people like John Kennedy, Jr., the Harvard education. But I'm doing a disservice to Sloane, Christine thought. He had much more to offer than an impressive background.

She felt warm breath in her ear as Jeremy whispered loudly, "Is that minister guy *ever* gonna stop talking?"

Christine dipped her head to hide a smile. Jeremy had merely whispered what everyone else was probably thinking, but she had to stop him before he continued in an even louder tone.

"He'll be done in a minute," she whispered back. "We have to stand still and be *quiet* or Ames will be mad."

Another gusty sigh from Jeremy. Sloane saw the exchange and winked at her. She winked back and looked away.

Her gaze met Bethany's. She looked beautiful in a hunter-green suit. She'd pulled her chestnut hair into a French twist, and Christine caught the glitter of small diamond-cut gold hoop earrings. Travis had bought them for her at Prince Jewelry last Christmas. Bethany was one of the few people present who had come for Patricia, Christine thought. Bethany had been intimidated by Patricia, but she'd also grudgingly liked her. At least she hadn't *disliked* Patricia or she wouldn't have helped her restore Eve's garden. Or rather, transform Eve's garden into Patricia's garden, which Patricia would never see in bloom.

Beside Bethany, Travis looked stiff and a bit washed-out. She'd first seen Travis Burke seven years ago when she'd taken Biology 101 at Winston University. She'd dreaded the class, having little interest in biology—especially the lab, where she knew they had to dissect a frog and a sheep's eye—but Travis's enthusiasm for the subject, his good looks, and his general charisma had won her over. She'd found herself studying not only because she wanted an A in the class, but also because she wanted this professor to think well of her abilities.

Christine had not developed a crush on Travis Burke, but she knew many of his female students did. He didn't have the classic looks of Rey Cimino, but he had devil-may-care eyes and a rakish air that seemed irresistible to many girls. Girls like Dara. Dara, too, had groused about taking biology, but a couple of weeks into the course she'd asked Christine what she knew about Travis. By then Christine had become friends with Bethany, and she'd told Dara he was smart, handsome, and *married*. Dara had never mentioned him again, except to once say he was a charmer.

Charmer.

The word seemed to boom in Christine's head as a scene from the past rose like something dragging itself up from a deep pool of dark water. She remembered being a senior in college and rushing to an appointment with a professor. As she'd dashed by the warren of offices at the top of Hadley Hall, she ran into Dara coming out of Travis Burke's office. She'd looked flushed and beautiful. She'd placed her hand on Christine's arm with uncharacteristic friendliness and said, "I've been in to see the Snake Charmer." "Snake Charmer?" Christine had echoed. "That's what some of my friends and I call him," Dara had said. "He has all those awful snakes, but he doesn't get bitten because he uses the same charm on them as he does on his women. God, he's hot! The Snake Charmer."

Christine's mind came back to the cemetery with a jolt. That day she'd been worried about her appointment with the professor, fearing she was going to have to argue her way out of her first B, and she'd brushed Dara aside, never again thinking about the encounter. After all, Dara was man-crazy and indiscriminate in her tastes. She had crushes on a dozen men a year. What she'd said about Bethany's husband wasn't particularly important.

Or it hadn't seemed important at the time. But Christine now realized Dara hadn't just looked girlishly excited, she'd looked downright aroused, as if she'd just had a sexual encounter. And she'd called Travis "Snake Charmer." Could he be the S.C. she'd written about in her diary? Christine desperately tried to remember exactly when she'd seen Dara coming out of his office. A wreath. There had been a small holiday wreath placed on his door by Bethany. She'd seen Dara coming out of the office right before Christmas break. Three months later, she'd disappeared.

2

Michael knew Christine had not seen him at Patricia's funeral. He'd been purposely unobtrusive, doing what was probably a complete waste of time—studying people attending the funeral to see if anyone looked suspicious. *Suspicious* had never been fully defined for him, but many behavioral psychologists believe murderers like to come to their victims' funerals to see the havoc they've wreaked.

So, he'd sat through the endless church service, stood through the endless graveside service, and noticed only two people who looked extremely "suspicious." They were Streak Archer and, unfortunately, Christine. Streak Archer was a conundrum to him. Christine was not. She looked furtive and jumpy because she was miserably uncomfortable not being able to anticipate how Ames Prince would act toward her and Jeremy. Michael *knew* that was her problem, although Sheriff Teague had told him to watch her in particular. "And that half-witted brother of hers," Teague had added. "He was supposed to be at a party at the Torrance house, but it would have been easy for him to slip out for a while. You'll never convince me he didn't kill Dara Prince. I've never trusted his kind, and that sister of his will do anything to protect him. Stop looking at me that way. I don't want to hear any of your half-baked theories about how that big, dumb hulk wouldn't hurt anyone. You don't know a damned thing about him."

Jeremy's half-witted, I'm half-baked, Michael thought in amusement as he strained his peripheral vision to study the crowd without appearing to be looking at anyone. Teague's got us all analyzed as "halves." He probably considers himself the only person around who's whole. If that's true, Winston citizens are one messed-up bunch of people.

Christine caught sight of him just as Jeremy leaned down to whisper something to her. She tried to hide a smile, and Michael saw people around them doing the same. Jeremy had apparently whispered loudly but entertainingly. Then Christine had looked like she'd drifted off into space for a moment before coming back to earth with a bang. Her shoulders straightened, her eyes opened wide, and her lips parted. Michael watched as her intense gaze shot to the people standing directly across from her. He did his "looking without looking" routine and decided she was staring at either Bethany or Travis Burke with what could only be shock.

Something just came to her, he thought. She'd remembered something. Then he told himself he was an idiot. What was he now? A mind reader? A half-baked psychic?

When the service mercifully ended, Michael saw Sloane Caldwell approach Christine and Jeremy. The deputy lingered, studying other funeral attendees, particularly Streak Archer, who looked like he was ready to pass out. His mother divided her attention between Streak and Ames. Bethany and Travis Burke were making their way toward Ames Prince. Other people headed for their cars. Michael intended to continue uninterrupted surveillance until everyone attending Patricia Prince's funeral left. His concentration dissolved, though, when Christine tapped him on the arm and said urgently, "I have to tell you something."

He glanced at Sloane Caldwell, who was talking to Jeremy but looking at Christine. "Has anything happened today?" Michael asked, gazing into her troubled eyes. "Did you get another phone call? Something in the mail?"

"No. Nothing has happened to me except that I've remembered something." Christine told him quickly about a memory of Dara walking out of Travis Burke's office and that Dara and her friends called him Snake Charmer. "S.C. in the diary," she explained unnecessarily, "it might not be Sloane Caldwell. It might be Travis Burke. If you'd seen the way Dara looked . . ." She shook her head. "I feel awful for telling you this, because Bethany is my friend, but I think Dara might have been involved with Travis, not Sloane."

She seemed extremely agitated about having perhaps misdirected his attention to Sloane Caldwell, Michael thought unhappily. Maybe she still had romantic feelings for the guy and wanted to protect him. Then he told himself he was being foolish and unprofessional, overlooking the importance of what she was telling him about Burke because he was worried about her feelings for Caldwell, which he shouldn't care about at all.

Except that he did.

"Have you ever heard anyone else call Travis Burke Snake Charmer?" he asked, dragging himself back to the subject.

"Snake Charmer!" Jeremy burst out behind him. "That's what Dara called Travis. He doesn't like me, but he sure liked Dara!"

Christine paled. "Jeremy, hush!" she hissed. "People will hear you."

"What did I say wrong?" Jeremy asked in confusion. "I only said what's true. Dara talked about Travis all the time and she called him Snake Charmer. I thought it was creepy that he keeps all those snakes, but she thought it was cool. She said he showed them to her—"

"I thought it was a really nice service," Michael interrupted loudly, but he was too late. Bethany Burke was already backing away, her skin pale, her eyes blazing at a crimson-faced Travis Burke.

3

An hour later Michael wondered exactly how angry Christine was with her brother right now. He could tell she hated ever getting irritated with Jeremy, but she wouldn't be human if she wasn't supremely pissed off at him for blasting out that Travis was Snake Charmer, which had drawn Bethany toward them. But Travis couldn't blame Christine or Jeremy for the questioning he was about to receive from Michael. That had been planned since last night.

He now called the Burke home and was glad when Travis answered. "I need to ask you some questions," he told the professor. "They aren't questions I think you want to answer at home. I'm willing to meet you someplace."

"Questions about what?" Travis had asked nervously.

"Questions about a CD player."

"A CD player? I don't understand."

"You will when we talk. And we *will* talk, so you might as well get it over with."

"All right. My wife went to see her father. I'm babysitting. I can't leave. You'll have to come here."

Michael hadn't realized how far out of town Travis Burke lived. When he pulled up at the house, he saw a concrete block building about half an acre away from the back of a nice but simple ranch-style home. That building must be where Burke keeps his snakes, Michael thought. He knew herpetology was a hobby growing in popularity, but it wasn't one he could fathom.

Travis opened the front door before Michael reached it. "I really don't know what this is all about," he began abruptly. "I don't understand why you want to question me."

"Let's go inside. You are going to let me in, aren't you, Mr. Burke?"

"Oh, sure. I didn't mean to seem like I was barricading the door." Travis seemed slightly breathless. "You want some coffee? I just made some."

"No thanks. I had a late lunch before I came. Let's just get down to business."

"Yes. Certainly. We'll sit in the living room. My wife will be back in an hour or so, though, and I think it would really disturb her to drive up and see a cop car parked out front. She's always so nervous about Jan. That's our little girl. She's four. Taking a nap, now. Bethany would have taken her to see Hugh—that's Bethany's father—but he has a bad cold. Beth worries constantly about Jan catching something. She's the most protected little girl in this city."

"Little kids need protection and constant attention," Michael said tersely. "I admire your wife's dedication."

"Well, so do I. Of course. I didn't mean to sound critical."

They had reached a medium-sized living room that was comfortably decorated. It didn't look like the formal living room many people reserved for company. The magazines and newspapers scattered around a big leather armchair indicated this room was actually used.

"Do you have kids, Deputy Winter?" Travis asked.

Michael tried to keep his face expressionless. "I did. A little girl. She . . . died."

"Oh. Damn. What a rotten break. I'm sorry."

"So was I." So much for stating the obvious, Michael thought but he could see Travis was too worried about what was coming at him to really notice anything Michael said about himself.

Travis made for the armchair as if it were a raft in the middle of the ocean. Michael sat down on a couch covered in a gay yellow-and-red country print. Beside him lay a coloring book and a lone green crayon. He picked them up and set them on a mahogany coffee table.

Travis glanced at the crayon and smiled. "Jan is in her green period. Everything she colors is green."

"Little girls are sweet," Michael said, bleakness in his voice. "I certainly miss mine." He cleared his throat. "I know you'd like for me to get out of here before your wife returns, Mr. Burke, so I'll get right to the point." Michael took out his notebook and looked at it a moment, although he really didn't need to. He wanted to see how nervous Travis Burke was going to get before the questions hit him. "You knew Patricia Prince, didn't you?"

"Patricia?" Travis seemed completely taken aback, as if Patricia were an unexpected topic. "Well, slightly. My wife and she are friends. Well, not really friends, but Bethany's been helping her with a garden. Beth's good friends with Christine Ireland and she introduced Beth to Patricia. I've really only been around her a few times. Patricia, that is."

Michael nodded. "You know that the circumstances of her death are under investigation."

"No. No, I didn't know that. She fell. That's what I heard. She just fell out of the barn loft."

"Fell or was pushed."

"*Pushed?* Nobody told me that. How do you know she was pushed?"

"I can't go into all the details. The police have to keep a few things secret." He smiled. Travis Burke tried to smile and failed. "You have a CD player, don't you, Mr. Burke? A boom box?" He glanced at his notebook again. "A portable RCA CD and radio with digital tuner, Model RCD-one-three-three?"

Burke's face went blank. Then wariness grew in his gaze. "Well, I *did* until a couple of weeks ago. It was stolen from my car."

"You didn't report it to the police?"

"I'd left the car unlocked, so I figured it was my fault. The car wasn't damaged and nothing else was taken, and frankly, I just didn't want to make a big deal over a CD player and have to fill out a lot of forms with the police. But how did you know about it?"

"Several years ago, the Winston police department offered to put identification strips on home furnishings, electronics, that kind of thing, so that items taken in burglaries could be tracked."

"Oh." Michael saw memory dawn in Burke's eyes. "I'd completely forgotten about the ID system. Bethany had it done."

"I see. Well, your boom box has turned up."

Travis seemed to relax. "So that's what this is all about? My boom box? Well, I'll be glad to have it back. I was planning on buying a new one this week." He stopped, the tension returning to his face. "But what does my CD player have to do with Patricia Prince?"

"It was found in the barn loft she fell from," Michael said mildly. "Would you know how it got there?"

Travis went so white Michael thought he was going to pass out. He swallowed and said loudly, "No! How should I . . ." He swallowed again. "You mean someone stole it from me and then hid it in the Princes' barn loft?"

"It wasn't hidden. When Christine Ireland discovered Patricia's body, music was playing on it. Later we found it set out in plain view and surrounded by candles. Lit candles."

Travis stared at him, opened his mouth, then closed it. He lifted his hands.

"Are you still saying you don't know how it got there, Mr. Burke?"

"Yes, that's what I'm saying. I have absolutely no idea how it got there. How should I?"

"According to one source, Patricia Prince had a lover. She used to meet him in the barn."

Travis leaned forward aggressively. "Who says it was me? It wasn't *me*! Who's this source?"

"I can't reveal that." Michael wondered how Travis would react if he told him the source was Jeremy Ireland. Michael could probably guess. Travis would relax, because he didn't believe anyone would take Jeremy seriously. Christine had told him she sensed Travis didn't like Jeremy, although he tried to hide it. "I just wondered if you knew anything about Mrs. Prince's affair, Mr. Burke."

"Positively not!" Travis stated.

"Because it was *your* boom box that was up in the barn loft. Playing music. Candles set around it."

"I told you that boom box was stolen."

"But you didn't report it. And nothing else was taken from you."

"That's right. The CD player was stolen. Nothing else. There wasn't anything else in the car to take."

"And you didn't want to bother making out a police report on just a boom box."

"That's right." Travis lifted his chin a bit. "Is that all you had to ask me, Deputy?"

"No. Would you mind telling me where you were around one o'clock on the afternoon of Patricia Prince's death?"

"I do mind, but I'll tell you anyway. I was at the university. In my office, but I'm sure dozens of people saw me. At least, a few."

"Good."

"Yes. A lot of people can give me an alibi."

"That's fine, sir."

"Now listen, Deputy, I really can't help you with this Patricia Prince thing. And now that I know where my boom box was found, I don't care about having it back. I don't *want* it back!"

"I wasn't offering it. For now it's evidence. We'll see what Sheriff Teague says later about giving it back to you."

"I just told you I don't want the damned thing back!"

"All right, Mr. Burke," Michael said calmly.

"Is that all? Are we done?"

"Let me see." Michael looked back at his notebook. "Oh, there's one more thing. Did Dara Prince call you Snake Charmer?"

This was it. This was what Travis had been expecting to be asked right off the bat. But now he was unprepared and he sat blinking as he mentally shifted gears. "Dara Prince? I hardly knew her."

"Or Patricia Prince."

"That's right. Two women in town whom I had contact with but hardly knew. Is that a crime?"

"No. I didn't accuse you of a crime. I just wondered about this nickname. Snake Charmer."

"I've heard that some students called me that for a while. I think the name died down."

"So it's not a widely known nickname."

"I said some *students* called me that. Do you know how many students are at Winston University?"

"Around thirteen thousand."

"Yes. There you go."

"But you said use of the nickname had died down."

"To the best of my knowledge. Probably some students still call me that. A lot of them could be calling me that." Travis paused. "What does this have to do with anything?"

"Dara Prince was involved with someone she called Snake Charmer."

All Michael really knew was that Dara had been involved with someone she'd identified as S.C. But Christine thought in hindsight that Dara had at least had a crush on Travis and had gone by his office not acting like the typical student. And Michael was certain enough of Christine's instincts to not worry about stretching the truth to see Travis's reaction.

And the reaction was worth it. Travis first looked as if he were going to splutter out an indignantly defensive denial that would make him sound guilty. Then he got hold of himself. A caginess appeared in his gaze. "I've never heard that in the three years since she disappeared. Who suddenly came up with this so-called information?"

"I'm not at liberty to say."

"Again. You're certainly at liberty to make accusations."

"I haven't made any accusations. I've just asked questions."

"Your accusations are implied."

Michael startled Travis by laughing. "Well, now, sir, you're going to lose me if you get into all this *implied* and *inferred* business. That's for the lawyers. I'm just here to ask a few questions like a simple cop should."

Travis's eyes narrowed. "Simple cop, my ass. You know a lot, but you're not telling anything."

"A lot about what, sir?"

"A lot about what people are saying about me!"

"I think you have a case of paranoia going there, Mr. Burke."

"Do I need a lawyer? Because Sloane Caldwell is a good friend of mine. I can get him here like that!" Travis snapped his fingers.

Michael smiled. "You can call him if you like, but I have only one more question. By the time he gets here, your wife might be back."

"Okay. One more question. *One.*"

"Were you romantically involved with Patricia Prince or Dara Prince?"

"No! For God's sake! And I resent—"

"All right, sir. You can sit here and resent all you want when I'm gone. I just had to get a few answers." Michael stood. "Sorry to bother you," he said pleasantly, as if this had been a friendly visit. "You take good care of that little girl. Did you say her name was Jan?"

"What? Yes. Jan. But—"

"I'll bet she's a cutie. Well, good day to you, Mr. Burke."

As Michael walked to the police cruiser, he glanced back at Travis Burke. He stood in the doorway staring at Michael. He looked dreadful, Michael noted, almost sick.

4

The minutes following Jeremy's outburst at the funeral had been agony for Travis. Bethany had stalked ahead of him to the car. He'd asked if she wanted to drive and she'd refused—an extremely bad sign. After they'd driven about a mile, Travis had lowered the music volume and said, "Bethany, let's talk about this." She'd responded by leaning forward and turning up the volume until the New Age sound of John Tesh, whom Travis detested, boomed through the car. They'd driven the rest of the way home with the car windows nearly rattling from the sound waves and Bethany's seething.

He'd made another attempt at détente after they'd paid the babysitter and sent her on her way. "Beth, if you would let me explain—"

"I think you've said enough for one day," Bethany had snapped after settling Jan down on her canopied bed with a cup of apple juice and her coloring book and second-favorite green crayon, and then stomping off to their bedroom.

"What are you talking about? *I* haven't said anything." Travis had pursued her to the bedroom. "Jeremy Ireland has done all the talking."

"And he spoke volumes."

"Oh yes, that impeccable source Jeremy Ireland," Travis had said witheringly.

"He said Dara called you Snake Charmer."

"So? A lot of students did. Still do."

"He said you liked Dara a *lot*."

"Well, Jeremy would certainly be an expert on my feelings. We're such good friends. Best buddies." Travis had rolled his eyes in disdain. "Beth, he's retarded! What does he know?"

"He's *mentally challenged*, he is not a vegetable. I think he reads people quite well, not to mention that Dara probably told him things."

"Dara Prince—a paragon of truth, an astute analyzer of other people's emotions—talking things over with the highly intelligent and perceptive Jeremy Ireland. That would be a conversation to intimidate even the gods!" Bethany had glared at him. "Look, Beth, even if Dara thought I particularly liked her, it wasn't true. You know what an inflated ego she had."

"No. *I* didn't know her that well."

"Christine told us about her. She said Dara thought half the men in town were smitten with her."

"Nice try, but it won't work. I sensed something when Dara was your student, Travis," Bethany had said as she began removing the suit she'd worn to the funeral. "And after that body washed up from the river, you said her name in your sleep."

"Oh. I said *Dara*. I didn't slur like most people who talk in their sleep. I distinctly said *Dara*."

"Yes, you did."

"I don't believe it."

"I wish I'd had a tape recorder running."

"I'm surprised you didn't, Beth. You have *always* been suspicious of me and female students."

"Maybe I've had reason to be." Bethany had hung up her suit with the careful precision that indicated suppressed fury. "I remember how you pursued me when I was your student."

"I wasn't married to someone else, dammit!"

"Keep your voice down. Jan is in the next room."

"You're talking as loud as I am."

"I am not. And I don't wish to discuss this any longer. I'm going to my father's."

"You're moving out?"

Bethany had whirled on him. "Oh, you'd like that, wouldn't you? You'd be free to play your little games. Who is it this time? Another nubile nineteen-year-old?"

"I'm not involved with anyone, Beth, and you know it. Don't go to your father's now."

Then, to make matters worse, the doorbell had rung. Bethany had thrown him a damning look, as if she expected it to be Dara herself come calling. "Who could that be?" Travis had asked. "Did you invite anyone to come after the funeral?"

"Not specifically, although I mentioned to a couple of people I thought it was awful that Ames Prince wasn't holding some kind of after-service gathering. Maybe it's Chris and Jeremy."

"Oh, wonderful," Travis had said. "Just who I want to see—Jeremy."

But to his surprise and relief, it was Tess and Reynaldo Cimino. "I hope we're not intruding," Tess had said. "I just didn't want to go home."

Bethany had looked nonplussed for a moment, then quickly recovered. "We're happy you dropped by, aren't we, Travis?"

Travis had nodded, although he wasn't at all happy about the visit. Neither was Rey, by the looks of him. Travis had noted that Cimino's locally famous drop-dead looks were dimmed by a slightly gray skin tone and eyes reddened by sleep deprivation. Even his small smile at Bethany was tight and forced.

"I'm in the mood for Baileys Irish Cream," Bethany had said lightly. Her guests would never know that fifteen minutes earlier she'd been in a rage. "Can I interest anyone else in joining me?"

Everyone else was interested. While Tess and Bethany fixed drinks, Travis and Rey had sat down in the living room. They weren't good friends, but they were friendly, and the Ciminos came to dinner a couple of times a year and to Bethany's annual Christmas party. Rey had even taken a tour of the snake house with Travis and seemed extremely interested in them, not afraid or repulsed like a lot of people. Travis had begun to like the guy then, although he was a bit envious of Cimino's looks. But Travis had felt distinctly uncomfortable today with Rey as they sat waiting for their drinks. He hoped Rey hadn't heard Jeremy blast out that Dara had called Travis Snake Charmer and that Travis had especially liked Dara. After all, Cimino had been in love with Dara at the time she'd gone missing. But Rey's hard, dark stare and monosyllabic replies to conversation attempts had let Travis know Rey had heard Jeremy loud and clear.

"That was the most dismal funeral service I've ever attended," Travis had begun when everyone settled in the living room. "No reception afterward. Patricia's plot placed so far away from Ames's. Strange."

"I think Ames knew Patricia was having an affair," Bethany had pronounced.

"Affair?" Tess had echoed. "I never heard about an affair."

Her face had stiffened and her voice had turned high and insincere. Travis had given her a searching look and suddenly realized she *had* known Patricia Prince was having an affair and she'd known it for a while, not just since Patricia's death. But why was she acting so odd? Did she think the affair had been with Rey?

Conversation had limped along. Travis had desperately wished the Ciminos would leave after one drink. Rey looked like he would have gladly picked up the alabaster ashtray on the coffee table and smashed his wife on the head with it when she'd accepted Bethany's offer of a second drink. Afterward there was more meandering, stilted conversation. Everyone had nearly fallen on Jan when she entered the room carrying a teddy bear and her coloring book. "We have comp'ny," she'd said in her adult little voice. "No one told me we have comp'ny. How do you do?"

Gushing. Compliments. Baby talk from Bethany and Tess. A lackluster, "What are you going to be when you grow up?" from Rey.

"A artist," Jan had answered firmly. "I'm gonna send my pictures to New York City to hang in a gowery where people can pay money to go in and see them and buy them. I'm gonna make tons of money and buy lots of puppies and kittens. And diamond earrings."

Everyone had laughed at the adorable child, who looked confused. She didn't see anything amusing about what she'd just said. Then, to Travis's huge relief, she'd yawned loudly.

"We should go. Jan needs a nap," Tess had said.

"I'll just use the bathroom first, if you don't mind," Rey had said. "Be back in a minute."

A minute had turned into ten. "I don't know what's taking him so long," Tess had fretted after the first six minutes. "He hasn't been well lately. Maybe I should check on him."

The poor guy wasn't even allowed to go to the bathroom in private, Travis thought, although he was nearly fidgeting with anxiety. He wanted these two out of his house. Something was wrong. There was an agenda for this visit, but he couldn't figure out what it was. Did it have anything to do with Jeremy's announcement at the cemetery? God, he hoped not.

But when Rey came back and his gaze met Travis's, Travis felt jolted by its cold hatred. Travis flushed. Now he was certain that Cimino knew he'd been having an affair with Dara at the time of her disappearance. But he couldn't know she was pregnant. Or did he?

Travis broke into a swift, drenching sweat. He shifted his gaze to Tess. She was watching him and Rey closely. Then her mouth had stretched in a false smile. "Well, now it's definitely time for us to go." She stood up and looked at the child. "Jan, you're a doll. Beth, do drop in the store next week. I have a new shipment of books coming in I think you'll like. Rey, come on. Do you need for me to drive?"

"You had more to drink than I did," Rey had said grimly. "I'll do the driving."

As soon as the Ciminos cleared the driveway, Bethany had picked up her purse. "I'm going to Dad's now. He'll be wondering where I am."

Travis wanted to be alone, but he also knew Bethany's visit to Hugh could make the home situation even worse. "Bethany, I really wish you'd stay here," he said. "You're already mad at me and he gets you even more fired up."

"Don't blame Dad for our problems. He's never been anything but supportive of our marriage."

"I hope that was a joke," Travis had said dryly.

She'd given him the slitty-eyed look that meant she was mad as hell. "I'm just going for an afternoon visit. I promised him." She'd searched her purse for her car keys. "I can't take Jan. Dad has an awful cold. Maybe the flu. You'll have to stay here and babysit." She'd looked at him challengingly. "That won't cramp your style, will it?"

"Oh, for God's sake," Travis had muttered. "Run to Daddy if you must. Pour out your troubles, your paranoid suspicions, your stories of imagined infidelities. Get the old guy all whipped up. Make him dislike me even more. Maybe that will make you feel justified and happy and you'll act a little more bearable when you get home."

"That is an offensive thing to say, Travis Burke. And while I'm gone, don't you *dare* take Jan to that snake house."

"I have never taken Jan to the snake house and I won't until she's older."

"Not then, either. Not ever."

"Beth, she's my child, too."

"Then start acting like a father."

"When have I not acted like a father? Just tell me when I haven't acted like a good and devoted father."

Bethany had ignored him and headed straight for Jan, who was now sitting on the couch coloring assiduously. "Mommy's gonna go visit Grandpa, who's too sick to see his baby-waby," she'd babbled in baby talk, which set Travis's teeth on edge. "Mommy will be back quick as a bunny. Until then, you do everything Daddy-Waddy tells you to, except not going to that nasty old snake house where you might get eaten all up by the nasty old snakes with their horrible, dripping fangs." After painting this ghastly picture, she'd kissed Jan's forehead. "Bye-bye, candy cane."

"Candy cane," Travis had mumbled. "Sounds like the name of a stripper."

Bethany had glared. "You would know more about the names of strippers than I."

"Oh, for—"

"Take care of her, Travis."

"I *will*. God, Beth, she's my—"

The front door had slammed behind Bethany. He'd looked at Jan, who'd shrugged like a sophisticated adult, then returned to her coloring.

He'd fixed a pot of coffee, then sat in his armchair watching Jan happily color a clown entirely green. A Martian clown, he'd thought. He hated clowns. They should all look like Jan's.

The phone had rung and he'd had the absurd hope it was Bethany calling from her father's to apologize. But it had been Deputy Michael Winter, wanting to talk to him. He'd said he had questions that perhaps Travis wouldn't want to answer at home, which had sent a shiver of dread down Travis's spine. Winter must know something, he'd thought. But how? Travis had always been so careful.

He'd gone back to the living room to find Jan lying against a pile of pillows on the couch. The speed with which little kids could fall asleep always amazed him. He'd carried her gently into her bed, covered her, closed the door, and paced the living room until he saw the police cruiser pull up out front.

After Winter left, Travis threw himself down on the couch, feeling like someone had let the air out of him. Winter's questions had thrown him. He'd expected something bad, but not this bad. Damn that identification label he'd forgotten about on his boom box. If it weren't for that . . .

No, it wasn't the boom box alone, he'd thought, suddenly pumping with adrenaline. There was all that stuff about "Snake Charmer." Damn Dara Prince for starting that nickname. And who had told Winter about it? Christine Ireland, that's who. He remembered Sloane Caldwell going up to her and Jeremy after the funeral and her ignoring Caldwell to go tearing over to Deputy Winter and begin whispering urgently. Sloane had looked after her, clearly offended at being dismissed. Then that idiot Jeremy had blared out that Dara had called Travis Snake Charmer. He'd said that Travis didn't like him, but he'd *sure* liked Dara.

That guy should have been institutionalized, Travis had

thought savagely as he poured a shot of bourbon in a drinking glass and gulped it down. He didn't care how unfashionable his ideas about treatment of the intellectually "inferior" were. He couldn't stand them. They made his flesh crawl. Especially one like Jeremy, who looked so normal, even downright handsome, but was so lacking, so stunted intellectually and emotionally, and no doubt also a sexual pervert. He'd decided in that moment of fury at Jeremy that he would never be allowed to see Jan again. No matter what Bethany said, no matter what she did. Jeremy Ireland could never come *near* his little girl without serious consequences.

He poured another shot of bourbon, tramping back to his study room, breathing hard as he thought about damned Jeremy. And *Christine*. How much had Dara spewed out to her about him? How much had Christine been carrying around with her for three years and never said a word? Certainly it couldn't have been much.

Or could it? He'd never disliked Christine, but he'd never trusted her, either. For one thing, she'd always seemed immune to his sex appeal, and that offended him. For another, she was too devoted to her brother. It was unnatural. Christine and Jeremy. What a pair. And they'd been the ones to find Dara's diary.

When Travis learned the diary had been found, he'd been terrified. He'd wondered what was in it. He would have stopped Christine from giving it to the police any way he could. But he couldn't. Now, as he downed his second shot of bourbon after Winter's visit, he wondered dismally what was coming at him because of that cursed diary. Was his whole world going to crash around him? Would he lose Jan and Bethany and all the security being married to a rich woman had brought him the last few years?

He sat gloomily behind his desk. He had work to do. Papers to grade. But he sure as hell couldn't concentrate on grading now. He couldn't read; he couldn't watch television. His entire day was ruined. There was only one thing that could divert him. His snakes.

He started to open the drawer where he kept the keys to the snake house, then noticed that it wasn't closed tight. Jan, he thought in alarm. Jan had been messing around in here and had gotten the keys . . .

But both sets of keys rested in their usual places. He just hadn't completely shut the drawer the last time he used the keys, he thought. He'd have to be more careful. Really, since Jan was getting older, he should keep this drawer locked, so she couldn't even touch the keys.

As depressed as he'd ever been in his life, Travis grabbed a set of keys, looked in on a peacefully sleeping Jan, then walked back to his snake house. He opened the padlock, the deadbolt, and the regular door lock and stepped into what he called the entrance room. Here he kept the insects and rodents he fed the snakes. He also kept medical supplies. Vaseline and alcohol for ticks. Insecticides for mites. Sulfa drugs for mouth rot. Ivermectin and praziquantel for internal parasites. Penicillin and tetracycline for respiratory ailments. After all, the creatures had only one working lung. No veterinarians in Winston would treat poisonous snakes, so Travis had learned to perform his own medical care, and he was a good diagnostician if he did say so himself.

Travis walked into the main room. He wasn't sure what made him stop in his tracks. He didn't see anything out of the ordinary at first, but something felt wrong. Very wrong. He stood still, listening. A whisper of sound came from somewhere to his right. He looked over. A cage door was open. The cage door of the diamondback rattlesnake.

Never in the twenty years he'd been handling snakes had Travis carelessly left a cage door open. His father, who had passed on his love of snakes to Travis, had also passed on his absolute vigilance about their handling and maintenance. And Travis had learned well. *Heedfulness* had seemed etched in his brain. He knew he had not left that cage door open.

No time to worry about the cage door right now, he told himself. The important thing was to get the rattler back in his cage. The fluorescent lights were strong in here and the snake was large. "Hey, Hugh!" he called the bad-tempered, highly venomous snake he'd named after his father-in-law. "How about a rattle to let me know where you are?" Nothing.

Travis's heart had picked up its pace. He looked around and froze. The triangular-headed death adder was not in its cage, either. What the hell was this? His gaze shot from cage to cage. No black tiger snake, no desert horned viper . . .

Maybe someone had gotten in here and stolen the snakes. If that was the case, he'd be furious. He might never get them back. But it would be better than—

Behind him he heard a hissing noise so loud it sounded like a car tire deflating. Travis actually let out a tiny shriek and jumped as he realized he was hearing the distinctive noise of the Gaboon viper, the species with the longest fangs of any venomous snake. Then pain seared his ankle. He looked down to see his tan-and-rust-colored pine snake sinking its fangs into his ankle.

He had to get out of here. He didn't have a second to lose with all these snakes on the loose. He shook off the pine snake and made for the entrance room, for the door. Already his leg felt as if fire traveled from the ankle to the knee, but he wasn't about to take time to stop the spread of the venom. Too many other poisonous snakes were on the loose.

He reached the door and flipped open the inner lock. The doorknob turned easily. Five seconds, he thought. Five seconds and I'll be safe.

But the door wouldn't open.

He turned the knob again. Nothing wrong there. He pushed on the door, but it didn't give. And then it hit him. Someone had clicked shut the outside padlock he'd left hanging loose. Jan? Jan never came near the snake house.

No. No, the padlock could not be shut. Travis lurched against the door again and again. No, his mind screamed. No! Dear God, *no*!

Finally he heard the rattle of the diamondback. He whirled away from the door and headed for a long metal table in the middle of the room where he administered medications to the snakes. If he could climb on top . . .

He went down with a crash and realized he'd stepped on his own shoelace. Of all the damned stupid—

Pain scorched up his right hand into the wrist. The black tiger snake had struck, its head rising from its big body and the neck it spread when alarmed. When he looked at it from eye level, it seemed gigantic. And it didn't just look deadly—it *was*.

Two bites. I can recover from two bites, Travis thought. He knew not to suck on the wounds, because oral flora could enter them, making things even worse by spreading the venom to his upper digestive tract. Local hospitals weren't experienced with treating bites from exotic snakes, but they could contact a poison control center. And he knew other things to do. He needed antibiotics and a tetanus shot. And he needed antivenin. But before the administration of antivenin, he needed an intravenous dosage of an antihistamine to limit an acute reaction to it. He had some of the medications he needed in a refrigerator, but he couldn't begin to adequately care for himself while trying to escape the snakes on the loose.

"Bethany!" he screamed in the hope that she hadn't stayed long at her father's. "Beth, help me!"

But even if she was home, could she hear him? And what about the padlock? She would have to get the second set of keys, because one set was in his pocket. Or she could break it. There were rocks outside. One good blow could smash open that padlock and he'd be free. Now he had to get to the table, partially out of harm's way—

"God!" he screamed. More pain. The death adder was at his thigh. It struck, drew back, and struck again. That leg was already blazing from the bite of the Gaboon viper. Travis made a weak effort to fling the snake off his leg. He didn't look to see whether or not he'd been successful. He dragged himself to the metal table and grabbed one of its legs. He looked up. The tabletop seemed to loom fifty feet above him. He'd never make it up there. Never.

His whole body burned with pain. And he was so weak. And dizzy. But his mind still functioned. With horror he thought of what was going on inside him right now. Different venom had different effects. Some would be causing small hemorrhages. Others were killing healthy tissue, while some were depressing cardiac function. And then there were the ones blocking nerve impulses. If he didn't get help, he would become paralyzed and his heart would stop.

Already Travis knew he'd sustained too many bites and too much time had passed for him to make a full recovery. Panic abruptly vanished, to be replaced by a deep melancholy. He would probably never smell fresh air again. He would never feel the silken touch of a woman as she made love to him. He would never again hug and kiss the love of his life, darling little Jan. Warm, helpless tears ran from the corners of his eyes.

"Help me," he moaned weakly as he lay on the floor, giving up his effort to climb onto the table. It was too late now. "Oh, God, please help me."

His cloudy gaze traveled up to light, the sunlight pouring in through one of the unbreakable Lexan windows. He wasn't sure if it was real or imagined, but there he saw the face of Bethany. She stared at him with her big brown eyes. "I'm sorry," Travis murmured with his last, labored breaths. "I'm sorry for everything."

18

1

According to the medical examiner's office, there was no doubt that snake venom had caused Travis Burke's death. No other signs of injury had been found on the hideously swollen corpse that had once been the handsome, charming professor. For a number of reasons, though, Michael Winter wasn't satisfied.

For one, Travis Burke had been handling snakes since he was a teenager, almost twenty years. Everyone, even his wife, Bethany, who had hated his hobby, told Winter that Travis took every precaution he could. For another, Travis had just come under suspicion in the Patricia Prince case. Michael was always troubled by coincidences, and the timing of Travis's bizarre accident was in Michael's mind one hell of a coincidence.

Sheriff Teague was beside himself. He didn't like trouble in his town. It meant he actually had to do something, although he was a master at delegating authority. His first move in this direction was to turn the Travis Burke case, which might prove to be a homicide, over to Michael Winter. After all, Winter had been the one who'd interrogated Burke on the day of his death about the boom box found in the Prince barn loft. Less than twenty-four hours after Travis's death, Michael found himself at the Burke house again.

Bethany Burke opened the door. Her long hair hung limply around her face, and dark circles surrounded her large brown eyes. Her face seemed thinner than it had at Patricia Prince's funeral, if it were possible for a face to get thinner in one day. She gave him a tired, bleak look and invited him inside.

Michael had seen Christine Ireland's car in the driveway when he pulled up. She and Jeremy sat on the couch Michael had occupied yesterday. Christine gave him a subdued greeting. Jeremy looked like a puppy ready to come over and lick him. Michael saw Christine blanch as she placed a restraining hand on her brother's thigh after he'd blasted a delighted, "Hi, Deputy! Do you know who killed anyone yet?"

"No, Jeremy, I don't," Michael had said mildly. He turned to Bethany. "Could I see you alone for a few minutes? I have some questions."

Christine rose abruptly. "Jeremy and I will be going."

"Oh, please don't! I want you to stay." Bethany looked at Michael. "We went to my father's right after . . ." She swallowed. "We had to because some of the snakes got out of the building when they went in for Travis. But Daddy's cold has turned into the flu and I didn't want to risk my daughter catching it. So we came back, but of course, Daddy couldn't come. Tess can't get here until later and I don't want to be alone."

"Christy and me could go in the kitchen and have some cake and coffee," Jeremy said helpfully. "You wouldn't believe how much food people have brought!"

"Standard procedure when a family member dies," Bethany said dully. "You're deluged with food when you least want to eat."

Michael nodded. "All right. I don't want to run off anyone."

"Let's go to the kitchen for a while, Jeremy," Christine said. "You can have another piece of carrot cake."

"Oh, great! I *love* carrot cake. I know there's a bunch of Jell-O molds, but I don't want any Jell-O. It's squirmy."

They disappeared with Jeremy still expounding on Jell-O. Bethany gave Winter a wan smile. "Thank you for letting them stay. They just got here."

"I understand why you wouldn't want to be alone right now."

"Would you like something to drink?"

"No thanks, Mrs. Burke. I don't want to take up more of your time than I have to. And I want to express my sympathy."

"Thank you." She gestured to the couch for him, then sat down in the armchair where her husband had sat the day before. "Travis was so strong. He always seemed indestructible to me, like my father. I just can't believe this has happened."

"I'm very sorry," Michael said. He'd been called to the scene yesterday, but he hadn't been able to question Bethany. She'd been hysterical and had to be sedated. But he'd seen Travis. He was barely recognizable from swelling and grotesque discoloration. "Mrs. Burke, when I arrived, the door to the snake house was shut and the padlock was closed."

She winced. "Yes. I'd just gotten home from my father's. I heard Travis screaming and I knew something was wrong. I just *knew* at least one of those horrible snakes had gotten out. So I looked through the window of the snake house. He was writhing on the floor. Snakes were all around him—" She shuddered. "I beat on the window, as if that would do any good. He looked up at me. His eyes . . . they had a dying look. He was already mostly gone. Shaking. Contorting." Her mouth trembled. "I ran to the door, but I couldn't open it. The padlock was shut. I didn't have a key. I just stood there and screamed like a ninny while my husband died."

"There was nothing you could do."

"I could have broken that padlock, but I went blank. I didn't do *anything*!"

"Mrs. Burke, as cruel as it sounds, with all those snakes loose it's better that you didn't get that door open. If you'd managed to get in, your daughter would have lost both parents."

"I know. But still . . ." Her eyes filled with tears. "I'll always remember that I did nothing. As usual. Helpless Bethany. It was several minutes before I even ran to the house and called nine-one-one. Time seemed . . . I don't know. Suspended."

"Even if you'd called immediately, it would have still been too late, Mrs. Burke. The ME's office has confirmed that there was a massive amount of venom in your husband's blood—too much venom for him to have survived even if the EMS had arrived at the same time you did. And even when they got here, they couldn't enter until the Department of Natural Resources arrived to get the snakes under control. You don't have anything to feel guilty about."

"I have *always* detested those snakes," Bethany said fiercely, wiping at one tear-filled eye with a fist like a child. "I can't bear to look at them. They scare me half to death! I've never set foot in the snake house. I begged Travis to give up that awful hobby. I knew he had it years before we got married, but I thought he'd abandon it if I pleaded with him enough, especially after we had a child. But he could be so stubborn! He wouldn't give in. I don't understand how he could be so entranced by a bunch of *snakes*, for heaven's sake! They're repulsive!"

"I guess they weren't repulsive to him."

"Oh no. He thought they were beautiful." A small, ragged laugh escaped her. "I suppose beauty really is in the eye of the beholder."

"You kept saying yesterday that your husband was always so careful with the snakes. Yet after the Department of Natural Resources went into the building to collect all the snakes, they found almost every cage open. How do you explain that?"

"I can't. Travis kept that place locked, padlocked, and dead-bolted. And when he went inside, he locked the door from the inside so that no one could wander in on him when he was handling a snake. The windows are unbreakable." She lifted her shoulders. "I don't know, unless someone actually broke the locks to get in. But Travis would have noticed broken locks."

"The police and the Department of Natural Resources had to break down the door to get in, but they looked at the locks first. There was no damage to them. No one broke into the building. So they had to have a key."

Bethany rubbed a line between her eyebrows as if her head was beginning to hurt. "There were three keys—one for the lock, one for the deadbolt, one for the padlock. Travis kept them in his desk drawer."

"There was only one set of keys?"

"No. There was an extra set, also in the desk drawer. It's still there. I checked when we got back around noon."

"Your husband had one set of keys in his pocket. So that accounts for both sets. Are you sure there wasn't a third set?"

"If there was, I don't know about it. I don't know why he'd want a third set. He always took one out with him and left one inside."

"He left one inside in case he ever got locked in the snake house?"

Bethany looked surprised. "No. He had a second set made in case he ever lost the first, although I don't know how that could have happened. He didn't carry them around like car keys."

"But the padlock on the outside of the door was shut. Someone locked it *after* your husband went in."

Bethany nodded. "I know. But who? There aren't kids around here."

"Didn't Mr. Burke ever worry about something like that happening? Why didn't he take the padlock off the door while he was inside?"

Bethany frowned. "I think he usually did. Besides, he usually took his cell phone in with him. If he did get locked in, he could call me and I could get the second set of keys."

"Except that this time he went in when you weren't home. And he didn't have his cell phone. And he did leave the padlock hanging on the outside door. Quite a set of unfortunate coincidences."

"Yes," Bethany said vaguely.

"You don't think your daughter, Jan, could have shut the padlock, do you?"

Bethany's gaze suddenly grew sharp. "No, she didn't. I won't have people suspecting my baby of such a thing!"

"It was an innocent but reasonable question, Mrs. Burke. I didn't mean to offend you."

"That's the kind of accusation that can follow a child around, warp her for life!"

"I didn't make an accusation. I just asked a question. We'll drop it for now."

"We'll drop it forever!"

"All right. Please calm down." She looked hostile but too angry to be on her guard. "What do you know about your husband's stolen boom box?"

Her voice rose. "His boom box? It was stolen?"

Michael thought Bethany's color rose, but he couldn't be certain. Her words definitely revealed strain, though. "He didn't mention it to you?" She stared. "I suppose not. Well, he didn't mention it to the police, either. He told me it had been taken out of his unlocked car about two weeks ago. He said nothing else was taken or damaged, so he didn't want to make a big deal over it."

"Oh." He waited for her to ask why he was bringing up the boom box now. She continued to stare. Then she managed, "I gave him that boom box."

"The one that was stolen?"

"Uh, yes. I mean, he only had one."

"But he didn't tell you it had been stolen." She shook her head. "Maybe he thought you'd be upset."

"Maybe."

Michael waited a few seconds. He had the impression Bethany was coiling like one of her husband's snakes. "I stopped by here yesterday while you were at your father's to tell Mr. Burke the boom box had been found."

"Oh. That's good."

"In the Prince barn. Up in the loft. It was playing when Patricia Prince's body was found."

Bethany seemed to swell, her face growing red, her throat working, her chest coming forward as she pulled air into her lungs. He watched, fascinated, not knowing what move to make next, waiting for her to set the tone. At last she said, "Well, isn't that odd?"

Michael felt as if he were going to fall off the couch from the anticlimax. He wondered what he had expected. For her to leap up, declare, "Yes, I knew my husband was having an affair with Patricia Prince, so I turned his snakes loose so they could kill him"? Maybe not something so dramatic. But some sign that she knew about Travis and Patricia, because he was certain they'd been having an affair. And he was *almost* certain Bethany suspected it.

But she sat without another word, her gaze daring him to push her further. He wasn't going to get anywhere, he thought in disappointment. Not now, at least.

He leaned forward in sincerity. "Mrs. Burke, do you know of anyone who would want to hurt your husband?"

"Hurt him? *Murder* him? You think he was murdered?"

"I'm sure your husband didn't open all those cages of poisonous snakes at the same time. Someone wanted to set those snakes free."

"Like animal rights people?"

He looked at her closely. Did she want him to think she was stupid? Or too stunned by the thought of murder to have even considered it? "I can't see animal rights people freeing a bunch of highly venomous snakes for your husband to walk in on. I know some of those rights people are dangerous fanatics, but I've never heard of anyone like that around here."

"Well, that's good." Back to vagueness. "It would be awful to think of people like that just wandering around."

"Yes, it would. Mrs. Burke, did your husband have clashes with anyone lately?"

"Clashes? What kind of clashes?"

"Arguments. Even with a stranger. Let's say he had a run-in with someone suffering road rage. Anything like that?"

"Not that I know of," Bethany said slowly. "Of course, there was a lot he didn't tell me." She immediately looked as if she wished she could swallow those last words. She seemed to coil again. "But if there was trouble of any kind, he couldn't have kept it from me. We were so in love and I knew him so well."

Michael had been on the verge of letting the interview drop, but the attempt to blind him with sugary words and a sticky sweet smile urged him on. "Mrs. Burke, at the cemetery Jeremy

Ireland said loudly that Dara Prince had called Travis 'Snake Charmer.' He said that Travis certainly liked Dara. You obviously overheard, and you looked like you were going to cry."

Bethany hesitated, then said stoutly, "Who said I looked like I was going to cry? That's ridiculous."

"I saw you, Mrs. Burke. It was my observation that you looked as if you were going to cry."

"Well, you misread me."

"I don't think so."

"Yes, you did."

"All right. But did you know Dara Prince called your husband 'Snake Charmer'?"

"I think a lot of students did. So what?"

"Did you know Dara Prince?"

"Slightly. Through Christine."

"What did you think of her?"

"I didn't care for her. She was spoiled. Arrogant. Awful to Christine."

"Did your husband know Dara?"

"I think she was his student."

"Did he like her? Jeremy said he liked her a *lot*."

Bethany flushed. "Sometimes Jeremy gets carried away. He probably knew Dara was Travis's student."

"He said Travis had shown Dara his snakes."

"He doesn't know what he's talking about. Oh, maybe she told him that to impress him, but Travis wouldn't have taken a student into the snake house."

"He's never had a student interested in herpetology?"

"Well, yes. He's shown the snakes to *serious* students. Males."

"He's never had a serious female student."

Bethany's lips compressed. "Deputy, I feel like you're making fun of me."

"I'm not."

"I think you are. I *know* you are!" She stood up. "I don't want to continue this discussion. I'm tired and I'm sick with grief and I'm—"

Jeremy strode into the living room. "Bethany, I didn't mean to eat so much, but there's only one piece of carrot cake left. Do you or Deputy Winter want it?"

Christine appeared behind him. "Jeremy! Honestly, I turned my back for a second and you're gone. We're supposed to stay in the kitchen."

"But I just wanted to ask—"

A high-pitched shriek from outside cut off Jeremy's explanation. Every bit of blood seemed to vanish from Bethany's face as her eyes flew wide and her hand went to her throat. "That's Jan," she croaked. "She was watching cartoons in the den, but that sound came from outside."

Bethany whirled to look out the back window, which was raised a couple of inches. Winter was right behind her. Outside, four-year-old Jan Burke sat huddled on an old, spindly lawn chair.

"Mommy, it's Daddy's Gabby wiper!"

"Gabby wiper?" Michael echoed.

"Gaboon viper," Bethany said in a strangled voice. "Oh, my God!"

And then they saw it raising its head, testing the distance from the ground to the low-seated chair. Jan's eyes fastened on the snake in terror, her body drawing into a ball.

"Do not move, Jan!" Michael called, already reaching for his gun. "Do not move one tiny bit!"

Jeremy seemed to move like quicksilver, Michael thought later. He was already headed out of the living room as Michael drew away from the window, his mind clicking a hundred horrible pictures of his missing the snake and shooting the child instead. A little girl. Just the age his own daughter would have been . . .

With horror he felt a tremor in his hand. He couldn't shoot at a snake with a shaking hand, he thought, outraged by his own body. He strode ahead, though, vaguely aware of Christine and Bethany behind him, one of them crying. When they got outside, the snake would be between them and the child. He *had* to shoot it.

Another shriek. "Mommy, it's coming closer!"

Another tremor. He *couldn't* shoot it. He'd kill Jan. He knew it. "I need a hoe! Or an ax!"

"What?" Bethany wailed. "I don't know where—what?"

"A weapon!" Christine yelled over Bethany's cries. "He needs a weapon. Beth, *please!*"

"I can't think!"

"Mommy!"

Bethany pushed past Michael and ran out the back door, heading directly for Jan. Michael grabbed her and pulled her back.

"Let me go!" Bethany screamed.

"The snake will strike you or Jan."

"I have to get her!"

Michael looked at the snake raising its head, which was now only inches away from the terrified Jan, who had begun to shake, drawing its attention. Then he saw Jeremy, moving with the graceful stealth of a panther, circling behind the child.

Bethany broke free of Michael and dashed to the side of the porch, grabbing up a shovel. She ran into the yard, directly toward the snake. "Beth, no!" Christine cried.

The snake's head was motionless as it poised to strike Jan. Its bite would be fatal to such a small child, Michael thought as he raised his gun, his hand suddenly steady, reliable. And then Bethany moved directly between him and the snake.

"Oh God," Christine moaned. "Oh no."

Jan let out one tiny, hopeless whimper. Then, just as the snake's head darted toward her, Jeremy swooped down and in one incredibly fast movement, so fast it seemed almost a blur, he scooped Jan up into his arms.

The snake lunged at the empty chair as Bethany began to strike at it with the shovel, missing time after time in her frenzy. The upper part of the snake's body turned. Its mouth now faced her. It tensed. Bethany swung wildly again as it prepared to strike.

Jeremy took three steps back from the chair, looking at

Michael. "Shoot it!" he yelled as Michael aimed. The thing coiled so close to Bethany. So fatally close. He turned, shut down his anxiety, and focused only on the snake as he raised his gun. Aimed. Pulled the trigger.

Bethany shrieked as the gun went off. She fell backward and Michael thought he'd hit her. He stood rooted, ready to shoot at the snake again so it couldn't bite the fallen woman, but then Bethany raised her head and Jeremy shouted, "You got it! You killed it, Deputy!"

Jan began to whimper against his chest. Michael ran to Bethany, who was already struggling to scoot backward, away from the long, strong body of the snake that still writhed in its death throes. Michael aimed and shot the snake again. Its body jerked, almost whipping up into the air, then collapsed. Motionless. Dead, finally, Michael thought. He put his arm under Bethany's back and under her lifted knees, raising her from the ground, carrying her a couple of feet away from the snake. Then she struggled out of his arms and ran to Jeremy and Jan.

Jan lay limply in Jeremy's arms, her face blank with blind terror. "Oh God," Bethany moaned. "It got her."

"It didn't," Jeremy said as the child clung to him while Bethany and Christine hovered, touching Jan, shaking. "It didn't bite her, honest."

Michael reached them. He touched Jan's arm and she began to squirm and cry in long, loud howls, emerging from the paralysis of freezing fear. "She's just scared, Mrs. Burke."

"Bethany!" She began to sob. "I don't want to be called Mrs. Burke. That stinking, selfish son of a bitch and his snakes! If she'd been killed, it would have been his fault. Even in death he's hurting us, sacrificing our happiness, our *safety*, for his pleasures! I hope God damns him to hell!"

And so the hatred she'd coiled herself around earlier during their interview came flooding out in a torrent of tears and cursing and shuddering. Jeremy handed Jan to her and she clutched at the child, kissing her, crying into her hair, before she turned viciously to Michael.

"You people said you took all the snakes away!"

"It wasn't the police who took the snakes away. It was the DNR. They must have missed one. You told them there were twenty snakes. There must have been another one."

"The Gaboon viper," Bethany said. "One of the worst!"

"Jan said that's what it was. How did she know? Travis didn't take her into the snake house, did he?"

"Do you think I'd allow that?" Bethany asked fiercely. "He showed her pictures. In books. And he took Polaroids of *his* snakes and showed her. He made her learn a lot of names."

"You have a Polaroid camera?" Michael asked.

"Yes." Bethany crooned over her little girl. "My sweetheart. My darling."

"Mrs. . . . Bethany, we need to get both of you to the emergency room," Michael said. "She might be going into shock. And you, too."

"Oh God." Bethany hugged Jan tighter. "I'm all right. But she's getting hysterical."

"Christine, you take Bethany and Jan to the hospital," Michael said. "I'll call the DNR. I want them to come back out here and search for any other snakes that might be loose. And, Bethany, I don't think you and Jan should stay here."

"After the hospital, we're going to check into a hotel," she announced. "And we are *never* coming back to this house. I'm going to level that snake pit to the ground, then sell this place. I can't live here anymore."

Michael watched as Bethany's spine seemed to stiffen with resolve. She marched into the house with Jan in her arms and Christine and Jeremy behind her, resolve and anger seeming to emanate from every line of her posture.

She's not a little mouse anymore. But then, maybe she never was, Michael thought as he remembered Bethany, who'd said she was terrified of the snakes, going after a deadly viper with maniacal vengeance.

2

Four hours later, Michael stopped at Christine's house. Although his visit had been unannounced, she and Jeremy both seemed happy to see him. They ushered him into the beautiful house that smelled of coffee and cinnamon buns Christine had just baked, and Michael felt warmth spread through him, a warmth that frightened him just a little. These people were beginning to mean too much to him, he thought. He should pull back, guard his emotions that were still raw, live in safe solitude for at least another year. That's what he should do, he told himself. But that's not what he wanted to do.

In a few minutes, the three of them sat at the dining room table drinking coffee and eating the cinnamon rolls. Rhiannon sat sphinxlike on the buffet table, her paws tucked beneath her, her beautiful golden gaze taking in all the activity.

Jeremy reached for one of the still-hot rolls. "So the doctor said that Jan's just fine, didn't he, Christy?"

"Yes. Like you said, she was just badly frightened, but she's a tough little girl. She'd stopped crying and seemed to be relaxing by the time we dropped off Beth and her at the hotel. Tess came by the hospital. She said she'd gone to the house and found you and the Natural Resources people and you'd told her what happened."

Michael sipped coffee and nodded. "She was off like a rocket when I told her about Jan almost being bitten. I should have given her a speeding ticket the way she tore away from the house and headed down the highway. Her tires squealed."

"Really?" Jeremy asked in delight. "That's so cool. Christy drives like a snail. She never makes the tires squeal."

"I don't drive like a snail!" Christine said indignantly. "I'm just careful."

"You're a slowpoke. You drive slower than Bethany."

"Honey, *no* one drives slower than Bethany," Christine laughed.

They ate and talked meanderingly for a while. Everyone seemed relaxed, almost giddy from the excitement of the day.

Michael once again felt like part of something, a member of a family, and the feeling scared him a little. This kind of happiness was too tenuous, too easily lost. Still, he couldn't bring himself to leave.

He was lost in contemplation of his feeling of ease and contentment in this lovely house with Christine and her brother when Jeremy suddenly announced, "I think someone let out Travis's snakes on purpose. I think someone wanted him to get killed."

Michael knew Christine had not said anything to Jeremy about the possibility of murder. "Who would want him to die?" he asked casually.

"Someone who didn't like him. Or someone who was jealous." Jeremy bit into another cinnamon roll and said around it, "Maybe he was Patricia's boyfriend."

Christine looked shocked. "What makes you say that?"

"Well, I told you about that day I heard her with somebody in the barn. I kind of knew the guy's voice, but I couldn't get who it was."

Michael couldn't keep the excitement from his own voice: "And now you think it was Travis?"

"I'm still not sure, but maybe."

Michael had not told Christine about identifying the owner of the boom box the police had found in the barn loft. He could see that the idea of Travis Burke being Patricia Prince's lover was a new thought for her, although she'd told him Jeremy was certain Patricia had a "boyfriend." "If you think about it some more, could you remember for certain?" Michael asked Jeremy.

"I don't know, but I'll try really hard. But if someone did want Travis to die, who would it be?"

Bethany, Michael thought. If she knew. Ames Prince. If he knew. He wanted to get Jeremy off the subject before these disturbing possibilities cropped up in his mind.

"It could have been an accident, Jeremy. The pathologist—"

Jeremy frowned. "The *doctor* who looked at Travis's body after he was dead did a test on his blood that revealed he'd been drinking. Maybe he just got careless."

"I try really hard not to be careless, but I am sometimes," Jeremy said earnestly. "But you don't think someone like Travis would be careless. With *snakes*." He shivered a little. "I sure hate snakes."

"Some are harmless," Michael said, "but it's best to be careful around all of them." He looked at his empty plate. "I can't believe how many of those cinnamon rolls I ate. They were great, Christine."

"Why, thank you. I took the dough right out of the can and put it on the cookie sheet all by myself. I'm exhausted."

Jeremy laughed. "Christy makes some stuff really good, but not this kind of thing. Her cakes come out all lopsided and her cookies are hard as rocks."

"I never claimed to be a good cook. Our mother was wonderful. I think being a good chef is a gift, like being a musician or an artist."

"Wouldn't know myself," Michael said. "I'm prone to opening a can of beans and eating over the sink."

"I love to do that, but Christy won't let me!" Jeremy exclaimed.

Michael laughed again, realizing he felt happy—too happy to worry about being cautious. He wanted this evening to last forever, as silly as he knew that was. But he didn't feel like worrying about being silly, either.

The beautiful weather had not held. Although the rain did not resume, the day had been gloomy and was now spinning down into an early dusk.

Jeremy finally retired with Rhiannon to his room, vaguely claiming he had "stuff to do." When he'd gone, Christine said, "He has a TV show at this time he never misses, but he didn't want to seem rude."

"I don't mind being abandoned for a TV show," Michael said. "Everyone has priorities."

"Television is one of Jeremy's. But I'm glad. He watches quite a range of shows for someone with his IQ and he learns from them, although I haven't quite gotten him to watch more than a little of PBS."

"A little PBS is fine. But you need action/adventure and fantasy as well."

Christine poured the last of the coffee into his cup, then said thoughtfully, "Even in all the excitement, I didn't miss your asking Bethany if she had a Polaroid camera," she said. "You were thinking about the photos I got." He nodded. "You can't think Bethany would send pictures like that."

"I'm just trying not to overlook any possibilities. And let's not forget that the camera belonged to Travis, too."

"What possible reason could he have had to send those pictures to me?"

"The same reason someone attacked you in the gym and made that phone call to the hospital. To scare you into a shell, to make you stop nosing into who might have killed Dara Prince. And I'm pretty sure the *S.C.* in her diary did refer to Travis."

"You think he was one of her lovers."

"Yes, and I'm guessing Bethany suspected it. And his other infidelities."

"I hate that for Bethany."

"I do, too. Why risk a marriage by fooling around, especially when you have a child?" He shook his head. "Anyway, back to the photos. I did some investigating I haven't had a chance to tell you about. The card they came in was put out by a company named Wonderland. The only place in town I've been able to find Wonderland greeting cards is Ned's News. No one there could remember who had bought the card, although I showed a copy of the cover to the staff. The owner said they sell thirty or forty Wonderland cards a month. So I've hit a dead end on tracing the buyer of the card."

"And I'm sure there weren't any fingerprints on it."

"Nope. The sender was careful."

"I'll bet if you could get those letters supposedly from Dara away from Ames, you wouldn't find any fingerprints on them, either."

"I'm pretty sure of that, too. I think they were sent by whoever killed her to stop an intense investigation by making everyone think she was still alive."

"She isn't," Christine said flatly. "I know that body in Charleston is hers. Her ring, the pregnancy . . ." She shook her head. "In spite of the way Ames is treating me, I feel so sorry for him. There can't be any greater pain than losing a child."

"There isn't," Michael said softly.

"You sound as if you've experienced it."

He nodded. "My little girl, Stacy."

Christine paused a moment before saying, "I assumed her mother had gotten custody after your divorce. You mean she's—"

"Dead. At two years old."

"Oh, Michael, I never dreamed!" She reached out and touched his hand. "I'm so sorry. How did it happen? No, forget I asked that. It's none of my business and the memory must be terrible for you."

"It is, but I feel like I need to talk about it if you don't mind listening."

"Of course I don't mind, Michael. Talk all you need to."

He reached out and took her hand, holding it tightly. "Stacy was such a beautiful child. She looked like her mother—auburn hair, green eyes. Lisa is an actress. Well, she wants to be an actress. So far all she's gotten are commercials. But she's driven where her career is concerned."

Michael drew a deep breath. "One day she was giving Stacy a bath. The phone rang. We had an answering machine to screen calls and normally Lisa wouldn't have answered while Stacy was in the tub, but it was her agent. So she left Stacy in the water, answered the phone, and got completely carried away when she heard she'd been given an audition for a situation comedy. We had a cordless phone. She could have stayed with Stacy while she took the call, but she didn't. Apparently Stacy tried to get out of the tub by herself and fell, hit her head, and knocked herself unconscious. She slid back into the water and drowned."

"Oh, Michael. How terrible!"

"I didn't get the truth out of Lisa for a couple of weeks. She said she'd only left Stacy alone for a minute while she went to get a towel. Then one day her agent called and I picked up the phone. The agent was abject. She said if she hadn't called exactly when she did, if she hadn't gotten Lisa so involved in conversation, the accident might not have happened. I confronted Lisa and she broke down." He closed his eyes. "She could have been prosecuted for negligent homicide, even with the towel story, but I had a lot of good friends on the force and they backed off. They knew how much I loved Lisa, and they thought I'd been through enough. But it was the end of my marriage."

Christine squeezed his hand. "You must have been through hell the last couple of years."

"That's why I left Los Angeles. My grandfather lived in Winston all his life. When he died, he left his house to me. He always worried about me in LA. He thought I'd be safer here. You might have known him. Corbin Winter."

"Corbin Winter was your grandfather?" Christine exclaimed. "He owned that old-fashioned general store and played Santa in the Christmas parade."

"The very one."

"I met him right after Jeremy and I moved here. Jeremy loved to go into the store."

"Well, I'll be damned," Michael said slowly. "He wrote to me about a boy and his sister who had just moved to town. He said the boy was like my cousin. I don't think he ever called Jeremy by name, but he must have been talking about you two."

"Yes!" Christine giggled delightedly. "Can you believe that we actually met?"

"Fate or chance?"

"I have no idea." Christine smiled. "Jeremy was so fond of Mr. Winter."

"The feeling was mutual. Anyway, my grandmother died years before Grandpa. When he died, he left his house to me. I planned on selling it. It had been on the market for nearly a year when Stacy died. I left LA a month later and came here. I'd spent a lot of time with my grandparents in Winston when I was a kid. I liked it here. And I had to get away from Los Angeles. I needed a new start."

"Has moving here helped?"

"A little. But I still haven't shaken the memory, the sadness."

"You never will, Michael," Christine said gently. "Jeremy and I adored our parents and I can tell you that the pain will dull, but it will never completely go away. That doesn't mean you can't rebuild your life, though. Giving up would be a betrayal of Stacy."

He looked at her and she saw a slight glimmer of tears in his eyes. "You think so?"

"I *know* it would. The people who loved us would want us to go on, even if they couldn't go on with us."

"I'd like to believe that."

"I know it sounds kind of sappy, maybe too easy and just an excuse, but remember Stacy and how much she must have loved you. Then you'll believe it. She wouldn't want her daddy to give up and never be happy again."

Michael closed his eyes. Then he brought Christine's hand to his mouth and kissed it lightly on the palm. "Thank you for giving me that thought. It helps."

Christine's hand tingled from his kiss. When he looked at her, his mahogany eyes were soft, penetrating. She felt as if he were gazing into her soul. She'd never had that feeling before. Not with anyone.

They heard Jeremy pounding up the stairs from the basement. He arrived in the dining room breathless, his face red. "Christy, someone's outside hanging around, looking in."

"You saw someone?" Michael asked.

"Yeah. Well, Rhi saw him first. She was sitting in the window and she growled like kitty cats do. Then I looked. He went behind some trees, but I don't think he ran off." He pointed at the sliding glass doors leading on to the deck. "He would've been looking right in that window."

"Damn," Christine muttered. "I should have shut the blinds, particularly after what happened the night Streak was here. Someone can stand out there and see everything going on in the kitchen and dining room."

"You two stay here," Michael said, rising. "I'm going out."

"No, don't!" Christine was surprised by the fear in her voice. "He could have a gun!"

"So do I. Jeremy, you keep your sister safe."

"Yes, sir!"

"Michael, please . . ."

"Christine, I'll be fine. Just don't either one of you follow me. I'm going out the front door and around the house. Don't stand in front of the window. Get back into the living room just in case he's armed," Michael said, then gave her a glancing kiss along the cheekbone before heading for the front door. Christine was too surprised to protest any further. She touched her cheek as Jeremy took her hand and pulled her toward the living room.

"I should go help him," Jeremy said after a few minutes. "He shouldn't be out in the dark all by himself."

"If you go out, he won't know it's you. He might shoot you," Christine said, grasping her brother's arm. "You stay in here out of the way. With me. I need you."

Jeremy put his arm around her protectively. They sat on the floor, out of the range of windows. Christine was just beginning to feel silly with their crouching and hiding when she heard Michael yell, "Stop! Police!"

A shot rang out.

For the first time in her life, Christine knew what it felt like to have her heart literally skip a beat. A quick pain in the chest, cessation of breath, then a hard thud as the heart jerked to life again against the ribs. Jeremy gasped and squeezed her harder.

A minute later, someone banged on the sliding glass doors in the dining room. They both froze until Michael called, "It's me! Open the doors!"

They scuttled into the dining room. Jeremy reached the doors first, unlocking one and sliding it back. Michael stumbled inside, breathing raggedly. "I didn't get him," he said weakly. "But he got me."

That's when Christine noticed the right side of his uniform shirt. It was drenched with blood.

19

1

"I'll call nine-one-one," Christine said in a high, thin voice.

"We can make it to the hospital faster by just driving," Michael answered. "If I can have a towel or something to press against the wound, I'll be fine. Damn. I've dripped on your carpet."

"Of all the silly things to worry about," Christine snapped the way she always did when she was frightened. "I think we should call nine-one-one. They're trained. You could bleed out before we even get you to the hospital—"

Jeremy had already gotten a towel, forced Michael to sit on a chair, and pressed the towel against his shoulder. "Christy, stop talking and let's get going," he said. He looked at Michael. "She always talks like crazy when she's scared."

Michael looked at her. "I'll be okay, Christine. I just need to get to the hospital before I pass out."

"Pass *out*?" Christine cried. "Oh, my God."

"Christy, chill out," Jeremy said, using a new phrase he'd learned from Ginger. "I'll carry Deputy Michael to the car."

"I don't need to be carried," Michael protested as Jeremy began to lift him. "Just let me lean on you."

Half an hour later, Christine and Jeremy sat in the hospital waiting room. Jeremy had been to the candy machine three times while Christine sipped a cup of bitter coffee. "They have crummy food here," Jeremy said.

"Hospitals aren't known for their fine cuisine."

"What's cuisine?" Jeremy asked. "Food?"

"Exactly."

Two policemen showed up just as Jeremy was debating whether or not to have another candy bar. "Evening, Ms. Ireland," the younger one said. "We heard you had some trouble at your place this evening."

"That's putting it mildly. How did you know?"

"A neighbor called." Christine immediately knew that neighbor had been the ever-vigilant Mrs. Flint. The younger, good-looking one gave her a smile. "My name is Lasky. My partner is Anders. Mrs. Flint told us there was a policeman with you. One that has been at your house a lot lately." Christine felt her color rise although the deputy's voice was neutral, even kind. "Was it Winter?"

"Yes. Deputy Winter had come by to update me on his search for the person who sent me Polaroid photos of Dara and Patricia Prince."

"We know about the pictures and the card," Lasky said.

"Then you know he hadn't been able to learn much, yet, but he knew how worried I was and he wanted me to know the police hadn't dropped the matter." That wasn't exactly a lie, Christine told herself virtuously. They *had* talked about the cards, although that's not really why Michael had stopped by.

"Anyway, my brother saw someone lurking outside on my lawn, looking in windows, sort of hiding behind trees. Deputy Winter felt it wasn't just someone passing through the yard. He made Jeremy and me stay inside while he went out to check on things. We heard him say, 'Stop! Police!' Something like that. Then a gun fired. We thought Deputy Winter had shot someone. But when he got back to the house, we saw it was he who'd been shot."

At last a doctor emerged from an examining room to speak to them. "Deputy Winter wanted me to apprise you of his condition. Luckily, the bullet didn't hit any bones or major blood vessels. He'll have limited use of the arm for a few days, but he should make a full recovery. We'll keep him here tonight."

When the doctor finally allowed visitors in to see the patient, Michael asked to see Christine and Jeremy first. Michael smiled, but Christine thought he looked extremely pale. "Are you sure you're all right?" she asked. "You're not just playing tough guy, are you?"

"He *is* a tough guy," Jeremy corrected reprovingly. "The toughest guy I know."

"Thanks for the vote of confidence, Jeremy, but to be honest, I'm not feeling all that tough tonight. I was lucky. They recovered the shell casing. It was a twenty-two."

"A twenty-two?" Christine repeated. "Isn't that considered a kind of wimpy caliber?"

Michael smiled. "You wouldn't think that if it had hit *you* in the shoulder."

"Oh, I'm sorry. I didn't mean to minimize your injury."

"It's okay," Michael laughed. "You're right. A twenty-two is usually used by a woman. Or the Mafia when they want to shoot someone in the head at close range. The bullet just bounces all over the place in the skull, tearing up the brain."

"Oh. How interesting to know," Christine said, trying to smile to hide her distress over Michael's condition.

"Sheriff Teague called and insisted on being put through even though they were still working on me. He's not too happy about this, but he has a brilliant theory. He thinks I might have been shot by hunters."

"Hunters?" Christine replied blankly. "In a residential neighborhood? What were they hunting? Cardinals?"

"Maybe skunks," Jeremy said seriously. "I saw a skunk in the backyard once."

"I don't think skunks rate high on the hunters' list of favorite prey," Michael said, then yawned.

Christine spoke up. "We'd better get out of here. I think those two policemen outside want to talk to you."

"Who is it?"

"Lasky and Anders."

"They're good guys."

"Is there anything I can do for you?" Christine asked.

"Well, one thing. You know where my grandfather used to live—where I live now. Get my house key out of my pants pocket, drop by there, and get some clothes for me to wear in the morning. My uniform is pretty well drenched in blood. Just jeans and a T-shirt will be fine. You can drop them off in the morning."

"Has he got you running errands already?"

Christine looked up to see a tall, slender young woman with masses of long auburn hair and the most mesmerizing green eyes she'd ever seen. The young woman wore skintight black leather pants, a black leather jacket over a gold mesh T-shirt, and huge gold hoop earrings. Christine thought she was one of the most beautiful, amazing-looking creatures she'd ever seen.

"Hi," the woman said, smiling to reveal perfect teeth. Her smile was particularly wide when she reached for Jeremy's hand. He looked dazzled to the point of incapacitation. "I'm afraid I didn't catch your names."

"Ch-Christine Ireland," she said, hating that she'd stumbled over her own name. "And this is—"

"Jeremy Bartholomew Ireland." Christine slanted a glance at him. "I'm Christy's brother."

"How lovely to meet you, Christine and Jeremy Bartholomew." Her voice seemed to tinkle around the room, young and care-free like a child's without being silly.

She turned to Michael. "I stopped by your house and found a policeman outside. Imagine my horror when he said you'd been shot!"

Michael had not said a word since the woman entered the room. He simply stared at her with his mouth slightly open, his expression dumbfounded.

She walked over to him and slowly brushed his dark hair back from his forehead before running her fingers across his cheek-bone and down to his lips. The motion was so proprietary and intimate that Christine felt herself blush.

The woman smiled at him lingeringly, then turned back to Christine. "Well, since Michael seems to have forgotten his manners, I'll introduce myself. Christine, Jeremy, I'm Lisa Winter. Michael's *wife*."

2

"I thought Deputy Winter wasn't married anymore," Jeremy said out in the car.

"He isn't. He's divorced."

"Then what's *she* doing here?" Jeremy demanded truculently.

"I guess she came for a visit. You're allowed to visit when you're divorced."

"You're not supposed to. Not that I ever heard of," Jeremy spluttered as if he knew all the rules of etiquette for divorced people. "She shouldn't be here! She's just gonna mess up everything!"

"What do you think she's going to mess up?"

"You and Deputy Michael getting together."

"What makes you think we were going to get together?"

Jeremy rolled his eyes at her. "Oh, Christy, come *on*! You two have a crush on each other. Anybody can see it. And I think you're just right for each other. And I'd like to have a policeman for a brother-in-law. Darn her! She's just messing up everything!"

Jeremy continued to fume as they drove home, but Christine barely heard him. The degree of misery she felt surprised her. That woman! She was gorgeous, Christine thought. She was nearly as tall as Christine, but the height looked right on her. And she'd never seen auburn hair quite that color. Maybe it wasn't real, but it was beautiful, long, and lush. Christine unconsciously touched her own short blond hair. Even if she let it grow long, it would never be as thick and wavy as Lisa's. And her eyes! They looked like emeralds.

"I didn't think she was one bit pretty," Jeremy announced as if reading her thoughts.

"Yes, you did."

"No, Christy. She looked like pictures of movie stars in *People*. Not like you."

"Oh, good. I'd hate to look like a movie star."

"You're prettier than any movie star. You've got a sweet look on your face and in your eyes, like you'd be nice to little lost kids and hurt animals."

"Jeremy, could you please quit extolling my looks? You're making me feel worse."

"What's extolling?"

"Praising. Complimenting."

"What's wrong with getting compliments?"

"Nothing. It's just the kind of compliments—" She broke off and sighed. "Let's change the subject."

When they got home, darkness had completely fallen. Christine could see no stars, and the moon was a thin crescent. The dusk-to-dawn light had completely failed. She would have to call the electric company tomorrow and get it repaired.

Christine knew police had been all over the grounds and that at least one cop was on surveillance. Whoever had shot Michael probably wouldn't have the nerve to return. Still, she felt uneasy, as if she were being stalked. She pulled all the draperies in the house and sat down to watch a television show with Jeremy.

During a commercial break, he looked up at her and smiled. "You feel bad now, but you'll feel better tomorrow. I bet the deputy's wife just came to get money or something and she'll leave." Oh dear, I hope so, Christine thought. Yesterday she would not have believed the return of Michael Winter's ex-wife could leave her so profoundly depressed. "And we have work tomorrow," Jeremy went on. "I'm glad the store will be open again."

Christine sat silently for a moment. She knew Jeremy was watching her closely, sensing that something was wrong. Finally, she asked, "Jeremy, would you be terribly sad about not working at Prince Jewelry anymore?"

He looked at her as if she'd just said the world was going to end. "Not work at the store anymore? You mean lose my job? Did I lose my job?" Oh God, Christine thought. Just as she'd expected. "Why?" Jeremy continued, his voice rising. "What did I do wrong?"

She took a deep breath. "You did absolutely nothing wrong. Remember when we found Dara's diary?"

"Sure I remember, but what does that have to do with my job?"

"Just let me explain. I felt I had to give the diary to the police, and Ames found out about it and got really mad." Jeremy's face flamed. "Yes, I know you're the one who first told him I was going to give the diary to the police."

"I'm sorry, Christy. It just sort of came out. I felt guilty 'cause I knew Dara didn't want anyone else to read it, but I knew you were going to give it to Deputy Michael and, well—" He looked like he was going to cry. "I'm real sorry."

"It's all right, Jeremy. Ames would have found out anyway. But as I said, he got terribly angry and . . . well . . . he fired me."

Jeremy stared at her in disbelief for a moment, then burst out, "Fired *you*!"

"Yes, I'm afraid so. He didn't say anything about you. Maybe you still have a job there, but I'm not sure."

"Well, I am!" Jeremy flared. "If you're fired, I'm not gonna work there, either!"

"You don't have to quit because of me. I know how much you love the job."

"Not without you! I think it was real mean of Ames to fire you! And if he's gonna be that mean, I don't want to work for him anymore."

"He's been very good to us for a long time, Jeremy."

"Yeah, but that doesn't mean he can treat you bad. I'll never work at Prince Jewelry again!"

Christine went to her brother and gently touched his golden hair. "I believe you should talk to Ames. You should tell him not to hold you responsible for what I did. After all, you didn't want *anyone* to read the diary. Ask him if you can keep your job."

Jeremy shook his head vehemently. "Not without you, Christy. Don't worry. We'll find other jobs. Even better jobs."

Christine wished she had her brother's confidence. Certainly there was another job for her, but what about Jeremy? Where would he get another chance to use his talent for jewelry design?

Christine knew Jeremy was more desolate than he was letting on. The making of jewelry meant everything to him. At last he'd found something at which he excelled. And now it was unlikely he'd ever get the chance to show Ames the beautiful Dara Pin.

But in a few minutes her mind had skittered away from the prospect of finding another job to the subject of Lisa Winter. She wondered why Michael's ex-wife had shown up. Did she hope for a reconciliation? She was so beautiful. Michael had told Christine how much he'd loved Lisa. Dear God, shouldn't she be happy for him instead of sitting around in a complete funk? How selfish could she be? Right now she felt as if in the selfish department, she was running a close second to Dara.

Later Christine heard the television going downstairs in Jeremy's room. The volume was turned up louder than usual, and apparently Captain Kirk was fighting off the Klingons again. One of the things Christine had always admired about Jeremy was his ability to push troubles out of his mind for long periods of time. Christine lacked that capacity.

After checking every lock in the house, even those on the windows, while trying to duck out of sight, Christine had holed up in her bedroom, where she lit three gingerbread-scented candles that reminded her of the cookies her mother used to bake. Cookies with cinnamon and raisins. Back then Christine had thought those secure days would go on forever. She was glad she didn't know then what lay ahead of her.

Like murder. Dara had been murdered and her body thrown in the river. Christine was certain Patricia had been murdered. There could be no doubt that someone had set the scene for Travis Burke's grisly death. But why? Who had hated the three of them enough to take their lives?

And who wanted to take hers? A shiver passed over her as she thought of the card she'd received with the lovely blond girl on the cover. "Pretty maids all in a row/Who will be the next to go?" She thought she had been the next target. Instead, it had been Travis Burke. But then, he was not a "pretty maid." Travis's death did not mean she was out of danger.

Christine sat up in bed, horrified at her thought. Had she hoped Travis would take her place on the murderer's hit list? No, of course she hadn't, she assured herself. He had a little girl. And a wife who loved him.

A wife who surely suspected him of infidelity. A wife who claimed to be terrified to the point of paralysis in the presence of snakes, but who had attacked a deadly Gaboon viper with the unhesitating fierce bravery of a Greek Fury.

Bethany. Sweet Bethany. One of the kindest, most generous people Christine had ever known. Bethany could not have been capable of killing her husband. Or his lover. Or lovers, if Dara had indeed been a precursor of Patricia.

Christine's thoughts went in circles and she suddenly felt a pain at the base of her neck. A headache. Exactly what she did not need. What she needed was a good night's sleep so she could have a clear head tomorrow. After all, she had to start investigating job possibilities. She had herself and her brother to support.

But how could she sleep peacefully on a night when someone had lurked outside her house and had the nerve to shoot a police officer who had come to her aid? How could she sleep when she was worried sick that she might be the next to die and that Jeremy would be left all alone?

And how could she sleep when she was eaten up by jealousy at the thought of beautiful Lisa Winter spending the night with Michael, a man Christine had just realized meant more to her than any man had for a long time? Maybe ever.

She groaned aloud, turned off the bedside light, and lay quietly on the bed, closing her eyes and smelling the delicious scent of the candles. Breathe deeply, she told herself. Breathe deeply and relax. Think of gingerbread cookies. Think of a home and family where you were loved and protected. Think of when life was happy and simple.

The phone on her bedside table rang and Christine had the absurd hope it was Michael. She snatched it up on the second ring, then listened to a background cacophony of country music and people talking, singing, yelling. Then her spine stiffened with fear and dread as the noise dimmed and she heard Dara's haunting, undulating voice drifting over the boundary between life and death:

> "Everywhere I go
> Dark eyes peer at me.
> I wish they meant me love,
> But I know they desire me harm.
> I want to live long and full,
> But sadly, I am certain that
> All too soon, death waits for me."

3

Christine quietly laid down the receiver and rushed downstairs to the answering machine's Caller ID. The number read: 555-9794. She lifted the receiver. The music had ended. "Hello," she said, not really expecting an answer. "Hello." The phone clicked in her ear.

What should she do now? she wondered. Normally she would have called Michael, but not tonight. Not with Lisa in his home. He might think she'd made up the call as an excuse to call him. She waited five minutes, then dialed the number that had appeared on her ID box. Nothing. Five minutes later, she tried again. A rough-sounding male voice shouted, "Yeah?" over a din in the background.

"Hello," she said tentatively. "I received a call from this number a few minutes ago. May I ask whose home this is?"

"Lady, this ain't no home!" he yelled back at her. He had a ferocious West Virginia accent and spoke at machine-gun rate. "This here's Ernie's Pool Hall."

"Ernie's Pool Hall?" she repeated, picturing the large combination grill, bar, pool, and dance hall on the outskirts of town. She knew at least one arrest was made there a week for disorderly conduct. "I got a call from there," she repeated lamely.

"Boyfriend out on the town?" the guy laughed. "Leavin' a pretty lady like you at home while he has a good time?"

"How do you know I'm a pretty lady?" Christine pounced nervously.

"Hey, don't get snippy. I just meant ya sound pretty. And refined, like. Not like the usual gals around here. Ya know, if you're lonely, why don't ya come on down and we'll have a few drinks and a couple of spins around the dance floor?"

"That sounds very nice," Christine said sweetly. If she made this guy mad, she wouldn't get any more information from him. "But I'm ready for bed."

"At this hour? Hell, honey, the fun's just getting started around here. Put on a pair of real tight jeans and your dancin' shoes and get yourself on down here."

"I'm afraid I really can't." Christine paused. She wanted to keep him on the phone but short-circuit the flirting. "I have to stay here with my little girl. And my twin baby boys."

The thought of her being the mother of three small children seemed to dampen his enthusiasm for her. "Oh. Well, that's too bad."

"Tell me about it. They're into everything. And they cry *all* the time."

"Oh." Christine could almost see the man recoiling. "Well, wouldn't want to keep you from them. I'll say so long now."

"Just a minute. I wonder if you had any idea who called me a few minutes ago."

"Lady, there's been people at this phone all night."

"But this person must have had a small tape recorder, because he played a song over the phone. A song sung by a dead friend of mine."

"That so?" Now he sounded wary, as if he were talking to a definite nutcase. With three squalling children.

"You didn't see anyone holding a tape recorder up to the phone?"

"No, lady. I've been havin' myself a good time. Look, I gotta go. Been nice talkin' to ya. Hope you find your guy with a tape recorder. Vaya con Dios."

He hung up.

So she now knew the phone call had been made from Ernie's Pool Hall, a cavernous place that could hold a hundred people. A hundred rowdy people who didn't pay much attention to one another unless they were trolling for a pickup. Well, that made sense, Christine thought. What fool would make a threatening phone call from his house, even if the threat was only implicit by the selection of music? She didn't know any more now than she did after the first call she'd received in the hospital.

Except that her tormentor wasn't going to give up.

Christine recited aloud, "'Pretty maids all in a row/Who will be the next to go?'"

She would.

4

Christine jumped when the phone rang twenty minutes later. Could she bear listening to that song again—a song Dara had written and sung so plaintively when death had been breathing down her neck? I have to, Christine thought. Maybe the caller has gotten bolder. Maybe he's calling from a private phone.

She picked up the receiver and said, "Hello?" in a strong voice to hide her fear.

"Christine? Is that you?"

Michael Winter. The trapped air in her lungs fled with a loud sigh. "Michael. I . . . How are you?"

"I'm fine, but you're not. What's happened?"

Aside from your beautiful wife coming to Winston? she almost said. But she didn't want to sound like a jealous harpy. Besides, she'd never even had a real date with Michael. "I got another call," she said in a businesslike voice. "The caller played the tape of Dara singing the same song I heard in the hospital. The one about her feeling that someone wanted her dead. I called back the number that showed on the Caller ID. It was Ernie's Pool Hall. Some guy answered. He knew nothing about the call, of course. Hadn't been paying attention to the payphones. I think they have several."

"About six."

"Well, anyway, the place was rocking tonight. Lots of people, lots of noise. I doubt if anyone would have paid much attention to someone at one of the payphones." Michael was silent. "What's wrong?"

"Christine, didn't you realize you might have been talking to the caller?"

She was so surprised she couldn't say anything for a few seconds. "The caller?" she finally managed. "But he had an accent. His voice was totally unfamiliar." She drew in a deep breath. "He could have been faking the accent and the voice. God, what a fool I am!"

"You're not a fool. You were frightened. And it's not like you're an old hand at receiving anonymous calls."

"I'm a fool."

"Stop it. You'll know better next time. And I won't have any trouble getting a trace on your phone after my shooting at your house. Oh, you'll have surveillance tonight, too. Don't be alarmed if you look out and see a patrol car."

"I feel safer already." She paused. "Are you sure you're all right?"

"I'm great. Well, not great, but pumped full of enough pain-killers that I'll get a good night's sleep." He paused. "Lisa came as a surprise."

"You can say that again." The silence spun out for a moment before Christine said, "I suppose she'd like to get together again."

"I didn't ask her to come, Christine."

Christine longed to hear him say he hadn't *wanted* Lisa to come, that he was sending her right back to Los Angeles, but he didn't. He was quiet for a few seconds. Then he said, "Goodnight, Christine."

"Goodnight, Deputy Winter," she returned, but he'd already hung up.

20

1

Christine spent a long and miserable night drifting from one bad dream to another. She knew rapid eye movements proved that dreams only lasted a few seconds, but each one of hers seemed endless.

She had just awakened from a dream in which Jeremy wandered through a city, aimless, alone, and dressed in shabby clothes, when she decided she must talk to Ames. She would not beg for her own job, but she would ask that Jeremy not be fired. He had done nothing that Ames could consider wrong.

Dawn had barely broken when Christine rose and wrapped up in a long robe. Downstairs she made coffee and peeked out a window. A patrol car sat in front of her house, but she knew Sheriff Teague wouldn't agree to wasting manpower more than a day.

In spite of the patrol car, she did not immediately open the blinds pulled over the sliding glass doors as she usually did to see birds come to the feeder. How strange to think someone might be lurking out there in the dim misty morning to take a shot at her, she thought. Things like that should only happen in novels. It was hard to believe this was happening for real.

While she waited for the coffee to brew, she glanced over the morning paper she'd retrieved from the front porch. The river level was almost back to normal, the headline announced, but the following article detailed the damage left behind. Cleanup operations would continue for at least two weeks, and some businesses and houses would have to be demolished because they were beyond repair. This flood had been worse than the one three years ago, the weather service announced. Christine knew this was one she'd never forget.

Jeremy stumbled upstairs from his lair a couple of hours later. He muttered, " 'Morning," without his usual gusto and headed for the coffeepot. "We got doughnuts or anything?"

"You'll have to settle for toast and jelly. I need to go to the store today."

"Toast is okay." But he did not reach for the bread. Instead, he sat down near Christine and looked at her with troubled eyes. "Christy, I had bad dreams last night."

"No wonder after the shooting," she said, not mentioning her own bad night. "But Michael is going to be fine."

"I'm real glad about that, because he's one of my favorite people, but my dreams weren't about him. I dreamed about Dara."

"Oh." Dara again. How Christine wished she could wipe the image of the beautiful, destructive girl from Jeremy's mind. "Maybe you dreamed of her because I told you about our jobs at Prince Jewelry. You always thought Dara would be impressed if she knew you had such a talent for jewelry design. Now you think she'll never know."

"It wasn't that, Christy. It's . . . well, I know where she is." Christine stared at him uneasily. "She's on the island." Jeremy always referred to the peninsula of land between Crescent Creek and the Ohio River as "the island." "I think Dara's over there with the Mound Builders."

"Jeremy, what would make you think such a thing?" Christine asked gently.

"My dreams told me. Besides, she loved it over there. She thought the land was magic."

Christine put her hand over his. "Honey, she wouldn't have stayed over there for three years. What would she have lived on? She wouldn't have had any food or new clothes or a place to get in out of the cold."

Jeremy looked frustrated. "You don't understand. I think she's . . ." He drew a deep breath. "I think she's dead and her *spirit* is over on the island. Her spirit could go there because the island's magic, Christy."

"Jeremy, the island *isn't* magic—"

"It is, too!" he said loudly. "You're just scared of it. I think we should go over there and look for her."

"We are not going to the island, particularly in this weather."

"*I* am!" His tone was increasingly loud and defiant. "I'm gonna find her spirit and tell her not to be scared and I'll always be her friend and everybody loves her!"

He started to rise from the table, but Christine grabbed his hand and held tight. "Jeremy, Dara is *not* on the island. The police looked for her there three years ago. There was no sign of her."

"They weren't looking for her spirit!"

"But you've been to the island a dozen times since she disappeared. Don't you think you would have sensed her spirit?" Doubt crept into Jeremy's eyes. "Well, don't you? Not me. You're right—I never understood your and Dara's love for the place. I was afraid of it. But you understand it. You understood Dara. You were closer to her than I ever was. And *you* would have sensed her spirit on that island if it were there. It isn't."

"But my dreams . . ."

"Dreams don't necessarily mean anything, Jeremy. Sometimes they're just a jumble of images. You've been thinking about Dara. You've been thinking about the island. You were trying to go there the night Streak and I found you. You've just gotten Dara and the island all mixed up in your head. But believe me, Jeremy, Dara's spirit is not haunting the island."

"I didn't say she was *haunting* it! She's not a scary ghost!"

"She's not a ghost at all." Christine realized her voice had grown harsh in her anxiety. "I mean that if she's dead, which she probably is, her spirit is in heaven. With God. Where it's peaceful. And there's harp music. And you can sit on a cloud."

Jeremy stared at her for a moment. Then the anger vanished from his eyes and he said, "Heaven sounds real boring for somebody like Dara."

Christine smiled in relief. "You're right. For Dara, heaven would be a big party with loud rock music and a karaoke machine she could sing into—"

"And Rhiannon!" Jeremy added, smiling.

"Yes. But Rhiannon is here with us, not over on the island, so we know Dara isn't there."

"Okay. Maybe you're right," Jeremy conceded.

"Well, what do you have planned for the day?" Christine asked in a chirpy voice, hoping to keep him off the subject of Dara.

"We should be going to work," Jeremy said listlessly.

"But we don't have to today. We can do what we want. Would you like to go bike riding? It's going to be a pretty day."

"Nah. I don't feel like riding my bike. I want to go into the store and work on a bracelet to go with the Dara Pin."

"Let's just forget about the store today. Hey, why don't you go to the fitness center? I'll bet Danny would like to have your company, and you can help spot people while they're lifting weights."

Christine had no fear of the fitness center as long as it had plenty of clientele, as it would by midmorning. Besides, she had already cleared this plan with Danny twenty minutes earlier. She was glad to see Jeremy's eyes brighten. "That sounds like fun! I haven't been to the gym for a long time. And I like to help Danny!"

"Good. I'm going to take a shower and then I'll drop you off."

"Where are you going?"

"Uh, to see Tess. I thought we might have lunch together."

"That sounds like fun, too. Don't eat too much at Gus's Grill."

"What makes you think I'm going to Gus's?"

"That's where you *always* eat lunch with Tess, Christy. And you always have the same thing."

"Then I'll have something different today, smarty, just to show you I'm not as predictable as you think."

Jeremy laughed. She was glad. At least his first day of un-employment would not be spent lying in front of the television sunk in depression. Too many days of that state would be bad for anyone, but especially for Jeremy.

An hour later Christine left Jeremy at the gym, then drove to Ames's law office. She did not need to confirm that he was in today. She knew he would not have taken off more than one day after Patricia's funeral. Ames usually had a strong sense of de-corum. She wondered why he was so blatantly flouting it after the death of his second wife. Was it because he now knew she'd had a lover? Or had he known for quite a while and brooded about it until his anger boiled into action? This was a thought she didn't want to entertain.

His receptionist looked startled when Christine walked in smartly dressed in a rust-colored tailored suit. She'd even worn her three-inch heels, putting her over six feet. It wouldn't hurt to look commanding, she'd told herself as she dressed, even if she didn't feel commanding. "Is Mr. Prince free this morning?" she asked.

The receptionist made a show of looking at an appointment book. "I'm afraid he's with someone now, Miss Ireland, and booked up for the rest of the day. Maybe tomorrow or later in the week . . ."

"What I need to speak with him about will only take a few minutes. I'll wait until he's done with his present client." Christine walked into the tan-and-burgundy waiting room and sat down on a wing chair, picking up a magazine.

"Um, I'm afraid he's going to be a while, Miss Ireland," the receptionist said uncomfortably. Her face was growing pink. "Maybe an hour. Or longer. If you'll just let me make an appointment . . ."

"No. I'll wait."

Christine's voice was firm and confident. Then she looked at her magazine to see that she was holding it upside down. She continued to hold it steady until the receptionist glanced away, then she turned it right-side-up and told herself to stop being nervous, even if it was clear Ames had given orders that Christine Ireland was not to be admitted. He probably thought she'd come crawling back for her job and he would show her who was boss, send her out with her tail between her legs like Patricia's dog, Pom-Pom, with all his false, collapsible courage. Well, she would show Ames a thing or two. She would sit here all day if necessary.

But such a bold move wasn't necessary. She heard Sloane's voice before she saw him, walking with a client out into the waiting room. Sloane shook hands with the man, assured him his new will would be ready by the end of the week, then glanced over with pleasure at Christine. "Well, Miss Ireland! What a pleasant surprise!"

"I'm sure. Especially for Ames. I'm told he'll be busy for days and days."

"I didn't say *that*," the receptionist returned indignantly. "I said he's busy *today*. And she doesn't have an appointment."

"Since when does Christine need an appointment?" Sloane asked.

The receptionist turned from pink to cerise. "Well, Mr. Prince actually said that . . . well, that—"

"That he doesn't want to see me," Christine supplied. "But he's *going* to see me."

"Well, of course he is." Sloane gave her one of his conspiratorial winks. "I happen to know he's just sitting in his office drinking coffee as we speak. Christine, come with me."

The receptionist nearly leaped from her chair. "Oh, Mr. Caldwell, I really don't think—"

"Don't worry," Sloane said easily. "I'll take the blame for any fallout that might occur."

As they walked down the long, heavily carpeted hall to Ames's office, Christine looked at Sloane gratefully. "Sloane, I don't know how to thank you for going out on a limb like this. Ames is going to be angry with you."

"He's been angry with me before and I've survived. So will you." Sloane tapped on Ames's office door, then opened it without waiting for a reply. "You have a guest, Mr. Prince."

Ames looked at Christine. "Go away this instant. I do not wish to talk to you."

For a moment Christine felt as if she'd been slapped. Then her back stiffened. "I will *not* go away. I will take exactly ten minutes of your time. Then you never have to look at me again if you don't want to."

Ames stared at her with his cold gray eyes. Then, to her amazement, she saw a flicker of admiration in them. "All right, Miss High-and-Mighty. Say what you have to say."

Christine was aware of Sloane slipping quietly out of the office as she composed herself for a succinct, if not abject, speech. "Ames, I know you and my father were roommates in college and close friends in law school. Then you drifted apart. Therefore, your generosity in taking in his two orphaned children was an even greater act of kindness and generosity than it would have been if you'd been bosom buddies until the end."

She drew a breath. "Dara and I never got along, as you know. But Jeremy adored her. Not in a licentious way that you could possibly find offensive. He just loved and revered all of her good qualities. He would never have done anything to hurt her, and that includes handing over her diary to the police. He had nothing to do with that action. In fact, he warned me to not even *read* the diary because Dara wouldn't want us to. But I did and I found information in it I thought might lead to finding out who killed her."

"My daughter is not dead," Ames said without emotion.

"Yes, she is. You know she is. But that's not the issue." Ames continued to look at her steadily and she rushed on, not wanting to give him a chance to interrupt. "I understand your being so angry that you fired me from the store. I haven't come here to ask for my job. But I want you to consider keeping on Jeremy. He's shown a remarkable talent for jewelry design. As a matter of fact, he made something as a surprise for you. I took it from his room this morning. He doesn't know I'm here, and he doesn't know I brought this to you." She opened her purse, withdrew a small black velvet box, and handed it to him.

Ames flipped up the lid on the box. "Jeremy calls it the Dara Pin," she said. "Rey told him that the Incas called silver 'tears of the moon.' He remembered that, so he made the leaves of silver. He read an old superstition that coral wards off evil, so he carved the rose of coral to protect Dara. Also, he knew Dara loved roses like the ones in Eve's garden. There's a bush in the garden with blooms exactly that color. It was Dara's favorite rosebush."

She watched Ames closely. His hands trembled a bit, but he did not look up at her. "Jeremy made this for Dara. And for you," she told Ames. "But besides considering the sentiment involved, I want you to look at the workmanship. He did a beautiful job on it without any help from Rey. Ames, I am begging you not to take this accomplishment away from him because you're angry with me. Let him continue to work at the store under Rey's guidance. He's taught Jeremy so much. They like each other immensely. Please. I will never ask you for another thing."

Ames continued to stare at the pin. Finally he said, "I didn't fire Jeremy, Christine. Only you."

"He doesn't want to stay without me. He says he *won't*. But I believe he'd change his mind if you asked him. Asked him sincerely, not as a matter of courtesy. If you told him you *needed* him at the store, I know he'd stay."

She saw no change in Ames's expression and her heart sank. She fully expected him to snap shut the box, hand it back to her, and tell her to leave. Instead, he slowly raised his cool gray gaze. "I will think this over, Christine. That's all I can say for now. I will—" He broke off and reached for a glass of water sitting on his desk. He took a tiny sip. "Please leave now. I'm tired."

Hardly the response she'd hoped for, but better than nothing, Christine thought as she stood up. "Thank you for hearing me out, Ames." He held out the jewelry box to her. "No. Jeremy made it for you. And for Dara. I'm sure he'd want you to keep it for her."

She walked on steady legs out of his office, closed the door behind her, and lapsed into trembling. She'd never realized until this moment that she'd always wondered what lay beneath Ames Prince's chilly, contained exterior and that he had always frightened her just a little.

2

Christine dreaded her next stop even more than the one at Ames's office. When she arrived at Prince Jewelry, she found that Reynaldo had already opened the store as she knew he would. Ginger looked at her with shock. "I've worked here for over a year and you've never been so much as one minute late!" she burst out. "And here it is ten o'clock. Did Mr. Prince forget to tell you we were reopening today? And where's Jeremy?"

Christine had not told Reynaldo and Tess that Ames had fired her, but she could see from the look of sympathy on Rey's face that he'd guessed there was trouble. "Mr. Prince called me last night and told me to open up today," Rey told her. "Is something wrong, Christine?"

"I will no longer be managing Prince Jewelry," Christine said in a formal tone to hide the tremor in her voice.

"What!" Ginger exploded. "You're not the manager anymore? Why? What happened? Is it because of Dara's stupid diary?"

"How did you know about the diary?" Christine asked.

"Half the people in town know about it. You know how gossip flies around here."

"Well, yes, it is about the diary," Christine said, knowing Ames had been partially vindicated. So many people knew about the diary. How many knew what Dara had written in it? "He's angry that I turned it over to the police, because there were personal matters recorded in it."

"You mean about all those guys Dara was sleeping with?" Ginger asked in amazement. "Like about a hundred people didn't already know!"

"I didn't know," Christine said. "She didn't confide in me."

Ginger rolled her eyes. "Well, she didn't have to *confide* in you. You just had to keep your eyes open—" She broke off abruptly, as if suddenly remembering that Rey had supposedly been Dara's one and only boyfriend. "Oh, gee, Rey, I'm sorry. I forgot you were in love with her, although I always thought you were nuts for choosing *her*!"

"Ginger!" Christine snapped.

"Well, I did think so!" No one could shut up Ginger when she got on a roll. "I mean, there was Tess, salt of the earth and just adoring him, and he didn't even *see* her because he was so over the moon about Dara, who was just anybody's for the taking!"

Rey had gone white and Christine intervened sharply. "Ginger, I think you've said more than enough for one day. Besides, the subject here was my being fired, not Dara's love life. Anyway, I don't know how soon Ames plans to replace me. In fact, he'll probably turn the store over to Rey. But I did want to stop and say good-bye to everyone."

"This stinks, Christine," Rey said weakly, clearly still reeling from Ginger's diatribe. "I don't know what Ames is thinking."

The irrepressible Ginger flung herself into Christine's arms. "Mr. Prince will realize he's being a jerk. I'll bet you'll be back here in a week. This store can't get along without you. None of us can. Right, Rey?"

"Yes. That's certainly true," Rey said woodenly, his mind clearly back on Dara's infidelities.

Christine forced a smile. "I want everyone to go on working as if nothing has happened. And don't worry about me. I'll be just fine. And Ames didn't fire Jeremy. He says he's not coming back without me, but I'm hoping Ames can change his mind about that." Rey and Ginger gave her wide, false smiles. They both knew it was nearly impossible to change Jeremy's mind about anything. "Well, I'm going next door to see if I can talk Tess into taking an early lunch. Bye, you two. I'll see you soon."

Christine turned and strode to the front door, hoping neither Ginger nor Rey had seen the tears welling in her eyes.

3

Calliope was the first store besides Prince Jewelry Christine had visited when she moved to Winston. She loved books, devouring at least three every week, and she'd been intrigued by the store's name. She'd been even more fascinated when she discovered the bookstore actually housed a working calliope that had belonged to Tess's great-grandfather. It stood at the back of the store on a sort of dais, a large mahogany machine painted with gay pastoral scenes that had been carefully restored when the calliope was moved into Tess's store. Once Christine had talked Tess into playing it. Tess had launched into a raucous version of "Bicycle Built for Two." The keys emitted a cacophony of harsh steam whistles that had sent them both into a hysterical laughing fit. Afterward, they'd both agreed the calliope served better as a conversation piece than to provide a musical background for the store.

Tess stood behind the counter ringing up two paperback novels for an elderly lady whose hair had been dyed an unfortunate shade of electric blue. Christine vowed to herself that even if in the future her own gray hair grew in with a yellow tinge, she would not venture into the blue and violet realms of false color meant to be flattering. She thought they made ladies look like elderly punk rockers.

The last time Christine had seen Tess was when she'd driven her and Jeremy home after Jeremy showed everyone the Dara Pin. She'd been furious that day, clearly jealous because when she'd come into the store, Rey's arm had been around Christine's shoulder. Tess's reaction was ridiculous, but Christine had worried about it. She valued their friendship. She wanted to make sure today everything was okay between them.

"How's business today?" Christine asked when the woman had left.

"Unbelievable. When the cable TV went out during the height of the flood, I think most people realized the value of books. They're stocking up for another disaster." Tess's tone was bright, her smile sincere. Some of Christine's tension eased. "How's it going at the jewelry store?"

"I . . . uh, okay." Christine had decided not to tell either Tess or Bethany about the loss of her job until she'd informed Rey and Ginger. Now, after facing Ames, as well as Reynaldo and Ginger, she'd decided she didn't have the energy for another emotional scene. "Unfortunately, people didn't feel the lack of jewelry as much as they did the lack of reading material during the flood."

"No, I think sweatsuits were the order of the day," Tess laughed. "Oh well, high school and college graduations will be coming up in a month, not to mention June weddings. Rey will be working overtime and loving every minute of it."

A bell over the door tinkled and they looked up to see Bethany. Her usually carefully groomed hair was pulled back carelessly, she wore no makeup except for a dash of lipstick, and her chartreuse sweater clashed jarringly with her burgundy slacks. "You're both here!" she said as if there was no one in the world she'd rather see. "I have a million things to do today. Funeral arrangements, mostly. They're so depressing. Picking out a casket. Choosing what clothes to bury Travis in. What flowers to pick for the casket blanket."

She smiled brightly at both of them, then suddenly burst into a torrent of tears. "Oh, my God, I'm burying my husband in two days!"

Christine rushed to her and enclosed her shuddering body in her arms. "Beth, I'm so sorry. I know that's an inadequate thing to say, but—"

"But what else *is* there to say?" Bethany sniffled loudly and Tess dashed around the counter holding a box of tissues. "I'm so damned mad at him about a dozen things, including dying. He was thirty-eight years old. He had a child. He was so bright. And he was also compulsively unfaithful and sneaky, but I miss him and I don't know how to live without him right now."

Christine went on patting Bethany's shoulder, at a loss for any words that could ease her pain. She remembered when her parents died. People had tried so hard to say the right things, the comforting things. But it had all sounded like meaningless gibberish to her ears. She appreciated the kind thoughts behind the words. She recalled none of the platitudes.

A male customer came in and Bethany quickly turned away to hide her tears. The man ignored her and asked in a rather pretentious voice for a manual listing publishing houses and agents. "I haven't decided who I'm going to let have my book yet," he announced to Tess. "I thought I'd flip through the manual until a name caught my eye. I believe that's the only way to go about this kind of thing. Instinct."

Good luck with that fabulous instinct, Christine thought sarcastically. The man was so full of himself in the face of Bethany's misery that Christine felt like slapping him. But he didn't know what Bethany was going through. And he was proud of his accomplishment, although judging from his un-bridled confidence, Christine was immediately suspicious of the book's quality. But then, she was always leery of people who indulged in self-aggrandizement.

The phone rang while the man chattered away to Tess, and another customer entered, yelling, "You got any good romances? Something sexy to spice up my evening?"

"I'll get the phone!" Christine called to Tess, who looked grateful. As soon as she announced, "Calliope Books," an older woman said, "This isn't Tess. Who *is* this?"

"My name is Christine Ireland. May I help you?"

"Oh, Christine, this is Thelma Brown, Tess's mother!" the woman shouted into the phone. Tess had said her mother refused to wear her hearing aid. "I haven't seen you for a coon's age!"

"Yes, it's been a while," Christine said loudly. "I'm afraid Tess is swamped at the moment. Do you want me to give her a message?"

"Well, I think you're a mighty good friend to leave your own business just to come over and answer Tess's phone!"

"I just happened to drop in." Christine glanced over at Bethany, who stared without seeing at a rack of cookbooks.

"Mrs. Brown, is there something you wanted me to tell Tess for you? Or would you like her to call you back when she gets a chance?"

"Well, she can call me back, but you can also tell her she and Geraldo are invited to Sunday dinner." After two years of marriage, Thelma Brown still couldn't master Reynaldo Cimino's name. "I haven't seen that girl of mine for ages. Asked her to come help me during flood time, but she didn't show up. Called and said her car conked out on her."

"Her car? I didn't know she'd had car trouble."

"Probably just some excuse so she wouldn't have to come," Mrs. Brown said petulantly.

"I'm sure it wasn't an excuse, Mrs. Brown," Christine returned slowly. Tess had said nothing to her about having car trouble. In fact, the car had seemed fine when Tess had picked her up at the hospital that morning. "I'm glad you came through the flood all right and I'll have Tess call you right back."

"Fine and dandy. Oh, and you can come to dinner, too. Nothin' fancy, mind you. Just good country cooking."

"Thank you. I have to go now. Tess will call back."

Christine hung up slowly, her thoughts whirling. Although Michael was convinced Travis was Patricia Prince's lover, no one knew for certain. What if it had been Reynaldo, who was so clearly unhappy with his marriage, who had looked positively ill at Patricia's funeral? And if Rey had been the mysterious lover, where was Tess on the afternoon when she'd claimed she'd been at her mother's moving items up from the woman's flooding basement, the afternoon when Patricia had been pushed to her death in the barn?

21

1

Christine looked at the clock again. Seven o'clock. The hour would seem early to most people, but she could not remember a time when Jeremy had been unaccounted for this late at night.

When she'd stopped by the fitness center at three in the afternoon, Jeremy had been having so much fun she'd hated to drag him away. "Let him stay awhile, Christine," Danny had said. "When he got here, he seemed pretty bummed over getting fired from Prince Jewelry."

"He didn't get fired—I did," Christine clarified.

"My parents think Ames walks on water, but just between you and me, I always thought the guy was a sanctimonious jerk with a stick up his you-know-what," Danny said, making Christine smile. "Anyway, Marti's not feeling great today—I think she's getting this flu bug going around—and he's actually being a big help to me. He's fairly knowledgeable about the proper way to use all the equipment and he's got a great personality. Give him a couple more hours. I'll call you when he's ready."

Christine had glanced into the main part of the gym and seen Jeremy looking happy as he showed a middle-aged man the proper way to do crunches. At least he wasn't mourning over his lost job at Prince Jewelry, she thought, and decided to take Danny's advice.

But now it was seven and Danny hadn't phoned to tell her Jeremy was ready to come home. She called him. "Danny, did you forget to call?" she asked. "I'm coming to get Jeremy now, so tell him to get his stuff together and be waiting at the door."

"You're coming to get him *now*?"

"Yes," Christine laughed. "Are you going to tell me you still can't do without him?"

"No. It's just that . . . well, I thought you already picked him up."

"Why would you think that? Oh God, he's gone, isn't he?"

"Well . . . yeah. The place is packed. I think everyone who didn't come during the flood is here now. Anyway, I was looking around for him about half an hour ago and couldn't find him. I thought he must be in the restroom. I finally went in to look and he wasn't there. Not the refreshment room, either. That's when I thought you must have stopped by to pick him up and I just didn't see you with all the people here and the activity."

"Danny, I wouldn't have left with him without telling you."

"That's what Marti said. We were just getting ready to call you because we thought maybe he'd decided to walk home."

"Three miles in the dark?" Christine's heart had begun to race. "You know he's got this superstition about walking at night, even though he'll ride his bike in the dark. He didn't have his bike with him, though. Danny, he must have left with someone."

"Doesn't he know not to go places with strangers?"

"He could have left with someone he knew. Have you asked around? Did anyone see him leave?"

"I've asked a bunch of people, but no one saw him go." Danny took a deep breath. "Listen, Chris, maybe someone he knew *did* offer him a ride home and he'll be there any minute."

"*Maybe*? And what if that's *not* what happened? Danny, I left him under your supervision," Christine said furiously. "You were supposed to watch him."

"I *did* watch him, Chris, but I couldn't keep my eyes glued to him. You know I love him like a brother. God, I'm *so* sorry—"

"It's a little late for that," Christine snarled, and slammed down the phone receiver, knowing she was more upset with herself than with Danny. Jeremy was *her* responsibility, not Danny's. She shouldn't have left him for so long at the gym.

Maybe he'd gotten his lost job at the jewelry store on his mind again and gone into a funk no one noticed. She should have dragged him out at three in the afternoon. She should have . . .

What? Kept him like a dog on a leash and made him feel helpless and incompetent? It was a sense of independence, of control, of responsibility, that had spurred Jeremy to accomplish all that he had in spite of his mental challenges. It had been an effort, but she'd worked hard to make herself give him enough freedom so he could develop confidence in himself.

But now what she constantly feared had happened. Jeremy was missing, and she had no idea where to look for him. Or with whom, because she knew in the core of her being that if he hadn't left the fitness center on his own, anyone offering him an innocent ride home would have delivered him by now.

Christine immediately thought of calling Michael. But Michael was off duty, no doubt at home with his newly returned ex-wife. The image brought pain dulled only by her anxiety over Jeremy. She had to find him. And she prayed when she found him, he would be alone, not at the hands of whoever was stalking her.

"Idiot!" she said to herself when she finally remembered the policeman still keeping surveillance on her house. She ran out to the patrol car parked in front of the house. The policeman's name was Morris, and she told him quickly that Jeremy had left the gym. Naturally he was not alarmed, giving her all the arguments Danny had already tried.

"Look, you know my brother is mentally challenged," she said. "It's not safe for him to be out at night without supervision. He's afraid to walk in the dark, but he's been upset about something going on at Prince Jewelry, where we work, and he might have gone there."

"But the place is closed," Morris said. "Does he have a key?"

"Yes. I'm going to the store to look for him. Will you go with me?"

"My orders are to keep an eye on you, ma'am," he said with a smile. His face was broad and good-natured, his eyes a pleasant dark blue. "If he's not there, we'll just keep looking. Does he have a cell phone?"

"Yes, if he remembered to take it with him today."

"Well, hop in the car and we'll head for the store."

"I'm afraid a patrol car might scare him. I'd rather drive my car and have you follow me."

"Whatever you think is best, Miss Ireland. And you calm down. We'll find him."

Christine hated evenings at this time of the year, when darkness closed in around six o'clock. Summer was her favorite time of the year, when daylight lasted until nearly nine o'clock. It was easier to find people in the daylight, and fewer dangers seemed to linger than in the spectral semi-darkness of a late March evening.

Parking spaces were plentiful on downtown streets after five o'clock when the stores closed. She pulled up in front of Prince Jewelry and Morris pulled in behind her. She went to his open car window again. "I'll only be in the store for a few minutes and I won't leave the lighted display room, so you can just wait in the car."

"Sure you're not afraid to go in alone?"

"I'm sure. Thanks anyway."

She still had her store key and unlocked the front door. Lights were always left on over the window display cases, but she turned on all of the showroom lights. "Jeremy!" she called. "Are you here?"

No answer. Christine walked to the door of the storeroom, flipped on the lights, but didn't enter. "Are you back here?" Once again, nothing. Jeremy would not play games with her. If he were in the store, he would answer.

She heard a crash outside, metal grinding against metal, shouts, and a shrill scream. Christine ran out to see a pickup truck gouged into the side of Morris's patrol car. The pickup had hit with such force that the patrol car had been pushed up on the sidewalk, the front rammed into a parking meter.

Morris was out of the patrol car holding a hand up to a bleeding forehead. Inside the truck, a woman with clown red hair above a ravaged face shrieked rhythmically as if for the pure drama of it. Beside the truck stood the driver—weaving, shouting, definitely drunk. His flannel shirt had been buttoned unevenly, he wore no jacket although the temperature had dropped to about forty-five, and his face looked like a water-drenched beet.

"Goddamn car stuck halfway out in the street!" the drunken driver shouted. His sweaty face sported a three-day growth of gray and black stubble. "No way I coulda missed it. Where's the police! I wanna report an accident! Look at my truck!"

"I *am* the police!" Morris shouted back. "You hit a patrol car and you're DWI."

"I am *not* insane!" the driver yelled, irate. Then he bellowed at the crowd gathering in the street, "He says I'm drivin' while insane!"

"Driving While Intoxicated, you dope!" Morris shouted back.

"Ain't had no dope, neither. I'm clean as a whistle! Dope'll rot your brain!"

Christine went to Morris, handing him a packet of tissues from her purse. "Press these to your forehead. I have a cell phone. I'll call nine-one-one."

"Thanks," Morris said. "And tell them to send backup. This drunk is going to do more damage if he's not put away fast."

While Christine called, the drunk stood in the middle of the street, waving his arms in rage as he insisted this was no way to treat a veteran of Desert Storm. Christine hovered, not sure what to do next except entreat Morris to sit down in his car. "Can't," he said tersely. "This guy might drive away."

"Well, you can't stop him in your condition. Besides, I've written down his license plate number."

A faint smile passed over Morris's battered face. "Good work." His smile passed. "God, I feel dizzy."

Morris consented to sit in his car with the door open just as Christine's cell phone rang. She answered with a distracted, "Hello?"

"Christine?"

"Jeremy! I've been looking for you! Where are you? I'll come get you right away."

"I . . . I'm over on the island."

"The island?"

"Dara's island. I came looking for her, only I fell. I think I broke my leg."

"Jeremy!"

"You gotta come get me. I don't think I can cling on much longer, it hurts so bad. Oh, uh, the bone's stickin' out."

Christine's hands began to tremble and perspiration popped out on her forehead in spite of the cool air. "Where are you on the island?"

"I'm not sure. Over near the river, not the creek." His voice sounded slurry with pain. Maybe he was losing consciousness, she thought frantically. "You know where the biggest mound is, the one Dara saw the people dig into and find the bones? I think I'm near that one."

Christine didn't remember the exact location, but she'd find it. "All right. I want you to lie very still, Jeremy. Don't do anything that might further injure your leg. You're going to be all right. I'm coming to get you right now!"

"Okay, Christine. But hurry. I *really* need you."

2

Christine turned to Morris. "That was my brother. He's on the island—I mean, the land across from Crescent Creek where the Indian mounds are. He's hurt. I have to go to him."

"I can't go with you."

"It's all right. I can find him by myself."

"You're not supposed to go anywhere by yourself. Let me call this in. We'll get some other patrolman to go with you."

"I don't have time for that, Deputy. My brother's leg is broken. He's bleeding. I'll call nine-one-one on the way."

"An emergency van can't get across that old bridge. It would collapse."

Christine was almost breathless with panic. "We'll work out something. I have a first-aid kit in my trunk."

"You can't drive across the bridge, either. Don't you understand me? The damned thing will crumble into the creek!"

"I have to go, Deputy. I have to!"

She heard him calling after her, weakly over the shouts of the drunk and his still-shrieking female companion, but Christine blocked out the words. She knew how rickety Crescent Creek Bridge was. But she couldn't leave Jeremy over on the island, injured, bleeding. She'd drive to the bridge and walk across. Run across. Swim the creek. Anything to get to him.

As she raced through town, ignoring speed limits, she did call Streak. Maybe he had an idea. But he didn't answer his phone, and she knew he wasn't merely screening her out. Not for something this important.

Next she dialed 911. They told her the accident had already been reported by Deputy Morris and for her to wait at the bridge for aid. She wondered what kind of aid they could offer. Not something involving an EMS van that couldn't cross the bridge.

Desperate, she tried Sloane Caldwell's number. No answer. She tried Reynaldo and Tess's number. Busy. Dammit, where was everyone when you needed them? Busy with their own lives. Busy when the life that was most important in the world to her might be fading away on an eerie deserted piece of land that should have been left to the ancient Indians who'd buried their dead there to slumber in peace.

She drove down the rutted lane to the bridge, then stopped the car. The site of the mound to which Jeremy had referred was at least a quarter of a mile away. She could make much faster time in a car than on foot, not to mention that she would have a way to get Jeremy back to the mainland and a hospital.

Christine looked at the bridge in the car headlights. The boards were gray from years of suffering through the elements unprotected by paint or wood treatments. Part of the railing had fallen away, and a hole was visible in the flooring.

She looked back at her car. It was a Dodge Neon, one of the lightest cars made. The bridge could never support an EMS van, but possibly it could support her car. She knew trying to cross the bridge in a vehicle would be incredibly risky, but Jeremy was worth the risk.

She got back in the still-running car, put it in drive, and cautiously crept onto the bridge, cringing as it creaked beneath the car's weight. Halfway across, something groaned and she tensed, waiting to be dumped into the high-running creek. But she had the sense not to take her foot off the accelerator. She shot forward so fast she barely knew what was happening. She felt faint with relief when she bounced off the boards and landed in the mud on the other side. Another light tap on the accelerator sent her up onto solid ground.

Christine leaned forward and rested her forehead on the steering wheel for a moment. She'd made it this far. Now all she had to do was find Jeremy.

She raised her head and looked ahead at total darkness, the moon obliterated by drifting clouds, the land growing ghostly from a fog creeping in from the river. The only light came from her headlights. She started out slowly, at first remembering only that the mound was near the Ohio River and somewhere to the north, meaning that she needed to veer right. The car bounced over ruts and holes, then over patches of smooth land, all of which archaeologists believed had once been a Mound Builders' village nearly 600 years ago.

Finally Christine thought she must be near the mound and stopped to get her bearings. She got out of the car, leaving the headlights on and the doors open for more light. Armed only with a flashlight, she walked around the ghostly deserted land, repeatedly calling Jeremy's name. At last she reached the mound where Dara had watched archaeologists unearth the skeletons. Hadn't there been eight? This place had been almost sacred to her. And to Jeremy because it had meant so much to Dara. Odd what Jeremy would latch on to as important. Singing. The mounds. *Star Trek*.

Christine stopped. *Star Trek*. When they were young, he'd

thought up a secret code word for them. "Whenever one of us is in trouble and can't say so out loud because bad people are listening, we'll say a word from *Star Trek*," he'd told her. "We'll say *Klingon*. The Klingons are the big enemies of Captain Kirk." Her mind fled back to the phone call she'd gotten from him at the store. "I don't think I can *cling on* much longer." And *Christine*. Twice he had called her Christine. Ever since he'd learned to talk, he'd called her Christy. *Never* Christine.

"Christine, is that you?"

She whirled and saw Sloane Caldwell. "Sloane! What are you doing out here?"

"I got a call from Jeremy. He said he was in trouble. Hurt. I came immediately."

Christine looked at him with a rush of relief. Then her thoughts seemed to slow and reorganize themselves into a dark, damning realization. Jeremy wouldn't have the number for Sloane Caldwell's cell phone. Why would he? He had little contact with Sloane these days. Something was wrong. But she couldn't show it, although her heart felt as if it were going to crack a rib with the force of its terrified beating.

"I'm so glad he called you," she said in a high voice. "I've been out here all by myself looking for him. He said he thought he broke his leg. I called nine-one-one. The police will be here any minute."

Sloane gave her a long, steady look. "You never could lie, Christine. You were just rotten at it." He paused. "You should have taken lessons from Dara. She was as good at it as my mother."

Christine had begun to shake, but she couldn't think of anything to do except keep talking until she found out where Jeremy was. "Your mother? Catherine? Wasn't that her name?"

"No, it was Lula. Lula was well known in certain circles as a woman of many exotic talents. Or perhaps I should more accurately say *erotic* talents."

Christine was at a loss. Sloane had told her all about his parents, lovely and graceful Catherine, handsome and prestigious Preston. He'd told her of his beautiful younger sister, Amelia, an artist. He'd described the majestic ancestral home they'd lived in so idyllically on the impressive River Road. His hazel eyes had filled with tears when he'd talked of the threesome's tragic deaths in a car wreck while he was away at Harvard. She'd even seen his photograph album. There was a picture of him at age twelve splashing in the family pool. Another had been taken when he was a teenager and clowning in front of a strip bar in the French Quarter. But her favorite had been an unforgettable image of the four of them together, posed in front of their Greek-columned white home, Sloane at least twenty, Amelia clinging to his arm, all of them looking so happy. What on earth was he talking about?

"I don't understand, Sloane," she said, trying to keep her voice kind and calm. "Who's Lula? Your mother was Catherine Caldwell."

"I think I know who my mother was," he said sarcastically. "My father is a different matter. My biological father, that is. I know very well who lived with Lula from the time I was four. Bobby Ray. He lived off her 'earnings,' called himself her husband, and 'reared' me with a gentle wisdom that included frequent beatings and constant badgering and belittling."

"But you showed me photographs. The house, your family . . ."

"The photographs are of a family named Devereaux. I started helping the gardener with their lawn work when I was twelve. They were wonderful people and they became quite fond of me. They always told me how smart I was, how ambitious, how handsome, how they wished they had a son like me. Amelia loved me and her parents thought that was fine. I believe they had plans for us to marry. Amelia was delicate. She needed someone strong to look after her."

He seemed to drift off into his memories for a moment before snapping his attention back to Christine. "They treated me like family, Chris. They even sent me to Harvard. I was there when they were all killed in that car wreck. I thought I'd die, too. But they'd always been thinking of me, always looking out for me. In his will, Preston left money for me to finish my education, to go on to law school." Sloane laughed harshly. "Don't think Lula didn't try to get that away from me! She tried every trick in the book, but Preston had anticipated her. That will was ironclad. She didn't stand a chance. And so, I became a graduate of Harvard Law School." He looked at her and smiled. "That's why Dara called me 'the Brain.'"

"Oh, my God," Christine breathed. "So you *were* one of her lovers."

"*One* being the operative word."

The clouds had moved across the moon, and Christine realized how big Sloane looked against the silvery landscape. Big and cocky and a little crazy around the eyes. "Sloane, where is Jeremy?" she asked gently.

"I never dreamed Lula would find me in a place like Winston," Sloane went on as if he hadn't heard her. "But somehow she got the money for a private detective. I don't think it could have been her former means of employment, given what she looked like by that time. Especially with AIDS. And Bobby Ray was long gone. I'll give it to Lula, though. She always was wily. She hunted me down like a bloodhound when I'd been here less than a year. Wanted money. A steady income or she'd let everyone in this town know what I really was—the illegitimate son of a prostitute. So I had to kill her. It was remarkably easy. I should have done it years earlier." He looked around. "She's buried over here. I can't remember exactly where."

Christine's mouth had dried to the consistency of cotton. She felt her vision dim, as if she might faint. She clung to consciousness fiercely, though. As much as she would like to simply fade out of this nightmare scene, there was still her brother.

"Jeremy," she almost whispered. "Sloane, please tell me you didn't . . ."

"Can't quite get it out? Didn't what? Kill him?" He stared at her and she felt weightless, without substance, hung suspended in the night with a cold breeze that had come out of nowhere. "Christine, I pride myself on personally dispensing only with worthy adversaries. Dear, dim-witted Jeremy hardly falls into that category."

Her breath came out in a rush. "Where is he?"

"At my house. Drugged. I stopped at the fitness center after work and saw him. A plan just fell into place like it was meant to be. I offered to take him to your house so you wouldn't have to bother, but I said I needed to pick up something at my place first. Then I offered him a cup of that nasty hot chocolate he likes, only I'd put a little something extra in it—forty milligrams of Valium. Then I held a gun on him and made him call you." He smirked. "He was quite obedient about it."

"He trusted you, Sloane. He's always looked up to you. How could you do that to him?"

"I can't help it if the fool trusted me."

"Did Dara trust you, too?"

His smirk vanished. "At first."

Christine swallowed. She'd caught a dim glimpse of the gun Sloane held by his side. If she tried to run for her car, he'd shoot her. The only thing she could do was keep him talking until, or rather *if*, the police could get here. "Did you begin seeing her before or after we were engaged?"

"After."

"Did you love her?"

"Love Dara?" He shook his head. "I loved Dara's looks. I loved Dara's expertise in bed. But I did not love Dara."

"Then *why*?"

"Because I didn't love you, either. I didn't even find you all that appealing." Christine recoiled. "So why the proposal? Because you were the perfect wife for the rising young lawyer. Excellent background. Excellent student. Behavior beyond reproach. And a very attractive trust fund."

Christine asked in a small voice, "Didn't you love me at all?"

"No, Christine, I didn't. But I wanted you to be Mrs. Sloane Caldwell. I would have had to put up with Jeremy for a year or two before he had an unfortunate, fatal accident, but having a class act like you, and Ames Prince for a pseudo-father-in-law, would have been worth the trouble."

Christine felt as if her heart had turned into a small chunk of ice. "You planned all along to kill Jeremy?"

"Well, I certainly couldn't put up with him for long. Aside from being an embarrassment, he set my nerves on fire. You don't know the strength it took for me to be nice to him. But if it was what I had to do to have you, then I made myself do it."

"You didn't love me, but our engagement, our marriage, was important to you."

"Extremely."

"But you had to have Dara, too."

"Dara was an unfortunate carnal lapse on my part. Very unfortunate."

"She thought someone was following her around in the last weeks of her life. Was that you?"

"I'm embarrassed to say that it was. I knew she had another lover. Oh, not Reynaldo. I knew she kept him around for show. But there was someone else who really meant something to her. And *that* bothered me. She finally even stopped having sex with me. Claimed she had an ovarian cyst that made intercourse painful. And then she turned up pregnant."

"She told you that?"

"Oh yes. It seems the little bastard's father refused to marry her. She was terrified of abortion, certain that it would kill her. And she couldn't stand the thought of marrying Reynaldo because she knew if she did, he'd never let her have a divorce. She'd never be free of him. So she came to me. She said we only had to stay married a year and then get a divorce. I refused. After all, I was engaged to you, and if I married Dara, I'd lose you forever. So finally she tried to blackmail me. 'Marry me or I'll tell everyone about us,' she said. 'My father will fire you. Christine will never have anything to do with you again. You'll be finished in this town.'"

"And that's when you snapped and killed her?"

"Not then. I did try to be reasonable. I tried to scare her first, scare her so badly she'd have an abortion. But after she made a spectacle of herself at that party, after she did everything except announce her pregnancy and you walked out on me, I knew what I had to do. In just a week the perfect time rolled around. The night of the Black Moon. She talked that witchcraft shit all the time, and I knew she'd be down at the creek. So I paid her one last visit."

"You killed her and your unborn baby."

"It wasn't my baby, Christine. It belonged to either Cimino or the other guy she was screwing. What a whore. Just like my mother." Disgust twisted his face for a moment. "Then I wrapped her in the plastic I'd brought along and threw her in Crescent Creek."

"Why didn't you bury her over here with your mother?"

"It was flood time. I wasn't sure I could get over here with her and back safely. Besides, she loved this place. She didn't deserve to be buried somewhere she loved."

"You smashed out her teeth. You cut off her fingertips. All that so she wouldn't be recognized. But you left her ruby ring with the body."

"That was an accident. It must have fallen out of my pocket while I was wrapping her up. I was nearly in a frenzy to get back to the house and gather up some of her stuff so it would look like she'd run away and they wouldn't launch a full-scale investigation immediately. I didn't realize I didn't have the ring until I got home."

"And the notes that have come to Ames from around the country?"

"A friend, or rather a man on whom I have some damaging information, has obliged me by sending those notes Ames sets such store by."

He stepped closer to her. Dear God, she wondered, where are the police? She knew a 911 call had been placed. They should be rushing to her rescue. Then she remembered the bridge. And she thought about the police cruisers. Crown Victorias. They weighed approximately two thousand pounds more than her car. They'd never make it across Crescent Creek Bridge. If the police were coming, they were coming by foot.

"Who was Dara's other lover?" she asked suddenly. "Didn't you ever find out?"

Sloane glanced away for a moment. The wind lifted his thick hair to expose a high, noble forehead. So much for facial features revealing the mind, Christine thought dryly. "I'm rather embarrassed to admit it, but I didn't know who it was at the time. She assured me she'd stopped having sex with Cimino, and by the hangdog expression that had become habitual with him I was certain she was telling the truth." He looked at her, then reached out and delicately touched her cheek. She forced herself not to draw away, not to show fear or revulsion. "Actually, Christine, Jeremy finally told me who the lover was."

"Jeremy?"

"Yes. 'Snake Charmer,' Travis Burke. He was supposed to be my friend, but suddenly it all made sense. Dara used to talk about his class. Then suddenly she stopped. I didn't notice at the time. Now I know she'd become wary. And of course, she said in the diary she was in love with S.C. I learned that by listening outside the night you were reading the diary with Streak, even though I still didn't know who S.C. was." Sloane sighed. "Then he compounded his error with Patricia."

Christine's lips parted in surprise. "You were involved with Patricia, too?"

"Well, I had to pass the time with someone until you calmed down enough to come back to me. You see, I never gave up on the goal of marrying you. But I wasn't meant to be a monk."

"There are other women in the world besides Ames's daughter and wife," she said waspishly, and immediately regretted it when he looked as if he were going to hit her.

"I know that, Christine, but they were convenient. And attractive. And for a while, quiet about our liaisons."

"But then Travis took Patricia away from you, too."

"He did *not* take her away from me," Sloane said harshly. "I was through with her."

"Not jealous?"

"Worried. You see, I'd kept a few things of Dara's. That ring of her mother's she always wore on a chain around her neck. Her mother's crystal ball—by the way, that's what I crushed her skull with." Christine thought of the beautiful crystal ball crashing down on Dara's head, covered in her blood and strands of her hair, and her stomach turned. "I never washed her blood off that ball," Sloane said, smiling. "I kept it wrapped in plastic along with Dara's hair. She had such lovely hair, and I cut about six inches of it off. Tied a red ribbon around it as a keepsake."

He was quiet for a moment. "Then, one day near the time I was about to end things with Patricia because her lovemaking had lost its luster, she stopped by my house with that horrible little dog. I'd left a closet door open. While I was talking to Patricia, the dog went in the closet, climbed into a box, and started trying to gnaw through the plastic to the hair and the blood-covered ball. Before I could stop her, Patricia had dashed into the closet after the damned mongrel. I wasn't sure how much she'd seen or if she'd even realized *what* she'd seen. After all, the ball was covered with blood that had turned dark. And what's a bit of hair and an unremarkable little necklace? I decided not to worry about the incident.

"Then I learned Travis was Patricia's new lover. He thought we were friends, the fool. He told me in that annoying way he had—like a sniggering little boy getting away with something bad. He even went into details about how he left notes for her in her garden under the statue and how they met in the loft of the barn and made love while listening to music on his boom box. It was so ridiculous, I almost laughed in his face in spite of my anger, but I listened. I always listen, and I always remember.

"By this time, Patricia had begun acting jumpy around me. I thought her nervousness could have something to do with our affair, but that answer didn't feel right. I think after the body turned up and she was sure Dara had been murdered, she'd begun to dwell on Dara's last weeks, on the way Dara had begun to act around me, and figured out that I'd been involved with her. And perhaps she'd gotten an inkling of what she'd seen in my closet. Black hair, a spherical object, a grayish ring on a chain. So I decided not to take any chances. I pushed Patricia out of that barn loft and set up Travis with his very own boom box I'd taken out of his car and left playing as loud as it would go in the loft."

"But you had an alibi the afternoon Patricia died," Christine said weakly. "You were in that deposition. How many people were witnesses to your presence?"

"Christine, don't be stupid. We *do* take lunch breaks. That day we took two hours. I billed for one of those hours, though. Old lawyer's trick, adding on billable hours."

"How clever."

"Don't look so disapproving, dear. It's almost expected these days." He seemed faintly amused; then his face abruptly turned bitter. "It was at Patricia's funeral, when your brilliant brother blasted out that Travis was S.C., that I realized he'd been Dara's lover and probably the father of her baby, the baby that had forced her into trying to make me marry her, into the flagrant behavior that drove you away from me, into the position of having to kill the little bitch."

My God, he sounds peevish, as if he's the injured party, Christine thought. The man she'd thought was so strong, so stable, so kind, so generous, was actually a lunatic. A lunatic she'd almost married.

A cold anger washed over her and she said in a steady knife-like voice, "So first Travis took Dara from you, and then he took Patricia. But why should you have cared? You said you didn't love them."

"I didn't, but they were *mine*. I don't give up what is mine until I'm ready to, Christine. All my life I've had to fight for every good thing I have, and I will *not* give up unless I'm forced to, and then not without retribution."

"And Travis got his."

Sloane smiled. "Oh yes. I was a frequent visitor at the Burke home. I knew where he kept the keys to the snake house and picked up a set during a casual visit. I came back in the early hours of the morning, entered the snake house, and opened the cages. I know how to move slowly, smoothly, quietly, so as not to set off the damned things."

He frowned. "It wasn't as easy as setting up Patricia's murder, but I had quite a sense of accomplishment when I made it out of the snake house unscathed. I'd left a window slightly raised in Travis's study. I just went back in, deposited the second set of keys in his desk, and went home for a good night's sleep. And the next day was a triumph. Travis's death was exquisitely gruesome, just as he deserved." He laughed. "He didn't die looking like any girl's dream man."

Christine felt a wave of nausea so strong she almost retched. "You are so sick, Sloane. I can't imagine what your childhood must have been like to make you like this."

Sloane's gaze seemed to turn inward. "I don't know why Lula didn't give me away. It would have been the kindest thing. Maybe that's *why* she didn't do it, although I remember her babbling something about a man she was with who wanted a child. Clearly he didn't want one for long, because he was gone before I was old enough to remember him. And then Lula found out I could actually help in the money department. At first, I was a cute little kid begging on street corners and outside of shopping malls. Later . . ." He shuddered. "Some men like little boys, you know."

Christine went cold to the bone. "Oh God."

"Yes. I used to ask that powerful gentleman to help me, but apparently he's selective when it comes to handing out help. I'd given up on him when I met Preston Devereaux. I'm surprised he gave me the time of day. I was scared to death of him at first, rude and hostile. But he understood me. He was patient. And he changed things for me. He taught me how to dress well; Catherine taught me manners; Amelia tried to teach me about art and literature. I'm afraid I didn't have any natural proclivities for the arts, but I took in everything they said. I watched all of them; I copied Preston's style, his speech, his ways. I tried *so* hard to become a gentleman."

Christine remembered how conscious Sloane had always been about always doing what was socially acceptable, always dressing to perfection, always worrying about making a good impression. His strict protocol had annoyed her during their months together, making her feel stifled. But now she understood from where it sprang. None of it came naturally. All of it was learned and therefore adhered to more strictly than if it had been a natural part of him.

"Life was looking good to me back then," Sloane went on in an almost dreamy voice. "Life suddenly wasn't squalor and gutter-mouthed women and cheap liquor. It had beauty, and grace, and limitless possibilities." He smiled bitterly. "And then that good fellow, God, took them all away. So, I started over. Preston taught me that when life knocks you down, you don't stay down in the mud. You get up and fight. So that's just what I did here in Winston. I had a good job, the perfect fiancée, respect, and limitless prospects. And just when things were looking up again, along came Dara."

"I'd say Dara suffered more at your hands than you did at hers," Christine muttered.

"You didn't always have such a smart mouth, Christine."

"Maybe I just didn't used to say what I felt."

Sloane frowned. "Well, perhaps that's true, because after Dara died, I saw a side of you I hadn't known existed. Like insisting to the police that Dara hadn't taken just the right things with her if she'd run away. Then digging, digging, digging into her death years later. Coming up with that diary and giving it to the police. Pointing the finger at me as S.C. You were wrong about that, but I'm certain at some point you would have found something damaging to me."

He shook his head. "I didn't want to murder you, dear, I really didn't. That's why I tried to scare you off by calling you and playing tapes of Dara singing that I'd taken from the Prince house. And the photos inside the card. And then the stunt at the gym. I did get a little carried away with that one. I came very close to raping you, but I'd already wasted enough time on you that morning. But I think the final blow was when I saw your interest in that *cop*. I saw it at Patricia's funeral. You walked right past me to talk to *him*. And the way you looked at him . . . You never looked at me that way. Not *ever*."

"Sloane, I cared for you. And I didn't mean to slight you at the funeral. I'd just thought of something I had to tell Michael—"

"*Michael*, is it? Just stop, Christine. Nothing you say can change what's going to happen to you."

"And what is going to happen to me?" Her voice was surprisingly strong given the fear coursing through her. "Are you going to shoot me, then run back over the bridge right into the hands of the police?"

"I am not going to shoot you unless I have to. You are going to have a terrible accident. You'll end this night in the *river*. In your car."

A black wing of panic fluttered in Christine's chest. "In my car? Why would I be in my car?"

"This peninsula inclines as it nears the river, as I'm sure you know. There's a drop of fifteen or twenty feet into the river. You will go speeding across the peninsula and drop right off into the Ohio at flood time. You won't remain in it as long as Dara did, but you'll be just as dead."

Christine stared at him, picturing the scenario he'd created. There was a flaw in it. "No one would believe I was over here just cruising around. And they'd never think I'd commit suicide and desert my brother."

"Do you honestly believe I didn't have the reason for your uncharacteristic behavior figured out? It will seem that Jeremy indulged in some alcohol and some Valium, then got the bright idea of luring you over here to the land of the Mound Builders to look for his precious Dara. Only his game backfired. Blundering around on unfamiliar ground on a foggy night, you drove right into the river. And poor old Jeremy, retarded to begin with, drunk and drugged on top of it, decided to run away, only he collapsed on the train tracks outside of town. Of course, I will have placed his unconscious body on the tracks, where it will be severed by the one o'clock A.M. run. Double tragedy. The town will be talking about it for months."

"Double tragedy?" Christine asked, hating the shakiness of her voice. "A little too coincidental, don't you think? You know, Deputy Michael Winter just *hates* coincidences."

"Back to Michael. I hear his ex-wife is back in town. His gorgeous ex-wife who is living in his house. I don't think he'll be so persistent when it comes to you as he has been. You were a passing fancy for a lonely man. And Ames sure as hell won't be as concerned about your case as he was his daughter's. He'll probably be glad you're gone."

"You're wrong," Christine said fiercely. "Michael and Ames will know something isn't right. And have you forgotten Rey and Tess and Bethany?"

"Dear heart, Rey is too sunk in misery over his marriage to think about much of anything else. And Tess is too obsessed with him, and no doubt glad that one more competitor for Rey's attention is out of the picture. And Bethany? What can we say about weak little Bethany? She's lost her husband. She has a little girl to care for. She's not going to waste time delving into the deaths of you and Jeremy." He shook his head. "You're flat out of luck, girl. So let's just walk over to your car."

My car. The agent of my death, Christine thought. "No."

"*Yes.* I'm certainly not going to carry you. You're not exactly a dainty little thing, Christine. That's another thing about you I never liked but I was willing to ignore." He laughed softly; then he reached in his pocket and withdrew a gun and pointed it at her head. "I said *walk*!"

Christine slowly headed for her car, her mind madly searching for a way out of this. She could run, but he would shoot her. She'd still end up in the river. She could turn and fight him for the gun, but she knew how strong Sloane was. Much stronger than he looked. She could never wrest the gun away from him.

"Walk *faster*!" he commanded.

Because the land of the peninsula had once been used for farming, few trees littered the area except for some locusts, which seemed to spring up everywhere with the determination of weeds. The clouds had moved across the moon again, throwing the land into darkness. Between the shadows and the fog, she could hardly see where she was stepping. Most people would not have trouble believing that on such a dark night, on unfamiliar land, and distracted by panic over her brother, she had plunged off the edge of the peninsula into the water. Sloane had worked it all out quite well, but then, she'd always known he was smart. She just hadn't counted on his wiliness.

"You've come up with a brilliant plan for disposing of me and Jeremy," she said. "No wonder Dara called you 'the Brain.'"

"Compliments won't help you, dear. Ah! Here's your car!"

Christine turned to face him. She had nothing to lose now. "What are you going to do? Handcuff me, put me in the car, and send it over the cliff?"

"The bank isn't high enough to qualify as a cliff," Sloane said in irritation. "Besides, your being handcuffed wouldn't exactly make this look like an accident, would it?"

"I suppose not. But I'll make a bargain with you. I will not fight you. I'll let you kill me without a struggle if you let my brother live."

Sloane rolled his eyes. "I can't let him live after having him make that call to you."

"You've said it yourself. He's retarded. Half the people— probably more than half the people—in this town wouldn't believe a word he said. But you have an excellent reputation. Who's going to believe that *you* of all people kidnapped my brother, drugged him, and forced him to make a call luring me here? They'll think he's just making an excuse for playing a game with me that ended in disaster. On the other hand, you might be seen placing him on the train tracks at one in the morning. Or he might come to and move out of the way. Or the conductor might get the train stopped. A dozen things could go wrong with your plan for Jeremy."

She had him. He looked like he was thinking over what she'd said, weighing the pros and cons, realizing just how hard it would be to place the body of a six-foot-three, almost 200-pound man on the tracks without something going amiss. A surge of hope rose in her only to be immediately dashed.

"I don't plan to dump him here in town, Christine. About two miles out ought to do it. No houses. Few cars passing by at night, but not too far for him to have wandered by himself. He has enough Valium in him to keep him out until morning. And as for the conductor miraculously stopping the train in time, just look at this fog. He won't even see Jeremy. But you'll have the comfort of knowing that Jeremy literally won't know what hit him."

"You bastard," Christine hissed.

"Yeah," Sloane agreed, smiling. "But I'm a smart one."

His hand shot forward so fast she barely saw it coming. Then he slammed her on the side of the head with the gun barrel and she fell, slipping into merciful unconsciousness.

Christine awakened behind the wheel of her car. The car was moving. Her head hurt violently and for a moment she had no idea where she was or what was happening. Then the memories came rushing back as quickly as the edge of the peninsula came rushing at the front of the car Sloane had put her in. He had started the car and placed her foot on the gas pedal and a heavy rock on top of it. Then he'd thrown the car into drive and sent her flying toward the river that would swallow her in its murky depths.

"Stop!" she heard someone shouting dimly behind her. "Caldwell! Police! Stop running!" And then a shot.

The edge of the land. The little car speeding forward.

"Christine, open the door!" someone screamed at her. "Open the door! Jump! Open the door and jump *now!*"

The front of the car tilted forward. She fumbled along the door panel until she found the knob. With sweating fingers she flipped it open and dived, hitting rough ground and rolling, rolling, until she smashed against a jutting rock. Just before she lost consciousness again, she heard her car splash into the deep, cold waters of the great Ohio River.

EPILOGUE

Two Months Later

A pale early-morning sun shone on the tender emerald grass of June. The mist of dawn had slowly receded, leaving the cemetery looking fresh-washed and gleaming.

Christine had discreetly stayed away from the funeral the day before, but today she'd felt compelled to come. Naturally Jeremy wanted to visit, too, but she'd been surprised when Michael had insisted on coming with them.

The results of the DNA test proving that the body retrieved from the river was Dara Prince had come back a week ago and the medical examiner's office had finally released her for burial. No headstone marked her grave. That would come later. For now she rested beside her mother with only the large rose granite stone bearing the word *PRINCE* behind her. Baskets of flowers from the funeral covered the fresh grave.

"I still think she woulda been happier buried over on the island near the mound," Jeremy commented.

"It's against the law to bury someone on land not officially decreed a cemetery," Michael told him. "But it's really pretty here. And Dara is beside her mother."

Jeremy carried a bouquet of white carnations and roses the same color as the one he'd carved of coral for the Dara Pin. "Why don't you put your flowers at the head of the grave where her stone will be?" Christine suggested.

Jeremy laid down the bouquet and stood looking at the grave reverently. Finally he said, "Dara, I miss you lots. I'll remember you forever and ever."

Christine's eyes filled with tears for the confused, unsettled girl who had finally found rest in this beautiful, peaceful cemetery awash in sunshine. Michael put his hand on her shoulder. She smiled shakily at him, happy both that her brother had finally been cleared of any suspicion concerning Dara's fate, and for Dara, who'd had a chance at all the good things in life and lost them all because of her own childish heedlessness. Maybe if her mother, Eve, had lived, things would have been different, but now they would never know.

"I don't think Ames Prince would have objected to you coming to the funeral," Michael said. "After all, he did offer you your job back."

"But there are still bad feelings between us, particularly since he learned I'm going to start my own jewelry store and that Rey and Ginger are coming with me."

"And Jeremy, of course," Michael said.

Jeremy beamed. "Christy said I get to name the store, even though I haven't thought up anything good yet."

"You will," Michael assured him.

"I hope so." He glanced around. "I'm goin' over and look at the swans on the pond."

Jeremy wandered over to the pond and began talking to the swans as they glided placidly on the still, clear water. "Well, it's finally over," Michael said. "Have the wounds begun to heal?"

Christine closed her eyes briefly. "I still can't believe Sloane was capable of such destruction. I know he was a monster, but when I think of the childhood that made him that way, the childhood he was so ashamed of, I feel sorry for him in spite of everything he did."

"Most people wouldn't have, and he knew it. That's why he shot himself rather than let himself be taken into custody and put on trial. He couldn't face having that image he'd created of himself destroyed in a courtroom," Michael said. "Every time I think that you almost married the guy, I cringe. God knows what he would have done to you."

"Well, we know what he had in store for Jeremy. But I'll never tell Jeremy that Sloane planned for years to kill him. And thank goodness, he doesn't remember a lot about the abduction."

"That's because of the drugs. But he remembered to say your secret code word to let you know something was wrong."

"Klingon," Christine said with a small smile. "And he called me Christine, not Christy. I just wish I'd picked up on the clues before I went to the island." She looked at him. "But just like in the movies, you showed up in the nick of time to save me."

Michael grinned. "Thank God Lasky called me at home to tell me what was going on after Morris reported to headquarters that you'd gone tearing off to Crescent Creek to look for your brother. Lasky remembered I have a car small enough to cross that wreck of a bridge."

"And you came over Lisa's protests."

Michael reached out and touched her hair. "Lisa and I were wrong from the start. I was taken by her looks. Smitten, if anyone still uses that word. We had nothing in common except our child. I know Lisa loved Stacy, but she couldn't love anyone more than herself, and *I* could never really love anyone so self-involved, so irresponsible. I didn't ask her to come back to me. I didn't want her here."

"But she might have changed since you were apart, Michael. She might have grown up, decided what was really important to her. You."

He shook his head. "She was only here because her career was lagging in spite of her fabulous fabric softener commercial. She was bored and a little scared. But she wasn't in love with me any more than I was in love with her. As soon as I saw her when she walked into my hospital room, I knew it was really over. I didn't even want her sexually. Nothing happened between us those days she stayed at my house. I wish her well, but I'm glad she's gone. Although we've been divorced for almost two years, I finally *feel* divorced."

"I don't know whether to feel happy for you or sad."

"Happy, I hope." Michael reached out and took her hand. He brought it up to his lips and delicately kissed the palm. "Happy that I'm free to start over."

Christine felt as if her heart had stopped as she gazed into his dark brown eyes, eyes filled with tenderness. "Is that what you want? To start over?"

Jeremy walked up to them. "The swans didn't have much to say. Hey, Deputy Michael, you're kissing my sister!"

"Jeremy!" Christine said in embarrassment.

Michael laughed. "Hey, Jeremy, do you think you could design a really super engagement ring for me to give her?"

"*Could* I! Wow! Are you gonna marry Christy?"

"I hope so. How about it, Christine? Are you ready to take a chance?"

"So soon? You've only known me a little over two months and you've never even said you love me."

"I haven't? Where's my mind these days?" Michael laughed. "Christine Ireland, I love you madly. And as for the short time we've known each other, when it's right, it's right."

"Yeah, Christy," Jeremy blurted. "When it's right, it's right! He said he loves you. And *you* love *him*. I can tell. You love him like crazy!"

"Yes, I guess I do love him like crazy," Christine said, smiling and blushing.

Michael pulled her into his strong arms, lifted her slightly off the ground, and whirled her around. "Then let's throw caution to the wind and take a chance on loving each other like crazy for the rest of our lives."

SHARE NO SECRETS

After her husband died four years ago, Adrienne Reynolds and her teenage daughter Skye moved to the quiet town of Point Pleasant, West Virginia. But their sense of safety is brutally shattered when Adrienne discovers the body of her best friend Julianna in an abandoned hotel. *La Belle Rivière* has a dark history, but Julianna's death is by far the most gruesome.

When the elderly hotel caretaker is burned to death in his cottage in the hotel grounds, Adrienne knows that her friend's killer will do whatever it takes to keep his identity hidden. Even if that means coming after her and Skye . . .

HODDER

SINCE YOU'VE BEEN GONE

Clairvoyant Rebecca Ryan became famous a decade ago when, only a teenager, she helped the police solve a number of high-profile cases. But when her younger brother was kidnapped she was mysteriously unable to provide any information. When Jonnie's dead body was discovered, Rebecca was overwhelmed with guilt.

After making a fresh start in New Orleans, Rebecca thinks she's finally coming to terms with what happened. But then she starts experiencing dark and disturbing visions again. When she hears that her cousin's son has been kidnapped, and that he was the same age as Jonnie, Rebecca is determined to use her second sight to help him, despite her own pain.

But when she returns to her hometown it becomes clear that many of her old friends and neighbours, and even some members of her own family, have never forgiven her for failing to help Jonnie all those years ago. And someone is determined to ensure that the Ryan family will once again pay a deadly ransom.

HODDER